ALSO BY CLAIRE KINGSLEY

Haven Brothers

Obsession Falls

Storms and Secrets

Temptation Trails

Whispers and Wildfire

Captivation Creek

A SMALL-TOWN ROMANCE

CLAIRE KINGSLEY

sourcebooks casablanca

Published by Sourcebooks Casablanca, an imprint of Sourcebooks
1935 Brookdale RD, Naperville, IL 60563-2773
(630) 961-3900
sourcebooks.com

Cataloging-in-Publication Data is on file with the Library of Congress.

Printed and bound in Canada.
MBP 10 9 8 7 6 5 4 3 2 1

For all the hot messes who would totally leave the house with paint on their face.

CHAPTER 1

Theo

The noise of locker doors, shuffling feet, and murmured conversations filled the Tilikum High School hallway as students made their way to lunch. I paused, leaning against the doorway of my classroom, and crossed my arms, surveying the mostly controlled chaos.

A group of girls clustered in a tight circle, heads bent together, trading news or gossip or maybe just deciding where to sit for lunch. A few of the sophomore boys, currently caught up in the school's latest nerd fad, raced to see who was the fastest to solve a Rubik's Cube before grabbing their lunches and heading for the commons downstairs.

One of my students, a big junior with a history of…well, being a jerk, came up behind a freshman boy. I cleared my throat. When the junior looked up and realized I was watching, the beginning of a grin left his face, and he moved on.

Not on my watch.

My football players were easy to spot. It was a Friday—game day—so they wore their jerseys to school. A few walked by, decked out in green and white with the Timberwolves logo, heading for the stairs.

"Hey, Coach."

I tipped my chin to them.

Glancing up and down the hallway again, I made sure none of the current couples were making out by the lockers. Teachers emerged from their classrooms, some lingering to keep an eye on the kids. Others ducked around the congregated students and beelined for the teachers' lounge, ready for a break.

Down the hall, the last door opened and Penelope Fallbrook emerged from the art room.

She was a mess, as usual. Dark hair in a bun that was probably not that loose on purpose, and a bit of paint on her beige blouse. She pushed her dark-rimmed glasses up her nose as she turned and made sure the door shut behind her, then glanced in my direction.

She smiled and nodded toward the stairs. I returned her nod. I'd see her in a few.

My eyes narrowed as I watched the boys watch her walk down the hall. Heads turned, eyes fixated on her chest or backside.

Penelope didn't dress provocatively. She was a professional and wasn't intentionally giving all the walking hormones in the building spank bank material. She just turned heads, no matter what she was wearing.

Not mine, though. Pen was supercool, but we were just friends.

No, really. Not "just friends" who were secretly pining for each other or destined to hook up. *Actual* friends who had no interest in each other romantically. Penelope lived with her longtime boyfriend. And I'd graduated from dating and moved into my single-forever phase.

Which wasn't just a phase, it was a life choice. And the forever part? I was serious about that.

Three of my five brothers had walked down the aisle over the past couple years, and we all figured Luke wasn't far behind. They were busy having babies and being family men. Which was great. I love having nieces and nephews. All the cool stuff about kids without the crushing pressure and responsibility. Or the need for a wife.

Because that was a hard no.

The hallway cleared, and I headed down the wide staircase that led to the commons—a big multipurpose area. Students sat at round tables, eating cafeteria food or packed lunches. One of my players held up an apple like he was getting ready to throw it at someone. I pointed at him, and he lowered his arm while his buddies snickered.

"Watch it," I said. "Or you're all running laps."

"Sorry, Coach."

I gave them my best serious-coach look and kept going.

The teachers' lounge was behind the front office, near the main entrance to the school. It offered a student-free space with some tables and a couple armchairs next to the window, plus a fridge and a counter with a sink. I'd always thought it looked more like the waiting room at a doctor's office than a place to relax. Penelope and I had been lobbying for a remodel—or at least some better furniture—but so far, no luck. Budgets and everything.

I went in and nodded to the other teachers congregated with their lunches. Penelope already had a spot, so I grabbed my lunch from the fridge and joined her.

"How's it going, Pentacular?" I asked. She had a black speck on her nose, so I reached over and tried to wipe it off with my thumb.

"Do I have paint on my face again?" She rubbed the bridge of her nose and checked her fingers as her glasses slid out of place.

I tilted my head and looked at her nose. "Still there. But it's not very big."

She adjusted her glasses and rolled her eyes. "I'll get it off later."

"Were students flicking their paintbrushes again?"

"We weren't even painting today. Which means I did it at home and left the house this morning without noticing."

I chuckled. "You're a mess."

"Tell me about it. Thanks, Sean, for the heads-up before I walked out the door."

I grunted a noncommittal reply. It wasn't that I didn't like her boyfriend. It was just that—

No, I didn't like him.

Not because he was with her. I wasn't jealous or anything. He was just one of those guys who made you want to put a fist through his face just for existing. You know the type. Douchey and a little doughy with a cocky sneer he couldn't back up.

I didn't know what Penelope saw in him, but it wasn't any of my business. I tended to avoid saying anything when he came up in conversation. Getting my sandwich out of my paper lunch bag and taking a bite was a good excuse not to comment on Sean and his lack of warning that she had paint on her nose.

"Why are your lunches always so boring?" she asked.

"What's wrong with a ham sandwich?" I asked around a bite, eyeing her glass container filled with a colorful salad-like concoction. "Why are your lunches always so pretentious?"

"At least tell me there's cheese on that."

I pulled open the bread slices to look. "No. Forgot."

"Ugh, just ham? And this isn't pretentious; it's a chopped salad. It's healthy and also delicious, thank you very much."

I swiped her fork out of her hand, dug into her salad, and shoved a big bite in my mouth. Damn it, she was right. It was good.

"Okay, fine. This is better than my sandwich." I stuck the fork in her bowl and started to drag it in front of me. "Can we switch?"

Our fingers brushed as she put her hands around the container and pulled it back. "Absolutely not. It isn't my fault you suck at packing lunches."

Involuntarily, I flexed my hand—the one that hers had touched—and I jokingly scowled at her before taking another bite of my stupid sandwich.

"The recipe isn't hard," she said. "I use variations of it for meal prep all the time. You can make a big batch, portion it out, and then eat it for lunch every day."

"That sounds like planning and work."

"Theo, you're a teacher and football coach. You plan things all the time. Lesson plans, practice drills, formations, starting lineups."

"I know, which is why I don't meal prep. You think I have time to do more than throw some ham on bread?"

She snort-laughed. "You're a big boy. I'm sure you could figure it out."

"Boy?" I gave her a crooked grin. "Honey, I am all man."

Another snort-laugh. She was actually pretty cute when she did that. "Sure, you are."

I opened my mouth to fire back when Ashley, another of our colleagues, came in. She was around our age and taught English. But that wasn't why Pen and I pretended we weren't watching her, while absolutely watching her.

She was totally hooking up with Jeremy, who taught history and social studies. At least, Pen and I were convinced they were hooking up. We'd been trying to find out if we were right since school started in September.

I kept an eye on Ashley while Pen shifted in her seat so she had a view of Jeremy. Ashley got a drink out of the fridge, then chose the seat right behind him.

"So there's that new movie out," Pen said.

"Yeah, looks good. Maybe I'll go this weekend."

There wasn't a movie. We were just covering. It wasn't like we were going to spread gossip about our coworkers if we did find out the truth. Pen and I wouldn't tell anyone—we just wanted the tea for ourselves.

Don't judge. It made work more fun.

Pen nudged me and I cast a quick glance at Ashley and Jeremy. They were leaning down, as if one of them had dropped something. And they were whispering.

I raised my eyebrows at Pen. She raised hers back. Yep, there had to be something going on there.

"Do you think the weather is going to hold out for the game tonight?" Pen asked.

I took the last bite of my sandwich. "I think so."

Jeremy got up to leave, and sure enough, Ashley followed a moment later.

Well, wasn't that interesting?

I met Pen's eyes again and she nodded. Without a word, we cleaned up our lunches, tossed our trash, and slipped out of the teachers' lounge.

"Which way?" she asked, leaning closer so I could hear her over the din coming from the commons.

Narrowing my eyes, I glanced around. I knew all the good make-out spots in the building. Not from my time as a teacher. But I'd been a horny teenager once. A horny teenager with a bunch of brothers. We'd discovered ways to make out with a girl without getting caught, even at school.

"Let's try outside by the field."

She nodded and we made our way toward the back doors that led to the football field.

The fall air was crisp, but fortunately, it wasn't freezing. We crept around the base of the stands—they were raised above the level of the track—and peeked around the other side. But no one was there.

"Maybe they went into the home ec room," Pen suggested. "I thought I saw them coming out of there last week."

"Did you? Why didn't you tell me?"

"I thought I did." She glanced around. "The home ec window is right over there."

Grinning, I waggled my eyebrows at her. She stifled a giggle, and we tiptoed our way to the window. Not that we needed to, but tiptoeing seemed like the thing to do.

The bottom of the window was set high in the wall—slightly above my head. I looked to make sure no one was around and crouched down, motioning for Pen to get on my shoulders. She set her purse on the ground and slipped a leg over one side, and I held on to her while she climbed on.

Holding her legs, I carefully stood, bringing her up to window height.

"See anything?" I asked.

"No. Wait! No. It's empty. No one in there."

"Damn." I lowered her down and she slid off my shoulders. "It was worth a try."

"Maybe they're just going into one of their own classrooms and locking the door so no one barges in."

"Yeah, could be."

She opened her mouth to say something else when we heard a buzzing sound.

"What is that?" she asked, patting her pants as if it might be coming from one of her pockets. "Is that my phone?"

I patted my back pocket, but I didn't have my phone. I'd probably left it in my classroom. I did that a lot.

Something buzzed again, and Pen kept looking around. Cracking a smile, I picked up her purse and handed it to her. "In here?"

She clapped a hand against her forehead. "Oh. Yeah. That was dumb."

With a sheepish smile, she dug around until she found her phone. A look of alarm crossed her face, and she almost fumbled it trying to answer.

"Sean? Hi, sorry. I almost missed your call." She held up a finger, indicating she'd just be a minute.

Crossing my arms, I glanced away, trying to keep my expression neutral.

"Well, we could, but it's Friday." She paused. "It's football season. There's a game."

Keeping the irritation off my face grew harder by the second. Why was he calling her during the day? Did he have to bother her at work? It didn't sound like an emergency, but it did sound like he was messing with her plans.

She always went to the games. Not because of me. She just knew it was important to support the kids, even in their extracurriculars.

"Sean, that's not… Okay… Yeah, I get it… It's all right, I can make it work… What time do we need to leave?" *Sorry*, she mouthed at me. "Sure, I'll see you at home."

She ended the call and dropped her phone in her purse. I didn't miss the second she took to collect herself—the way she wrinkled her nose, adjusted her glasses, and brushed a few loose strands of hair off her face.

"Sorry," she said. "Just... You know... Sean."

"Don't worry about it." I wanted to ask if she was still coming to the game, but from her side of the conversation, it sounded like Sean had made other plans. "Everything okay?"

"Yeah. Great." Her eyes widened a little too much and her tone was too bright. She was lying. "We're hanging out with some of Sean's work friends tonight."

Watching her try to act happy about that was about as fun as being tackled by a three-hundred-pound defensive end on the opponent's field while the crowd cheered for your demise.

"Cool. That sounds fun." At least we were both lying about it.

"I'll try to get to at least part of the game if I can. I might only make it to the fourth quarter, but then I can be there to see you win."

"If you do, you do. If not, no big deal."

Her fake smile faded a little and she started rambling. "Yeah. Of course. You don't need me there. I'm just hanging out in the stands anyway."

"Hey." I held out my fist. She gave it a bump, then we spread our fingers wide and made a quiet explosion sound. "It's fun when you're in the crowd."

The way her cheeks flushed slightly when she smiled did uncomfortable things to my insides. That was my cue to head back to my classroom.

I gestured toward the doors leading into the building. "I've got a bunch of grading to do, and I'd like to check out for the weekend after the game if I can."

"Good call. I do, too."

We went inside and up the stairs, passing students heading to their lockers and preparing for their afternoon classes. I paused outside my room. "See ya, Pennywise."

"Ugh, don't call me that. I'm not a murderous clown creature."

"Fine, Penny Lane."

"Better."

I winked at her, then unlocked my classroom and went in.

I was a little disappointed that she couldn't make the game. I'd miss looking up into the stands and seeing her wave at me like the cute little nerd girl she was. She was always alone, though. Sean never went with her.

But he was her boyfriend. I was just her work bestie. He took precedence.

Even if he was kind of a dick.

I flopped into my chair. Whether or not Pen was at the game wasn't a big deal, and I really did have a ton of grading to do. Before I started on the pile of tests I needed to deal with, I got out my phone and tapped to check my email.

A knot twisted in my stomach, and I wasn't sure if it was anxiety or excitement. Maybe a bit of both. I had an email from the athletic director at the University of South Carolina.

I blew out a breath, hesitating before opening it. They'd reached out to me over the summer, inviting me to come for an interview and a campus visit. I'd gone in July but hadn't told anyone. Not Principal Larson or any of my colleagues. Not even my family.

It was a huge opportunity. As much as I loved coaching high schoolers, moving to the college level would be incredible. I'd played in the pros until a career-ending injury left me sidelined for good. And I couldn't deny that I wanted a taste of the big time again.

I opened it and the knot tightened as I read.

The athletic director wanted to meet with me. He was even offering to come to Tilikum for an in-person meeting the following week.

There was only one reason he'd fly all the way out to meet with me. They were serious. I was really in the running.

I replied, letting him know that would be great.

Leaning back in my chair, I let out another breath. It was a great opportunity. A prominent school with a first-class program. Tons of responsibility. A chance to take my career to the next level.

But it would also mean leaving Tilikum.

I'd done it before. I left to play in college. Then I'd been drafted into the pros. But that had always felt temporary. Granted, I'd thought my pro career would last a lot longer than it had. Still, I'd gone into it assuming I'd play for as many seasons as I could and probably wind up back in my hometown after.

This would be different. More permanent.

With the very real possibility of a job offer on the other side of the country staring me in the face, I had no idea what I was going to do.

CHAPTER 2

Penelope

My feet hurt.

I'd worn a new pair of shoes to work and, cute as they were, they hadn't done my feet any favors. That was what I got for trying to be stylish. Why had I even bothered? My shoes barely showed beneath the hem of my slacks. Who would even notice? Especially on me.

My pinkie toes, that's who.

It was too bad. The shoes really were cute—lace-up ankle booties with low heels. Sitting on the edge of the bed, I flexed my feet and checked the red spots where my shoes had rubbed the skin. No blisters, so at least I had that going for me.

Fortunately, I could dress down for the evening. Sean and I had plans, but his friends were pretty casual. Except Chad's wife, Jordyn. She always dressed like she expected paparazzi to follow her around taking pictures, even when we were just going out for drinks at the Timberbeast Tavern.

I stood and adjusted my glasses as I walked over to the closet. Speaking of dressing down—or up—I needed to figure out what to wear. Fall had settled over Tilikum, the little town in the Washington Cascade mountains where I'd lived for the last few years.

It had been a longtime dream of mine to become the art teacher at Tilikum High School. I loved teaching art, and my grandma—the only close family I had—lived in an assisted living home in town. Staying close to her was my priority. Several years ago, I got a job at Tilikum Middle School, and eventually the position at the high school had opened up. I was in my second year and absolutely loved it.

Standing in front of the open closet, I tilted my head. A sweater and jeans would work. I moved the rack of clothes aside to inspect a burnt-orange sweater. It was a nice fall color.

My THS hoodie hung right next to it. With a sigh, I fingered the sleeve.

Sean poked his head in the bedroom. He'd recently cut his blond hair super short—almost a buzz cut—and for reasons I did not understand, he'd grown a mustache.

"Hey babe," he said, although the word *babe* sounded habitual, not really like a term of endearment. "What are you doing?"

I glanced over my shoulder. "Picking out something to wear."

His forehead creased. He was still in the jeans and T-shirt with his company logo he'd worn to work. "Why? You don't need to change."

"I want to."

"Just don't take forever. You already got home late."

"I was trying to catch up on grading so I don't have to do it this weekend."

"Fine, just don't take forever." He turned and left, disappearing down the hall.

I was about to reach for the sweater when I paused and eyed the hoodie again. It wasn't that it was any cuter or more comfortable than other items in my wardrobe. It was just a hunter green sweatshirt with a kangaroo pocket and the Tilikum Timberwolves logo on the front. But I wore it to the football games, and that was what I wished I was doing. Not getting ready to hang out with Sean's work friends all night.

High school football over a night out with grown-ups? Maybe that made me weird—especially for a girl who'd never been into sports—but the Timberwolves football games were so much fun. I'd started going the previous year to show my support, and it had quickly become my favorite Friday-night activity.

But Sean had made plans, so…

Irritation flashed through me, and I yanked the hoodie off the hanger. If I couldn't go to the game, I'd support the team from afar.

Pairing it with jeans and pulling my long brown hair up in a ponytail, I dabbed on a little lip gloss and went to find Sean so we could get going.

He stood in the kitchen, barefoot, looking at his phone, which was odd because I thought we were leaving. His eyes flicked up and down when I walked in.

"That's what took you so long to pick?" he asked.

"You said we were going to the Timberbeast. Last time I checked, Rocco doesn't enforce a dress code."

"Whatever, it's fine. We're not going to the Timberbeast anyway."

"Oh. Then where are we going?"

"Nowhere." He set his phone on the counter. "Everyone's coming here. They'll be here any minute."

My lips parted in surprise, and I sputtered for a second, fishing for a reply. "What? Here? What do you mean, they're coming here? You said we were meeting everyone at the bar."

"Change of plans."

"Why?"

He checked his phone again and typed a message before looking up at me. I didn't miss the annoyance in his expression. "Does it matter? It's just what we decided."

"*We* didn't decide anything." I pointed back and forth between us. "You and the homeboys maybe, but not *we*."

"What's the problem? It's just the guys. It's not like they care if the place is clean."

"That's not the point. You could have at least asked if I mind having guests over."

"What difference does it make if we hang out here or at a bar?"

I was about to reply that it made a big difference, especially if his friends were expecting food, when there was a knock at the door.

My shoulders slumped. Great. Guests already.

"Can you get out some chips and salsa or something?" he asked.

I gaped at him while he went to answer the door. It was his buddy Mark. They greeted each other with an elaborate handshake, and Sean shut the door behind him. Mark wasn't married, and he hadn't brought anyone with him. Just a six-pack of beer.

As irritated as I was with Sean, I wasn't going to be a bad hostess. I went to the pantry and found a bag of chips and a jar of salsa. He and I would have a conversation about inviting people over without consulting me later.

With the chips and salsa laid out on the dining table, I went back to the kitchen and poked around, looking for more snacks—and hoping the other guys brought more than beer.

Chad and Jordyn arrived next, and of course Jordyn looked like she'd just come from a photo shoot. I went to the entry, ready to greet them and take whatever food they'd brought to the kitchen. But Chad handed me another six-pack—without so much as a smile or a thank-you—and Jordyn wasn't carrying anything.

"Hi," I said, trying to be friendly. "Welcome. Happy Friday."

Jordyn turned to me and her smile faded slightly as her gaze flicked up and down. "Hi, Penelope."

"I like your outfit," I said. "That sweater is so pretty."

"Yeah, thanks." She eyed me again but didn't say anything else.

A blush crept across my cheeks, and I held up the beer. "I guess I'll put these in the fridge. Did you eat before you came?"

"No," Jordyn said, her tone matter-of-fact.

"Oh." I swallowed, feeling so awkward I wanted to crawl into a hole. "I put some chips and salsa on the table."

I couldn't tell if she'd actually heard me. She was already walking away to join her husband and the other guys in the living room.

"Awesome," I muttered as I went to the kitchen. "Great to have you here."

A few more couples arrived—guys Sean worked with and their

girlfriends or wives. One of the women had at least brought a prepackaged veggie platter. All the men had brought beer.

Was I at a frat party? All beer and almost no food?

I stopped and watched Sean as he stood with his friends—talking and laughing. I could probably walk right out the front door and he wouldn't notice. Until he wanted something.

When had he changed? Things hadn't always been like this.

That was too much to grapple with while guests were descending on our house. With a little shake of my head to clear it, I opened the freezer to see if we had anything to feed almost a dozen people. There was an unopened bag of pizza rolls. That was something. I set them on the counter and was about to turn on the oven when Sean called from the other room.

"Hey, babe? Can you bring me a beer?"

My back stiffened. With a slow, deliberate motion, I pushed my glasses up my nose, then turned to look at him. The smile melted from his face.

One of his friends guffawed loudly and smacked him on the chest. "Oh dude, you're in trouble."

"Shut up," Sean said with a glare and stalked into the kitchen. He stood close and lowered his voice. "What's going on?"

My eyebrows shot up. "Are you kidding me?"

"What?"

All too often, I would have said nothing was wrong just to avoid conflict—especially in front of other people. But I was tired, and the noise of laughter in the other room crawled up my spine like a spider.

Still, I lowered my voice so I wouldn't make a scene. "It's Friday and I'm exhausted, but I was going to do my best to rally since you made plans with your friends. Without asking me if I wanted to go, I might add. And then, without telling me a thing, you changed the plans, inviting everyone over to our place. Now there's a house full of people and no food and you want me to bring you a beer?"

He looked at me like he had no idea who I was—or why I was mad. "I thought you'd be happy about this. You never want to go out."

"That's not true."

"You complain about it every time. Look, who cares about the food? No one in there gives a shit if there's not a four-course meal. They're our best friends. We don't have to worry about that crap with them."

Our best friends? More like his best friends.

I crossed my arms. "That's not what I meant. There's just a whole lotta beer and not much to eat. But if you don't mind dealing with a bunch of drunk dudes after they finish all that beer on empty stomachs, be my guest."

He opened his mouth, and for a second, I thought he was about to start yelling. But one of his buddies shouted, "Shots! Shots! Shots!"

Kind of made my point for me.

"What the fuck do you expect me to do?" Sean snapped.

With my arms still crossed, I glanced away. *Kick them out and tell them to go home.* "I don't know. Home Slice will be busy, but we could probably still order pizza."

"What time is it? They deliver, right?"

I was going to say yes, they do, when I got an idea.

"Why don't I go pick it up? It's a Friday. It could be hours for delivery. If I go down there, it'll still take a while, but I bet it'll be faster."

"Probably." He glanced over his shoulder at his friends all chatting and laughing, then turned back to me.

I grabbed the bag of pizza rolls and stuffed them back in the freezer. I didn't want him to decide we could scrounge something at home. "I'll take care of it."

"Fine. Whatever works." He grabbed a six-pack out of the fridge and went to join his friends.

I wrinkled my nose and fought down a very un-Penelope-like urge to flip him off.

Our guests didn't seem to notice me as I got my purse out of the hall closet. My hoodie would be warm enough—I didn't need a jacket—but I took my green and white knit beanie off the shelf and stuffed it in my purse. With a quick glance at Sean, who was busy talking to his friends with a beer in his hand, I left.

The sudden onslaught of people in the house had raised the temperature, so the crisp fall air was refreshing. I took a deep breath and went to my car, smiling at my stroke of genius.

Getting in and turning on the engine, I took out my phone and found the number for Home Slice Pizza.

"Home Slice, can you hold?" someone answered.

"Sure."

Surprisingly soothing piano music came on. I waited for a moment, swaying in my seat, until someone at the restaurant picked up again.

"Thanks for waiting." The same voice—a teenage boy maybe?—prompted, "Can I help you?"

"Yeah, I'm going to need six large pizzas. What's the wait looking like?"

"Oh man." The poor kid sounded stressed. "Pickup or delivery?"

"Pickup."

"That's going to be at least ninety minutes. I'm really sorry, we're slammed."

A big grin stole over my face. "Ninety minutes is great."

"Really?"

"Yep. I can totally make that work."

"Okay. What can I get you?"

I ordered four pepperoni, an all-meat, and a veggie pizza. Still smiling, I ended the call and put my phone down.

"That's a pretty long wait," I said aloud. "Whatever shall I do in the meantime? Oh, I know."

I pulled out my ponytail and fluffed my hair, then grabbed my green and white beanie and put it on. It matched my hoodie. Then I backed out onto the street and headed toward the high school.

The stadium lights glared in the evening sky, and I could hear the crowd as soon as I opened my car door. With a tingle of excitement in my stomach, I got out and hurried to the entrance.

Showing my staff ID at the gate, I went in and made my way up the stairs to the packed stands. The scent of popcorn filled the air, and the pep band played a quick tune while the kids in the student section cheered.

Following the railing, I looked down onto the field. The game was in progress, but it must have been a time-out. The players were circled up, listening to Theo.

Coach Haven, that is.

A little smile crossed my lips. He was dressed in slacks and a half-zip fleece with the Timberwolves logo embroidered on the left side of the chest. I was too far away to hear what he was saying, but his expression was intense as he gave direction to his players. They clapped once in unison and ran back onto the field.

Willing him to turn around and look in my direction, I practically leaned out over the railing.

And then he did.

He turned and looked right at me, as if he knew I'd be there.

The smile that stole across his face made my belly flutter like a girl with a crush. I scoffed at myself. Obviously, I didn't have a crush on Theo Haven. He was just my work bestie. That was why I was so happy to see him. He was a great teacher, sure, but I knew football was his passion. I just liked seeing him in his element. Totally a friend thing. Nothing more.

He stretched out his fist. I did the same, then we opened our hands and made a little explosion sound. Long-distance fist bump.

With a smile still on my lips, I took a seat and settled in to watch the rest of the game.

CHAPTER 3

Theo

Grabbing a small cart, I headed into Nature's Basket Grocery. I was on my way to my parents' place, and my mom had asked me to pick up a few things.

I whistled softly as I walked, steering around a woman who appeared to be lost in thought in front of the forty-seven different apple varieties. Slowing, I eyed the pile of big, juicy Honeycrisp apples, wondering what Penelope would do with them. Seemed like the sort of thing she'd put in a salad. But not a plain iceberg lettuce salad. One of those hearty ones she made that looked like an actual meal.

Her accusation that my lunches were always boring came to mind, encouraging me to grab a few apples. Maybe if I tossed one in with my sandwich, she'd stop giving me a hard time. Produce was healthy, right? An apple a day and all that.

Mom had said she needed dinner rolls, so I moved on, heading for the bakery. It hadn't escaped my attention that my parents invited me over for dinner about once a week. And I was pretty sure it was because I was the last single Haven brother.

Well, the last single Haven brother in Tilikum, at least. Who knew where my older brother Reese had gone? He'd disappeared almost twenty years ago.

Family gossip had it that he called Mom every now and then to let her know he was alive. But that was it. No idea what he was doing, where he was living, or what was going on in his life.

Or why he'd left and hadn't come back.

Thinking about Reese tended to put me in a bad mood, so I decisively pushed that jerk out of my head while I grabbed a package of rolls. I was still riding high from the previous night's win and I didn't want to start brooding over my brother.

My team had played their asses off, coming back from a two-touchdown deficit in the fourth quarter, squeaking out a win with a field goal. I was so proud of them. Morale had taken a hit and the vibe in the locker room at halftime hadn't been good. But they'd turned it around—proved to themselves they could.

I glanced toward the deli, still thinking about options to improve my lunches, when a woman with long dark hair caught my eye. She stood in front of a refrigerated display of prepackaged foods, reading the label on a container of guacamole.

My mouth twitched in a grin. Penelope. She wore a sweater and jeans and pushed her glasses up her nose as she kept reading.

"Hey, Penultimate," I said, walking over to her. "What's so riveting about that guac?"

She gasped and the container flew out of her hands. Sidestepping, I reached out and caught it with one hand.

"You startled me," she said as I handed it back to her. "Nice move, though."

"I'm basically a ninja."

She snort-laughed. "Sure, you are. It's not riveting, I was just checking the ingredients."

"Why? Isn't it just avocado and jalapeño or something?"

"It should be. That's why I'm checking. Some of these have a bunch of additives." She grinned. "Not this one."

I smiled back and felt a weird sense of shared triumph at her successful guacamole find. "Awesome."

"It's not like I don't eat junk food. I do. But if there's junk in the stuff you think isn't junk, then it's that much more junk in your diet. You know?"

I nodded. "Yep."

Her smile grew. "See, you get it. I don't know why Sean doesn't get it."

Maybe because he's an idiot. I didn't say anything. Just shrugged.

"Congrats on the win last night, by the way," she said.

"Thanks. They played their hearts out."

"I was so nervous at the end, I was actually biting my nails." She held up her hand, but I couldn't tell if her nails looked any different. "And my throat is still scratchy from cheering."

"Sorry about the sore throat, but I'm glad you were there to see it."

She smiled, her blue eyes sparkling behind her glasses. "Me too."

The warmth that spread through my chest when she looked at me like that was both pleasant and uncomfortable. She had a pretty smile, no doubt about that. Any guy would agree. But there was something about the way she smiled *at me* that I both loved and hated a little bit at the same time.

I figured it was a consequence of a guy-girl friendship. There was always going to be some tension, even if it was only on my side.

Clearing my throat, I gestured to the closest aisle. "I should probably…"

"Yeah, of course. Sorry, I didn't mean to keep you."

"Hey, babe?" a male voice said behind me.

My back stiffened, and the smile disappeared from Pen's face, her eyes darting between me and the guy approaching.

Sean.

"Are you done yet?" he asked, his tone irritated.

"Found it." She held up the guacamole. "This is the good kind that I was looking for. No additives."

He didn't reply, just dropped a few things in their cart, and my jaw hitched at the way he dismissed her.

His eyes flicked toward me and his brow furrowed, as if he was wondering why I was standing there. "What's your deal, Haven?"

As much as I would have enjoyed stepping into his personal space and staring him down until he cowered, Penelope's worried expression held me back. I didn't want to make things hard on her.

So I ignored him the way he'd just ignored her and grabbed a container of the same guacamole off the shelf. "Thanks for finding this. I didn't even think to look at the ingredients."

She smiled. "Sure."

"See you Monday."

"Yeah, see you," she said.

I didn't bother glaring at Sean. Without another word, I turned and pushed my cart in the opposite direction.

"Dick," I muttered under my breath, irrationally annoyed that he hadn't been grateful to Pen for finding an additive-free brand of guacamole.

I wandered down an entire aisle before I realized I couldn't remember what else my mom had asked me to get. I patted my back pocket, looking for my phone, but it wasn't there. Damn it. I wondered if I'd left it at home.

Butter. She'd said butter. After grabbing some, and hoping it was all I'd needed, I checked out and left.

My parents lived a short drive outside town, up a long gravel driveway. Pine trees surrounded their hand-built log home. The side yard had a picnic table on the grass and a swing set for the grandkids, and my dad had a big shop out back.

I parked my truck, grabbed the groceries, and went to the front door. Mom had decorated the porch with a bunch of pumpkins.

"Hey, Mom. Dad," I called as I walked in. "I'm here."

"Hi, Theo," Mom's voice came from the kitchen.

The short hallway was decorated with years of old photos—mostly me and my siblings as kids. There were seven of us—six brothers and one sister. My parents each had three little boys when they'd gotten married, then they had Annika together. Somehow they'd brought us all together and created a family.

It had been a good way to grow up. Kinda hard to get too full of yourself, no matter who you are, when you have to share your space with so many brothers.

The hallway opened into a living room with a woodstove, cozy furniture, my mom's knitted throw blankets everywhere, and more family photos on the mantel. Mom was in the kitchen, so I brought the grocery bags in and set them on the counter.

"Thank you, honey," she said as she got the bread and butter out of the bag. She was dressed in a black cardigan over a T-shirt and jeans, her signature blue-rimmed glasses perched on her nose. "This saved me a lot of time."

"No worries." I gave her a quick kiss on her hair near her temple. "How's everything going?"

"Oh, good. We're fine. Dad's out tinkering with the snowblower. Will you go tell him dinner is almost ready?"

"Sure."

The back door opened onto a path that led to the shop. It had metal siding and two large garage doors. One was wide-open, and I found my dad with his handheld snowblower on a workbench surrounded by tools. His broad shoulders and barrel chest filled out his well-worn plaid flannel shirt, and his dark hair and thick beard were peppered with gray.

Paul Haven wasn't my biological father, but he'd adopted me when I was little. More importantly, he was my dad in every way that mattered.

"Hey, Dad."

He looked up and didn't exactly smile, but the slight softening of his features was as telling as a giant grin on any other man. "Son."

"Mom says dinner is almost ready."

Straightening, he grabbed a shop towel and wiped his hands. "Great game last night."

"Yeah, they played their hearts out."

"I don't know where Owen got those wheels of his, but, man, is he fast."

He was right. My nephew was a talented athlete. "He's not just fast; he has incredible instincts. That kid smells the end zone and it's all over."

Dad met my eyes. "He has a good coach, too."

Gratification spread through me like warmth from a fire. "Thanks, Dad."

Walking by, he patted me on the arm, but didn't say anything else. He'd always been a man of few words, but once in a while he sure knew how to make them count.

I wasn't about to puff up at his praise, though. The implications of taking the university job—assuming they offered it to me—were still swirling through my head.

Owen was brimming with natural talent, but he didn't need me to shape him. If I left, Assistant Coach Lewis was sure to take over, and he was top-notch. He'd guide Owen, and the rest of the team, through each season like a pro. He cared. I knew I could count on him.

But how would my parents, and the rest of my family, feel about me leaving?

I followed Dad inside. As we sat down and ate—chicken with roasted vegetables—that question lingered in the back of my mind. I'd planned to bring it up. Let them know I was in the process of interviewing. But as the evening went on, I found myself avoiding it.

We chatted about the usual stuff. Dad and my brother Josiah's latest house they were remodeling. My nieces and nephews, especially the three baby girls who'd been born earlier that year—Garrett and Harper's surprise baby, Isla; Zachary and Marigold's Emily; and Josiah and Audrey's daughter, Abby. Mom was in Grandma heaven.

There was town gossip and news about a few of Mom's friends in her knitting group. And of course, football. As we talked, I tried to ignore the increasing stiffness in my neck and the slight shimmering at the edges of my vision.

Even in the midst of chatting all things sports, I still didn't tell them about my upcoming interview.

Eventually, I said goodbye and headed home. I didn't know why I'd kept it from them. If I took the job, they'd be thrilled for me. I couldn't imagine them making me feel guilty or giving me a hard time about it. That wasn't who they were.

My brothers, on the other hand, would give me endless shit about leaving. But that was their job. And they'd be happy for me, too. Even if they didn't admit it right away.

Maybe it was just the fact that change was hard. Even though it was an incredible opportunity, taking a job across the country meant a lot of uncertainty. Staying where I was would be the easier path. But was it what I really wanted?

When I got home, my house felt chilly—and very empty. It was odd. I'd lived alone for years and it never bothered me. I was too busy to be bored or lonely. There were always lessons to plan, tests to grade, football formations to tweak, plays to develop. But somewhere deep down, I knew all that stuff was covering up a very real emptiness inside me.

An emptiness I didn't particularly want to face.

My house was a three-bedroom, two-bath rambler with a garage—typical in Tilikum. Small, but livable. Especially since it was just me. I hung my keys on the hook my sister Annika had given me as a housewarming gift. It was in the shape of a football and looked like it belonged in a kid's room, but I liked it anyway.

For some reason, I thought about the fact that there were no pumpkins decorating my porch. No idea why. I'd probably just noticed the fall vibe at my parents', and the key hook made me think of Annika, who was super crafty, and probably had an elaborate fall display around her front door.

But it was weird how the lack of pumpkins tugged at that empty spot in my chest.

I went to my bedroom and shucked off my jeans. By now, I could hardly turn my head from side to side, and the vision disturbances were making me squint.

A severe neck injury did that to you.

The migraine was too far gone to avoid, so I took a dose of my prescription, hoping it would ease the pain once it hit. Cold usually felt good when I was in the midst of one, so I grabbed an ice pack, lay on the couch, and pressed it to my forehead.

And for some reason, I wished I hadn't left that container of guacamole at my parents' house.

CHAPTER 4

Penelope

Planters filled with orange and yellow mums decorated the walkway outside Tilikum Gardens Village. Although the automatic doors weren't exactly homey, the rest of the lobby was. Overstuffed armchairs sat near a window by the check-in desk, and there were garlands of autumn leaves and mini pumpkins everywhere.

I stopped to sign in at the front desk and said hi to Sarah, the attendant. The entrance lobby opened to a cozy living area with a double-sided gas fireplace in the center of the room. Several residents sat on the couches or chairs, reading or chatting with each other, and a man in a wheelchair thumbed through a magazine. They looked up as I walked by.

"Good morning," I said with a smile.

There was a chorus of, "Good morning, Penelope!"

"I think Colleen is outside," one of the ladies said.

"I'll look there first. Thank you."

Colleen Wilson, my grandmother on my mom's side, was born and raised in Tilikum. She'd chosen to move into the assisted living facility about five years ago. She had her own apartment and was still able to do some things independently, but back and hip injuries, coupled with other elements of age, had left her in a wheelchair.

Fortunately, Tilikum Gardens Village was a nice place, and she was thrilled to have someone else cook for her every night.

I visited her every week or two, usually on weekends. She wasn't the only family I had, strictly speaking. I didn't have any siblings, and my parents had divorced when I was ten. My dad had been distant from that point on. He'd remarried and moved around a lot, and hadn't seemed particularly interested in making me a part of anything. My mom had eventually remarried as well, and after I graduated from high school, she and my stepdad had moved to Ohio to be closer to his family.

That had left me and Grandma Colleen. It was why I'd been so adamant about moving back to the area after college and worked so hard to get hired at Tilikum High School—so I could live and work as close to her as possible.

I walked past the fireplace into another sitting area with tables. Two men sat at a table, deeply embroiled in a game of chess, and another resident worked on a puzzle. A few magazines and newspapers were set out, a show played on a mounted TV, and a console table held coffee, tea, and water.

Another set of automatic doors led to a large patio. More yellow and orange mums spilled out of pots next to benches. A path wound through the lawn and large trees bent their branches over the yard, offering shade.

Grandma sat in her wheelchair just past the first bend in the path. She kept her pure white hair long, tied at the nape of her neck, and she'd wrapped a lavender knit shawl around her shoulders.

Before I could say a word, she held up a hand, palm out. I stopped, my lips parted.

Leaning down, she tossed something onto the grass. A moment later, a gray squirrel approached.

"There you go, little one," she said.

A few more squirrels appeared, scampering over happily to devour the snacks. She sat back and maneuvered her wheelchair so she was facing me. Her warm smile lit up her face.

"Penny," she said, wheeling herself closer. "How's my darling girl?"

"Hi, Grandma." I leaned down to give her a kiss on the cheek. "I'm well. How are you?"

"It's a beautiful day, and Spritz over there finally decided to come check me out."

"Spritz?"

She gestured to the squirrels still picking up treats from the grass. "He's just a baby. Wasn't so sure about me for a while. But I got him. I always do."

Tilikum had a love-hate relationship with the squirrel population. They were known thieves and could be quite a nuisance. But Grandma adored them. She'd been making friends with the squirrels for as long as I could remember.

"He's very cute. Do you know it's a he?"

She shrugged. "No, but I don't think he cares if I get it wrong."

"I'm sure he doesn't," I said with a laugh. "So, what do you want to do today? Do you need more treats for your squirrel friends?"

"Those greedy little things have had quite enough. Until tomorrow, at least. How about you get us some tea and we have a sit?"

"Outside or inside?"

She took a deep breath of the crisp air. "Outside, as long as you're warm enough."

I'd worn a plaid shirt-jacket over a long-sleeve shirt and jeans. Even with a slight chill in the air, I'd be comfortable. "Outside is great. Let's do that while we can, before winter sets in."

"My thoughts exactly."

I went inside and poured hot water over tea bags I dropped into two white ceramic mugs at the coffee and tea station. Hanging on the wall above it was an oil painting portraying an old barn in a field with a river in the distance. It had been donated by the artist—Edwin Morris. He was a local, and you could find his paintings in various places throughout the central Cascades.

The painting brought a little smile to my face as I stirred a teaspoon of sugar into Grandma's tea. I'd taken one of Edwin Morris's painting classes the previous summer and had learned a lot. Seeing his art made me feel a bit like I knew a celebrity. Not a real celebrity, of course. Hardly anyone outside the art world knew who he was. But he was something of a mentor to me, and I was hoping to take another class next summer.

With the tea bags steeping, I took our mugs outside. Grandma had wheeled herself up to a patio table and I set her tea down before taking a seat.

Tilting her head, she took a long look at my hand wrapped around the warm mug. "Still no ring?"

With a sigh, I let go of the mug and spread my fingers wide. "Obviously not. I would have told you if he'd proposed."

She brought her mug to her lips. "Mm-hmm."

"And what would you say if there was a ring on my finger?" I asked, my tone skeptical.

"I'd say I was happy for you."

"Really?"

"Of course. If that's what you want, it's what I want for you."

It was no secret Grandma wasn't Sean's biggest fan. She'd liked him fine when we'd started dating. But as time had gone on, her approval had diminished. Considerably.

"But…" she said, trailing off.

"But, what?"

"Do you really want to know what an old woman has to say about it?"

I wasn't sure if I did, but I knew she'd tell me whether I wanted to hear it or not. "I want to know what *you* have to say about it. *Old* doesn't have anything to do with it."

She opened her mouth to reply, but Janine, one of the facility's caregivers, came out through the automatic doors. She was a sweet lady in her fifties, dressed in a polo with the facility logo on the front.

"There you are, Colleen." There was a hint of something in her voice. Concern, maybe? Or possibly irritation.

Uh-oh.

"Oh hello, Janine," Grandma said, and by her tone, I could tell she was trying to sound innocent.

What was she up to this time?

"Do you know what happened to Maury's reading glasses?" Janine asked.

Grandma clicked her tongue as she shook her head. "Can't say that I do."

"So, you didn't take them when he put them down at breakfast this morning and hide them? Again?"

She gasped. "I would never."

"You've done it three times, Colleen."

I could see Grandma pressing her lips together, trying not to smile.

"If Maury is so worried about his glasses, he ought to keep better track of them." She took a sip of her tea.

The doors opened again, and Maury Haven wheeled himself through. He was completely bald with a bristly gray beard and deep wrinkles, especially on his forehead and around his eyes.

"Colleen, what did you do with my glasses?"

"Hello, Maury," Grandma said. "Lovely day we're having, isn't it?"

His lined forehead creased even more, and his voice was rough and gravelly. "Don't give me that *lovely day* bullshit. Where'd you hide my glasses this time?"

Grandma let out an exasperated sigh. "I don't see how it's my problem if you can't figure out the clue I left."

"Clue?" he barked. "What clue? I didn't see a clue!"

"That's because you weren't looking."

"Colleen, just tell him where you put his glasses," Janine said.

I bit the inside of my lip. Part of me felt like I ought to help coax Grandma into revealing where she'd put Maury's glasses. And part of me wanted to laugh because those two had been pranking each other for years. All because Maury was a Haven.

He was probably related to Theo, although I wasn't sure how.

Maybe a great-uncle or something. There were a lot of Havens in Tilikum. Back in the day, there'd been a generations-long feud between the Haven and Bailey families. My grandma had been on the Bailey side.

Maury and Grandma didn't seem to realize that the feud was over. Or maybe they just didn't care. I wasn't sure who'd started it, but there'd been a regular back-and-forth between them ever since Grandma had moved in.

And despite Maury's surly expression, I knew he dished it out just as much as she did.

With a growl, Maury turned his wheelchair around. "Don't let them touch my table. There's a clue somewhere."

Janine sighed and followed Maury back inside.

"What clue did you leave?" I asked.

"A pencil."

"How is a pencil a clue?"

"Isn't it obvious? There's a cup of pencils on the game cabinet." She giggled softly, as if it were quite the joke. "I hid his glasses in one of the cupboards and put the pencil right where he left his glasses sitting out."

"I suppose that's a decent clue. He'll find them."

"Oh, of course he will." She waved her hand in the direction he'd gone. "He's a Haven, but he's not an idiot."

"I know we've had this conversation before, but you know the feud ended, right? The other Baileys and Havens stopped pranking each other. Mostly. I guess they still do it for fun sometimes."

"Why on earth do you think I do it? Somebody has to. Besides, that crotchety old man loves it. Gives him something to look forward to."

"What do you think he'll do to retaliate this time?"

"It better be something good. Last time all he did was replace my sugar with salt. Maury Haven thinks I won't drink some salty tea? Ha!"

I winced. "You drank tea with salt in it instead of sugar?"

"Absolutely. Didn't make a single face while I did, either. I couldn't let him win, could I?"

"What if he puts something worse in your tea next time?"

She shrugged and took a sip. "We'll see if he's good enough to get something worse by me."

I had a feeling she kind of hoped he would.

It had not escaped my attention that our conversation about Sean had been interrupted. And I was hoping Grandma wouldn't notice and bring us right back to where we'd left off. Because despite what I'd said about wanting to know what she thought, I mostly didn't. And the implications of that were getting harder to ignore.

To be honest, I was starting to feel pretty pathetic.

But things had been so different in the beginning. He'd been fun and sweet and so romantic. Not in the sense that he'd showered me with gifts or flowers all the time. But he had showered me with his attention, and I'd loved it.

Thrived on it, even.

He'd made me feel like I was important to him—maybe even the most important person in his life. Like his favorite thing was to just be with me, regardless of what we were doing.

Somewhere along the way, things had changed. And it had happened so slowly, I'd hardly noticed. Not until it seemed like I was dating a different guy.

But maybe that was just how relationships went. We'd been living together for a couple of years, so the newness had long since worn off. We were both busy. As much as I loved teaching, it took a lot of energy. And he worked for his dad's HVAC company, which could be physically demanding.

Luckily for me, Grandma didn't bring up Sean again, so I didn't have to keep pondering what I was doing with my life.

We chatted more about her squirrel friends, and how she wasn't supposed to be feeding them but did it anyway. That was no surprise. Colleen Wilson had never been one to be told what to do.

That probably had as much to do with why she kept pranking Maury Haven as the old feud. If the staff told her not to do something, that was a great way to get her to do it. Repeatedly.

When our mugs were empty, she pulled her shawl tighter around her shoulders. "Let's go inside. It's getting a bit too chilly for me."

"Do you want to go up to your apartment, or maybe sit by the fireplace downstairs?"

"Fireplace."

"All right. I'll get our dishes."

I gathered up our mugs and followed her inside. There was a busing station next to the coffee and tea, and while she made her way to the fireplace, I put our dishes in the plastic bin.

"Ha!" Maury held up a pair of glasses as she wheeled by him. "Found 'em!"

"Took you long enough," she said.

He grumbled something under his breath, but I didn't catch the words.

Probably for the best.

I pulled a chair from a nearby table and moved it closer to Grandma. She'd grabbed two copies of the local newspaper, the *Tilikum Tribune*, and handed one to me. A lot of what I did when I visited was just hang out while she did whatever she wanted to do—even if it was just reading the paper by the fireplace. I figured it made her happy to have some companionship, and it was nice that I didn't have to worry about entertaining her.

I was also pretty sure she'd chosen to sit in the common area instead of going up to her apartment so she could keep an eye on Maury Haven.

But that was fine. I opened the paper and scanned a few of the headlines. There was a Hometown Spotlight on the front page featuring Gerald McMillan, longtime Tilikum resident and owner of The Art of Manliness, one of the barber shops in town. I smiled as I read it. The Hometown Spotlights were always so charming. They made me feel like I knew the people in the community a little better, even if they were people I'd never met.

Below that, a name caught my attention. Edwin Morris. He was in the paper now and then, usually when he put on a special gallery display or opened a class to the public. But the headline made my breath catch.

Local Painter Edwin Morris Dead at 64

"Oh no," I said. "How sad."

"What's that?" Grandma looked up from what she'd been reading.

"Edwin Morris died."

"Who?"

"He was a painter." I pointed to the canvas above the coffee and tea. "He painted that."

"Did you know him?"

"A little. I've always been a fan, and I took one of his classes over the summer."

"How did he die?"

I scanned through the brief article. "It doesn't say. Just that his wife came home from visiting a family member and found him. Oh, that poor woman. How awful."

"I bet it was a heart attack," Grandma said. "With the men, it's always a heart attack."

"Who had a heart attack?" Maury asked, his gravelly voice booming across the room.

"Not you, obviously," Grandma fired back.

"Don't you wish."

"Don't worry, Maury, I'll be sure to wear red to your funeral."

He chuckled and waved a hand at her. "I've got a suit picked out for yours, Colleen. With a pink tie."

She gasped. "You wouldn't."

"Your least favorite color." He wagged a finger at her. "Don't think I won't remember."

She clicked her tongue and rolled her eyes.

"You two are terrible," I said with a little giggle.

"When you get as old as we are, you either joke about death, or you start to long for it. I'd rather go out laughing."

"That's oddly wise." I glanced at the paper. "Hopefully Edwin Morris went out laughing."

CHAPTER 5

Penelope

Sunlight was starting to filter through the kitchen window while I waited for my morning tea to steep. Absently, I dunked the tea bag a few times, my mind wandering to the day ahead.

I was working with the freshmen and sophomores on sketching on paper with charcoal pencil, and we'd be moving into shading. It would mean a lot of gray fingerprints all over my classroom before the day was done.

Glancing down at my outfit, I wondered if I should change. I'd put on an off-white blouse and tan slacks. Not that the students would touch me, but I had a feeling I'd wind up with charcoal smudges everywhere anyway—most of them my own doing.

If I was being honest, I wasn't a neat artist.

I went to the bedroom to change, opting for a black shirt and dark gray pants. Problem solved.

Sean was still in the shower, and I wondered if he'd want to bring lunch to work. I decided to pack him some of the cranberry walnut chicken salad I'd meal prepped the night before. Hopefully he'd eat it instead of going out for fast food with his buddies.

I sipped my tea as I packed our lunches. Sean came out not long after, his short hair damp and his mustache trimmed. He grabbed his half-empty mug, dumped out the cold coffee, and poured a fresh cup from the coffee maker.

"I packed a lunch for you if you want it." I held up the bag. "Just please bring the container back."

He grunted. I wasn't sure if that meant yes or no, so I set it on the counter. When he took his coffee to the table and sat, I grabbed my tea and joined him.

He took a drink of his coffee, and I sipped my tea. It was weird, but I couldn't think of anything to talk about. I almost launched into an explanation of what was in his lunch, but didn't. He wouldn't be interested in the ingredients of a cranberry walnut chicken salad. The only other thing that popped into my head was the Friday-night football game, but I stopped myself before I blurted out anything about the win. He didn't know I'd been there.

"So," we both said at the same time.

"Sorry," I said. "Go ahead."

He sighed. "No, what were you going to say?"

I hadn't been about to say anything. I'd just instinctively tried to fill the silence. Although his sigh probably meant he didn't really want to hear what I had to say, I jumped into the next topic that came to mind.

"You know that painter, Edwin Morris? I took his class last summer. You came to the picnic with me at the end."

"Is he the one whose wife looks like a skeleton?"

"She doesn't look like a skeleton."

"Yes, she does. She has those cheekbones and weirdly large eyes."

I sighed. "Okay, so she has a face that's…memorable. Anyway, Edwin Morris died."

Sean's brow furrowed, like he had no idea why I'd brought that up. "Oh. What happened?"

"I don't know. There was an article in the newspaper, but it didn't say. Grandma Colleen figures it was a heart attack."

"Probably. Was he old?"

"Not really. He was in his sixties."

"Old enough, I guess."

Wrapping my hands around my mug, I sighed again. "Yeah, I suppose."

Silence crept between us again and I found myself gazing at the painting on the dining room wall. It wasn't a Morris, it was one of mine, but I'd painted it while taking his class. We'd gone to Salishan Cellars, a lovely winery in the neighboring town of Echo Creek, and painted one of the vineyards. Instead of capturing the whole landscape, I'd focused on a small section of vine with plump grapes glistening with early morning dew.

"Are you upset about this or something?" Sean asked.

"Oh, um..." I sat up in my chair and blinked a few times. "Actually, yes. He was a little bit like a mentor. I learned a lot from him. And I've always loved his work."

He made a noncommittal noise.

"Anyway, there's a celebration of life at his gallery on Saturday. I was thinking about going."

"Why?"

"I don't know. To pay my respects. It's open to the public." I hesitated to ask the question on my mind because I had a feeling he was going to say no. But I didn't want to go alone. "Would you come with me?"

Getting up from the table, he groaned. "On Saturday? It's my day off."

"Right, which means you could come with me. We won't stay long."

"Fine, but in and out. Funerals creep me out."

"It's not so much a funeral as a—"

"I gotta get to work." He put his mug in the sink and picked up his lunch bag.

I didn't reply. Just watched while he put on his shoes and grabbed his coat. He left with a mumbled goodbye.

"Bye," I said to the closed door. "Have a good day."

Suddenly overwhelmed, the feeling washed over me like a cloudburst on a previously sunny day. Gripping my tea, I closed my eyes, wishing I could open them and find myself somewhere else. Not on the cusp of a life-shattering choice.

But I couldn't keep grasping at something that wasn't there. I didn't have a boyfriend; I had a roommate who gave me emotional whiplash. Did he even care about me anymore? It seemed like he had, once.

The implications of that train of thought were so overpowering, I had to push it all aside. A decision point was coming, and I'd face it. But not two minutes before I had to leave for work. I had a bunch of teenagers to educate.

I gathered up my things and drove to school. I liked getting there early so I had plenty of time, not just to prep for the day, but to relax a little before the students descended on the building. My mouth turned up in a smile as I parked next to Theo's truck. He was the same way—always got there early.

Absent the hustle and bustle of students, the building was eerily quiet. I needed to put my lunch in the fridge, so I veered toward the teachers' lounge. Maybe I'd make myself another cup of tea.

A low hum of voices greeted me when I went in. Several of my colleagues had gathered at the tables, sitting and chatting with their coffee.

"Pen Diggity," Theo said behind me as I put my lunch in the refrigerator.

"Ooh, nineties hip-hop reference." I closed the fridge door. "I like it."

He held out his fist. I bumped it with mine and we spread our fingers, making our familiar explosion sound.

We took a seat at the open table. His hair was a little disheveled and he had dark circles under his eyes. I could tell by the way he held his head that his neck was stiff, and I wondered if he'd spent his weekend nursing a migraine.

"How was your weekend?" he asked. "Oh, wait. I made you tea."

He got up and I noticed the subtle rigidity to his movements. Poor guy. I hoped it hadn't been too bad. He handed me a cup of tea and sat with his travel mug of coffee.

"I probably left the tea bag in there too long. Sorry."

"Oh, that's okay. Thanks for making it for me."

"You bet. So, weekend?"

I took a sip. Hot and not too strong or bitter. And most definitely appreciated.

"It was fine. Pretty quiet. Just visited Grandma Colleen yesterday."

"How's she doing?"

"She's well. Feisty. She hid Maury Haven's reading glasses again."

He chuckled. "Those two are so funny."

"Aren't they? She said the last time he retaliated, he replaced her sugar with salt. She put some in her tea but drank it anyway."

"Solid prank. Solid response. I like it."

"How was your weekend?"

He lifted one shoulder and took a sip of his coffee. "Didn't do much."

A lock of his hair flopped down over his forehead. Without thinking about it, I reached over and brushed it back. He flinched a little, his reaction almost imperceptible, and a flash of surprise crossed his features.

I pulled my hand away and was about to apologize, but just as quickly, his expression returned to normal.

He ran a hand through his hair. "I should have gotten it cut."

My cheeks warmed, and I had the sudden desire to crack a joke to cut the tension. "I hear mullets are making a comeback. Maybe you should go for one."

"No. No mullets."

"Are you sure? That'd be a good look on you."

He eyed me like I was crazy.

I kind of wanted to reach around and run my fingers through the back of his hair. Make another joke about how he was already halfway to growing one. But my stomach tingled a little and the flush in my cheeks grew.

"Anyway," I said, my mind racing with the sudden need to change the subject. "Something else did happen over the weekend. I found out Edwin Morris died. He was a local painter."

"Oh, really?" He leaned closer and his forehead creased with concern. "Is he the one whose class you took?"

"Yeah." I was surprised he remembered. "I loved his work, and I learned so much from his class."

"He passed away? Man, that sucks. Do you know what happened?"

"No. There was an article in the paper, but it didn't say."

Theo hesitated for a moment, his eyes full of concern. Finally, he reached over and put a hand over mine. "Pen, I'm sorry."

The warmth of his hand made my head fuzzy, and the tingles spread from my stomach all the way to my fingers and toes. "Thanks."

Pressing his lips together, he nodded and squeezed my hand before letting go.

I glanced away and swallowed hard. The mix of butterflies, flushed cheeks, and the sensation of his hand on mine were all getting a little overwhelming.

Which was so weird. It was just Theo.

He cleared his throat. Not a regular throat-clear. It was a signal. When my eyes lifted to meet his, he flicked his gaze to the table next to us, then raised his eyebrows. I cast a quick glance at the table. Everyone had gotten up and gone, but one of our coworkers, Sharon, had left her phone.

No one else would have seen his subtle nod, nor the one I gave him in reply.

My eyes flicked around the room, but Sharon wasn't there. Trying to look as innocent as possible, I deftly reached over and took the phone.

Theo immediately scooted his chair next to mine. "Is it unlocked?"

"Yep."

He picked it up and tapped to open the camera, then held it low, at the most unflattering angle possible. We leaned in so we were both in the frame and pressed our chins down. Theo took several of the ugliest pictures of us imaginable, looking right up our nostrils.

I stifled a giggle behind my hand as we looked at our handiwork. "Those are awful."

"Yeah, so bad." A few swipes and taps later, he'd changed Sharon's background to the terrible photo of us.

He handed the phone back to me, and I slid it onto the table.

"That's going to scare the poo out of her when she opens her phone," I said.

"She should know better than to walk away without it."

"True, she really did bring this on herself." I checked the clock on the wall. "I should get to my classroom."

"Yeah, same." He stood and picked up his travel mug. "The chaos will soon begin."

I got up. "Indeed."

"Good job, by the way."

"Good job with what?"

He grinned. "Not coming to school with paint on your face."

Rolling my eyes, I smacked his arm. He just kept grinning.

And that was when I realized Theo Haven had dimples under his stubble.

How had I never noticed them before?

The rush of butterflies in my stomach threatened to make me start babbling. I got so awkward when I was nervous.

But why was Theo making me nervous? What was wrong with me?

We left the teachers' lounge and walked through the commons and up the wide staircase leading to the second floor. The feel of his hand on mine still lingered for some reason, and I found myself wanting to tuck it against my chest, as if I could preserve the sensation.

On the way up, we passed Sharon going down. She was probably heading to retrieve her phone.

Theo turned and waggled his eyebrows. Suppressing a giggle, I followed him to his classroom, but we didn't go in. Crossing his arms, he leaned against the doorway. I tapped my chin, as if lost in thought about something very important.

A moment later, Sharon let out a startled scream.

Theo's mouth turned up in a triumphant grin. Without a word, we fist-bumped. He gave me a quick wink, then unlocked his classroom and disappeared inside.

I scurried down the hallway, feeling decidedly less brave about our little prank without Theo there. Sharon had a good sense of humor, so I knew she wouldn't be mad or anything. But still. Theo was the one who gave me the courage to do silly things like play harmless pranks on our coworkers.

The flutters were still fluttering and tingles still tingling as I went into my classroom. I picked up a book from my desk and fanned myself. I needed to get myself together before my students started showing up.

But all I could think about as I started prepping for my day were Theo Haven's dimples.

CHAPTER 6

Theo

Running a hand through my damp hair, I got out of my truck. A storm had blown in right when we'd hit the field for practice, drenching everybody. There hadn't been time for me to go home and change, but fortunately, I'd found a Timberwolves hoodie in my truck. A hoodie and shorts were a far cry from interview attire, but Kevin Wilkins, the athletic director for Carolina, knew I was coming straight from practice. He'd been there to watch me coach for about the first hour from the safety of the covered bleachers.

I'd asked to meet him at a sports bar near Tilikum College. It had been a strategic decision on my part. The area around the college was somewhat separate from the rest of town, which substantially decreased my chances of being seen by nosy neighbors who'd be apt to start rumors.

The gossip line in Tilikum was no joke.

I went in and spotted Kevin at a bar-height table, perusing a menu. He looked up as I approached.

"Theo," he said, reaching out a hand. "Thanks for meeting with me."

I took his hand and shook. "Absolutely. Sorry if I kept you waiting. Practice went a little long."

"You're good. I just got here." He gestured to the high-backed stool across from him and I sat. "Can I order you a beer? Something else?"

"A beer would be great. Thanks."

The server came over, and after a brief discussion of what they had on tap, he ordered two Blue Moons.

I'd had a couple of phone conversations with Kevin, but he'd been out due to a family emergency when I'd gone to interview back in July, so I hadn't met him in person. He was probably in his fifties, with light brown hair going gray at the temples and a trimmed beard, and was dressed casually in a half-zip fleece with the Carolina logo on one side of the chest.

"Thanks for flying all the way out here," I said. "It must be a quick turnaround."

"Yeah, in and out. But I really wanted to meet you in person. I like to get a feel for my people, and you just can't do that the same way on a video call."

When the server set our beers on the table, Kevin lifted his drink. "To new opportunities."

I clinked my glass against his and took a sip.

He set his down. "So, tell me about your career. I'm familiar with your résumé, but talk to me about your progression. What's led you here?"

"Sure. After leaving the pros, I moved back here to my hometown. I decided to go back to school, get my masters. While I was doing that, I took the assistant coach position for the high school. A couple of years later, I was hired as a full-time teacher and head coach. So, here I am."

"What about your time in the pros?"

I tapped my thumb on the table a few times. "Shorter than I would have liked."

"You got injured in your first season? Second?"

"Second season. Game three. I got taken out by the human equivalent of a freight train, although the severity of the injury was mostly bad luck. If I'd landed a little differently in one direction, I probably would have walked off the field."

He shook his head. "That's tough."

"Although an inch in the other direction, and I might not have walked again at all, so there's that."

"I remember it. I was watching that game. You could hear the entire crowd gasp when you went down. I don't know how much you were aware of as things were unfolding, but I'll never forget the silence. Tens of thousands of people holding their breath, waiting to see if you'd get up."

I did remember it. Part of me wished it wasn't so clear. "Yeah, it was quiet. That was eerie. I think that was part of how I knew it was bad."

"It's remarkable how you've bounced back. A lot of guys in your position wouldn't have picked themselves up and moved forward."

"It didn't happen overnight. Recovery took a while. But that was what motivated me to go back to school. After months of not doing much other than physical therapy, I was itching to do something. Find a way to stay in the game, you know?"

"Absolutely." He took a drink. "What interests you the most about this opportunity?"

"It would allow me to up my game as a coach. Get into stuff that's more advanced and complex. There's a ceiling on how far you can take your players, and in college, that ceiling is higher."

The conversation turned to my coaching style and ideas for Carolina's offensive strategy, as well as the team's strengths, challenges, and opportunities. Kevin nodded along as I spoke, and the longer we talked, the more my excitement grew.

He took another drink and set down his glass. "As a coach, I'm sure you're used to trusting your instincts."

I nodded.

"My instinct has always been that you're our guy. Watching you coach and talking with you today has really confirmed that. Honestly, you're great with those kids. I feel a little bit guilty trying to steal you away."

I smiled through the sudden knot of nerves in my gut. Was this really going to happen? "Thanks."

"Having said that, I am going to try to steal you away. No pressure to accept right this minute. You'll get an official offer letter and you can take your time. I know it's a big move, and a big decision. But we'd love to have you on board as our offensive coordinator starting next season."

"Wow." I took a deep breath. "Thank you. I'll definitely consider it."

He reached across the table and shook my hand.

"I hate to cut this short, but I'm catching a red-eye home. I need to get going."

After he paid the tab, we both stood and I thanked him again for flying all the way out to Washington to meet with me. He assured me the offer letter would be in my inbox in a day or two.

Once he left, I slid back onto the stool and signaled the server to order another beer. I had a lot to think about.

When Carolina had reached out to me to see if I was interested in the position, I hadn't really thought things would get this far. I'd figured I would fly out to South Carolina, chat with the coaching staff, go home, and never hear from them again. But this was actually happening. I had an offer.

An offer that would take me to the other side of the country.

The server brought my second beer, and I sipped it. I was glad Kevin hadn't pushed me to answer immediately. He was right. It was a big move and a big decision. I didn't have a wife and kids to think about, but I did have a family—a family who meant a lot to me.

This opportunity meant a lot to me, too.

In the back of my mind, I'd thought if I actually got an offer, I'd know if it was the right call. As if somehow the reality of the job would immediately sink in, and my gut would tell me which way to go.

My gut was strangely silent.

Or maybe not silent, but uncertain. I could see it both ways—staying in Tilikum or taking the job. Both had some big pros and cons. And in that moment, neither stood out as being the obvious choice.

Oddly, I thought of Penelope. I kind of wanted to talk to her about it. See what she'd think.

Of course, if the tables were turned, and she was the one contemplating a job offer on the opposite side of the country, I'd probably hate it. The thought of Tilikum High School without her was weirdly depressing.

This was just something I'd have to figure out for myself—sooner rather than later.

CHAPTER 7

Penelope

Tilting my head, I studied the canvas. I'd been working on a new painting—acrylic on canvas—for a few weeks and I was finally starting to feel like it was coming together.

It was an ocean beach, similar to one I'd visited when I was a child. The sun had just dipped below the horizon, staining the sky with shades of pink, purple, and orange. White-tipped waves stretched as far as the eye could see and the gray sand contrasted with the colorful sky.

My painting area was in a storage room off the garage. A space heater provided enough warmth that I'd taken off my cardigan, and the window let in just enough natural light. It wasn't the ideal space, but it was what we had room for. Sean didn't want to share his home office.

Although I wasn't sure why. He hardly ever used it.

I checked the time. The celebration of life was that afternoon, and while I still felt a twinge of anxiety about going, paying my respects in person felt like the right thing to do. I was just glad Sean had agreed to go with me—grudgingly or not. I really didn't want to go alone.

After adding a few more brushstrokes, I took another long look, recalling something Edwin had said in class—sometimes a painting is finished even when we don't think it's perfect.

That was how my beach painting felt. It wasn't exactly what I'd intended to paint, but continuing to tinker wasn't going to improve it. I needed to let it be what it had become.

I put everything away and went to the kitchen to clean my brushes, idly wondering what Sean was up to. We still had some time before we needed to leave, but I had to plan ahead in case he headed into the bathroom. I didn't know if it was an over-thirty thing, or just a guy thing, but he could spend forty-five minutes in there like it was nothing.

Before I could call for him to see where he was, he came out of the bedroom and started putting on his shoes.

"Are you going somewhere?"

"Yeah."

"Um…where?"

"Chad's."

I hesitated, waiting for him to explain, but he didn't. Just tied the lace on his shoe.

"What's going on at Chad's? Will you be gone long?"

"We're testing out his new home theater."

"But…"

"What? Are you going to be mad because I didn't invite you? It's just the guys."

My heart sank and my shoulders slumped. "No. The celebration of life is today."

His eyebrows drew in. "What celebration of life?"

"For Edwin Morris. You know, the painter?"

"Oh. You actually want to go to that?"

"Yes, I do."

He shrugged. "I forgot."

I glanced away. Of course he forgot. He'd probably only been half listening when I'd told him the day and time.

By the way Sean hesitated, his eyes on me, I knew he was waiting for me to tell him it was fine. That he should go hang out with his friends. And in that split second, I realized that was exactly what I was going to say.

I didn't even want him to go with me anymore.

"It's fine," I said. "I'll go by myself."

He nodded, as if that was exactly what he'd wanted—expected—me to say. "Good. I gotta go."

He grabbed his things and left.

Leaning against the kitchen counter, I let out a long breath. Maybe I'd just stay home. It wasn't like I knew Edwin's family. No one would expect me to be there. I'd met his wife once, but that hardly counted. I doubted she'd even remember me, especially with what she was going through.

The real problem was, I was shy, especially around strangers.

I was just about to go change into pajama pants and bury myself in a throw blanket with a good book when Theo popped into my head.

Would Theo go with me?

No. That would be weird. You didn't take your work bestie to a funeral.

But once I'd thought the thought, I couldn't seem to stop thinking it. Because if he didn't have other plans, I had a feeling Theo would go with me. He was the type of guy who'd be there for a friend.

And despite the fact that none of Edwin Morris's family or friends would care if Penelope Fallbrook attended his celebration of life, I cared. I wanted to go.

I grabbed my phone and sent Theo a text.

Hey. Weird request. Is there any way you'd go to a celebration of life with me this afternoon? Sean can't go.

It only took a moment for him to reply.

Sure. What time?

My lips curled in a little smile. Yep, the type of guy who'd be there for a friend. We texted back and forth a few more times, working out the details. I told him the place and time. He offered to drive, so he'd pick me up in an hour.

With that settled, I went to my room to shower and get ready. Knowing me, I had paint on my face again.

The celebration of life was at the Painter's Loft, the gallery in downtown Tilikum owned by Edwin and his wife, Gina. It was housed in a restored brick building a block from Main Street. We had to circle to find parking a short walk from the gallery.

Theo turned off his truck and I adjusted my glasses. I'd chosen a simple long-sleeve black dress I'd had forever and knee-high black boots. My hair was down and I'd triple-checked to make sure I didn't have paint anywhere—on my clothes or my skin. Theo looked nice in a button-down shirt and black slacks.

"Thanks again for coming with me," I said. "It's probably weird. But I don't think I'll know anyone and I still want to go, even if it's a little bit uncomfortable."

"I don't mind weird."

"We don't have to stay long or anything. And I'll make it up to you somehow."

One corner of his mouth lifted. "Pen, it's all good. You don't owe me anything."

Oh my. One of his dimples was puckering. A rush of tingles swept through me.

"Besides," he said, "there's always food at these things. I'll just hang out by the refreshments."

We got out and walked up the sidewalk toward the gallery. I wondered if there were so many cars because of the celebration of life. The obituary had said it was an open-house style event, and the public was welcome. It was nice to think that a lot of people would come pay their respects. I hoped that brought some comfort to his family.

Theo opened the glass door and ushered me inside. The interior was spacious and open, with pale birch floors and paintings on the walls illuminated by gallery lighting. Stairs ascended to a loft with a matte black railing where more artwork was displayed, and a door near the back led to a large space used as a classroom as well as Edwin's personal painting studio.

The displays that were usually in the center of the room had been moved to accommodate the guests, and there was a table set up in the entrance with a guest book. A woman in a black pantsuit and a name tag that read *Lisa* stood behind the table. She greeted us with a warm smile.

"Welcome. Please sign the guest book." She gestured to the book, then to a small stack of blank white stickers. "And if you don't mind, a name tag would be appreciated."

I wrote our names in the guest book while Theo made us name tags in his blocky all-caps handwriting. For a second, I thought he might write a nickname instead of Penelope. He hesitated after writing the first three letters of my name, but seemed to decide it wasn't the time for too much silliness.

He handed me the sticker and I attached it to my dress while he pressed his name tag to his shirt.

"Shall we?" he asked.

Feeling a little self-conscious, I followed Theo into the gallery. People stood in small groups, talking in low voices, and an air of melancholy hung over the room. That was certainly understandable considering the circumstances.

Theo leaned closer as we took a few more slow steps deeper into the gallery. "Do you see anyone you know?"

I glanced around, scanning faces and name tags. There wasn't anyone I immediately recognized, other than the familiarity of Tilikum residents I could recall seeing around town.

"Not really."

He nodded, and there was something about his calm demeanor

that put me at ease. A room full of people I didn't know, especially if there could be small talk involved, was basically my nightmare. But Theo didn't seem the least bit anxious. He exuded his typical casual confidence—relaxed body language, laid-back expression. It slowed my racing heart and made me feel considerably less jittery than I would have otherwise.

As Theo had predicted, there were two large tables with food and beverages along one of the side walls. Theo and I glanced at each other and simultaneously shrugged as if to say, *Why not?* We walked over and started putting various finger foods on small paper plates.

With several pieces of cheese, some crackers, a dollop of fig spread, and a few green olives on my plate, I stepped aside so I wouldn't be in the way. It felt better to have something in my hands.

Theo stood next to me and took a big bite of bruschetta. "Not bad," he said, still keeping his voice low.

Glancing around the room again, I nibbled on my food. I thought I should probably find Gina Morris and say hello. I'd only met her once, so I didn't think she'd remember me—especially with everything she'd been through—but it seemed like the right thing to do.

"I can't believe she showed her face here," a woman on the other side of Theo said to her companion. She looked to be about Edwin's age, probably in her sixties, as did the woman she was talking to. Her name tag read *Jean* and her friend's said *Kathy*.

Theo's eyebrows lifted as he met my eyes. We both took a subtle step closer. It was like being in the teachers' lounge when someone was about to spill the tea.

"I can't, either." Kathy shook her head and appeared to be looking across the room at someone.

"Who?" Theo whispered.

I shrugged. I couldn't tell.

"Gina is showing so much class," Jean said. "I'd have asked her to leave."

"Does Gina know she's here?"

"She must. I saw them standing quite near each other just a few minutes ago."

"Are we sure Gina..." Kathy paused. "Knows?"

The way she said that word dripped with suggestion. Theo and I widened our eyes at each other.

I lowered my voice. "Affair?"

Eyes still wide, Theo nodded. "Maybe."

I adjusted my glasses and started searching out every woman in the room. Had Edwin Morris been having an affair with one of them?

"If she doesn't know, she's blind," Jean continued. "It was more than obvious."

"Look at her. The least she could have done is worn something a little less revealing. It's a funeral, for goodness' sake."

That left little doubt which woman they were gossiping about. She stood talking with a bald man wearing a suit and black-rimmed glasses. Dark hair spilled around her shoulders and the neckline of her dress plunged so low, her name tag was affixed to her skin above her ample cleavage. The hem of her dress rode high on her thighs and she wore the type of stiletto heels that made me wonder how she'd ever be able to walk in them.

I didn't want to be judgy, but it really wasn't a funeral dress. Although it was black, it had a shimmer to it. She looked like she was ready to go clubbing.

Why did she seem familiar? In a flash, I remembered. She'd been in Edwin's painting class. Her named started with an A... Ashley? No. Allison? Amanda? That sounded right. I couldn't quite see her name tag, but I was pretty sure her name was Amanda.

Theo met my eyes, and we moved from our place near the food, gradually making our way to the stairs. A few people came down, passing us as we went up to the loft.

The low hum of voices seemed even more hushed upstairs. Like the main floor below, the loft had been cleared of most of the usual displays. People stood in small knots, some with food or beverages, some without.

I spotted Gina Morris talking with a tall man in a black suit. She wore a long-sleeve black dress and her thick silver hair was styled in a straight bob. With a twinge of guilt, I remembered what Sean had said about her—that she looked like a skeleton. I didn't want to be mean, but he wasn't wrong. She wasn't unattractive, but her large eyes and prominent cheekbones, along with her slender limbs, did give her a slightly lurid beauty.

The man was probably of a similar age, with mostly gray hair and a neatly trimmed beard. His name tag said *Curt Redfern*. Gina dabbed beneath her eyes, and Curt reached into his pocket and handed her a tissue.

"That's Gina, his wife. Well, I guess widow," I whispered to Theo.

"Do you want to say hello?"

"Kind of, but I'm suddenly feeling very shy. What do I say?"

"Just tell her your name and that you're sorry for her loss."

"I have a name tag. Do I have to say my name?"

Theo placed a gentle hand on my back and rubbed a few circles. "Don't overthink it."

His touch was calming and pleasant—probably too pleasant. But it gave me the courage to talk to Edwin's wife.

I took a step, but Theo gripped my elbow softly and maneuvered so he was partially in front of me. Before I could ask what he was doing, a man wearing a dark gray suit staggered by. He was probably in his thirties, and I didn't have to read his name tag to know who he was. He looked like a younger version of his father.

It was Michael Morris, Edwin and Gina's son.

"Tim-may," he said, his voice jarringly loud in the quiet gallery. "Waz up, my man?"

The man he was addressing turned with concern in his expression.

If the staggering gait hadn't given it away, the volume and slurred speech did—Michael Morris was drunk.

Gina's lips pinched and she shook her head slightly as she watched her son. The man with her—Curt—put a hand on the small of her back, leaned in, and said something close to her ear. She dabbed the corners of her eyes with the tissue.

Theo moved to my other side, as if to shield me from Michael Morris. Michael had lowered his voice, thankfully, but you never knew what people would do when they were intoxicated. Especially when they'd also suffered a deep loss. I felt sorry for him.

I figured I should offer my condolences to Gina, and then Theo and I should leave. The tension in the gallery was growing thicker by the minute. I had a feeling there was a lot of family drama simmering just beneath the surface.

Theo walked with me, and I gathered my courage as I approached Gina.

She met my eyes and gave me a polite smile. I had a feeling she'd been doing a lot of that. Curt Redfern stood next to her like a sentinel.

"Hi, Mrs. Morris." I nervously adjusted my glasses. "I'm Penelope Fallbrook. Sorry, that's on my name tag. You probably don't remember me, but we met briefly last summer. I was one of your husband's students. I'm so sorry for your loss."

"Thank you," she said with a small nod.

I opened my mouth and inhaled, although I didn't have anything else to say. Theo gently took my elbow again, turned me around, and led me toward the stairs.

"Thank goodness you did that," I said on the exhale. "I was about to start rambling."

"You did great. I'm sure she appreciates that you came."

"Can we just stop?" Michael's drunk voice rose again. "Like he was so great. Didn't even want me here. Go ahead, Mom. Kick me out. Iss fine."

Theo and I stepped out of the way as Curt Redfern, his expression grave, grabbed Michael by the arm and led him to the stairs.

Michael laughed as they moved to the lower level. At the bottom, he stumbled, but Curt yanked him upright.

"You all think he was so great," Michael said. "The bastard cut me off. Cut off his own son. Piece of shit."

Gina moved to the railing and silently watched her son get dragged out of the gallery, her expression filled with sorrow.

Theo and I made eye contact again, and without a word, headed down the stairs. We needed to get outside. There was a lot to discuss.

We'd just gotten to the bottom of the stairs when a male voice interrupted our escape.

"Excuse me, Penelope Fallbrook?"

It was yet another man in a suit. He had a professional air about him, as if that were his everyday attire.

"Yes, that's me."

"I'm Jerry Turner, Edwin Morris's attorney." He held out his hand.

I clasped it and shook. "I'm sorry for your loss."

"Thank you. Edwin earmarked a number of his paintings that he wished to be gifted to his students in the event of his passing. One of them is for you."

I touched my chest. "He wanted to give a painting to me?"

"Yes. Your name is on the list. I can give it to you now, or if it's more convenient, I can take your contact information and make other arrangements."

I glanced up at the loft, but Gina was no longer at the railing. "Is it okay with Mrs. Morris? All his things must be hers now."

"She's happy to respect her husband's wishes."

"What a lovely gift. Sorry, I'm just very touched." I brushed my hair off my forehead and glanced at Theo. He nodded. "I can take it now. That would be fine."

"Wonderful. This way."

We followed Jerry to the back of the gallery and through the door that led to the large classroom workspace. The walls were exposed brick, and it was cluttered with paintings on easels—the pieces that had been moved to make space for the gathering.

A chill hung in the air, and I crossed my arms while Jerry sorted through a stack of framed canvases leaning against the wall. He took one out of the middle and held it up.

It wasn't very large, maybe eighteen by twenty-four, with a simple wood frame. A creek meandered across the landscape, and a big rock formation rose on one side. Mountains loomed in the background and trees blazed with fall color, their cheerful tones a stark contrast to the cloudy sky.

"It's beautiful," I said as he handed it to me. "Thank you so much."

"You're welcome. Thanks for coming."

Theo offered to carry the painting, so I handed it to him. We went back through the gallery, and it was a relief when we stepped outside. I didn't want it to look like we'd stolen something.

We paused on the sidewalk and looked at each other open-mouthed. There was so much tea, we didn't know where to begin.

CHAPTER 8

Theo

Penelope and I walked to my truck in silence. I wasn't sure where to start. The gossipy ladies accusing the deceased of having an affair? The woman in question, wearing a dress that barely concealed her boobs? The drunk son, going on a tirade about his father and getting kicked out by his mother?

So. Much. Tea.

It wasn't that I was a gossip. Not like the Tilikum busybodies who spread rumors like it was their job. I wouldn't tell anyone. But discuss it—at length—with Pen? Heck yeah, I was doing that. How could I not?

I unlocked my truck and when Penelope got in, I handed her the painting before heading around to the driver's side and climbing into my seat.

"Wow," I said, not sure what else to say.

"You can say that again."

"Where do we start?" I shifted in my seat so I was partially facing her.

She did the same, angling toward me. "Those ladies meant he was having an affair, right?"

"That's totally what they meant. Did you know anything about it?"

"No, but I don't really know anything about his personal life. I've seen the woman before, though."

"Amanda? Really?"

Her brow furrowed. "Do you know her?"

I winced. "I sort of went on a date with her."

Her eyes widened and her mouth dropped open. "You did not. When? How long did you date her?"

"No, no, no. Wrong idea. I didn't date her. We went out one time a few years ago. My aunt Louise set us up."

"Why didn't you go out again?"

"If I remember, it felt a lot like a job interview. She asked me my annual salary."

"That's rude."

I nodded. "Yup. But that's what I get for agreeing to an Aunt Louise date. Anyway, do you know her?"

"She was in the painting class I took last summer."

"So she definitely knew Edwin. Did you notice anything going on between them?"

She paused and pressed her finger to her lips, like she did when she was thinking. "Maybe? He did seem to pay her a lot of attention. But I assumed it was because…"

"Because what?"

"This is going to sound bad, and I don't mean it that way, but she wasn't a very good painter. So it seemed like he was spending a lot of time working with her because she needed the help. Like, so much help."

"Or maybe because he was interested in her. Or they were already boinking on the side."

"Boinking?" she said with a laugh.

"You know what I mean." I made a circle with my thumb and forefinger and used my other hand to stick my pointer finger in and out.

She laughed harder. "Nice visual. Thank you for that."

"In case I'm not being clear, this is the dick." I held up my pointer finger. "And this is the—"

She smacked my hands. "Stop. I know."

I chuckled. "All right, so renowned painter, and married man,

Edwin Morris might have been having an affair with one of his students. Interesting. Also, disgusting."

Penelope's face fell. "I know. It's very disappointing. I hope those ladies were wrong."

"Yeah, adultery is fucked up."

She raised her eyebrows. I was careful with my language at school, so she wasn't used to hearing me swear.

"It is," I said with a shrug.

"You're right. Very."

"So the drunk guy was their son?" I asked, needing to move on so I didn't start staring at Penelope's very full mouth.

"Yes, Michael. I've never met him, but he looks so much like his dad."

"Man, he was not okay. I saw him stumbling around that loft, and for a second, I thought he was coming toward you."

"I'm glad he wasn't."

"Me too. I didn't want to have to drop the guy at his dad's funeral."

Pen's lips parted like she was going to say something, but she didn't. Just gazed at me, like she was seeing me for the first time.

"What?" I asked.

"Nothing." She shook her head a little. "Anyway, he was a mess. I wonder if that's normal behavior for him or if it was the result of grief."

"I don't know. He was yelling about his dad cutting him off. And his mom just watched that other dude escort him out."

"My guess is ongoing conflict, and Gina and that Curt guy were prepared for the worst."

"I bet you're right." I put my hand on the steering wheel and looked out the windshield for a moment. "I feel bad for his wife. Lost her husband and has a messed-up son."

"I can't even imagine. She looked like she was holding herself together, though."

"She did. Probably one of those people who's good at putting on a brave face in public."

"Who knows how she's coping in private."

"Where do you think Michael ended up?" I asked. We hadn't seen any sign of him when we'd left the gallery.

"Hopefully he got a ride home. Now I'm so curious. Is he married? Does he have a family? Where does he live? Did his dad cut him off because he has a drinking problem? What does cutting him off even mean?"

"What if Michael found out about his dad's affair and that's why they had a falling-out?"

She gasped. "Ooh, that's a good theory. Or maybe Michael was a talented artist who threw it all away to study math and his dad never forgave him for it."

"Hey, I have a math degree."

"I know, but your dad isn't an artist."

"True. And he never tried to get me to follow in his footsteps, either."

She moved the painting so it was flat on her lap, face up. "I guess we'll never know."

"Probably not. Although you know the gossip line is going to pick up on the Edwin-Morris-was-cheating story, whether it's true or not."

"Poor Gina."

"Yeah, it's brutal." I looked down at the painting. "That's really nice. Where are you going to put it?"

"I don't know. I'm not sure where we have room."

She hadn't said it, but all I heard was, *I'm not sure where Sean will let me hang it.* I resisted the urge to grip the steering wheel in frustration.

"Can I ask a favor?" Pen's voice was soft. "You already did me a big favor by coming, so I don't want to impose, but hopefully this is a small one. Except—"

"Hey," I said, gently interrupting her. "It's fine. What do you need?"

"Could you keep this for me? Just until I figure out where to put it. I wouldn't want anything to happen to it, you know?"

"No problem." I hesitated, wondering if she was going to explain further. There was something in her voice—a sense that she meant more than just needing a place to keep the painting until she decided where to hang it.

Was this about more than wall space? Was she thinking about leaving—

"Anyway," she said, talking fast, "thank you so much. I'm afraid I would have frozen up if I'd gone in there alone. And I did not expect that to turn into the opening scenes of a soap opera."

"It was morbidly entertaining. Even better than trying to figure out if Jeremy and Ashley are hooking up at work."

She laughed. "We still haven't figured out if we're right."

"If they are messing around at school, they're good at not getting caught."

"Ugh, I know. It makes me even more curious."

"Same. We'll have to watch them a little bit closer."

She held out her fist. "Done."

I bumped my fist against hers and we did the explosion thing.

Light rain started to fall as I turned on my truck and pulled out onto the street. We chatted a little more about the goings-on at the celebration of life on the way back to Penelope's house. When I dropped her off, I thought about walking her to her door, but ultimately didn't. Seemed kinda weird. And I didn't know if Sean was home. I didn't want to make trouble for her.

I waited until she got inside, then hesitated with the truck still running. Rain pattered on the windshield, obscuring my view of her front door. I was strangely reluctant to leave, although I didn't know why.

With a glance at the painting she'd left on the seat, I backed out of the driveway. I'd see her Monday at school.

And it would have to be enough.

CHAPTER 9

Penelope

I wasn't sure when Sean would be back. Either way, his absence after Theo dropped me off was a relief. I had a lot on my mind, and I wouldn't have been able to think clearly if he'd been there.

Because it was Sean I needed to think about. Specifically, my relationship with him.

Suddenly overwhelmed, I wandered through the house, looking from room to room, wondering what on earth I was going to do.

How could I get out? I didn't have anywhere else to go. But I couldn't keep avoiding the truth. I needed to leave him.

The situation was so daunting. We weren't just dating. We lived together. Leaving him would mean finding a new home. Would I be able to find something quickly enough? And if I did, would I be able to afford it on my own?

It wasn't like I had a fallback. My parents lived in another state. And Grandma didn't have her own place anymore. Her one-bedroom apartment couldn't fit me, and there were probably rules against it anyway.

To make things worse, I didn't exactly have a lot of friends.

But I'd stayed with Sean too long as it was—stuck in a rut and not sure how to get out. I needed to face the reality that this relationship, whatever it had been in the beginning, wasn't good for me. It was time to move on.

You're not getting any younger, you know.

"Yeah, yeah, I know," I said aloud, pushing away the whispering voice in my mind reminding me how hard it would be to start over in my thirties. "Don't remind me."

With a deep breath, I grabbed my phone and took it to the living room. A new place to live wasn't going to find itself. I needed to take care of that first, because as soon as I told Sean I wanted to end things, staying in his house would not be an option. I needed a place to land.

Before I had a chance to start my search, the front door opened and Sean came in, carrying a bouquet of red roses.

"Hey, babe." He shut the door behind him and brought the flowers to me. "Here."

I took them and the floral scent surrounded me. "What are these for?"

"Just because."

"You bought me flowers just because?"

"Sure, why not?"

I couldn't remember the last time he'd brought me flowers, except as an apology. Was that what they were? Apology flowers? Was he trying to make up for not going to the celebration of life with me?

"They're pretty." I leaned in and sniffed them. "Thank you."

I got up and took them to the kitchen so I could put them in water. Flowers weren't going to change my decision, but I wasn't ready to have that conversation with him.

He disappeared into the bedroom while I unwrapped the flowers, cut the stems, and placed them in a vase.

"Hey babe?" he called as he came out. He'd changed out of his work clothes into a navy T-shirt and a pair of cargo pants. "I was thinking we should just go out to dinner tonight. There's this new place the guys have been talking about. Sounds good."

My stomach rumbled at the mention of food. I certainly wasn't in the mood to cook. It would mean sitting awkwardly across the table from Sean, but I could handle it.

"Sure, we can go out."

"Awesome. Do you need to change or anything?"

I glanced down at my black dress. "Where are we going? Is this too dressy?"

"No, it's a nice place. You look great."

"Okay." I put the last rose in the vase and cleaned up the cut stems before grabbing my purse and putting on my black trench coat.

We left and I climbed into his truck. Hard rock blared from the speakers as soon as he turned it on. I leaned back against the seat, as if the wave of noise had shoved me.

He turned it down without comment as he pulled out of the driveway.

I'd assumed we were going into town, but he took the route to the highway and went south.

"Where are we going? It's not in Tilikum?"

"No, Echo Creek."

"Who told you about it?"

"Some of the guys at work."

I wondered if that meant it was a sports bar.

The hard rock he listened to was not my style—I was more of a nineties pop girl—but after long moments of silence, I was grateful there was something in the background. Several minutes later, he turned up the volume, and his playlist kept us company for the rest of the drive.

Echo Creek was a cute town about half an hour from home. We parked outside the downtown restaurant and he held the door for me as we went in. The ambiance was nice. Very classy with white tablecloths and flickering flameless candles. It was packed, with only one or two empty tables to be seen, and servers dressed in black maneuvered in the dim light.

Definitely not what I'd been expecting—it wasn't a sports bar at all.

I was still looking around in surprise, wondering which of his friends had suggested such a nice place, when Sean told the hostess he had a reservation. I teetered on the edge of annoyance. Once again, he'd made plans without asking me first. Was it because he wanted to treat me to a nice dinner? Or was he just barreling forward, doing what he wanted and assuming I'd go along with it?

The host led us to our table. It was roughly in the center of the dining room, with tables on either side of us. He set menus at each place setting and told us our server would be with us shortly.

I shrugged off my coat and let it drape over the back of my chair, then picked up the menu.

"What do you think?" Sean asked. "Nice place, huh?"

I glanced around. "Very."

"Should we get a bottle of wine?"

"A whole bottle? I don't think I'll have more than one glass."

"Come on, babe. Why not? They're supposed to have really good wine here. It's from the winery up the road."

I didn't think we needed an entire bottle, but I decided it wasn't worth arguing over. "Okay, wine would be nice."

The server came and Sean ordered a bottle of cabernet and calamari for an appetizer. I kept perusing the menu, trying to decide between something with chicken and a pork dish that sounded good.

A few minutes later, she came back with our wine, poured, and took our orders. I opted for the chicken and Sean ordered a New York strip steak.

"So, Penelope, I've been wanting to talk to you about something."

"Oh?"

"We've been together for a long time. And it's been great."

Wait. What was he talking about?

"Which is why," Sean said, but then he paused and looked over at something behind me.

"Which is why, what?" I asked.

He nodded, and I glanced over my shoulder, but didn't see anyone. A second later, the server appeared next to our table holding a glass of champagne on a plate. Smiling at me, she set it on the table.

Why was there champagne? We had wine. An entire bottle. Confused, I looked at it like I'd never seen a champagne flute in my life and had no idea what it could possibly be.

"Go ahead," Sean said.

With my brain swirling in a hundred directions and blood pounding in my ears, I lifted the glass. Suddenly, I realized what was happening. At the bottom of the champagne flute, surrounded by rising bubbles, was a diamond ring.

Oh, no. Oh, no, no, no.

My eyes widened and my mouth dropped open. The server moved back and Sean slipped out of his chair, getting down on one knee in front of me.

This can't be happening.

I watched him as if I were in a dream. There'd been a time when it would have felt like the moment I'd been waiting for. I'd moved in with him assuming it would eventually lead to a proposal. But now? When I'd finally come to terms with what I needed to do? I couldn't marry him. I was going to leave him.

"Penelope." He took my hand, and before I could stop him, continued, "Will you marry me?"

It seemed as if the entire restaurant took a collective breath. It was dead silent. Not the tiniest clink of silverware could be heard. We were in a packed restaurant on a Saturday night, sitting right in the middle, and every single eye was on us.

"No." My voice sounded strange, as if someone else were speaking. It was too matter-of-fact. Too straightforward and emotionless for the sheer destructive force of that one word.

Still on one knee, Sean blinked in confusion. "What?"

I shook my head slowly, sadly, my eyes losing focus. "No."

An uncomfortable murmur rippled through the restaurant. I had enough presence of mind to feel a little bit bad about that. I took my hand out of Sean's and held it close to my chest, as if I'd been burned.

"No, Sean. I'm so sorry, but I can't marry you."

"Are you kidding me?" he asked.

The server backed away slowly as Sean stood. People averted their eyes as he glanced around. His face flushed, and a vein stuck out on his forehead. For a second, I wondered if he was going to do something outrageous, like flip the table. He'd never been violent, but I'd never seen him look quite that angry.

He took a deep breath, his nostrils flaring. Then he smoothed down his shirt, and when he spoke, his voice was even. "Can we talk outside?"

I nodded and stood, grabbing my coat and purse, and followed him out.

The night air was cold. I put my coat back on and tied the belt. Considering what I'd just done, I didn't know how I could be so calm. But my hands didn't tremble, and I didn't feel the least bit anxious or jittery.

"What the hell is going on?" He gestured to the restaurant. "Isn't this what you wanted? Isn't this what I'm supposed to do?"

"Supposed to do? What does that even mean?"

"What you think it means?"

My shoulders slumped. "That you're comfortable. And you probably figure that's good enough."

"What are you talking about?"

"We're not good together, Sean. Maybe we were at first, although it's hard to remember anymore. But we certainly aren't now."

"Sure, we are. What's the problem?"

"Why do you want to marry me?"

"Because…" He paused, his mouth slightly open, like he'd intended to say more, but realized he didn't have an answer.

I raised my eyebrows.

"Because this is what you do," he said, finally. "We've been together for a long time. We live together. Shouldn't we just get married?"

"No," I said with a slow shake of my head. "We shouldn't. We're not in love with each other. We're barely even friends."

Resting his hands on his hips, he shook his head. "This is fucked up, Penelope."

"I'm sorry. If I'd realized what you were planning, I wouldn't have let it happen."

"Well, you did, didn't you? Made a fool out of me in front of an entire restaurant full of people."

"That isn't my fault."

"You know what? Fine. If this is what you want—if you want to be single again—great. Good fucking luck out there." He pointed a finger at me. "But you're going to realize, sooner rather than later, that you just made the biggest mistake of your life. Because no one else is going to want you."

That arrow struck a bull's-eye. My eyes filled with tears, and I furiously bit the inside of my lip to keep them from spilling.

He shook his head again, as if he'd reached the point of being more disappointed than angry, and started to walk away.

"Wait," I called after him. "Where are you going?"

"Home."

"You left the ring in there. We didn't pay."

"I'll deal with it later."

He kept walking, and I wondered if he expected me to run after him. "Sean."

"What?" he snapped and paused to look at me over his shoulder.

"Are you leaving me here?"

"You just left me. Find your own damn ride."

I gaped at him as he kept walking and got in his truck. He couldn't seriously be leaving me on the side of the road at night in a town thirty minutes from home.

Home? I didn't have a home. Not anymore.

My mouth hung open as I watched his truck roar to life. Music blared, and with a squeal of tires and a whiff of burning rubber, he left.

"Excuse me, ma'am?"

Still half dazed, I turned toward the host standing in the partially open door of the restaurant. "You were watching all that, weren't you?"

He stepped outside. "I didn't mean to intrude. I just wanted to make sure things didn't escalate."

"Thank you." My voice sounded far away, and I gazed past him, not really focusing on anything. "He didn't pay. Do you need me to—"

"No, no. Don't worry about that. Do you need help getting a ride?"

I blinked a few times to clear my head, realizing I was standing there like an idiot, doing nothing. I pulled my phone out of my purse. "I'll call someone."

"All right. I'll be right inside if you need anything."

"Thank you. I'm really sorry about all this."

"Don't apologize. It's not the first time this has happened."

He quietly stepped back into the restaurant, but I had a feeling he was going to watch out the window until he was sure I'd gotten a safe ride.

I stared at my phone. Who was I supposed to call? I had no family except a grandmother in assisted living who couldn't drive. And as I'd already realized, I wasn't exactly swimming in friends.

Just Theo.

My eyes brimming with tears I knew were about to fall, I brought up his number and called.

CHAPTER 10

Theo

The movie I'd turned on was boring. I was sprawled out on my couch with an equally boring sandwich for dinner. Maybe I'd go out. A beer at the Timberbeast didn't sound half bad. Better than sitting around by myself, at least.

I turned off the TV and got up to change out of the pajama pants I'd put on when I'd gotten home. Penelope's Morris painting was on my dining table, ready for her to take home when she decided where to put it. I still wondered why she'd asked me to hang on to it for her. Not that I minded. It wasn't a big deal. It just struck me as odd.

I grabbed my keys, and right as I was about to slip my phone in my pocket, it buzzed with a call. Penelope.

A jolt of alarm hit me. Why was she calling?

"Hey, Pen."

"Hi… Um…" She trailed off for a second. "I'm sorry to bother you, but…"

"But what? What's the matter?"

"It's a long story." She sniffled and seemed to be having trouble talking.

Oh, shit. She was crying.

"Pen, what's wrong? Where are you?"

"Echo Creek. I just…I need a ride."

I was already out the door. "I'm on my way. Where in Echo Creek?"

"Outside…a restaurant," she said between sobs. "Sage Bistro."

"Don't worry, I got you." I got in my truck and fired up the engine. "What's going on? You're outside?"

"Ye—" She hiccupped. "Yes."

"Are you safe? I'm half an hour away. Can you wait inside?"

"N-no. I…um…can't… Don't…want to…go back in."

"Okay, hang tight. I'll be there as fast as I can. Stay on the phone with me, okay?"

"Uh-huh."

Tension rippled through me as I drove, listening to the sound of her crying on the other end. I knew it was Sean. That douchebag piece of shit. What had he done to her? Why was she outside a restaurant in another town? That fucker. I'd rip his face off.

My hands gripped the steering wheel as I navigated the winding highway. Every time her end went quiet, I checked to make sure she was still there. She was. The sobbing died down, but she didn't talk much. Just replied with a soft yes when I asked if she was still on the phone.

The drive went by fast—probably because of my complete lack of attention to the speed limit. Once I got into Echo Creek, I peered into the dark as I drove down the main road through town, looking for Pen. Finally, I caught sight of her standing on the sidewalk outside Sage Bistro.

"I'm here," I said as I pulled into the no-parking zone in front of the restaurant.

Without a word, she ended the call. I slammed my truck into park and unlocked the door. She climbed in and shut the door.

"Hey," I said, keeping my voice soft despite the mix of worry and anger clenching my chest. "What happened?"

Her lower lip trembled, and it took her a moment to answer. "Sean proposed."

My eyes flew to her hands, rage pouring through me at the mere thought of seeing that jackass's ring on her finger. But it wasn't there. Because of course it wasn't. That's why she was crying.

"Oh, shit," I muttered. "You turned him down."

Eyes on her lap, she nodded. "The whole restaurant saw." Although she was no longer sobbing, her voice shook. "He was pretty mad. So he left."

"He left you out there alone?"

Still not looking at me, she nodded again.

"Fuck," I said under my breath. Yes, I was furious, but more than anything, I was concerned about her. I turned up the heat. She had to be cold.

"Thanks." She held her hands in the warm air coming out of the vent. "I, um…"

It looked like she was going to start crying again, so I waited. I wanted to reach over and pull her to me, but the center console was in the way. What was I going to do, drag her into my lap?

I glanced at the space between me and the steering wheel. Actually, if I moved the seat all the way back—

Big tears rolled down her cheeks from beneath her glasses. "I don't have anywhere to go," she whispered quickly, as if it was almost too much for her to get the words out.

Of course she didn't. She lived with him and had just ended their relationship. The piece of shit had left her there, alone in the dark, with nowhere to go.

"Yes, you do." My voice was decisive as I put the truck back in drive. "You're coming home with me."

"I can't ask you to let me stay with you."

I pulled out onto the street. "You didn't. I'm telling you, you're coming to my place."

She took a shaky breath. "Thank you."

We spent the drive in silence. It didn't seem like she was ready to talk, and I didn't want to make her start crying again.

About halfway home I decided fuck it, and reached over to hold her hand.

Maybe it was weird to hold hands with your best friend when

she'd just broken up with her boyfriend, but I didn't care. I had to do something. I couldn't let her sit there in misery.

I twined our fingers together and squeezed. With another shaky breath, she squeezed back.

It felt good. Really good.

When we arrived at my house, I parked and reluctantly let go. We got out and went inside, Penelope taking slow steps into the living room, like she wasn't sure where to go or what to do.

I set my keys on the counter. "Do you want to take your coat off?"

"Oh." She looked down at herself as if she'd forgotten she was wearing it. "Sure."

She untied the belt, and I stepped in to hold her purse and take her coat as she slipped it off. She still wore the black dress she'd had on earlier, and damn, it looked great on her. But I couldn't start thinking about the way the dress hugged her curves when her life had just fallen apart.

I hung her coat and purse on the hook by the door. "Do you want something else to wear?"

Her hands skimmed her hips, which did not help. "That would be great. Thank you."

"I'll be right back."

I went to my bedroom, forcing my brain—not my groin—to stay in control. She needed clothes. A place to sleep. I probably had an extra toothbrush I'd gotten at the dentist's office. There'd be more to deal with—a lot more—but that should get her through the night.

Grabbing my THS hoodie, a white T-shirt, and a pair of pajama pants that were going to be big on her but were the best I could do, I fished a toothbrush and some toothpaste out of a drawer in my bathroom and took it all across the hall to the spare bedroom. It was a bit of a mess in there. I used it mostly for storage, although I had a futon that folded flat. No one had slept on it in years. Probably not since my brother Zachary, back in his troublemaker days. He'd needed a place to crash once in a while—usually after starting shit at the Timberbeast.

Those days long gone, the couch was covered in a pile of old clothes I'd been meaning to get rid of and one of the blankets my mom had knit for me. I tossed the clothes in the corner and moved the futon away from the wall so I could fold the back down. I couldn't remember where I'd put the extra sheets, but there was a sleeping bag in the closet. Not ideal, but it was better than nothing. I found a pillow and made the bed as best I could, draping the throw blanket over the sleeping bag to make it look a little cozier.

I laid the change of clothes on top and set the toothbrush and toothpaste on a side table. My makeshift hospitality wasn't exactly impressive, but at least I had a room to offer her.

"Sorry," I said as I walked back to the living room. "I was getting things set up for you. There's a futon in the spare bedroom. All I could find is a sleeping bag. But I put some clothes in there and I found a toothbrush that's still in the package."

She still stood in the living room, hugging her arms around herself, her expression as forlorn as a puppy left out in the pouring rain.

My entire body ached with the desire to hold her. To march over, put my arms around her, and crush her against me. I wanted to fix this. Not her relationship—she deserved so much more than that dick—but I wanted to make her feel better, almost more than I could stand.

"Thank you."

The way her voice still shook held me back. I was out of my depth and feeling way too many things. I had to be careful or I was going to do something monumentally stupid. Like kiss her.

Or worse, offer to be her revenge fuck.

No. Not a good idea.

I stepped aside and gestured toward the spare room. "It's through there."

With a nod, she went in and closed the door behind her.

Letting out a low groan, I raked my hand through my hair and wandered into the kitchen. I needed to keep moving—keep doing things. Tea. She liked tea.

Did I have tea?

I rooted around and found a box of green tea in a cupboard. Turning it over, I wondered why I had it. And how old it was. Did tea expire? I didn't even have a teakettle—just a coffee maker—but all I needed was hot water. That I could do. I pulled out a small pan and got some water heating on the stove.

Was she hungry? I wondered if they'd made it through dinner before he'd popped the question. Curiosity about how that had gone down poked at me. I opened the fridge, but I hadn't been to the store recently and didn't have much on hand.

I turned around at the sound of the bedroom door opening. She emerged, dressed in my hoodie and the too-big pajama pants. Her hair was pulled over one shoulder, draping between her neck and the hood. She had the sleeves rolled up and her hands in the front pocket.

Why was that so hot?

None of it fit. The sweatshirt hung low, I had a feeling the drawstring was the only reason the pants weren't falling off, and her feet were bare. And it was sexy beyond belief. It called to mind an image of her coming out of my bedroom in the morning after a night of ravaging her.

Why was I thinking like that? I was the worst.

"Thanks again," she said. "This is much more comfortable."

My eyes swept up and down and her toes caught my attention. "Are your feet cold? Do you want socks?"

"No, I'm fine. This is great."

"I'm making tea." I jerked my thumb over my shoulder at the stove. "Not sure if it's any good, but it's all I have. Do you want some?"

"That's okay." She headed toward the couch in the living room. "I don't need any."

I turned off the burner while she sat down, then went to join her. Maybe I should have given her space, but I sat right next to her. I couldn't help it. The need to be close to her was killing me.

"I'm surprised I didn't see it coming," she said. "He brought me flowers. Do you know how long it's been since he brought me flowers?"

"I don't know."

"A long time. And they were usually apology flowers after we argued." She paused. "Sorry to just start babbling, but I think I need to get it all out."

"Go ahead."

"He took me to that restaurant. He'd made a reservation, which is also not like him. I wish I would have realized. Maybe I could have stopped him. But it wasn't until the server came out with a glass of champagne, even though he'd already ordered an entire bottle of wine, that I realized what was happening. There was a ring in the glass."

"He ordered a whole bottle of wine but put your ring in a glass of champagne?"

"That's weird, right? Good, I thought it was just me. It was sort of confusing."

"Yeah, not quite how you're supposed to make that move."

"Anyway, he did the whole thing. Got down on one knee and the entire restaurant went silent." She leaned her head back against the cushion. "Everyone was watching. It was so surreal and horrible."

I thought about taking her hand again, but it didn't feel right, so I waited.

"He asked, and do you know what I did? I said no. Just like that."

Relief washed over me like a hot shower after a hard-won game. Ever since the first time I'd met Sean, I'd been waiting for her to wake up. To realize she deserved better.

"Obviously, he got upset. We went outside to talk. I don't think it had occurred to him that I might say no. He thought, well, we've been together so long, getting married is just what you do." She paused again. "Do you want to know what's really bizarre?"

"What?"

"I'd already decided to leave him. Earlier today. I was feeling pretty overwhelmed, because it means starting over, finding a new place to live, all of that. I wanted to figure out where I was going to go before I told him."

"That's fair."

"You're probably wondering why I was with him for so long."

I'd wondered that more times than I could count, but I didn't want to be a jerk about it. "Yeah. Kinda."

"So am I. Things weren't like this when we got together. Not even when I first moved in with him. We had fun. He was always doing nice things and spending time with me. He showered me with attention, which felt really good at the time."

She shifted so she could tuck her legs under herself. Knowing I probably shouldn't, I lifted my arm, giving her space to nestle against me if she wanted. She gradually leaned closer, almost as if she wasn't aware of what she was doing, until she rested against my chest.

"I don't think I would have admitted it back then, but I was kind of desperate for attention. Or affection, maybe."

Her body settled against me, and I put my arm around her.

"Why?"

"Probably because of my parents. After they got divorced, they were really wrapped up in dating. And then they married other people. I spent most of my childhood being ignored. Or at least feeling ignored. So of course I loved all the attention from Sean. He was giving me something I'd never had before."

I gently rubbed her arm with my thumb. "Yeah, that makes a lot of sense."

"Now I look back and I think I mistook the way he showered me with attention for something more. For love. Because, the thing is, I don't think the attention was about me, or even for me. It was for him—the way he'd learned to make a woman like him. And once I was there—once he felt like he had me—it started to go away. He didn't need to try anymore, so he didn't. But the change was so gradual, I barely saw it happening.

"Lately I've been wondering how I got here. How did I let it go on so long? I kept trying to remember what it had been like at the beginning, as if somehow that would make it all better. And I kept making excuses. Like this is just what happens when you've been together for a while. Things get routine, and maybe a little boring."

She was quiet for a long moment. Resting my face against her hair, I inhaled her scent. She smelled so good. My eyes closed as I let it fill me.

"It wasn't just boring," she said, finally. "I don't think he cared about me very much. He wasn't even very nice to me."

"I'm so proud of you."

"Really?"

I caressed her arm with my thumb again. "Absolutely. What you did tonight was hard, but it was the right thing to do."

Sniffling, she nestled in closer. "Thanks."

A brief fantasy came to mind, of me pulling her into my lap, her legs straddling me. My hands digging into her backside while my tongue invaded her mouth. Our clothes coming off—the logistics didn't matter, it was just a fantasy—and me thrusting inside her, making her forget everything. I'd fuck the memory of that piece of shit right out of her.

But I shoved it away—decisively. She was my friend. Not even just my friend, she was my best friend. I didn't really want to be her revenge fuck, and banging her on my couch would only lead to complications neither of us needed. It would change things between us—change everything.

I couldn't let that happen. Especially now, when she needed me to be her friend.

The hard-on was annoying, but totally my fault, and thankfully not too obvious in the pants I was wearing.

I felt her body relax, and her breathing was slow and even. After sitting with her for a while, my arm still around her, I realized she'd fallen asleep. That made me crack a smile. The couch was probably better than my sorry excuse for a bed in the other room anyway.

I didn't want to wake her, and truth be told, I didn't want to leave her, either. Carefully, I slid her glasses off and set them on the other side of the couch. Then I grabbed a knit throw blanket—thanks, Mom—and draped it over the two of us. I still had my shoes on, but I didn't care. I propped my feet on the coffee table, leaned my head back, and let my eyes close.

Gradually, I fell asleep, knowing in the back of my mind a sore neck could trigger a migraine. But I didn't care. I wasn't letting go of Penelope. She needed me. That was all that mattered.

CHAPTER 11

Penelope

I woke to the faint scent of clean cotton and subtle cologne. My neck was stiff, but I was so warm, I didn't want to move—or even open my eyes. It was odd, because I wasn't lying down, and my arm was draped across—

Oh, no.

My eyes flew open. I'd fallen asleep on Theo.

We were still on his couch with my head tucked against his chest, and my glasses definitely weren't on my face. I'd stretched one leg over his lap and his hand rested casually on my thigh.

I tried to move, but he held my leg and grunted softly in his sleep. Biting my lower lip, I shifted again, but his other arm tightened around me.

We had a green knit blanket partially covering us. He must have done that. I'd been pouring my heart out to him and fallen asleep. Instead of waking me up, he'd gotten as comfortable as he could—he hadn't even taken his shoes off—and stayed there.

All night.

I wasn't quite sure what time it was, but it looked like the sun was up.

He made another low noise in his throat and shifted slightly, pulling me tighter against him. I wondered if he was dreaming. Instinctively,

I moved my hand up his torso and rubbed a few slow circles across his broad chest. His body relaxed and his breathing evened.

For a moment, I thought about trying to go back to sleep. But with my body angled the way it was, his thigh pressed between my legs. Once I noticed that, there was no ignoring it. Deep pressure filled my core and the desire to move—to get just a little friction—was so intense I almost did.

This was so bad. My body was on fire. It had been quite a while since my lady parts had been touched, let alone satisfied. I squeezed my eyes shut and tried to shift my hips away from him. As soon as I moved, he drew me closer, inadvertently dragging me against him. I gasped and forced myself not to rock backward again.

Do not dry hump your best friend's leg, Penelope. Do. Not.

Closing my eyes, I took deep breaths, and the sensation gradually eased. He'd rescued me, brought me to his house, listened to me babble about my now ex-boyfriend, and held me while I slept. He was such a good friend. I didn't want to think of him in any other way.

It would change everything if I did. Risk our entire friendship. The timing was bad anyway, but aside from that, it was a chance I couldn't take.

Besides, guys like Theo didn't want girls like me. Not like that.

He took a deep breath and let go of me, stretching his arms overhead. I pulled away, quickly moving my leg off him and sitting up. Without my glasses, everything was fuzzy, including Theo.

"Hey," he said. "Morning."

"I'm so sorry I fell asleep on you."

He shifted so he was sitting up and moved his head from side to side, stretching his neck. "It's okay. I didn't mind."

Feeling vulnerable, I pulled the blanket into my lap and clutched it beneath my chin. He reached to the other side of the couch and grabbed something, but I couldn't see well enough to know what he was doing. A second later, he gently put my glasses on my face.

His smile came into focus first.

"Thank you," I said.

"Coffee?" he asked, and his husky just-woke-up voice was stupidly sexy. "Wait, you don't drink coffee. I doubt that tea in there is any good. I'll go get us something."

"You don't have to do that."

"It's all good, Penini." He stood and stretched again. "Although I should probably change first."

I sat huddled on the couch while he went to his bedroom and shut the door. It was hard not to lose it again as the cold, hard realization of the mess that was my life washed over me. I had absolutely no idea what I was going to do.

It would have been much better if I'd been able to plan my exit. Broken up with Sean after I had a place to go and made arrangements to move out. As it was, I was homeless. The only things I had to my name—for the moment, at least—were a pair of boots, a dress I was never wearing again, a coat, and the contents of my purse.

Theo came out a few minutes later dressed in a plain black hoodie and gray basketball shorts.

"Do you want to come?" He picked up his keys. "Or stay here?"

"I don't have anything to wear."

"Oh, that's right. Sorry, my brain isn't firing on all cylinders yet. Don't worry, I'll take care of everything."

"Okay."

He winked at me, sending a flurry of tingles down my spine, and left.

I got up to use the bathroom. There was a hall bath he probably never used, so after grabbing the toothbrush and toothpaste he'd left for me, I went in there.

Biological necessities dealt with, I went back to the living room, but paused before sitting down. I eyed my purse hanging on a hook by the front door like it might contain a bomb. But it was my phone that filled me with a mild sense of dread.

Had Sean reached out?

Was I hoping he had, or hoping he hadn't?

It was truly over between us. I didn't want him to try to get me back. But silence from him would feel ominous. And a bunch of angry—possibly drunk—messages weren't an appealing prospect, either.

I decided knowing was better than not, come what may. Steeling myself for the worst, I fished my phone out of my purse and checked.

Sure enough, I had a string of messages from Sean.

You just made the biggest mistake of your life.

I hope you're happy.

Good luck being miserable and alone.

You know you're going to regret this.

Fuck you, Penelope. What kind of a name is that, anyway?

Don't show up to my house. You left, your stuff is mine now.

This is your fault. Don't fucking blame me.

With a sigh, I set my phone on the coffee table in case Theo called while he was out. Sean was not going to make things easy. In fact, I had a feeling he was going to do everything he could to be difficult.

I curled up on the couch. I was swimming in Theo's hoodie and plaid pajama pants, but I sort of loved it. They were so comfortable, and they smelled like him.

It wasn't long before I heard his truck outside. I got up to see if he needed any help, and he came in with a drink carrier and a to-go bag.

"Is there anything else?" I asked.

"No, I got it." He went to the kitchen and set everything on the counter. "The Steaming Mug had breakfast sandwiches. I got four. Don't judge, I didn't have dinner last night."

"Me neither."

"Good, my instinct was right. Two for you, two for me. And I got you a hot tea. There were too many choices, so I let the barista pick. I hope it's good."

I found the cup with my name on it, took off the lid, and pulled out the tea bag. English breakfast. "This is perfect."

"Why are there so many kinds of tea?" He pulled the breakfast sandwiches out of the bag and set them in a line on the counter.

"I suppose they're sourced from different plants."

He grabbed his coffee and took a sip. "Fair enough. These are all the same, so take whichever ones you want."

"Thank you."

I helped myself to one of the sandwiches. I was hungry enough I was probably going to eat the other one, too. Theo brought both of his, along with his coffee, to the living room and set everything on the coffee table. I followed and took my place next to him.

"All right, I did some problem-solving while I was out," he said.

"Solving what problem?"

"Yours."

"Which one? There's a list."

He grinned. "Yeah, no kidding. That douchebag left you in a shitty position. Anyway, first off, my brother and his girlfriend will be here in a little bit."

"Wait, what?"

"Luke and Melanie. She's a character, but she's supercool. I was going to call my sister Annika first, but Luke texted me, so I figured that meant they volunteered."

"Volunteered for what?"

"She's bringing you some clothes to tide you over until you get your stuff. I think she's around your size, or close enough."

I stared at him with my mouth open. "She is?"

"What, your size or bringing you clothes?"

"The second one."

"Yep." He took a big bite of his sandwich.

"That's nice of her."

"Yeah, just be prepared. She'll probably come in hot, ready to burn down his life. But don't worry, Luke will calm her down."

"Okay." I took a sip of tea, still feeling slightly bewildered.

"Second of all, I found you a place to live."

I spit out the tea—thankfully it hadn't been a big mouthful—and clamped a hand over my mouth. "What? Where?"

He started to answer, but there was a knock at the door. Not even a second later, it opened, and a woman with dark hair burst in.

"Where is she?" The woman stopped just inside and looked at me with sympathy. "Hi, Penelope. I'm Melanie. Our names almost rhyme. That's cute."

Theo's brother Luke came in behind her, carrying a blue duffel bag, and shut the door. I'd seen them both at games but never met either of them.

"Hi?" I said, still feeling a bit bewildered.

Melanie came over and sat on the edge of the armchair next to the couch. "I know this is weird because we don't really know each other, but if you want me to, I'll burn down his house."

My eyes widened. She sounded completely serious.

Luke chuckled. "Slow down, Mercenary Mel. She needs clothes, not arson."

"I'm just saying. I know what he did to you last night. Did he really propose, and you turned him down?"

I nodded.

She moaned, like she'd just taken a bite of something delicious. "I have such a girl crush on you right now. Good for you. Screw that guy."

Luke lifted the duffel bag. "Where do you want this? Your bedroom, or…"

"Spare room," Theo said quickly.

"Oh-kay," Luke said, and took the bag down the hall.

"I wasn't sure what you'd need, or what you like, but I packed some basics. And I happened to have an unopened three-pack of underwear, so I put that in, too. Theo didn't think to ask for panties, but a girl needs to keep things fresh down there."

"Wow. Thank you so much. I don't know what to say."

"Say you'll pay it forward by telling some unfortunate girl your story when the opportunity arises, so she dumps the jerk she shouldn't marry before it's too late."

I nodded decisively. "Okay. I will."

"Good. Do you need anything else? Chocolate? Pickles? Chocolate-covered pickles?"

"No, Theo brought breakfast. I don't think I've ever had chocolate-covered pickles. Are they good?"

"Oh, honey. They're to die for."

Luke came back in. "Anything else we can do? Do you need help getting your stuff?"

"My stuff," I said with a groan. "I didn't have a chance to plan this very well. Or, at all."

"Don't worry." Theo's voice was so calm and reassuring. "We'll get it all figured out. Doesn't have to be today. You've got clothes, and you can ride with me to work."

"Oh, and I brought you some cute blouses and slacks, in case you need work clothes." Melanie clapped a hand over her forehead. "I forgot shoes. Do you need shoes? What size are you?"

"That's okay, I have a pair of boots with me that go with just about everything."

"Is the guy going to be a problem?" Luke asked.

"Not sure," Theo said.

"Based on the string of angry texts he sent me last night, I don't think he's going to be very cooperative," I said.

Theo growled and met Luke's eyes. They nodded to each other.

"You can always call the Squirrel Protection Squad if you need help," Melanie said. "They're not just for squirrels."

"She won't need to," Theo said. "We'll take care of it."

Luke nodded.

"Is this your phone?" Melanie picked it up and held it toward me. "Can you unlock it for me?"

"Um…sure." I took it and unlocked it, then handed it back to her.

"I'm putting my number in your contacts." She swiped, tapped, and typed. "There. Now you can get in touch if you need anything. And I'm texting myself, so I'll have yours, too."

I smiled, feeling a little giddy. "Thanks. I, um… I don't have a lot of friends. Pretty much just Theo, actually."

She put my phone on the coffee table. "Now you have one more."

Theo winked at me again and my stomach fluttered.

"You two get back to your breakfast," Luke said. "Let me know when we're dealing with the rest."

"Will do," Theo said. "Thanks, man."

Melanie got up, and after saying goodbye, they left.

"Thank you for that." I hadn't eaten any of my sandwich yet, so I picked it up and took a bite.

"No problem."

I swallowed. "What else were you going to say before they got here? That you found me a place to live? Where?"

A slow grin crossed his face. "Here."

I blinked at him, wondering if I'd heard him correctly. "What?"

"You should move in here. I have plenty of space."

"Are you serious?"

"Yeah. What do you say? Wanna be roomies?"

I giggled and accidentally snorted a little. "Yes, I would love to be roomies."

He held out his fist and I bumped it. He was right, he had solved my biggest problems. Just like that, I had clothes to wear and a place to live.

Roommates with my best friend? It was perfect.

CHAPTER 12

Penelope

The stress that had been building for weeks—if not months or years— began to unravel as I got settled at Theo's place. We went grocery shopping, I meal prepped lunches, and he cleared out the rest of his things from the spare bedroom so I could get comfortable.

On Tuesday, we made a quick trip to Sean's house so I could get my car and some of my things—mostly clothes, toiletries, and my art supplies. Fortunately, I had my keys, so I was able to get in. And even more fortunately, Sean wasn't there.

I'd have to face him sooner or later. But I needed some space first.

Theo stood guard outside while I gathered what I needed. There was more that was mine, including some of the furniture, but I'd deal with it later. We grabbed takeout on the way home, and after dinner, I set about organizing my things.

The bedroom wasn't large, but it seemed enormous. Not because of its proportions or the small furniture—because it felt like freedom. There I was, standing in a space that was my own. I'd done it. Sure, it was because of Theo. But that didn't diminish my relief.

Maybe everything really was going to be okay.

"Hey, Pensicle?" Theo poked his head through the door.

"Hi. You can come in. I'm just putting away my clothes."

He stepped into the room. "I was thinking… Do you want my

room? I can move my stuff in here. I don't need a lot of space, and my room's bigger."

"No," I said, emphatic. "I'm not kicking you out of your bedroom. This one is perfect."

"Okay, but I do want you take over the third bedroom, too."

"There's a third? How did I not know that?"

"Yeah, it's empty. I figure it can be your art studio or whatever you call it."

"There's room for me to have a studio?"

He grinned. "Yeah. Let me show you."

I followed him down the short hallway to a closed door that I'd assumed was a closet. He opened it and flipped on the light.

It was a small bedroom with plain white walls and a window overlooking the backyard. There was beige carpet on the floor and an empty closet.

"What do you think?" he asked. "Will this work?"

"It's amazing. I'll put down drop cloths so I don't get paint on the carpet."

"You can, but don't worry about it. Carpet can always be replaced."

I took slow steps around the room, thinking about where to place my easel. "This is so much better than the storage room off the garage."

"That's all you had? A storage room?"

"Yeah. Once in a while, he'd say he was going to build an addition so I could have a proper studio, but it never happened." My shoulders slumped. "Why did I wait so long to leave him? Seriously, Theo, I feel like I've been the world's biggest doormat."

He moved closer and nudged me with his elbow. "You're not a doormat. You were just stuck in a rut."

"That's true. It's like I'm waking up after living in a fog. It's a weird feeling."

"Well, you can paint your feelings in here."

That made me smile. "That's exactly what I'm going to do."

"What are you going to paint first?"

I tapped my lips with my finger. "I keep thinking about a mountain creek. Not like the Morris painting he gave me—I'd never copy another artist's work—but I could honor him by creating my own. Use his as inspiration. I don't know if it really matters, but I'd like to pay tribute to who he was and what he taught me."

"That's awesome. I can't wait to see it."

"Thanks. Speaking of." I tilted my head and gazed at one of the bare walls. "Do you mind if I hang things? I can fix the holes later. I know how."

"Knock yourself out. You can put things anywhere you want."

I pointed to a spot on the wall near the window. "I think the Morris painting would look lovely right there."

"Do you need any help?"

"I don't think so. It's not heavy."

"Let me know if you need me. I've still got grades to enter, so I'll be in the other room."

I smiled. "Thanks."

He gave me a dimpled grin and left.

My stomach tingled with giddiness as I once again took in the room. A space to paint was a small thing, but it meant so much to me. I could already tell I was going to love working in there.

It only took a few minutes to move my art supplies into the room. A side table would be helpful. Maybe even a small cabinet. I set up my easel and glanced around in satisfaction. It was going to be great.

The Morris painting was in the dining room where Theo had left it. He smiled at me from behind his laptop and asked again if I needed help. I assured him I'd let him know if I did.

I took the painting into my new studio and held it up against the wall. Perfect. I set it on the floor and sat cross-legged while I figured out what hardware it needed for hanging. I had a little box of supplies—sawtooth hangers and probably a few D rings. I ran my hands along the back of the frame, wondering which would be best, when I noticed a rough spot that didn't feel like wood.

Picking up the painting, I tilted it so I could see the spot. It was at the top, off to one side. It looked like a bit of paper sticking out between the backing and the frame itself.

It was probably just there to keep the canvas secure. Maybe the frame hadn't fit snugly enough, so Edwin had tucked a bit of paper in the gap.

I was going to leave it—get up and find my box of picture-hanging hardware—but a whisper of curiosity crept through me. A shiver ran down my back, and suddenly I had to know what that little scrap of paper was doing there.

The backing board was held in place with small, flat pegs that turned so they tucked beneath the frame. I opened them to free the backing board and carefully lifted it.

What I'd thought was a small scrap—maybe even a ripped corner wadded up and stuffed into a gap—was actually a folded piece of paper. It was thicker than what you'd find in a notebook, but not as rigid as card stock. More like a page torn out of a nice journal.

I unfolded it and my eyebrows drew together as I read a note written in slanted cursive.

> *Someday, someone will search and find the answers. The hauntings that led to my demise. It was no accident.*

I stared at the note for a long moment. What on earth? Had Edwin written it? I didn't know what it meant or why it would have been tucked in the picture frame of one of his paintings.

So strange.

Turning the painting over, I held the note next to his signature. I was no handwriting expert, but it looked the same to me.

Hesitating, I chewed on my lower lip. I didn't want to bother Theo while he was busy. But my curiosity had gone from a whisper to an excited squeal. A secret note tucked in a painting? He had to see this.

Taking the note with me, I got up and found him still in the dining room.

"I hate to bug you, but—"

"What do you need?"

He started to get up, but I waved him back down. "You don't have to get up. I found something."

"Where? In the room?"

I pulled out the chair next to him and took a seat while he moved his laptop. "No, in the Morris painting. In the frame, to be specific. A note."

Spreading the note flat on the table, I slid it to him.

Confusion crossed his face as he read. "That's weird. Did he write it?"

"I think so. It looks like the same handwriting as his signature."

"*The hauntings that led to my demise*," he read. "Do you think he meant literal hauntings? Like he thought his house or his gallery was haunted?"

"Maybe. *Search and find the answers* could mean he hoped someone would discover what was haunting him."

We both paused, gazing at the note. Another similarly disturbing idea entered my mind. What if Edwin Morris didn't think he was being haunted? What if he thought he was being hunted?

"This is weird as hell," Theo said, interrupting my half-formed thought. "But it's even weirder considering the context."

"What do you mean?"

"Mostly what we saw go down on Saturday. There was clearly more to this guy's life than painting peaceful landscapes. Plus, you know, he's dead. This note almost sounds prophetic."

"Like he knew he was going to die?"

"Don't you think? It's not explicit, but it makes me wonder if he was worried something bad would happen to him."

I met Theo's eyes. "That's exactly what I was just thinking. But not only that something bad was going to happen, like he had health problems and knew he didn't have much time."

"*It was no accident*," Theo quoted.

"Exactly," I whisper-yelled, although I had no idea why. There was no one around. "What if he wrote this thinking someone was out to get him?"

"And he was right. They were out to get him."

"And they got him."

Theo nodded gravely.

I stared at the note. Edwin Morris's death hadn't raised any suspicions. He was a man in his sixties with a certain waist circumference. Statistically speaking, he'd been at risk of an early death. Nothing to investigate.

But what if the note meant he knew something might happen to him, and he'd been hoping someone would find it and search for the answers?

The most ridiculous idea popped into my head. And like the moment of curiosity when I'd noticed the scrap of paper sticking out from the frame, I couldn't resist it.

I had to figure out if Edwin Morris had been murdered. And if so, who killed him.

But I couldn't do it alone.

I looked up, my mind racing. How could I convince Theo? He was going to laugh and say I was being silly. That we were just a couple of high school teachers. What business did we have trying to solve a murder?

With no idea of what I was going to say, I opened my mouth. Only, Theo beat me to it.

"We need to find out what happened," he said, his voice definitive.

"Are you serious?"

He nodded again. "Pen, this could mean he knew he was going to be murdered. And then he *was* murdered. The cops have no idea. Everyone's just moving on with their lives like he was another victim of cardiovascular disease or something."

"Yes, exactly. But what if he wasn't?"

"What if someone killed him? We need to know."

My eyes widened. "You'll help me find out? I thought I was going to have to convince you."

He hesitated. "I thought I was going to have to convince you."

Adjusting my glasses, I laughed. "I guess we have more in common than meets the eye."

His dimples puckered with his grin as he held out his fist. "Okay, Penlock Holmes. Let's solve a maybe murder."

I bumped his fist with mine. "Later, though. You probably still have grades to enter."

"That I do." He slid the laptop back in front of him. "Let's keep thinking about it, and we'll figure out how to start looking."

"Deal." I got up and took the note. "I'll keep this in the empty bedroom. I mean, my art studio."

He grinned at me. "Sounds good."

I went back to my studio with a little flutter of excitement in my stomach. And of course it was just the anticipation of possibly solving a murder. It had nothing to do with Theo and his playful smile.

CHAPTER 13

Theo

Between school and football—and trying to make a potentially life-altering career decision—I'd been too busy to give much thought to the mysterious note Penelope had found. The official job offer from Carolina had come in, and I'd responded to let Kevin know I needed some time to think it over.

The salary was a distinct check in the pro column. I'd about fallen out of my chair when I'd read that part. It was really good money.

But somehow that didn't make the decision easier.

Wednesday night after practice, I'd run into my brother Garrett. Instead of taking the opportunity to get some brotherly advice on whether I should take the job in South Carolina, I told him about the note Pen had found. But hey, he's a sheriff's deputy. That's totally his area.

He'd agreed it was odd, but it wasn't enough to open an investigation. That was the answer I'd expected, but mentioning it to him ahead of time meant he couldn't get pissed at me later for not telling him.

I was free to investigate.

More accurately, *we* were free to investigate. Me and my new roommate.

That was a curveball I hadn't seen coming. I'd hoped she'd get rid of Sean—sooner rather than later—but it hadn't occurred to me that I'd wind up being the one to give her a place to land.

And while living with her was unexpected, I wasn't complaining. We got along great. We were work besties for a reason, and it wasn't any different at home than at school. Even though I told her it wasn't necessary, she insisted on sharing her meal-prep lunches with me. Sure did beat my boring sandwiches. And there was something about her being there that was just…nice.

Let's skip over the part where I found myself staring at her bedroom door late at night, a sense of longing tugging at my chest and a very annoying hard-on keeping me awake.

Didn't happen. We were just friends.

Thursday after practice, the temperature was dropping and the sun hung low in the sky as I watched my team head to the locker room. We were having a good season, but I'd worked them hard. Winning could spur good morale and make the next win more likely, or it could make them cocky, thinking the next win was guaranteed. I was not in the business of turning out cocky athletes.

But they were rising to the occasion, like I knew they would.

I said goodbye to Coach Lewis and was about to head to my truck when I realized I had no idea what I'd done with my phone.

Damn it.

It wasn't in any of my pockets, and I didn't find it in the locker room. So I went back to my classroom. Apparently I'd put it in my desk drawer.

At least I hadn't lost it. And I'd remembered it before I left for home.

My gaze drifted to the art room as I locked my classroom for the night. Penelope had already left for the day. I wasn't sure why I was thinking about her. I'd see her at home.

I cracked a smile, thinking about how we'd successfully put sticky notes on everyone's lunches in the fridge—with the wrong names. We'd kept mostly straight faces as we watched our coworkers' confusion. A simple prank, but funny.

Ignoring the strange tug of longing in my chest, I headed to my truck.

As soon as I got in, the real thing weighing on my mind burst in, like a loud, unwelcome guest at a party.

The Carolina job. I needed to make a decision.

My mind went through my list of pros and cons as I drove. The pros were significant. It was a great opportunity. But the cons were real, too. Particularly the distance.

Someone who wasn't close to their family might not understand why that was such a barrier for me. But it was. My family was the ones who'd been there for me. Who'd really had my back when my life had fallen apart after my injury. I wouldn't have admitted it when we were kids—or maybe even young adults—but my brothers were my best friends. And living in the same town, being around for them and their growing families really meant something to me.

On the other hand, the job was an incredible opportunity to do something new and even amazing.

Somewhere along the drive, I realized I wasn't heading in the direction of home. As if my intuition had taken over, I was on the road to my parents' place. Seemed like I ought to follow the gut feeling, so I kept going and eventually turned up their gravel driveway.

The windows glowed with soft light. I sent Pen a quick text to let her know I'd be home later. Seemed like the thing to do.

The door to their house was unlocked, so I went in without knocking.

"Hey, Mom? Dad?" I called.

Dad's voice came from the kitchen. "Yeah."

I went down the hallway lined with photos into the kitchen. Dad stood dressed in a dark green flannel shirt, the sleeves cuffed to his elbows, washing his hands in the sink. He glanced over his shoulder at me but didn't say anything. Just finished rinsing his hands, turned off the water, and grabbed a towel to dry them.

"Where's Mom?" I took a seat on one of the stools.

"Knitting group." He finished drying his hands and set the towel on the counter. "There's leftovers if you're hungry."

"No, I'm good. I..." I trailed off, not quite sure what to say. "I'm actually not sure why I'm here."

With a grunt, Dad nodded, as if that made perfect sense to him.

He went to the fridge and pulled out two beers. I smiled a little as he popped off the caps and handed me one of them. He took a long drink and so did I. Then he leaned against the counter with his beer in hand and raised his eyebrows at me, as if to say, *Go ahead.*

"I got a job offer. Offensive coordinator at the university level."

He nodded in acknowledgment.

"It's wild. They came looking for me. Reached out over the summer, wanted me to come out and visit the campus, talk to them about the position. So, I did. I didn't tell anyone. I guess mostly because I didn't think it would go anywhere."

"But it did."

"Yeah, it did. They offered me the job."

"You haven't said where."

I let out a breath. "Yeah. I know. That's because it's at the University of South Carolina."

Dad nodded slowly for a moment, then took another drink of his beer. I took a long pull of mine.

"Are you going to take it?" he asked, finally.

"I don't know."

"What does your gut tell you?"

"That there are a lot of good reasons to take it. And a lot of real reasons not to."

"Like what?"

"It's a great opportunity. Really good money. A chance to take my career in a new direction, work with more advanced athletes. But it's in South Carolina."

"Is that the main drawback?"

"Yeah, but it's a big one. Tilikum is weird as hell, but I love it here. I was feeling pretty settled. In a good way. And I've got nieces and nephews, and we both know Luke's gonna get married. I want to be here for all that, you know? I don't want to be like—"

I stopped myself before I said my brother Reese's name.

Maybe I'd just realized what had been bothering me. My brother

Reese had disappeared nearly twenty years ago. He'd missed…everything. Annika moving home, the end of the feud with the Baileys, weddings, babies—he was missing all of it.

"You don't wanna be like Reese," Dad said, echoing my thoughts.

It was strange to hear him say my brother's name without the slightest hint of emotion in his voice. My siblings and I avoided talking about Reese, especially around my parents. It was an unspoken agreement that he wasn't a safe topic of conversation. I suppose I'd expected Dad to spit out his name like a curse word, or at least grumble about him.

"No, I don't want to be like Reese. In case you haven't noticed, we're all pretty pissed at him."

Glancing away, Dad nodded again. "Yeah. I was, too."

"You're not anymore?"

He hesitated for a long moment, his eyes unfocused. "No. I'm not angry. And if I'm honest, I've always been a lot more pissed off at myself than I ever was at him."

I stared at him, my mouth slightly open. I didn't know what had happened when Reese left. It was one of those things we just didn't talk about. At the time, I'd been too wrapped up in my own stuff to understand the full extent and impact of what had happened—that Reese had gone and broken off almost all contact with our family.

Dad cleared his throat and took another drink of his beer. I knew him well enough to know the topic was closed. It wasn't going to do me any good to ask him what had happened between them, or what he meant by being pissed at himself about it. If I did ask, he'd probably just grunt and walk away.

"It's not the same," he said, his tone decisive. "If this job is what you want—hell, even if you're not sure it's what you want, but you know it's worth pursuing—then you should take it. What's the worst that can happen? You hate it, realize you made a mistake, and come back."

"Come back a failure? Twice?"

He met my eyes and pointed at me with his beer bottle. "Watch it.

You're no failure. And if you're worried about what the gossips around here would say, fuck 'em. Their opinions don't mean shit. You get to decide what's important to you."

I smiled. Any time my dad decided to string more than a few words together, he made you listen. And he was right. I was only a failure if I quit, not if I changed course.

"Thanks, Dad. You don't think Mom will be upset?"

"She'll have feelings about it. But you know as well as I do she wants what's best for her kids, even if it's hard for her. Besides, who says you can't visit?"

"Yeah, that's what planes are for."

"Exactly." He took another drink and put his bottle down. "Look, if this is a good opportunity, and you want the job, you should take it. If it's not, then don't. Simple."

I nodded again and finished my beer. "Good advice. I appreciate it."

"You're welcome."

He took our empties and put them in the recycle bin. With a grunt and a nod, he left through the back door, probably headed to his shop to tinker with something.

I lingered on the stool for a few more minutes, his words running through my head, before going back to my truck.

There was one factor I hadn't mentioned to my dad, mostly because I wasn't sure what to say.

Penelope.

Why did she make me hesitate? I wouldn't leave her high and dry. If I took the job, she could stay in my house. I'd already thought about keeping it as a rental. It would be perfect. I'd give her a good deal and she wouldn't be stuck in the tiny spare bedroom anymore.

Work would be different. If the tables were turned, and she was the one leaving, I'd be pretty bummed about it. So it stood to reason that she'd be disappointed if I left. But was that a reason to stay? To say no to a great opportunity?

Like I'd told myself already, Pen and I were just friends. The fact that she'd left her shitty boyfriend wouldn't change that. Being roommates wouldn't change it, either.

I knew what I needed to do—what I wanted. I wanted that job. I wanted the challenge. Dad was right, it was simple. I was making it complicated, but it didn't need to be.

It was a good opportunity. A great one, even. It was worth taking the chance. Sure, moving away from my family—and Penelope—was a downside. But I could visit, especially in the offseason.

I got out my phone and typed a reply to Kevin's email, accepting the Carolina offer.

That was that. I'd finish out the school year at Tilikum High School, and then I was moving to South Carolina.

Now I just had to tell my family. And my best friend.

CHAPTER 14

Theo

I got to the Steaming Mug a little early. I was meeting my mom so I could talk to her about my new job and the move. I needed to tell her in person—and before the rest of the family. I figured a coffee date would be a nice way to break it to her. There was already a Haven family dinner at my folks' place planned for that night, so I could tell everyone else then.

Tilikum's popular coffee shop was usually busy, and even fairly early on a Saturday morning, there were quite a few customers. Some sat in armchairs, others at small tables. Soft music played in the background and the scent of freshly ground coffee filled the air.

I hadn't broken the news to Pen yet. I'd thought about it when I'd come home after talking to my dad, but it had been late and hadn't felt like the right time. Friday had been too busy, and with an away game that night, I hadn't gotten home until after she'd gone to bed.

Since I had a few minutes, I texted Mom to see what she wanted so I could order for her. She replied that she'd be there soon and would love a spiced chai latte.

The front counter was painted teal and the chalkboard menu hung on an exposed brick wall behind it. Three baristas flitted around each other, filling orders and calling out names. The sound of grinding coffee beans and whir of frothing milk seemed endless.

When I got to the front of the line, I ordered my mom's spiced chai and a black coffee for myself. I loved coffee, but I tended to keep it simple.

"Amanda," one of the baristas called out and slid a drink across the counter.

That got my attention. It couldn't be *that* Amanda. Could it? What were the chances I'd run into her in public?

Actually, the chances were good. Small-town living and all that. I ran into people all the time.

Sure enough, *the* Amanda came to the counter to retrieve her order.

Dressed in a sweater with jeans, her outfit was a lot less revealing than what she'd been wearing at Morris's celebration of life. I watched from the corner of my eye as she took a seat across from a woman dressed similarly, with shorter blond hair.

There was an open table near her, so I casually walked over and sat down. Angling myself so I was facing the counter, not the two women, I rested my elbow on the table with my hand to my chin and leaned slightly in their direction.

"It's so weird, because I looked at his profile and I totally would've swiped left if I'd met him that way," the other woman said. "But we actually had a good time."

"That's the problem with online dating," Amanda said. "How can you tell anything from someone's profile? I'm so over it."

"You say that now, but give yourself a few months. You'll reactivate your profile."

"Maybe. I guess I haven't had luck the other way, either."

"Well..." Her friend paused. "I mean, the last guy was...you know."

Amanda sighed heavily. "I know. I don't expect you to understand."

"Good, because I really don't. Did you actually think he was going to leave her?"

"I do not want to talk about him," Amanda snapped. The sudden change in her voice almost made me shrink away.

"I'm sorry," the friend said, her tone sympathetic. "I know it's been hard."

"Theo!" the barista called.

I got up and went to the counter to get my order. As I brought the drinks back to my table, I studied the two women for a second. Amanda seemed agitated, and the way she'd snapped at her friend clearly meant it was a sore subject.

But why?

Unfortunately, they were gathering up their things to leave. When I sat down, I heard the friend say something about getting to work. A moment later, they got up and left together.

I took a sip of my coffee, mulling over what I'd heard. I'd have bet a million dollars the guy they'd been talking about was Edwin Morris. Amanda had been having an affair with a married man.

A married man who'd wound up dead.

Did Amanda have anything to do with it? Did she kill Edwin while his wife was out of town?

The plot thickened.

My mom walked in, and I had to push all thoughts of Edwin Morris aside. But man, I wanted to talk to Pen. I couldn't wait.

With a smile, Mom sat down across from me and tucked her chin-length hair behind her ears. As always, she wore her blue-rimmed glasses, and she was dressed in jeans and what looked like one of Dad's flannel shirts over a Squirrel Protection Squad T-shirt.

"Hi, Mom."

"Hi, honey." She set her purse on the floor near her feet and moved her mug closer.

I could see the concern in her expression. "Did Dad talk to you?"

"He just said there's nothing to worry about."

"Which probably made you worry."

She nodded and wrapped her hands around her mug. "A little. So what's going on? Is everything all right?"

"Yeah, everything's good. Great, as a matter of fact. I've been offered a job coaching at the college level."

Her eyebrows lifted. "Really? That's so exciting."

"It is. And it's in South Carolina."

"Wow, that's a big move. Tell me about the job."

"It's an amazing opportunity—offensive coordinator at the University of South Carolina. They have a great program, and the chance to coach at that level is huge for me."

Her smile was real, as was the hint of sadness she was trying to hide. "I'm really happy for you."

"Thanks. I know it's a long way away, and I took that really seriously. I don't love the idea of relocating, but this is such a great opportunity. I think taking it is the right thing to do."

"Good," she said, her tone emphatic. "Then you should take it."

"That's what Dad said."

Taking a deep breath, she reached across the table and took my hands. "Of course I'm going to be sad to see you go. But I'm so proud of you. You've come such a long way."

"Thanks, Mom."

She let go and took a sip of her drink. "When do you leave?"

"I'll finish the school year here and move down there next summer."

"I'm glad you have plenty of time. Have you thought about what you're going to do with your house?"

"I might keep it as a rental. I recently ended up with a roommate—a friend from work. She just went through a breakup and needed a place to live. If she wants to stay, I could rent it to her. And if not, I'll figure it out."

"You could talk to Josiah about it. He'd probably be able to manage it for you."

My brother Josiah had partnered with my dad, and the two of them had become small-town real estate moguls. They bought old houses and fixed them up. They sold some, but they kept a lot of them as rental properties.

"I'll keep that in mind."

"Sorry, I don't mean to jump in and start problem-solving. It's a mom thing. I can't help it."

"That's okay. I appreciate it. There are a lot of details I'll need to figure out. But like you said, I have time."

"And you have a roommate now? That's big news. Who is she?"

"Her name's Penelope Fallbrook. She's the art teacher. We've been friends for a while, and, like I said, she just got out of a relationship. Didn't have anywhere else to go."

"It's good of you to be there for her."

"Yeah, what are friends for?" I cracked a smile.

She nodded slowly, and the way her eyes lingered on me made me wonder what she was thinking. Hopefully she wasn't getting the wrong idea about me and Pen.

"Can I make one request?" she asked after a pause.

"Sure."

"Come home once a year. I know it seems like that isn't a lot, but it's amazing how quickly time goes by. And how easy it is to lose touch with the people you love."

"I'll come home *at least* once a year. How about that?"

She smiled. "I appreciate that. And I know Annika and your brothers will, too."

I let out a long breath. "Speaking of Annika and my brothers…I need to tell everybody."

She took another sip of her drink. "That's going to be fun."

I chuckled. "Not really."

"Don't worry. They'll give you a hard time, but they won't mean it. Do you want to tell them tonight?"

"Will everyone be there?"

"I believe so."

"Either that's perfect or it'll just give them a way to gang up on me. But yeah, that would be great. And thanks for not freaking out when I said South Carolina."

"I've had adult children long enough to know the best thing I can do is go with the flow and love you from afar, if that's all I can do."

Maybe she was talking about me, but she was also talking about Reese. She had to be. I needed to know what the hell was going on with him, or at least what she knew. I opened my mouth to ask her, but before I could get a word out, a little old lady in a gold velour tracksuit came in and immediately spotted us.

Aunt Louise.

Louise Haven was a small-town force of nature. If you had so much as a stuffy nose, she'd be at your house with soup or a casserole. But she was most famous, at least among my brothers and me, for having declared herself the Haven family matchmaker.

The problem? No one wanted their eccentric aunt to set them up on dates. Especially because she was notoriously bad at it.

"Marlene!" She gave my mom an air kiss next to her cheek. "What a lovely surprise."

"Hi, Louise," Mom said with a smile. "How have you been?"

"Can't complain." Aunt Louise pulled a chair to our table, sat, and dug a small notebook and pen out of her large handbag. "Theo, I'm so glad you're here. I've been working on something for you."

I didn't reply. Just met my mom's eyes with a look of alarm. She smiled, as if to say, *Don't worry*.

But I was worried. You had to worry when Aunt Louise was up to something. And she was always up to something.

Louise flipped through the pages of her notebook. "Here we are. What are you doing Friday evening?"

I hesitated and she looked at me expectantly, batting her eyelashes.

"You're free? Good—"

"Whoa," I said, putting my hands up. "Slow down, Aunt Louise. If you're trying to set me up on a date, the answer is no."

"Don't be silly. You haven't been on a date in ages, have you?"

"No, but—"

"Then it's the perfect time. You know you can trust me."

I blinked at her. "You once set me up with one of my former students, which was awkward enough. And I think she was still in college, and I was like thirty-one."

"If recall, she was mature for her age."

Mom clicked her tongue. "That is a bit young, Louise."

"Oh, fair enough." She batted my mom's comment out of the air. "But that was then, and my matchmaking skills have improved considerably. This one isn't one of your students; she's a teacher."

My brow furrowed. I hoped she wasn't talking about Ashley, the English teacher at my school. Even if she wasn't secretly hooking up with Jeremy, there'd never been any chemistry between us.

Not that it mattered. I wasn't dating anyone.

"Her name is Kelly. She teaches fourth grade, I think?" Louise went on. "Or maybe it's fifth. She's been in a relationship that's, let's say, not the best. It's an on-again, off-again sort of thing, and we all know that's not healthy."

"If she's in a relationship, why are you trying to set her up with me?" I asked.

"Well, if I'm being honest, I'm hoping you might be the thing that snaps her out of it."

I blinked at her. "You want me to go out with someone so she'll break up with her on-again, off-again boyfriend?"

A broad smile crossed Louise's face. "Exactly."

"No."

"Theo—"

"Hard no, Aunt Louise. I don't date, and I especially don't date women in toxic relationships in the hopes that they'll choose me over the jerk they keep going back to." I stood. "Absolutely not."

Louise sighed. "Well, when you put it that way."

"Bye, Mom. See you later, Aunt Louise. And no dates. I mean it."

"Don't worry, honey," she said. "I have a few other ideas. One in particular who I'm sure will be much more suitable."

I rolled my eyes and walked away. It didn't matter if she kept trying to set me up. I was going to keep saying no.

Besides, I was leaving town. Soon, it wouldn't matter anyway.

Later that evening, I went to my parents' place and joined the chaos. Their log home was filled with voices, laughter, the big kids playing, and the babies babbling or crying. Kind of reminded me of my childhood.

Pen and I had missed each other that afternoon, and she'd still been out when it had been time to leave to head to my parents'. I tried to ignore the pang of disappointment. I had no idea if she'd have wanted to go to a Haven family get-together. And it might have been a little weird, since we were just friends.

Plus, everyone—especially my brothers—would get the wrong idea.

Everyone but Luke and Melanie had already arrived. Dad sat on the couch with Annika's twin girls in his lap. Their brothers were wrestling with Owen on the floor, while Annika's husband, Levi, watched from a few feet away.

Josiah's daughter Abby looked tiny in his burly arms, and his wife, Audrey, walked around with my other niece Emily—Zachary and Marigold's daughter. Both babies were around five months old, if I had my math right, just a little younger than Garrett and Harper's daughter, Isla.

The Haven baby boom was a thing.

Mom and Marigold were busy in the kitchen and Zachary wandered in to help. The smile on my dad's face as he read a book to his granddaughters was a sight to behold. He wasn't exactly a smiley guy, but his grandkids melted him every time. It was pretty cute.

I leaned against the wall in the doorway to the living room, sipping a glass of red wine. I was debating whether to interrupt and make my announcement or wait until everyone was eating. The latter seemed like a smart move. If I could catch my brothers with food in their mouths, they'd be less likely to jump on me all at once.

I'd already talked to Owen, having pulled him aside to let him know when he'd first arrived. It affected him more than anyone. He'd taken it well, especially when I'd suggested he might come play for me in a couple years. We'd hugged it out and I knew I didn't have to worry about him. He had great parents, and a good head on his shoulders. He was going to be fine.

The front door opened, and I glanced over my shoulder to find Luke and Melanie. Between the two of them, they were carrying four bottles of champagne. That was suspicious. The smile on Luke's face rivaled our dad's.

Grinning at me, Luke said hi as he walked by and into the living room. They were up to something, and I had a feeling I knew exactly what it was.

"Hey, everybody," Luke said, pitching his voice to carry over the noise.

Mom stepped out of the kitchen, her eyebrows lifted. I'd have bet anything she already guessed what they were about to say.

That was when I caught sight of the ring on Melanie's left hand.

Oh, shit. It was happening.

"Melanie and I have an announcement." Luke looked at her, still grinning. "We're getting married."

The entire house erupted with cheers. Annika and my sisters-in-law grabbed the champagne, setting it down on the coffee table so they could hug Luke and Mel—and each other. Josiah offered Luke a chin tip—typical Josiah—and Zachary barreled in to hug them both. Garrett had somehow ended up with two babies in his arms, so he tipped his chin as well.

Dad still had my nieces in his lap. They sat, politely clapping, as if they'd just watched a stage performance. Mom eventually made her way through her daughters-in-law to give Luke and Melanie teary-eyed hugs. My handshake with Luke turned into a hug, and I hugged Melanie as well.

I felt like my news was going to be a downer after their announcement. Mom met my eyes from across the room and gave me a sympathetic smile, as if she knew exactly what I was thinking.

Annika and Harper took the champagne to the kitchen, and a few minutes later, clear plastic cups of bubbly were passed around. Mom had Sprite for the kids.

Dad cleared his throat and the room went silent.

He lifted his champagne. "To Luke and Melanie. Thanks for giving us another daughter, Son."

We all raised our glasses with a chorus of, "Cheers," and drank.

"Stop it, Paul, you're going to make me cry," Melanie said as she hugged him.

The excited buzz continued as dinner was set out and we all made our way to the dining room. Our family had grown so much, Dad had built a big new table. They'd had to move some furniture around to make more space, but even with that, it was a tight fit.

Conversations continued while we dished up and ate. I waited for a lull, then put down my fork.

"I actually have some news, too."

All eyes moved to me.

"Over the summer, the University of South Carolina reached out to me about the possibility of joining their coaching staff. They offered me the offensive coordinator position, starting next season, and I decided to accept."

For a few seconds, silence hung over the table, broken only by the sound of baby Isla babbling.

"Theo, that's amazing," Annika said, finally. "Congratulations."

"Yeah, congratulations," Levi said.

"South Carolina?" Zachary asked, his tone indignant.

Here we go.

"I know," I said. "It's a big move. But it's a great opportunity."

Making a fist, Zachary groaned. "Damn it, Theo. Congratulations. I'm actually really happy for you and simultaneously mad that you're leaving."

Marigold rubbed his arm. "It's okay. Sometimes we have big feelings."

"Same, but congrats," Luke said. "That's awesome."

More congratulations started coming from around the table. I nodded along, appreciative of the smiles and well-wishes.

"Thanks, you guys. I know it's a big change, but I'm really excited about it."

I answered their questions about the school and what my new job would entail. After a while, the conversation drifted to other things before returning to Luke and Melanie and their wedding plans.

I finished dinner with a sense of relief. Now that my family knew, it seemed real. It was actually happening. And they'd all be fine without me around every day. I'd visit as often as I could, and meanwhile, I'd be forging ahead on a new path.

I cracked a smile. New job, new city, new possibilities. It was exciting, and I was looking forward to seeing where life took me next.

CHAPTER 15

Penelope

A low hum of conversation filled the cafeteria in the assisted living home when I found Grandma at her table. She greeted me with a smile, and I gave her a hug before sitting down. They'd designed the dining hall to be as homelike as they could, with tables in a variety of sizes, seasonally themed tablecloths, and comfortable chairs. The food was usually good, but as my grandmother liked to eat early and I wasn't particularly hungry, I wasn't planning to take much of the chicken with rice pilaf they were serving.

"Well, Penny," she said as she laid her napkin in her lap. "What's new with you?"

Where did I begin?

"Let me start by saying, everything is fine. Better than fine. So don't worry."

"That's a surefire way to get your grandma to worry."

"No, I mean it. Everything ends well. First of all, Sean proposed."

"I told myself I was not going to say a thing if this day came. But you know what? I lied. I am going to say something. Are you sure this is what you want?"

"Not at all. I said no."

"Because, honestly, that man is—wait, what did you say?"

I couldn't help but smile. "I said no. Actually, I'd already decided to leave him. I wanted to find a new place to live first, so I hadn't told him yet. But then he suggested we go out for dinner, and I didn't realize what he was planning until it was too late."

"So he proposed but you broke up with him instead."

I nodded. "Pretty much."

She reached over and put her hand over mine. "Oh, Penny. That must have been hard. But I'm so proud of you."

"Thanks. That was definitely a low point. He got mad and left me outside the restaurant with no way to get home. Not that I had a home to go to. But like I said, it all turned out fine. I called my friend Theo, and he picked me up. And guess what else? He offered to let me move into his spare room. Housing problem solved."

"Theo? Who's Theo?"

"He's one of my coworkers."

She pressed her lips together. "Hmm."

"Don't worry, he's a great guy. We've been friends for a while, so it's not like I moved in with a stranger."

"Stranger danger wasn't my first concern."

I laughed a little and was about to explain that there was no reason for her to be concerned—Theo and I were just friends—when one of the staff came over to our table with a white envelope and handed it to Grandma.

"This was in your mailbox. You must have forgotten to pick it up."

"Well, goodness," she said, turning it over. "How did I miss this?"

She slipped her finger beneath the flap to pop it open and took out a card. It said *Thank You* in shiny blue and silver letters.

"Thank you for what?" she mused.

My eyes widened as I realized what it was. I opened my mouth to tell her to wait, but it was too late. She opened the card, and it released a puff of multicolored glitter.

"What on earth?" she shrieked, dropping the card.

Cackling laughter came from across the cafeteria. Maury Haven howled, leaning forward in his wheelchair and slapping his leg.

"I got you good, Colleen," he said between wheezing cackles. "Thought you'd open it in your apartment, but this was even better."

She glared daggers at him. "Maury Haven, you'll pay for this."

He just kept laughing.

I tried to help brush the glitter off her clothes, but I had a feeling she'd be finding more of it for weeks. Or longer. I picked up the card from where it had fallen. Inside it read *For the laughs*.

"Don't you laugh with him," Grandma said.

"I'm not. There's just glitter everywhere."

She brushed more off her shirt, sending it pooling in her lap. "Maury Haven is not funny. He's a menace."

"What are you going to do to get him back?"

"I have a few ideas." She shot another glare across the room. "Mark my words, he'll pay for this trick."

One of the staff came over with a vacuum, and we helped Grandma get cleaned up as best we could. I didn't miss the hint of a smile she gave Maury when she thought no one was looking. She was pretending she didn't find it funny, but I could see her laughing on the inside.

She'd probably crack up as much as Maury had when she was alone and wouldn't have to admit it to anyone.

Once we'd de-glittered her as much as we could, we got our dinner. I still wasn't hungry, so I mostly kept her company while she ate. She didn't bring up Sean—or Theo—again. I knew she was relieved to hear I'd finally left that relationship. There wasn't much more to say about it, now that it was over.

After dinner, I took her upstairs to her apartment, then said goodbye. I needed to go to the grocery store. And maybe I'd stop somewhere for takeout on the way home. Theo wouldn't be there—he had plans with his parents—and Italian sounded good.

Nature's Basket was packed, which wasn't unusual for a weekend. I maneuvered my cart around as best I could. The fact that there were only two cashiers didn't bother me. I felt sorry for them. Poor things were slammed. I felt a little silly, but I told the cashier she was doing a great job. Her grateful smile made me glad I'd spoken up.

As I loaded my groceries into my car, my stomach rumbled a little. Hunger had caught up with me and I was going to feed it with pasta. I planned to hit up a great Italian bistro I hadn't been to in ages, mostly because Sean didn't like it.

But that didn't matter anymore.

They had online ordering, so I put in the order from the grocery store parking lot, drove the short distance to the restaurant, found parking, and went inside.

It smelled like garlic bread, basil, and oregano. Tables were covered with red and white checked tablecloths and twinkle lights added a cheerful ambiance.

I checked in with the hostess and sat down to wait for my order. Only a few of the tables were occupied and a server dressed in black brought food to a couple seated on the far side. My eyes wandered, stopping on the people sitting at a table toward the back. Was that…?

It was. Michael Morris. He had a pint of beer and took a piece of bread from the plate in the center of the table. A man sat across from him, but I couldn't see much of his face. From what I could see, I didn't recognize him.

Michael was dressed casually in a long-sleeve T-shirt, while his companion wore a button-down shirt with the sleeves cuffed to his elbows. They both had a beer, although Michael's was already half-empty and the other man's was mostly full. They were talking, but I was too far away to even guess what they were saying.

Curiosity filled me. Ever since finding the note in the painting, I'd been pondering who might be a suspect. Michael Morris had been one of the first to come to mind. If Edwin had a strained relationship with his son—and it seemed clear that he had—he could have feared the worst.

I chewed on my bottom lip, wishing I could hear what they were saying. The table next to them was empty. *What if I…?*

But I was by myself. If Theo were with me, he'd give me a subtle gesture, nodding toward the table, and we'd both quietly get up and sit next to them.

Could I do the same thing alone?

There was no reason I couldn't. Other than my own fear holding me back.

Nervously, I adjusted my glasses. I was about to commit to staying right where I was—I couldn't do it alone—when a little spark flared inside me. I didn't know where it came from, but I straightened in my seat, imagining how excited Theo would be when I told him I hadn't let the chance go to waste. The way he'd smile with those dimples and give me a fist bump.

He'd be proud of me.

I glanced around. The hostess was on the phone, probably taking a to-go order. And the server was nowhere to be seen.

My heart beating hard, I slipped a menu from the front counter and walked as casually as I could to the table next to Michael and his companion. Choosing the chair that would put me back to back with the other man, I sat down and buried my face in the menu.

"I know that's not what you want to hear," the second man was saying. "But it's the truth."

"It's bullshit. The bastard can't get away with that."

"He can, and he did."

"That was supposed to be my money. I don't know how he talked my mom into screwing me over like this."

"I told you, her signature is on everything. You need to take it up with her."

Michael groaned. "She'll just cry again."

The other man cleared his throat. "She did just lose her husband."

"He was an ass."

"Which means she's not allowed to mourn?"

I heard a glass hit the table and I had a feeling Michael had just swallowed the rest of his beer. "She can wear black for the rest of her life for all I care. And don't look at me like I'm the asshole here. She had me thrown out of his funeral. Do you know how mad my wife is about that?"

"You were drunk and belligerent."

His tone was mocking. "Am I not allowed to mourn?"

"Look, I'm your attorney, not your therapist. Family strife is messy. Contracts are not. Whatever happened between you and your father that prompted him to make the changes he did is not my problem. My job is to tell you what it means. And it means that money is no longer yours."

"This is not how things were supposed to go down. I was supposed to…" He trailed off.

"I know you're not happy, but there's nothing else that can be done. You could try to sue your grieving mother, but you don't have a solid case, and I wouldn't recommend it."

Michael sighed, but he sounded frustrated, not apologetic. "I'm not going to sue my mother."

"Good, because I'd fire you as a client if you did."

"Thanks, I appreciate your loyalty," Michael said, his voice dripping with sarcasm.

"I've helped you out because we're friends. Or we used to be. So can I give you some advice, not as your attorney, but as a friend?"

"Sure."

"Be careful. I know there was a lot more to your father than his reputation as a beloved artist. But you need to quit rampaging around town, drunk off your ass, talking about how much he screwed you over to anyone who'll listen. It's not a good look. Especially if people start asking questions."

"What are you implying?"

"You know exactly what I'm implying. I can't protect you from everything."

"Excuse me?" a female voice said.

The server startled me so much, my glasses slipped all the way down my nose. I pushed them up and gave her a weak smile. "Hi. Sorry."

"Did someone seat you? I'm sorry, I didn't realize I had another table."

"Oh, no. You're fine. I'm waiting for a to-go order." I opened my mouth to keep explaining what I was doing at a table, when I should have been sitting in the lobby, but I had no idea what to say. So I said nothing and kept smiling at her like an idiot.

She didn't seem to know what to do about me, either. After hesitating for a second, she glanced toward the kitchen. "I'll go check on that for you. What's the name on the order?"

"Penelope."

"Great."

I squirmed in my seat as she walked away. Thankfully, Michael and his attorney were still talking. They didn't seem to be paying any attention to the weird girl eavesdropping on them. But I wondered if I should stay there or go back to the lobby. I was kind of committed, so maybe it was best to stay where I was.

A few moments later, the server came back with a to-go bag, and I breathed out a sigh of relief. Michael and the attorney's conversation had kept going, but I didn't hear anything else that seemed important. As soon as she handed me my food, I thanked her and scurried out of the restaurant as fast as I could.

My head was spinning as I got in my car. Michael was clearly angry at his father, and it definitely had something to do with money. That wasn't necessarily suspicious, but something about the way he'd said *This is not how things were supposed to go down* bothered me.

He might have just meant he'd expected to receive an inheritance when his father passed, and he hadn't. But what if it meant something else? Something worse? What if the falling-out hadn't just been an argument?

And what had his attorney been implying?

I really needed to talk to Theo. But he was at his parents' house. I couldn't interrupt a family dinner.

At least I wouldn't have to wait until Monday to see him again. Unexpected benefit of being roommates—it was going to make our little investigation that much easier.

CHAPTER 16

Penelope

Theo wasn't awake when I got up the next morning. He'd been at his parents' late, and I'd gone to bed before he'd come home. I made some tea and fidgeted for a while, impatient for him to get up.

Sean had texted again. Only once, and it wasn't as blatantly angry as his first string of messages. But it was easy to see he was mad. Or at least annoyed.

Sean: Will you just text me back?

I didn't. And I wasn't going to. Not yet, at least. And once I got the rest of my stuff out of his house, I was absolutely blocking his number.

Deciding to shower and get dressed for the day, I glanced at Theo's closed door as I headed for the bathroom, momentarily wondering if he had a migraine. I hoped not. It was still early. He was probably just sleeping in.

After showering, I went to my room to get dressed. I still had the hoodie Theo had let me wear after the proposal debacle. I'd meant to give it back to him. It wasn't like I needed it. I had a THS hoodie of my own.

But for some reason, I liked his better.

He hadn't asked for it back, so I slipped it on, pairing it with leggings and thick socks. I left my hair wet—I'd been blessed with hair that could air-dry without getting frizzy—and went out to see if Theo was up.

I found him in the kitchen, dressed in a T-shirt and pajama pants. He had his back to me as he poured a cup of coffee.

"Morning," I said.

He turned with a sleepy grin and my heart fluttered. His hair was a little messy, and why was the way he smiled at me like that so…?

I didn't want to say *sexy*. We were friends, and I'd just gotten out of a relationship. It was not the time to get swept up in his sex appeal.

Not that there'd ever be a time to get swept up in Theo's sex appeal. He and I weren't like that.

But a messy-haired Theo Haven standing in the kitchen in pajama pants, dimpled smile on display? It made my insides swirl in a way that was both tantalizing and uncomfortable.

"Morning," he replied.

His rough morning voice did not help.

"How was your visit with your parents?" I asked.

"It was good. How's your grandma?"

"She's doing well. Maury glitter bombed her."

He chuckled. "Classic. Were you there when it happened?"

"Sure was. It got all over. Not so much on me, but I have a feeling she'll be finding little sparkly bits for weeks."

He headed for the living room and I followed. Both of us took a seat on the couch, one in each corner.

"How's she going to get him back?" he asked.

"I don't know. I'm sure she has something up her sleeve." I tucked my legs beneath me. "I know this is going to seem like an abrupt subject change, and maybe you'd rather have more of your coffee to wake up first, but I've been dying to talk to you."

"Yeah? Me too. But you go first."

I adjusted my glasses. "Okay. Last night, I was picking up some takeout for dinner, and you'll never guess who was at the restaurant."

"Who?"

"Michael Morris."

"You're kidding."

"Totally serious. I almost couldn't believe it. He was sitting at a table with another man. I went to the table behind them so I could hear what they were saying."

"Nice move."

That made me smile. "Thanks. The other guy was his attorney, and it sounded like they're also friends. Or were friends at some point. Michael clearly has issues, so I'm sure it's hard to be friends with someone like that."

"For sure."

"Sorry, I'm making this too long."

One corner of his mouth lifted. "You're fine. Keep going."

"Okay, they were talking about Edwin, and Michael was upset. Apparently, he'd been expecting to get money from his father, but something had changed. Whatever it was, his mom had also signed it, so he was angry at her, too. He was so callous when he talked about her, it was awful."

Theo shook his head with a scowl.

"But that's not the part I've been dying to tell you," I continued. "The attorney told him to be careful. That he needs to stop rampaging around town, talking about how his dad screwed him over. That it's not a good look, especially if people start asking questions. And then he said he can't protect Michael from everything."

His eyes widened. "That's interesting."

"I know, isn't it?" I leaned closer. "Do you want to know what I think?"

He shifted toward me. "What?"

Although we were alone, I lowered my voice. "I think Michael and his attorney know, or at least suspect, that Edwin Morris was murdered."

"I bet they do."

"But the question is, how do they know? Is it because Michael had something to do with it? Or did the attorney just mean that Michael would be a suspect if the truth comes out about his father's death?"

"Good questions. That dude is definitely suspicious." He took another sip of his coffee. "You won't believe who I ran into."

"Who?"

"Amanda."

I gasped. "No."

He nodded. "I'd wonder how that's possible, but this is Tilikum. Anyway, she was at the Steaming Mug having coffee with a friend. I didn't hear much of their conversation, but it was enough."

"What were they talking about?"

"Dating. The friend said something about the last guy Amanda was with and how she couldn't have thought he'd leave his wife for her."

I gasped again. "What! No way!"

"Yep. They didn't mention any names, but Amanda snapped at her and told her she didn't want to talk about him."

"Wow. Oh my gosh, that's huge."

"I know it doesn't prove anything, but it's suspicious, right?" he asked.

"So suspicious. Maybe the gossipy ladies were right, and Morris was having an affair with her."

"Seems likely." He shook his head again. "What a dick."

"Such a dick."

I had to be imagining it, but for a second, it seemed like a flash of heat crossed Theo's face. His blue eyes smoldered as his gaze flicked to my mouth, and when he licked his lips, a tingle ran down my spine.

He shifted, glancing away as he took a sip of his coffee. And just like that, it was gone.

Definitely my imagination.

But the tingly spine and pulse of heat deep inside made me feel like I needed to get up. Put some distance between us and reset.

Tea. I'd make more tea.

I kept talking as I stood and walked to the kitchen. "I'm glad we got this intel. I wish I knew what it meant, but at least it's a place to start."

"That's what I'm thinking." Theo followed me in and poured more coffee while I started the teakettle.

"I almost didn't go over to the empty table in that restaurant," I said. "I was so nervous. I don't know why. It wasn't a big deal."

"You did good, Ball Point Pen."

He reached out and we bumped fists. His compliment filled me with warmth. And more tingles.

What was wrong with me? It was just Theo.

But maybe there was no such thing as *just* Theo Haven.

Turning toward the cupboard to get a mug, I hoped my cheeks weren't flushing. How embarrassing. I reached for a mug, but paused. The one I'd been expecting—it had a cute little cat curled up on a pillow—wasn't there. I hadn't brought it over from Sean's house yet.

Tears gathered in the corners of my eyes.

"You okay?" Theo asked.

"Oh. Yes." Blinking away the tears, I took out a different mug and set it on the counter. "I just thought I had one of my other mugs here. It must still be at Sean's house. It's totally not a big deal."

His brow furrowed. "Are you sure?"

"Of course." I pushed my glasses up my nose. "It's just a mug."

He hesitated. "Except, maybe it's not the mug? Maybe you're stressed because there's still a lot of stuff over there that you have to deal with at some point. The mug just reminded you."

Biting the inside of my lip so I didn't tear up again, I nodded. Because he was absolutely right.

Without another word, he set his coffee on the counter, stepped in, and wrapped his arms around me.

I inhaled, and his masculine scent filled me. His arms were thick and strong, his body warm and steady against mine. For a second, I thought he'd immediately let go, but he didn't. He held me tighter, resting his cheek on the top of my head.

Relaxing against him, I wound my arms around his waist and closed my eyes. The tension melted from my body. He felt so good, I didn't want it to end. Couldn't we just stand there in his kitchen, hugging for the rest of the day?

Or at least for another minute?

Eventually, he let go and stepped back. I dropped my arms and fixed my glasses, once again hoping my cheeks weren't bright red.

"It's going to be okay," he said, his voice soft. "You let me know when you're ready and we'll get your stuff out of there."

"Thank you." My voice was embarrassingly breathy. I swallowed, trying to pull myself together. But that hug had scrambled my brain. "I know I should probably—"

"Hey." He put a finger to my lips, and his voice was still gentle. "Don't *should* yourself. It's okay if this is hard. It doesn't make you weak."

I gazed at him in disbelief. He meant that. He didn't think I was weak—not for staying with Sean when I should have left, or for waiting to confront him again.

He was such a good friend. What would I have done without him?

"Besides, it's only stuff." He paused, concern passing over his features. "You don't think he'll get rid of it before you can move everything out, do you?"

I considered that for a moment. "I guess I can't put anything past him."

"Like I said, let me know when you're ready. I've got you."

Smiling, I resisted the temptation to hug him again. It would have been nice, but I had a feeling I needed to keep some distance. My feelings were getting stirred up in ways that were very inconvenient.

"There's actually something else I need to talk to you about," Theo said.

His voice had changed. He sounded hesitant. Maybe even a bit nervous.

That was odd. Theo never seemed to get nervous about anything. Oh, no. Was he about to tell me I had to find a different place to live?

"Sure, what's up?"

"I've been offered a job as the offensive coordinator at the University of South Carolina. It's obviously a big move, but it's a great opportunity. And I decided to accept."

It felt as if the floor opened and swallowed me whole. I stared at him in disbelief. He was leaving? Moving away? Across the country?

My lips parted, but I couldn't seem to get a word out. I needed to say something. Congratulate him and tell him I was happy for him. That it really was an amazing opportunity.

His expression shifted from hopeful to bleak.

This was bad. So bad. I was failing. Big fat F on this test of friendship.

I sucked in a lungful of air and finally regained the use of language. "Oh my goodness! That's incredible. Theo, I'm so happy for you."

His look of worry transformed into a big dimpled smile. "Thanks, Pen. I'm really excited about it."

Friend crisis averted.

"Wow, offensive coordinator. And that's a big university."

"It is. They have a solid program, too. It's going to be great."

"So great. You'll be amazing at it. You're such a gifted coach. When do you go?"

"Next summer. So I'll be able to finish out the school year here. And don't worry about the house. I thought about keeping it as a rental anyway, so if you like living here, you can stay."

"Thanks, I appreciate that." I gave him my best everything-is-great smile. "What have you done to celebrate?"

He shrugged. "Took my mom to coffee. Had dinner with my family. We had champagne, although that was because my brother Luke got engaged."

"Lots of big news in your family."

"Yeah. Now that I think about it, I'm kind of surprised no one announced another baby on the way."

I laughed a little, but the words *engaged* and *baby* bounced around in my head. Or maybe it was my heart.

They both hurt.

Because I was not engaged. And although I would have loved it, I was definitely not expecting a baby. I wanted a husband and a family, and I wasn't exactly getting any younger.

Realizing my smile had faded and I probably looked stricken, I turned away before Theo could see. My lackluster life was not his problem.

"You know what this means, though?" he asked.

Smoothing my expression, I looked at him and schooled my voice to sound cheerful. "What?"

"We have to figure out what happened to Morris before I leave."

"Oh no, a ticking clock," I said, my tone mock serious. "That ups the stakes."

He nodded. "It does. Although I guess if we haven't figured out what happened to him by next summer, maybe the answer is nothing."

"True. We don't have proof he was murdered."

"No. But doesn't your gut tell you he was? Because mine really does."

"Mine does, too. I feel like we at least need to look into it."

"Agreed." He held out his fist and I bumped it with mine. He gestured over his shoulder with his thumb. "I should hit the shower. What are you up to today?"

I glanced around the kitchen, as if I'd find the answer sitting on the counter. "Not much. I'll probably make lunches for the week."

"Meal prep for the win." He grinned. "And you know you don't have to make mine."

"I know, but it's easy to double whatever I'm making."

"Awesome. Thanks, Pen."

He turned to go, and I tried to focus on what I'd make for that week's lunches. But all I could think about was a time when I'd be eating lunch alone. No Theo. No little pranks on coworkers. No chin tips, shared office gossip, or fist bumps.

With a sinking feeling, I faced the fact that Theo was not just my only friend at work, but the only real friend I had. Everyone else I used to see socially were Sean's friends. And to be honest, I was happy to let him keep them.

But Theo was all I had. And I was losing him.

I was not going to cry. I breathed it all in, shoving it down as deep as I could, and stuffed all those awful feelings in the empty place Theo was leaving behind.

As I was pulling myself back together, he reappeared in the kitchen doorway. "Thank you."

His voice was so sincere, it almost ripped me wide open.

"For what?"

"Being happy for me. You're my best friend. I hope you know that. And if you were the one leaving, I'd be pretty bummed about it. School wouldn't be the same without you."

Trying desperately to hold in the wave of emotion threatening to overtake me, I blinked and glanced away. "Yeah, it'll be an adjustment. But this is what happens. People find new opportunities and move on. I'm happy for you."

His eyes searched my face, as if looking for evidence that I wasn't being honest. I smiled, hoping he thought it was real. Because if he said anything else—or worse, hugged me again—I'd be a puddle of tears in an instant.

Thankfully, he didn't. He pressed his lips together in a subtle smile, tipped his chin, and disappeared down the hall to take a shower.

With another deep breath, I crossed my arms, hoping it would be enough to hold the pieces of myself together.

CHAPTER 17

Theo

It was a good thing school and coaching kept me so busy. Otherwise I would have been in trouble. What sort of trouble? The guy-who-hugged-his-roommate-and-probably-shouldn't-have sort.

A week after hugging Pen in my kitchen, I still thought about it. I didn't want to admit how often. But damn it, she'd felt amazing. The way she'd melted against me had been better than scoring a game-winning touchdown.

It had been tempting to hold her again after telling her about the job, but I'd held back. I hadn't trusted myself to touch her like that without doing something stupid. Like kissing her.

I couldn't go there. She was still recovering from a breakup. What she needed was a good friend, not a make-out session in the kitchen.

But I was going to have to live with the knowledge of how good she felt, and that I was never going to feel her like that again.

So I threw myself into work, which, to be fair, wasn't hard. I had classes to teach, tests to grade, and lesson plans to tweak. Parent meetings and a staff lunch. Not to mention football, which was almost a full-time job in itself.

After a busy week at school, and another Timberwolves win, I got up Saturday morning with one thing on my mind.

Okay, two.

One was Penelope. Her bedroom door was open, but the door to her art studio was closed. That probably meant she was in there painting. Despite the strange pull I felt urging me to go see her, I resisted the temptation and went to the kitchen to make coffee.

The second thing—and the one I was determined to focus on—was the question of whether Edwin Morris had been murdered.

Pen and I had already talked about the possibility that there were notes in other paintings, but with everything else we had going on, we hadn't figured out how to find them. She'd mentioned the painting at her grandma's assisted living facility, and the possibility we could find a way to snoop around and check it. But that was only one painting. Ideally, we wanted to check more.

The gallery seemed like the best place. But how could we check there for secret notes without getting caught? It wasn't as if we could waltz in and ask permission to remove the frames.

And unless we could really narrow it down, anyone could be a suspect. Amanda and Michael had possible motives, but there was too much we didn't know. We couldn't let anyone find out that we'd found a note in the painting or that we were investigating Morris's death.

Leaning against the counter, I sipped my coffee. The idea hit me like a bolt of lightning and I almost dropped my mug.

Disguises.

I was either completely nuts or freaking brilliant. It remained to be seen. I found my phone and grabbed my laptop, taking them to the dining table. Sucking down my coffee like it was the elixir of life, I set about figuring out how to make my plan work.

About half an hour and another cup of coffee later, I rushed down the hallway and knocked on Pen's art studio door.

"Hey, Pennifer?" I called.

"Come in."

I opened the door and found Penelope looking like a hot mess. She held a paintbrush in one hand and a palette in the other. Her oversized T-shirt was paint-splattered, and her leggings had a hole in the knee. Her bun drooped to one side, and, to top it all off, she had a big stroke of blue paint across her cheek.

She was adorable.

"Morning," she said.

"Do you have a minute?"

"I have lots of minutes. I'm just working on a painting."

"Good. You know how we were talking about the note, and that we should see if we can find more?"

She nodded, her eyes brightening with interest.

"I have an idea. But we need to get moving. Marigold has time between clients, but we need to get to her salon soon."

She blinked at me in confusion. "Marigold?"

"My sister-in-law. She owns Timeless Beauty."

"I know who she is. I've seen her at the football games. But what does she have to do with finding out whether Morris left more notes?"

I checked the time on my phone. "I'll explain in a little bit. For now, you have paint on your face."

"Oops." She seemed to have forgotten she had a paintbrush in her hand and swiped another streak of blue across her cheek. "Did I just make it worse?"

My mouth turned up in a grin. Damn, she was cute. "Little bit."

"Shoot."

"It's okay. But do you mind getting cleaned up? And put on something nice, like a dress. It's all part of the plan."

She shrugged. "Okay. Just give me a few."

While Pen got ready, I went to my room to change clothes. My plan called for a certain look. Thankfully, I had a nice suit. That was one good thing about half my brothers getting married recently.

Decked out in my slate gray suit with a dark blue tie, I combed my hair off my face and added a bit of pomade. Checking my reflection in the bathroom mirror, I nodded. It should work.

"Theo, is this too fancy?" Pen called.

I stepped out of my room and my jaw dropped.

Pen stood in the living room, a knockout in a curve-hugging dark red dress. She was busy messing with her hair and didn't quite look at me as she continued.

"I don't know why I grabbed this dress when I was packing. Of all the dresses I could have chosen, this is the least likely to get worn. What was I think—"

Looking up, she stopped mid-sentence, and her jaw dropped.

"Wow, Theo," she said. "I don't think I've ever seen you in a suit."

Glancing down at myself, I tugged at the lapels of my jacket. "Not bad, right?"

"You look amazing."

A flash of heat swept through me as I looked her up and down. I probably shouldn't have been gazing at her like that, but I'd never seen her in something so sexy.

"So do you."

Pressing her lips together, she ran her hands down her hips. That did not help the hard-on situation.

"Is this okay?" she asked.

"Oh, yeah." I cleared my throat. "You look perfect."

The blush that crept across her cheeks heightened the pressure in my groin. I needed to stop looking at her like she was on the menu. That was not happening.

"I just need to do something with my hair," she said. "Or do I? Marigold?"

"Nope, you don't need to do a thing. Mari will take care of it."

"All right. I guess I'm ready."

I had to resist the urge to guide her to my truck with a hand on the small of her back. And the temptation to watch her ass while she walked.

Eyes up, Theo. She's your friend.

The fall air was chilly, but the sun was bright, and I slipped on a pair of sunglasses when we got in my truck.

"So why are we dressed like I'm your date for a wedding?" Pen asked.

I backed up and pulled out into the street. "Okay, check this out. We need access to the paintings in the gallery, but we don't want anyone to know what we're doing."

"Because anyone could be a suspect."

"Exactly." I held out my fist and she bumped it. I loved it when we were on the same page. "Even people at the gallery. So we're going in disguise."

"This is a solid plan. Who are we?"

"I'm billionaire Shepherd Calloway, and you're my wife, Everly. I think we look pretty good, except Everly is blond. Which is where Marigold comes in. I called her and she has a wig you can use."

"How did you land on a billionaire and his wife?"

I shrugged. "Wealthy people collect art. I figured no one would raise an eyebrow if a billionaire and his wife come to the gallery."

"True. They're real people?"

"Yeah. I googled handsome billionaires and found Calloway. They live in Seattle, so it's perfect."

"Handsome?" She snort-laughed.

"Hey." I pulled down my sunglasses and eyed her over the top of them. "I clean up good."

"You're okay. If you like that kind of thing."

I chuckled.

Timeless Beauty wasn't far—nothing was far in our town—and I found a parking spot right out front. We got out and I held the door to Mari's salon so Penelope could go in first.

Stacey, Marigold's front desk person, greeted us as we walked in. "Hi. Can I help you?"

"We're here to see Marigold."

"Sure. Do you have an appointment?"

I took off my sunglasses. "Sort of. I called her this morning. She knows we're coming."

Stacey blinked. "Oh, Theo. Sorry, I didn't recognize you. I'll let her know you're here."

I winked at Penelope. My plan was already working.

"Hi, Theo," Marigold said, her voice friendly, as she came out to the lobby. Her long brown hair was pulled up off her face and she wore a navy blue dress.

"Hey, Mari. Thanks for squeezing us in."

"Not a problem. My schedule is packed today, which is a good thing, but this won't take long."

"Do you know my friend, Penelope?" I gestured to her. "Pen, this is my sister-in-law, Marigold."

"Hi," Pen said with a shy wave. "I don't think we've met, although I've seen you before. That sounded creepy. I just mean I'm usually at the football games and you are, too. You know, with your whole family. And I'm just there because I work there."

"Pen's the art teacher," I said. "And…um…my roommate."

Marigold's eyebrows lifted. "Oh. That's news."

"Yeah, kind of a long story."

Marigold turned to Pen "It's so nice to meet you. Can I give you a hug? I'm a hugger."

Penelope adjusted her glasses. "I love hugs."

Marigold hugged her, then gestured to the back of the salon. "Let's get you all ready. I have a gorgeous wig for you."

We followed Mari back to her station and Penelope sat in the chair. Marigold ran her fingers through Pen's hair, brushing it out. "Penelope, your hair is gorgeous. Is this your natural color?"

She nodded. "I've never been brave enough to dye it."

"You certainly don't need to. It's beautiful. But let's have some fun making you blond for the day."

"I've never worn a wig before."

"Don't worry. They're easier than they seem."

Penelope took her glasses off, and I blinked a few times at her reflection in the mirror.

"Wow, Pen. You look so different without your glasses."

"Do I?" Her cheeks flushed a slight shade of pink, and she slipped them back on.

"Yeah. Take them off again."

She did, and it was like watching her turn into a different person.

"I guess I'm just not used to it," I said.

"I probably look better with them off, but I've never been able to wear contacts. They dry my eyes out."

"No, you look great with them on. Just different. I never understood how Clark Kent could just put on glasses and no one knew he was Superman. But now I kinda get it."

Her smile and soft laugh made my chest feel tight.

I really liked making her laugh.

Marigold got to work, and if Penelope had looked different without glasses, she was completely unrecognizable once Marigold put the wig on her. Instead of long, dark brown hair, she had thick blond waves that cascaded around her shoulders.

To be fair, brown hair looked better on her—probably because it was her natural color. Marigold would have explained it better than I could.

But the blond wig was kinda hot.

Marigold fluffed the wig and smoothed down the hair around her face. "What do you think?"

"I don't even look like me," Penelope murmured, gazing with wonder at her reflection.

"It's perfect," I confirmed. "Nice job, Mari."

"Thank you," she said with a smile.

I tried to pay Marigold for her time, and for the use of her wig, but she refused. She hugged Penelope again on our way out, and there was something about it that tugged at my chest again. I knew Pen was a little shy, and Mari was the type of person to make friends with just about everybody—and mean it. So when Mari asked for Pen's number so they could have coffee sometime, it was touching.

Holding the door open, I let Penelope go through, then put my sunglasses back on.

"All right, remind me who I am again?" Pen asked.

"My wife," I said and tried to ignore the way it felt to say those words to her. "Everly Calloway. And I'm your husband, Shepherd."

"What if the gallery assistant knows who they are?"

He shrugged. "I'm not worried about it. If we're questioned too closely, we can just act offended and leave."

"That's true. All right, Shepherd. How do I look?"

She fluffed her blond wig and turned in a little circle. I stifled a groan. Dangerous. That was how she looked.

"Hot," I said, then coughed as if I could cover up the word. "Perfect. You look perfect. Except…"

"Except what?"

"I'm pretty sure Everly Calloway doesn't wear glasses, so…" I reached out and gently slipped them off her face. "There. Disguise complete."

"You realize I'm almost blind without them."

I held them up to my face and peered through the lenses. The world was a distorted mess. "Geez, Pen. You really are blind."

"I told you. How am I going to look for secret notes if I can't see?"

"Once we're inside, take them out of your purse and put them on. Like they're reading glasses, something you don't wear all the time."

She smiled. "Good plan. I can do that. But seriously, I'm going to need to hold your arm so I don't trip over things."

"Don't worry, Penlock Holmes. I've got you."

"It's Everly Calloway, thank you very much."

"Oh, of course. Sorry, my lovely wife."

Her nervous giggle sent a rush of heat to my groin. Damn it, I was trying really hard not to get turned on by her in that dress. But I hadn't been kidding—she was hot as hell. It wasn't the wig, it was the whole package.

And my package was paying attention.

She put her glasses in her purse, and when I held out my arm, she tucked her hand in the crook of my elbow, and we started up the sidewalk.

CHAPTER 18

Penelope

The wig was surprisingly comfortable, but walking without my glasses was not.

I kept my hand tucked in Theo's arm as he led me up the sidewalk toward the gallery. It wasn't far from the salon, but my fuzzy vision made it hard to tell exactly where we were. Plus, I was still reeling from this slick, sophisticated version of Theo Haven.

And from him calling me hot.

I was not a hot girl. Sean had called me things like *pretty* or *cute*—in the beginning, at least, until the compliments gradually fizzled out. But never hot.

It was probably just the blond wig. And lack of glasses. I felt a little bit like a girl in an eighties movie who gets her braces off and starts wearing contacts, and suddenly she's the hottest girl in town.

Not that I was actually the hottest girl in town.

I needed to get my head together before we got to the gallery. I wasn't dressed up to look like a hot girl. We were looking for clues to a crime.

We got to the gallery and fortunately, it was open. It seemed like Theo had thought his plan through, so he'd probably checked to make sure we'd be able to get in.

He opened the door. "Watch your step there."

"Thanks."

My sight wasn't so bad that I was unable to see anything without my glasses. But unless something was right in front of me, it was fuzzy and indistinct. It made it hard to separate smaller objects from larger ones, and almost impossible to make out faces.

"Hello, welcome," a female voice said.

I could see the outline of a person, but other than the vague sense that she was wearing blue, I couldn't make out much about the gallery assistant. And I had no idea if she was someone I'd seen before.

"Can I help you?" she asked.

"Shepherd Calloway," Theo said and held out his hand. She shook it. "This is my wife, Everly."

"Hi." A tingle of nervousness swept through me, and I stuck my hand out a little too aggressively. "Nice to meet you."

"Nice to meet you as well." She took my hand and shook. "I'm Tina. Is there anything I can help you with, or did you just wander in?"

"We heard about the unfortunate passing of Mr. Morris," Theo said.

"I'm sorry for your loss," I added.

"Thank you," Tina said. "Yes, it was quite a shock."

"My wife and I enjoy his work," Theo continued. "We thought we'd come and take a look at his gallery in person."

Every time Theo said *my wife*, my spine tingled..

"That's wonderful," Tina said. "Please, allow me to show you around the gallery."

We didn't want a gallery tour, but maybe once she showed us the highlights, we could find a way to be alone.

"That would be great," Theo said. "Thank you."

It was the perfect excuse to put on my glasses. I let go of Theo's arm and started fishing in my purse for them. Where had they gone? They should have been right on top. I'd just put them in there.

"Sorry," I muttered.

Theo deftly took the purse out of my hands, and a second later, he carefully slipped my glasses on my face. The first thing that came into view was his smile, dimples and everything.

"Better?" he asked.

"Yes."

He winked at me and my knees did not almost buckle.

Okay, yes, they did.

I took my purse and put the strap over my shoulder, grateful that I could finally see clearly. The gallery still looked fairly empty, as if they were only gradually putting back the displays after the celebration of life. There were a few easels with paintings on them, but not as many as I remembered from times I'd been there before.

"I'm afraid you've come when quite a bit of Edwin's work is not being displayed," Tina said. "But I'd love to show you what we do have on display today."

We followed her toward the side wall where several paintings were hung, lit by gallery lighting. I wanted to tuck my hand in Theo's arm again, but I didn't.

"As you can see, Edwin is primarily known for his landscapes. These depict scenery familiar to the Cascade mountains."

"Are they real locations?" Theo asked.

"That's an excellent question, and I'd say it depends," Tina answered. "Some are specific locations. Others are more general. Amalgams of different places he painted from memory."

We took slow steps around the gallery while she shared more details. I was already familiar with his style, so it wasn't new information for me. He'd painted with both oils and acrylics, depending on his mood. He'd experimented with other mediums, such as charcoal, but had always returned to paint. He was known for his use of color and texture.

She led us to the loft, the scene of his son Michael's drunken drama. Without the small knots of people standing around, it was spacious and empty. Theo asked a few questions as she pointed out more of Edwin's work, as well as the works of a few other painters they had on display.

His paintings were beautiful, but I was getting anxious. Was Tina going to leave us alone? We only needed a few minutes—there weren't that many paintings to check.

One beach scene caught my eye. For some reason, I had a feeling about it. Maybe because it was one of several that weren't set in the mountains. Or maybe it was the moody sky, so similar to the creek painting I'd received.

I wanted a moment to check the frame.

Finally, the door downstairs opened, and someone came in.

"If you'll please excuse me," Tina said.

Theo gestured to the stairs. "Be our guest. My wife and I appreciate your time."

There he went with that *my wife* thing again. It gave me a very uncomfortable mix of feelings.

My heart started to beat harder as Tina walked down the open staircase.

That's it. Keep going. We're not doing anything up here. Just admiring the art.

When we heard her greet the person who came in, we sprang into action. I pointed to the ocean painting and Theo nodded. He took the one next to it—a typical Morris piece featuring a meadow dotted with wildflowers.

He'd seemed to like wildflowers. He'd painted a lot of them.

With my heart beating wildly, I gently removed the painting from the wall and checked the back. Nothing. I ran my fingers along the edges of the frame, but there was no sign of a note tucked inside. If he'd left one, it didn't have the edge of the paper sticking out.

There was no way we could remove the backing on any of them to get a good look. We'd just have to hope that if he had left more notes, he'd made them accessible like the one in my creek painting.

I rehung the painting and checked to make sure it was straight. Theo returned the meadow piece to the wall. He glanced at me and shook his head.

Shoot.

We moved on, checking the paintings on either side. No luck. Tina's voice carried from the first floor, as did a male voice, although they spoke too quietly to make out what they were saying. They didn't appear to be coming to the loft, so we kept searching.

Just as I was rehanging a painting of a pine forest—with no sign of a note—Tina and the newcomer started up the stairs, their footfalls carrying through the airy space.

Eyes wide, I whipped my head to the side. Theo looked at me with alarm. As if we were executing a choreographed dance, we both adjusted the paintings we'd been rehanging, then took big steps back so it wouldn't look like we'd been touching them. We sidestepped toward each other, and I tucked my hand in the crook of his elbow just as he turned us around so we were facing the stairs.

Tina and a tall man in a suit stepped onto the loft. Recognition hit me, and I dug my fingers into Theo's arm. He'd been at the celebration of life—the man who'd been standing with Gina Morris, and who'd escorted Michael Morris out of the gallery. Curt Redfern.

We were dead. He was going to recognize us. We'd been right there, in that very spot in the loft of the gallery. I'd babbled to Gina Morris right in front of him.

His eyes passed right over us, as if he hardly deigned to notice there were other people present. Tina smiled and gave us a slight nod.

Theo led me to the stairs, and a moment later, we were on the main floor, with Tina and Curt in the loft above us.

I cast a quick glance around. It would be much riskier to check the paintings on the main floor—too easy for Tina or Curt to move to the railing, look down, and see what we were doing.

But we hadn't found anything.

The door at the back caught my eye. The one leading to the classroom studio. There had been lots of paintings stored back there. Meeting Theo's eyes, I pointed. He nodded.

Tiptoeing so my heels wouldn't click on the wood floor, we hurried across the gallery. Theo tried the knob and at least a little bit of luck was on our side. It opened.

He ushered me through the door and softly shut it behind us.

The classroom studio looked almost the same as when the attorney had given me my Morris painting. Artwork on easels still cluttered the space, and there was a stack of paintings propped up against the wall. It looked smaller than when we'd been there last, as if more of the pieces had been distributed according to Edwin's wishes.

I beelined for the paintings leaning against the wall while Theo kept his ear close to the door so he could listen.

The wig was starting to get warm, making my face feel hot. I crouched down and tilted the first painting so I could inspect the back. Nothing. Same with the second. I glanced over my shoulder and Theo gave me a thumbs-up. No one was coming.

I checked the third and started to wonder if this had all been for nothing. Or if we simply didn't have time to look hard enough.

Come on, Edwin. Were you murdered? Give me a clue.

My breath caught in my throat as I felt along the back of the fourth painting. There was a rough spot, like the edge of paper. I whipped my head around and nodded to Theo.

"Hurry," he whispered.

My art-loving heart protested against the possibility of damaging the painting by unfastening the backing on the bare floor. But without time to do anything else, I gently released the backing where it was and pulled out a folded piece of paper.

Turning, I held it up in triumph.

Silently, Theo held out his fist. I closed my hand and did a long-distance fist bump, careful not to crumple the paper.

Theo's eyes went wide. He didn't have to say a word. Someone was coming. He twisted the lock on the doorknob and stepped backward, holding up his hands. A second later, the knob rattled.

Working as fast as I could with shaking hands, I tucked the note in my purse and replaced the backing. The doorknob rattled again, and voices carried through. They were probably trying to figure out why the door was locked. Thankfully, Tina didn't appear to have her keys on her; otherwise we would have been in big trouble.

Knowing I was pushing it, I grabbed my phone out of my purse and took a few pictures of the painting where I'd discovered the note.

Theo reached down to help me to my feet and lowered his voice to a whisper. "We need to get out of here."

I pointed to another door. I remembered it leading to a hallway with a restroom, but I couldn't recall if there was a way out beyond it. Still, it was better than staying where we were.

We went through and found ourselves in a dark hallway. The restroom door was ajar and a few feet down along the other wall, there was another door.

Voices grew suddenly louder. Theo and I froze. Tina and Curt had entered the classroom studio.

Theo put a finger to his lips. I nodded, and we took soft steps toward the other door. Was it a closet or storage space, or did it lead outside? I had no idea.

It was locked with a dead bolt. I bit my lip, my heart pounding, as Theo slowly turned it. There was a tiny click, and I held my breath as he eased the door open.

Daylight and crisp, cool air streamed in. We slipped out and shut the door, but didn't pause to bask in relief at our escape. Theo grabbed my hand, and we hurried down the alley behind the gallery. Running in heels was not exactly in my skill set, but thankfully, Theo's grip on my hand kept me steady until we reached the sidewalk.

We slowed to a fast walk and didn't stop until we got to his truck outside Timeless Beauty.

I put my hand over my heart and tried to catch my breath. "That was terrifying."

He grinned and pressed his key fob to unlock his truck. "Yeah, but we did it."

Gratefully, I climbed into the passenger side. It felt safer than being out in the open. As if Curt would come after us like some sort of art Mafia boss.

Art Mafia? That probably wasn't a real thing, but my imagination was running a little wild.

I pulled off the wig and removed the wig cap Marigold had put on me. My real hair spilled over my shoulders and I shook it out a little.

Theo's gaze was on me, an intensity in his eyes that made my stomach swirl.

He blinked, and it was gone.

"What does the note say?" he asked.

I took it out of my purse and unfolded it. It looked a lot like the one I'd found before. Written on thick journal paper, in the same slanted cursive, it read:

So sad. So pure. So blue. It will all catch up in the end. And I fear my end is closer than I think.

"Sort of ominous, but it doesn't tell us much more, does it?" Theo said.

"No, but it's interesting that there's more than one note. And *I fear my end is closer than I think* sounds a lot like he's expecting something bad to happen."

"Definitely. Which painting was it in?"

I got out my phone and opened the photo I'd taken of the painting. "This one."

The piece depicted an alpine lake, the mirrorlike surface reflecting clouds in the sky. A cabin stood to one side and mountains rose in the background.

"Does this have anything in common with the painting you got?" he asked.

"Not really. Mine is a creek with a rock formation. No buildings or anything."

Theo rubbed his chin, and I was momentarily distracted by the stubble on his very chiseled jaw. He said something else, but my brain was still fixated on his bone structure.

"Pen?"

I startled, blinking in surprise. "Sorry, what? I was just…thinking about the note."

"I asked if you want to swing by Angel Cakes Bakery and get something. Celebrate not getting caught."

"Celebratory cookies sound great." My smile slipped a little. "But I feel weird walking around in these clothes. What if Tina or Curt look for us?"

"They probably won't, but…" He twisted around and reached behind his seat, pulling out a gray plaid flannel. "Here. With this and no wig, you'll look completely different."

Theo loosened his tie and lifted it over his head, then unbuttoned his collar while I slipped on his flannel. It smelled amazing. Clean, with a hint of his cologne. Subtle, but so masculine. I resisted the urge to bury my face in it and inhale while Theo took off his suit jacket and unbuttoned the rest of his shirt, revealing a white T-shirt underneath.

I got the silliest thrill from sitting next to Theo in the cab of his truck while he half undressed. Turning toward the window, I reminded myself I really shouldn't have been thinking like that.

"Ready?" He leaned over to look at his reflection in the rearview mirror and messed up his hair a little.

"Yeah, ready," I said, almost wincing at how breathless my voice sounded.

Smoothing out the wig, I put it on the back seat. Theo said he'd take care of returning it to Marigold. I got out of his truck and fell into step with him as we walked in the opposite direction from the gallery.

Theo was right, with him in a T-shirt and slacks, and me wearing a flannel over my dress, my natural hair once again on display, we looked completely different. I would have bet we could run into Gina and she'd have no idea we'd just been in the gallery, posing as a handsome billionaire and his wife.

Feeling a bit giddy at the success of our sleuthing, I walked next to Theo, only wishing a little bit that I could tuck my hand in the crook of his elbow again.

CHAPTER 19

Penelope

The bell rang and my students jammed through the door in their rush to get to lunch. I finished collecting their sketching projects off the tables, noting that several had neglected to write their names on their work. Again. I set those aside to be claimed next class and finished picking up my classroom.

After our sleuthing adventure over the weekend, real life had arrived bright and early Monday morning. There were classes to teach, assignments to grade, lesson plans to finalize, supplies to secure. As much as I would have loved to dedicate my time to being an amateur detective, I had a job to do.

Which meant we didn't have any more information about the mysterious notes, or our suspicions about Michael and Amanda, by the time Friday rolled around.

I left the art room and shut the door. Students filled the wide hallway. Lockers clanged shut and conversations ebbed and flowed while I locked up for lunch.

When I turned, there was Theo, leaning against the doorframe outside his classroom, muscular arms crossed. His posture was relaxed but alert as his eyes scanned the hallway. He had such a way with our students, able to be both firm and supportive, friendly and tough when necessary. The kids respected him, and I think they also knew how much he cared.

It was a priceless combination in a teacher.

His gaze moved over the crowd of kids heading to lunch and stopped on me. One corner of his mouth lifted in a subtle grin, and he tipped his chin.

I nodded back. I'd see him in the teachers' lounge.

It took a lot of emotional energy to pretend I wasn't devastated over his impending move. I completely understood why he wanted the job, and I was genuinely happy for him. But I couldn't help but be sad for me.

I was going to miss him so much.

It was hard to decide if living with him made it better, or worse. On the one hand, living together felt so effortless. Navigating around each other in the kitchen each morning. Sharing meal-prep lunches. Chatting about our days or theorizing about the Morris mystery over dinner.

The tugs of longing I felt as we said good night were the biggest downside. He'd pause in his bedroom doorway and look over his shoulder with a sleepy smile. I'd wish him good night, and he'd say the same. We'd close our doors, and every single time, I'd go to bed trying not to think about how much I wished he was with me.

Or what it would be like when I was shuffling down that hallway to my bedroom by myself, because Theo was on the other side of the country.

My plan was to make the best of it until he had to leave. Enjoy our brief time as roommates and be grateful he'd been such a good friend, especially when I'd needed him most.

Several of my coworkers were already in the lounge when I walked in. Sharon sat in an armchair with a book, and Derek, who taught PE, was at a table looking at something on his phone while he ate. Jeremy and Ashley sat at separate tables, and I wondered if that was to avoid suspicion, or if something had gone wrong between them.

I got our lunches out of the fridge and sat at the open table. My phone buzzed in my purse, so I dug it out to check. My heart skipped—and not in a good way—when I saw who'd texted.

Sean: Hey, Penelope. Could you call me? It's important.

Pressing my lips together, I narrowed my eyes at his message. I did need to make arrangements to move the rest of my things out of his house. With a deep breath, I typed a reply.

Me: Not right now, but I do need to arrange to move the rest of my things.

Sean: Okay. And I have something for you to sign to take you off the lease. Can you come over tonight?

It was Friday and there was a home game. There was no way I was missing that to go sign paperwork.

Me: I'm not free tonight.

Sean: I need it ASAP.

I could practically feel his irritation. But if I was going to meet him face-to-face, I was doing it on my terms. Not his.

Strangely, I did want to meet him face-to-face. I wanted to get it over with. Maybe even prove to myself I could—that I was brave enough to handle it.

Me: I'll meet you on Sunday, 6pm, at the Timberbeast.

Sean: Why don't you just come here? You can pick up your stuff.

Me: I need to arrange movers for my stuff. If you need me to sign paperwork, we can do it at the Timberbeast on Sunday.

Sean: Fine.

With a smile, I dropped my phone in my purse, feeling a little bit proud of myself. We were doing things on my terms.

Theo came in, taking the seat next to me, and I slid his lunch to him—the last of our Polish sausage and veggie bowls.

"Thanks, Pentangle." He snapped off the lid and dug in. "Man, this is good."

"I'm glad you like it. It was super easy."

He shoved another bite in his mouth and his gaze flicked to Ashley and Jeremy. Meeting my eyes, he lifted his eyebrows. I shrugged. I wasn't sure what was going on between them.

"Did I tell you about Lindsay Mallahan?" Theo asked. "I have her for Algebra One."

"No, what about her?"

"She got an A on her test yesterday." He smiled, showcasing his dimples. "It's her first A of the year. She's one of those kids who thinks she can't do math. Which isn't true at all. She can, she just needed to get her basics down."

"That's great. Good for her."

"Yeah, I'm proud of her." He took another big bite and kept talking around his food. "She's a good kid. Needed the win."

We kept chatting about the goings-on at school while we finished our lunch, all the while keeping an eye on Ashley and Jeremy to see if they'd do anything interesting. Like try to whisper without anyone noticing or get up and leave together.

They didn't.

Just as we were finishing up, Derek pulled a chair over to our table and straddled it backward. "Dude, Theo. Did you see the game?"

"Which game?"

"Buffalo. Man, they got killed. It was hard to watch."

"Nah, I missed it."

"You should have watched; it was a total train wreck. Their O-line was asleep or something. It was ridiculous. They couldn't get a first down to save their lives."

Theo shook his head. "That sucks."

"Yeah." Derek smacked Theo's shoulder. "Too bad you don't

play for them anymore. You might have been able to get something done."

Theo looked down at the table. "That was a long time ago."

"Yeah, but you could have still been playing. You're not that old."

I watched the conversation in front of me with growing horror. Was Derek actually that clueless? Couldn't he see this was an uncomfortable topic for Theo?

I stood abruptly. "So, Theo, if you could help me with, you know, that thing in my classroom, that would be great. Sorry, Derek, I just need to borrow Theo for a minute. He's…taller than me."

"Right." Theo got up. "Yeah, let's go take care of that now."

"You guys need another set of hands?" Derek asked.

"No," Theo and I said simultaneously. He handed me his dish and I slid it into my lunch bag along with mine.

"You sure?" Derek asked.

"I've got it." Theo headed for the door. "Thanks, man."

I followed close behind him. "Have a good afternoon!"

We went upstairs to my classroom, and I unlocked the door. The art room smelled like crisp paper with a hint of graphite and the lingering scent of acrylic paint. Student artwork decorated most of the wall space from ceiling to floor. In the back was a large metal cabinet filled with art supplies, a stack of folding easels, and my desk, which probably dated from the 1960s. Adjustable-height tables with tall stools provided workspace for my budding artists.

Theo leaned against a stool. "So, do you have any plans for the weekend?"

"Not really. Just the game tonight. You?"

He shook his head. "Not unless we decide to infiltrate the art gallery again."

"I hope not. I don't think we'll get that lucky a second time."

"Probably not."

"Oh, actually, I do have one thing. I'm meeting Sean at the Timberbeast on Sunday to deal with some paperwork for the lease or something."

His expression hardened. “Can’t he just email it?”

“Maybe. But to be honest, I think I need to do this. I’m going to see him in person eventually. This town is too small to avoid him forever. If I do it on my terms, then I won’t be worried about accidentally running into him.”

He nodded slowly. “I can respect that.”

“Thank you.”

“What time?”

“Six. I’m sure I’ll be in and out. It’s just some paperwork.”

“Noted.” He stood. “I should get to my classroom. I’m torturing them with a pop quiz.”

“Right after lunch? You’re so mean.”

He grinned. “It’s like three problems. They’ll be fine.”

“I probably won’t see you before the game, so good luck tonight.”

“Thanks, Pen. You’ll be there?”

“Of course. I wouldn’t miss it.”

“Awesome.” He grinned again before leaving, and the things that smile did to my insides could not be healthy.

With a deep breath, I set about prepping for my next class.

Theo stayed with the team after school, while I went home to change and grab something to eat. I put on a pair of jeans and a tank top, then reached for Theo’s hoodie. He hadn’t said anything the last time I’d worn it. That probably meant he didn’t mind.

Or he hadn’t noticed.

Either way, I pulled it on. It was going to be cold, so I made sure to grab my hat.

When I got to the stadium, an excited buzz of energy filled the air. The game hadn’t started, but the crowd was already loud, and the scent of popcorn wafted from the concession stand.

I walked up the steps and went straight to the railing in front of the stands. Theo was on the sideline, talking to Coach Lewis. A few seconds later, he looked up and a big grin stole over his face. He reached out his fist and I did the same, long-distance fist-bumping him. We spread our fingers wide and made a little explosion sound.

Good luck tonight, Theo.

With a flutter of happy tingles, I turned to find a seat.

"Penelope!"

Had someone called my name? I didn't usually talk to anyone when I was at the games. Even when some of my fellow faculty members were there, they usually sat with their families.

I scanned the crowd to see who'd called for me. Melanie waved with a friendly smile. Her dark hair was up in a ponytail and she wore a black jacket and jeans.

Luke was next to her, and as my eyes flicked around, I realized the whole Haven family was there.

Melanie gestured for me to join her. "Come here."

Adjusting my glasses, I walked over to her. There wasn't room on the bench, but she leaned over Luke and yelled for everyone to move down one.

"That's okay," I said. "I can sit wherever."

"No, we've got it." She scooted over and patted the spot next to her. "Have a seat."

I sat down, feeling a nervous tingle.

"Do you know everyone?" She glanced around. "Never mind. It's too loud; they won't hear me. I'll introduce you later. How is everything?"

"Not bad. I'm sorry I haven't returned your clothes. I've just had a lot going on. I will, though, I promise."

She waved a hand. "Don't even worry about it. And my burn-down-his-house offer still stands."

A guy behind us cleared his throat loudly.

Melanie turned with a wide smile. "Oh hello, Firefighter Bailey. I would never do such a thing. It's a figure of speech. You know what I mean."

I glanced back at him and blinked in recognition. "Hi, Levi. You are Levi, right?"

He smiled. "Yeah. Hey, Penelope. I thought that was you."

"Do you know each other?" Melanie asked.

"Sort of," I said. "We met once, when his twin brother went behind his back and created a dating profile for him and then swiped right on me and pretended to be him and set us up on a date. Obviously that was like a million years ago, and look at him now, with his beautiful family. And here I am with a nice roommate. Yay, me?"

I twisted in my seat, my cheeks blazing.

Melanie put an arm around me and hugged me against her. "Honey, I feel your pain. I was married to a jackass for basically a decade. My life fell apart and I moved back to my hometown, divorced and broke." She squeezed me again. "It'll get better."

I straightened as she let go and pushed my glasses up the bridge of my nose. "That actually does make me feel better. Thank you."

"That's what friends are for." She smiled. "Speaking of friends, you and Theo are just friends, right? You're not…"

"Right, no," I said quickly. "Just friends. Definitely nothing else."

She nodded slowly. "Maybe you can help me solve a little mystery, then."

"What mystery?"

"Why Theo doesn't date."

I opened my mouth to reply, but I didn't know what to say. It had never occurred to me that Theo didn't date. He hadn't dated anyone since I'd known him, but that didn't mean he wouldn't. I'd sort of assumed he just hadn't met the right person yet.

"I actually don't know," I said. "What do you mean, he doesn't date? Ever?"

"That's what he told me. He said he doesn't, like it's a rule he's adopted for himself. I was wondering if he might have told you why."

"No."

"Well, shoot, now that I'm thinking about it, that was a rude thing for me to ask. If he did tell you, it could have been private, and I shouldn't be trying to get you to break his confidence. Sorry about that. Sometimes my mouth moves before my brain can tell it to stop."

"That's okay. It's not something we've talked about, so I really don't know."

She shrugged. "Oh, well. I'm sure he has his reasons."

The announcer came on the loudspeaker to call the starting lineups, and everyone got to their feet. I clapped and cheered with the crowd and tried not to worry about what Melanie had said.

It wasn't like it mattered. Whether or not Theo dated in general didn't have anything to do with me.

Pushing all thoughts of Theo and dating, and even my own relationship failures, out of my mind, I focused on the game.

It was thrilling, a nail-biter with an intense back-and-forth between the two teams. By the end of the fourth quarter, it was tied. Timberwolves had the ball, but they were on their five-yard line—ninety-five yards away from a win. The center snapped the ball, and I held my breath. The quarterback faked a pass, then handed it off to Owen Haven.

Owen broke free from the line and the crowd went wild, chanting his name as he ran, the other team's defense scrambling to catch him. Melanie and I clutched each other, watching as he passed the fifty, the forty, the thirty, the twenty, the ten.

Touchdown!

We threw our arms in the air and cheered, adding our voices to the roar of the crowd. Down on the field, the players jumped and danced and celebrated. The last few seconds ticked down and the game was officially over. A few of the players ran to get the big water cooler and dumped ice water all over Theo.

It was amazing.

Once the cheering and celebrating died down, people started to file out. I said goodbye to Melanie and Luke, then went to the railing to wave to Theo. He was busy talking to Coach Lewis, but right as I was about to give up and walk away—I'd congratulate him later—he turned and smiled at me.

My heart seemed to swell as I smiled and waved. He winked and held out his fist. I did the same, giving him another long-distance fist bump.

And tried not to cry at the thought that it was the last season of Theo's career in Tilikum. Soon, it would be over. And he'd be gone.

CHAPTER 20

Penelope

I spent Sunday afternoon visiting with Grandma Colleen while Theo went to his parents' house. For once, there weren't any Maury Haven shenanigans. The weather was nice, so we went outside and fed her squirrels for a while, then had dinner in the cafeteria.

It was almost six o'clock by the time I left. My stomach swirled with nervousness as I got in my car and drove to the Timberbeast to meet Sean. It was something I needed to do, but that didn't mean I was looking forward to it.

I parked and got out of my car, glancing down at my black sweater, jeans, and tennis shoes. I wished I would have dressed a little sexier—or at least cuter. It was a perfectly fine visit-your-grandma outfit, but not a great deal-with-your-ex-boyfriend outfit.

Oh, well. I adjusted my glasses, shouldered my purse, and went into the bar.

A little smile crossed my lips as soon as I heard the nineties grunge playing in the background. It felt serendipitous. I loved nineties music. Sean hated it.

I found him sitting at a table, facing the door. He had a beer, and it looked like he'd ordered a cider for me. I let out a frustrated breath. I wasn't there to have a drink with him. I just wanted to sign the lease paperwork and move on.

He stood with a smile when he saw me.

I walked to his table and stopped.

"Hey, ba—" He closed his mouth before he could finish the word *babe*. "Have a seat."

"What do you need me to sign?"

"It's right here. But have a drink with me. It's the One Tree caramel cinnamon cider that you love."

"Fine." I pulled out the chair and sat. That was one of my favorite ciders, but I wasn't sure if I was going to drink it or not.

"I know you're mad," he said. "And I don't blame you. I've been a real asshole and I'm sorry."

"You left me on the side of the road, at night, thirty minutes from home."

"Yeah, I was pissed off," he said, and his voice was sullen rather than defensive.

"And then you angry texted me half a dozen times."

"I was pretty drunk. I don't remember most of those."

I took a deep breath. "You know what, I have no reason to hold a grudge. Thank you for apologizing. I accept."

He smiled. "Good. I'm glad we got that out of the way."

I was too. I smiled back, feeling like that had been a success. We'd seen each other, cleared the air, and now it was over. I wasn't going to dread running into him in public.

"Is this the paperwork?" I slid it in front of me. It was an agreement stating that I was moving out and, surprisingly, that I didn't owe any additional rent or utilities. I dug a pen out of my purse and signed.

"Now we can both move on." I pushed it back toward Sean.

I noticed someone at the bar and did a double take. Theo sat on one of the stools. He looked over his shoulder and gave me a quick wink. My stomach fluttered and a flush hit my cheeks.

For a hot second, I forgot what I was doing there and started to stand, as if I were being drawn by gravity into Theo's orbit.

"Penelope, wait."

Sean's voice startled me. Blinking in surprise, I looked at him.

"I know I was angry before and I didn't handle it well. You took me by surprise. But I think all this..." He gestured between the two of us. "It's a big mistake."

"What do you mean?"

"I've had time to go over what happened, and I realized I didn't give you a chance to think things through."

"Think what through?"

"Us. Where we're headed."

"We're not headed anywhere. We broke up."

"It was a heated moment. Did you really consider the implications?"

"I don't think I understand what you're getting at."

He rested his forearm on the table and leaned forward. "Are you sure leaving a solid long-term relationship when you're in your midthirties is a good idea?"

My eyes widened and my mouth dropped open. For a second, I was so shocked, I couldn't seem to make any words come out.

"Excuse me?" was all I managed.

"I'm not trying to be a jerk here. It's just reality. I'm a guy who makes good money and who'll eventually take over a business. I'm stable. I'm not going to have any problem finding someone. But you? The cute nerd girl thing you have going on isn't going to last forever."

"What are you saying? I have an expiration date?"

"I don't make the rules. It's not my fault the world works this way." His expression softened. "You made a rash decision, and I want to give you the chance to come back before it's too late."

"Too late for what?"

"Let's just be real about all this, babe. I'm giving you another chance. You should take it. Come home." He gestured to the form I'd signed. "I can rip that up right now."

"Why? Because no one else could possibly want me?"

"I wasn't going to say it, but..." Pressing his lips together, he nodded.

A hand slid across my shoulders, and I looked up to find Theo standing next to my chair.

"Hi, beautiful," he said.

I stared at him in disbelief as he moved his hand to the back of my neck. It was not a friendly touch. It was possessive and intimate—almost dirty. Especially the way he slid his fingers into my hair and leaned down, his grip tightening as if he wasn't going to let me turn away.

With his face mere inches away, he spoke again in a deep voice. "Sorry I'm late."

Before I could respond—or even think—he closed the distance, and his mouth was on mine. The shock of his kiss reverberated through my body, sending sparks that burst between my legs. His lips were firm, but soft, moving over mine like he'd done it a thousand times.

Like he owned me.

And in that moment, he did.

A slight brush of his tongue almost made me moan. But then he pulled away.

My lips parted as we separated, my eyes fluttering open just in time to catch him licking his lips. The corners of his mouth turned up slightly, as if he'd enjoyed that kiss and was savoring the way I'd tasted.

I was dumbstruck, blinking at him like a moron as he straightened.

"Hi," was all I managed to get out.

Theo Haven had just kissed me, and it had short-circuited my brain.

He turned to glance at Sean and his voice was low and even. "You're in my seat."

I was almost afraid to look, but flicked my eyes to the side, risking a peek.

The color drained from Sean's face and his mouth hung open. I couldn't tell if he was mad, or just shocked.

Theo released his grip on my hair but kept a protective hand on the back of my head. His fingers moved, almost as if he wasn't aware of it, sliding through my hair and lightly massaging my scalp. My lips blazed with the heat of his kiss, and his touch was mesmerizing.

Finally, my brain caught up. Theo was pretending to be my new boyfriend—a man who wanted me.

I turned to look Sean directly in the eyes. "What was that you were saying about no one else ever wanting me?"

The grimace of horror that crossed Sean's face almost made me laugh. He'd actually thought he was doing me a favor.

Clearing his throat, he stood and almost crumpled the paper I'd signed in his fist. Without another word, he stormed out.

Theo stopped playing with my hair and the absence of his touch was almost jarring. He walked around the table and took the chair Sean had just vacated.

I opened my mouth, but I didn't know what to say. My mind was a swirl of thoughts and feelings.

That kiss.

But it had been fake.

I resisted the urge to touch my lips. It sure hadn't felt fake.

"Sorry," Theo said, giving me a sheepish grin. "I wasn't going to interfere, but he was seriously pissing me off."

"What are you doing here?"

He hesitated before answering. "I know you don't need me to fight your battles for you, but I wanted to be here, just in case."

I gazed at him for a moment. How did I get so lucky? He was such a great friend.

And an amazing kisser, which—for better or worse—I now knew.

"Thank you."

"You're not mad?" he asked.

"No, I'm not mad. And I sure don't think he's going to bother me again."

"He better not."

My lips still tingled, and I inadvertently rubbed them together. Theo's eyes flicked to my mouth, and I caught a glimpse of his tongue darting across his bottom lip.

I glanced away. The kiss had been fake. He'd only been pretending to be my boyfriend to make a point. The fact that I could still feel his mouth on mine wasn't because it was the best kiss I'd ever had. It was just because he'd surprised me. I hadn't been expecting it.

Okay, that was a huge lie. It was the best kiss I'd ever had.

And suddenly, it was killing me to know that I'd never get another one.

CHAPTER 21

Theo

I shouldn't have done that.

The thought kept running through my mind as I looked at Penelope sitting across from me. I shouldn't have kissed her.

I could have accomplished the same thing without the kiss. All I'd needed to do was touch her shoulder and tell Sean he was in my seat. That would have been enough to get the message across.

But no. I'd leaned down, and a second later, I was kissing her.

I could still feel her lips. Still taste her. And I was hard as steel thinking about what it would be like to taste more of her. To devour that mouth, and the rest of her along with it.

Fuck.

At least she wasn't mad at me for interfering.

She hadn't touched the drink Sean had bought her, which was weirdly gratifying. I wanted to get rid of the last remnants of him, so I grabbed his empty bottle and reached for hers.

"Do you want that, or…?"

"No." She shook her head. "I'm not going to drink it."

"Good." I stood and picked up her cider. Maybe staying for a drink—on me, not the douchebag—would be a good idea. I didn't trust myself to be alone with her yet. "I was thinking about getting a drink. Do you want something?"

"Sure, that sounds nice."

"One of these?" I lifted the cider.

Wrinkling her nose, she adjusted her glasses. "I think he ruined that flavor for me. Maybe just a regular cider."

"On it."

I took the bottles to the bar and waited while Rocco served another customer. Penelope seemed restless. She kept messing with her hair and glasses.

"Be right with you, Theo," Rocco said.

Glancing at him, I tipped my chin, and he disappeared into the back.

When I looked at Penelope again, she was touching her lips with her fingertips. Inadvertently, my tongue darted out and I licked my lips, remembering the way she'd felt. The way her mouth had tasted.

Our eyes met and we both froze. Looking away, she dropped her hand into her lap. I pressed my lips together, as if I could pretend I hadn't been thinking about how it had felt to kiss her.

Damn it. What had I done?

It was fine. I could fix this.

Rocco came out and I ordered a beer and a cider. He handed me the bottles and I paid, then took them to our table.

Just friends, Theo. We're just friends.

I sat and we both took a drink. We needed something to talk about—other than Sean. Or the fact that her mouth felt like—

"How's your grandma?" I asked, cutting off my own thoughts.

"She's fine. She likes to feed the squirrels, so we did that. Then had dinner. Luckily, the food there is good."

"How long has she lived there?"

"About five years. The nice thing is, it was her choice. She can still live independently, but she doesn't have to cook unless she wants to. There's medical help if she needs it. And activities to keep her busy."

"It's nice that you can visit her so often. I'm sure she appreciates that."

"Yeah, we only have each other. It was one of the reasons I wanted to move to Tilikum. I was in Pinecrest before, which isn't far, but it's nice to be able to pop over more easily."

"Sucks that you aren't closer with the rest of your family. Especially your parents. Do you have any contact with them?"

"A little. I usually get a call on my birthday and around the holidays. That's about it."

I shook my head. "Damn. Sorry for bringing up a crappy subject."

"No, it's okay. The good part about all of it was Grandma. My grandpa passed when I was a teenager, so I moved in with her when I was in college. It worked out great for both of us. After that, I got a teaching job in Wenatchee. That wasn't bad. I could still visit. But it made me realize I wanted to settle down here, so I could be as close to her as possible."

I nodded along as she talked. I certainly understood being close to your family. I was still struggling with the reality of leaving mine.

But another thought occurred to me. Penelope probably wouldn't leave Tilikum.

Maybe it would be an option once her grandma had passed on. But then again, maybe not. She'd worked hard and been patient for a long time before finally getting her job at Tilikum High School. This place meant something to her, as did being close to her grandma.

Not that I was thinking about asking her to come to South Carolina with me. That would have been a girlfriend conversation, not a friend conversation. Not even a work-besties-turned-roommates conversation.

But the realization that it wouldn't be an option, no matter what, kind of hurt.

Which was stupid. Just because I'd fake kissed her didn't mean anything had changed. And it definitely didn't mean we were more than friends.

"It's nice that you're so close with your family," she said. "I see them at the games, and it seems like you spend a lot of time with them."

"I think my parents invite me over a lot because they assume I'm lonely."

"Because you're single?"

I nodded. "Probably."

"Can I ask you a weird question?"

I took a drink. "Sure."

"Now I regret saying that. Never mind. I don't need to ask you anything."

"Well, now you have to ask me. What is it?"

"No, I'll just make it awkward."

"You're not going to make it awkward. What do you want to know? I'll tell you anything."

"I was just wondering." She paused, fidgeting with her bottle. "Is there a reason you don't date? I'm not judging you for being single. I'm just curious. You're such a great guy, it's almost impossible to imagine you not getting snatched up by some lucky girl. See? Awkward."

Had she just called me a great guy? A sense of warmth spread through my chest.

"That's not awkward. I get asked that a lot, actually. Mostly by my family. I, um..." I trailed off, trying to decide how much to say. "It's just what's best for me, I guess."

"So it wasn't because something happened? You just like being single?"

"Not exactly." My love life wasn't my favorite topic, but I had a strange desire to tell her. "I was dating a girl in college. We met my senior year and stayed together after I graduated and started playing pro ball. I thought everything was great. She was getting into sports journalism and got a great job working for one of the networks. I was living my dream, playing pro football. It was like we had it all. I actually asked her to marry me."

"Did you? I didn't realize you'd been engaged."

"It didn't last very long. A few weeks after I gave her the ring, I was injured in a game. It was clear pretty quickly that it was a career-ender. Neck and spine injuries are no joke."

"But…" she hesitated. "What did that have to do with your engagement?"

"It was too much for her. The injury, the rehab, the possibility that I'd have ongoing mobility challenges. She called it off."

She huffed. "Are you kidding me? She broke up with you when you were severely injured?"

"Yeah, pretty much."

"That's…" She scrunched her nose. "That's so awful. How could she do that?"

I appreciated that she was angry on my behalf, but I had to fight back a grin. She was cute when she was mad.

"I'm glad it happened. She wasn't the person I thought she was."

"Clearly not." Her voice softened. "So, that was it? You decided to stay single?"

"No. My recovery took a while, and then I went back to school to get my masters. After that, I decided to try dating again. Eventually, I met someone and we hit it off. We dated for a while, and things were getting serious. That was when my migraines got bad."

"Did you get them right after you were injured, or did it take that long for them to start?"

"I had mild ones for a while. I didn't even know they were migraines. But then they started getting really bad. One took me out for about four days, and I had no idea what it was. They were debilitating. Eventually, my doctor and I found ways to get them under control, but for a while, my quality of life was not great."

"So, you were getting serious with someone and the migraines got bad. Are you about to tell me she did what your other ex did? You had medical issues that were too much for her and she bailed?"

"Yeah, that's exactly what happened." I huffed out a resigned laugh and shook my head. "She couldn't imagine herself coping with my migraines for the rest of her life."

Her brow furrowed. "That's not right. If you love someone, you don't leave when things get hard. You stay by their side no matter what."

"I guess she didn't love me." I shrugged. "Anyway, that was it. I decided I was done. I was teaching and coaching, and that was fulfilling enough."

"I can't say I blame you."

Silence settled between us as we finished our drinks. But it wasn't uncomfortable. It felt natural to sit with her, quietly enjoying a beer. Sharing things I didn't usually share with anyone.

After a while, I broke the silence. "You ready to go, or do you want to hang out here?"

"I'm ready to go. The alarm will go off all too early tomorrow."

"Yeah, it will."

We stood, and as she came around the table, she dropped her purse. We both bent to grab it, and I found myself within inches of her face. Again.

Don't kiss her again, Theo. Don't do it.

I picked up her purse and straightened, handing it to her. Her cheeks flushed with a hint of pink as she took it.

Close call.

We went outside and I walked her to her car.

"I'll see you at home," she said.

"Yeah. See you at home."

I backed up a few steps while she got in and watched her pull out of her space and drive away.

See you at home.

That phrase sent a sense of warmth spreading through my chest. There was a very uncomfortable truth brewing inside me—something I kept trying to deny. I liked Penelope. A lot.

And not as a friend.

CHAPTER 22

Penelope

Everything was fine.

I went inside and hung my purse on the hook by the door. At least the meeting with Sean was over. There was still the issue of my furniture and the other things I'd left behind, but now that I'd seen him—faced him and stood my ground—it didn't seem so daunting.

Closure. Closure was good.

Unfortunately, I had the opposite of closure with Theo.

One fake kiss should not have sent my emotions into a tailspin. Sitting with him and talking—like friends—had helped. But the memory of his kiss remained, warm and visceral.

I went to the kitchen to meal prep for the week. I needed lunches, but more importantly, I needed to keep busy.

Theo's truck pulled up outside and my stomach fluttered. It felt like middle school all over again. I'd had a crush on a boy named Peter. A very unrequited rush. He'd been an athlete—cute and popular. Me? Not so much. In those days, the cool jocks never went for the awkward nerd girls.

They probably didn't when you were in your thirties, either.

I startled at the sound of the front door. Which was so silly. I'd heard him drive up. There was no reason for me to be surprised by his entrance.

He shut the door behind him and our eyes met. He smiled, displaying those irresistible dimples. It was a normal smile. Friendly. Like nothing had happened between us at the bar.

And really, nothing had. I needed to get that through my mind.

"Hey," he said. "I realized when I got in my truck I was almost out of gas. Glad I noticed it before tomorrow morning."

"An empty gas tank is never a fun surprise on a Monday morning."

"What are you up to in there?" he asked as he wandered into the kitchen.

"Just meal prepping."

His brow furrowed as his eyes moved across the counter. "What are you making?"

I glanced at the ingredients I'd pulled out. There was the chicken I'd already cooked. That made sense. But I'd also grabbed ketchup, a box of spaghetti, an orange, and a half gallon of milk.

How embarrassing.

"Um..." I pushed my glasses up the bridge of my nose. "I guess I wasn't paying attention. I forgot what I was looking for."

A flash of worry crossed his features. I didn't want him to know how much his kiss had flustered me, but it was probably too late for that.

"Do you need any help?" he asked.

"No, I've got it. Thanks, though."

I started putting things back in the refrigerator. He hesitated for a moment, watching me, almost as if he wanted to say something.

Or kiss me again.

But no, that was just my imagination. He left the kitchen, disappearing down the hall to his bedroom.

He hadn't kissed me because he wanted to. Because he was attracted to me. No, he'd done it to help me. It had been fake. Just pretend.

Friends. We were just friends.

With a deep breath, I went back to work on the chicken burrito bowls I'd been planning to make for the week. The familiar movements of chopping and mixing eased my jitters. By the time Theo came out of his bedroom, dressed in a clean T-shirt and plaid pajama pants, I was much less jumpy.

He paused in the kitchen doorway. "Are you sure you don't need help?"

"Nope. Almost done."

"Those look great." He went to the refrigerator and got out some leftovers. "You keep spoiling me, though. I'm going to have to learn to make better lunches for myself. I can't go back to boring sandwiches after this."

The subtle reminder of his upcoming move felt like a pinprick. A sharp one.

"It's not difficult." I tried to sound cheerful. "You just have to make time to do it."

He warmed his leftovers in the microwave while I finished the burrito bowls with a sprinkling of chopped green onions. I put the lids on, and he took his dinner out and gave it a quick stir.

"Thanks again," he said.

"For what?"

He hesitated, his eyes on mine. "Lunch."

"Yeah, of course."

I ran through the reasons that kiss had been fake—and couldn't be anything but fake—while he took his dinner to the other room, and I put our lunches away and cleaned up.

Just friends. South Carolina. Just friends. South Carolina. Just friends. South Carolina.

He turned on the TV and I joined him in the living room. I'd eaten with Grandma, so I wasn't hungry, but it was too early to go to bed. I probably should have gone to my room to read or something, but his magnetism was too strong. Even though I knew I was making it harder on myself.

Eventually, I got too drowsy to stay up any longer. I went to the bathroom to get ready for bed. When I came out, Theo was nowhere to be seen. He must have gone to his room.

With a long exhale, I went to my bedroom and quietly shut the door.

It was almost November. That meant about seven months until he left. Seven months of living under the same roof. Of bedhead and tired morning smiles. Of quiet good nights and sleeping one room away. Of knowing that Theo Haven was the best guy I'd ever met, but we weren't meant to be.

Hours later, I was still wide-awake, my thoughts a tangled mess. My body wasn't helping, either. The heat of that kiss—that one stupid kiss—flowed through me like fire. I was restless, antsy, unsatisfied. And apparently not sleeping any time soon.

After tossing and turning for a while longer, trying to find a position that would enable me to finally relax, I gave up and threw off the covers. Maybe chamomile tea would help.

I got out of bed and felt around the side table for my glasses. Without bothering to turn on the light, I put them on and quietly opened the door.

Just as I was about to slip down the hallway to the kitchen, Theo's door opened.

My heart jumped and I pressed myself against the wall, as if I could hide. He emerged with an uncharacteristic scowl on his face, wearing nothing but a pair of boxer briefs.

My wide eyes were glued to the dusting of chest hair and the happy trail that disappeared beneath his waistband. He was muscular and toned without being so ripped that he didn't look real. A flush hit my cheeks, and he didn't move.

Slowly lifting my gaze to his face, I realized that, like him, I was hardly wearing anything. Just a tank top and shorts that left very little to the imagination.

"Sorry," he said, averting his eyes. "I didn't know you were up."

"I couldn't sleep."

Don't look down, Penelope. Don't look at his—

Too late. I looked. And he was—

"Me neither," he said.

The scant space of the hallway was between us, I kept my back pressed to the wall and he stood still, as if frozen to the spot.

I was about to start babbling something about chamomile tea and wishing I'd put on a robe, or at least a bra, but he spoke first.

"I want to kiss you again."

It was so unexpected, I didn't know what to say. I opened my mouth to reply, but nothing came out.

"I shouldn't," he continued. "Shouldn't have before, either. But I can't stop thinking about how good it felt."

"Neither can I."

He stepped forward, cutting the distance between us in half, and his eyes roved over me. The brush of silk against my skin made my body tingle and heat pooled in my core.

"Tell me no." He moved closer.

My voice was barely above a whisper. "What if I don't?"

He stepped into my space and slid one hand into my hair, the other around my waist. "Then I'm going to kiss you again."

"I…" I hesitated. Was this actually happening? "I didn't think…"

His fingertips massaged the back of my head. "Didn't think what?"

"That you wanted me."

"You don't think I want you?" The hand on my waist slid down to cup my backside, and he pressed me against his hardness. When he spoke again, his voice was a low growl. "You feel that? That's what you do to me. You drive me fucking crazy. So tell me no, Pen."

"Yes."

In one smooth motion, he tilted my head back and took my mouth with his. Gone was the softness and restraint of the kiss in the Timberbeast. He invaded my mouth with his tongue, pressing my body against his.

Opening for him, I kissed him back, melting against him as he devoured me. The pressure between my thighs built so fast, I wanted to jump up and wrap my legs around his waist. I whimpered into his mouth as his velvety tongue slid against mine, and his fingers dug into my backside.

Still holding me against him, he backed us into his bedroom. I was in too deep to worry about the consequences. Too far gone to think about tomorrow.

In seconds, our clothes were on the floor. He took the time to carefully remove my glasses and set them aside. Then his hands were all over me, sliding across my skin as he kissed me. His mouth moved to my jaw, down my neck, and I leaned my head back, moaning as his fingers slid between my legs.

"You're already wet for me," he growled in my ear.

I had no words. I was nothing but a tight ball of heat and pressure, ready to burst, and he'd hardly touched me.

He nudged me onto the bed and climbed on top of me. His tip brushed my center.

"Do I need something?" he asked.

"I have it covered."

"Still yes?"

"Yes," I breathed. "Please."

I moaned as he slid inside me, pleasure exploding through my entire body. His mouth found mine and he kissed me deeply as he thrust in and out, his hips driving me up the bed.

I'd never felt anything like it. His skin was hot against mine, his body relentless. Pressure built as we moved together, and I clung to him, my fingers digging into his hard planes of muscle. I hiked my legs up, opening to take him deeper, and recognized with a sense of awe that he was going to finish me.

Easily.

Holding on as if my life depended on it, I let him take me—let him have all of me. He owned every inch, and I didn't want any of it back.

Our mouths separated and he lifted himself higher, looking down with hooded eyes and a slight curve of his lips, as if he liked what he saw. I felt so vulnerable, so exposed—and so safe, with no desire to hide.

He drove his hips harder, groaning with each thrust. I moaned and whimpered, draping my arms overhead, letting him have complete control of my body. The pressure built, almost to a breaking point, and he moved faster, as if he knew exactly what I needed.

His gaze was intense. Bracing himself over me with one hand, he grabbed my backside with the other and drove in so deep, my world exploded.

I burst into a thousand pieces, the pleasure so intense I cried out over and over as he thrust into me. His brow furrowed, and with a deep growl, he started to come, sending my climax to new heights. One orgasm drew into another until I was panting and whimpering with his rhythmic motion.

Finally, he slowed and came to a stop, lowering himself so his body draped over mine. I wrapped my arms around him, breathing hard, and felt his chest rise and fall against me. I was dazed—overwhelmed. I'd never experienced anything like it before.

I'd never known sex could be so incredible.

He nuzzled into my neck, brushing soft kisses across my skin. I ran my hand through his hair, relishing the feel of his body on mine. For long moments, we lay there together, and I drifted in bliss, enveloped in his scent, wishing it could last forever.

It couldn't. But I wasn't ready to face that yet.

Eventually, he rolled off me, and I turned onto my side. We were close enough that I could see his face without my glasses. His eyes were sleepy—half closed—and his mouth turned up in a subtle smile. He leaned closer and kissed me again.

I was so relaxed, but I needed to clean up. And I wasn't sure if I should stay or go back to my own bed. I wondered if he would say something, but his eyes closed. He reached out to caress me gently as I slipped out of bed and put on my glasses, and although he opened his eyes and smiled again, he didn't say anything.

I went into his bathroom and took care of necessities. When I came out, he looked like he was asleep. I thought about climbing back into bed with him—curling up with Theo all night sounded wonderful—but I hesitated. It wasn't that I thought he would mind. He probably wouldn't. But was staying all night a good idea?

It was probably better if I went to bed in my own room. In one night, he'd given me the best kiss of my life and the best sex of my life. That was going to be a lot to grapple with in the morning. A little distance might help me process.

Because I knew this didn't change anything. Theo and I were still just friends, and he was still moving away. And whatever happened next, I needed to keep my heart out of it.

But I wasn't sure that I could.

CHAPTER 23

Theo

The sound of a door shutting roused me from sleep. I opened my eyes, expecting to find Pen getting back into bed with me. Hadn't she just gotten up to use the bathroom? But the bed was empty.

She'd gone back to her room.

I let out a long breath. That was probably for the best.

I'd gone to bed telling myself I wasn't going to kiss her again. I needed to let it go. But the memory of her lips had tortured me, keeping me from getting any sleep.

The last thing I'd expected when I'd gotten up in the middle of the night to get some water was running into her in the hallway.

I'd been weak. She'd been too much to resist.

But fuck, it had been amazing.

The tension in my neck told me I needed to succumb to sleep and get some rest, otherwise I risked a migraine. I didn't know what the morning would bring, but there wasn't anything I could do about it then. I'd just have to hope I hadn't ruined everything.

And that I could live with the knowledge of what it felt like when I was buried deep inside Penelope without giving in to temptation again.

We all have those days when the alarm is especially jarring, and that Monday morning was one of them. It felt like I'd only just closed my eyes when the relentless beeping ripped me from sleep.

Waking up alone left me disappointed all over again. What would it have been like to open my eyes to the sight of her? To pull her against me and enjoy a few minutes of contact before we started our day?

Groaning, I hit the alarm to shut it up and stretched my neck a little in both directions. Vision was normal, no growing tension. No sign of a migraine. That was good.

I got up and did my best not to think about the previous night as I got ready for school. It was there—the memory of her body, her mouth, her hair fanned out over my sheets. But maybe if I ignored it long enough, it would stop torturing me.

Or maybe I'd made the biggest mistake of my life.

Showered and dressed, I hesitated in front of my bedroom door, a sense of dread knotting my stomach. She was up. I could hear her moving around. Was it going to be awkward? Had I crossed a line and ruined our friendship?

Time to face her, for better or worse.

I found her in the kitchen with all her meal-prep containers spread out in two rows on the counter. She cast a quick glance over her shoulder as I walked in, then turned back to what she was doing.

"Morning," I said.

"Morning."

"I thought you finished those last night," I said.

"Me too, but I forgot the salsa." She dropped a dollop into one of the containers. "I'm so glad I realized it in time. They would have been so bland."

I wanted to move in close and wrap my arms around her. Lean in and kiss her neck, inhaling her scent. But I just watched her, unable to move, as if my feet were rooted to the floor.

She put one more scoop of salsa into a container, then started snapping the lids on. Leaving two on the counter, she stacked the rest and put them back in the fridge.

"There, all fixed." She put the salsa away and shut the refrigerator door, then grabbed one of the containers and held it out to me. "This one's for you."

For the first time since I'd walked into the kitchen, she really looked at me. Granted, she was only waiting for me to take my lunch. But I realized with a sense of relief that everything seemed normal.

Did that mean we were okay? She hadn't woken up with regrets?

I took the container. "Thanks."

She smiled and I didn't miss the hint of pink in her cheeks. "You're welcome."

"Hey, Pen." I hesitated. "We're good, right?"

"Oh, yeah. Of course."

"You sure?"

She rubbed her lips together, making me wonder if she was remembering the feel of my mouth on hers. "Yeah, I'm sure. We're fine. I mean, I'm fine. Are you fine?"

"Yeah, I'm fine."

"Okay, good."

I nodded. It was good. Last night had happened, and it had been fucking amazing. And it hadn't changed anything. We were all right.

But as the day progressed, I realized I wasn't.

When I'd told her I was fine, I'd meant it—I hadn't been lying. Or maybe I'd just wanted it to be true. But the reality was, I was kind of a mess.

My mind wandered as I drove to school, thinking about Pen. I was distracted in my classes, losing track of what I was supposed to be teaching. My Algebra One students got half a lecture on geometry before I realized I was using the wrong material. And I passed out a quiz in Algebra Two they weren't supposed to take for another week.

Lunch rolled around and when I walked into the teachers' lounge, there she was. My eyes darted around the room, and I wondered if everyone knew. Could they tell? Did we look different? How could they not see it? How could they not realize that the world would never be the same?

Probably because it was just my world she'd rocked.

She'd already warmed up my lunch for me. She did that every day. Why did she have to be so fucking good? So sweet and generous and such a good friend?

I took the seat next to her. "Thanks for lunch. This looks great."

"You're welcome."

The room was half full of our coworkers, so I couldn't exactly ask if she'd spent her morning distracted by the memory of mind-blowing sex. And even if we'd been alone, what could I say?

So Pen, is it just me, or are you sucking at your job because you can't stop thinking about last night?

Yeah, no. Wasn't going there.

So, we chatted about normal stuff. Things going on with our students, whether it might rain for the game on Friday. Even a bit about Morris, although we were careful to keep it vague.

When it was time to get back to our classrooms, we both reached for my lunch container at the same time. The brush of our hands sent a jolt of electricity running through me. Our eyes met, and by her intake of breath, I knew she'd felt it, too.

The urge to kiss her was so overwhelming, I almost did, right there in the teachers' lounge.

Fortunately, I kept my head. That would have started a firestorm of gossip, which was the last thing either of us needed.

But was it my imagination, or did she hesitate before moving her hand, letting hers linger against mine for a moment?

I grabbed our dishes and rinsed them out in the sink. She was still there when I finished, so we walked upstairs together. I couldn't understand why I was struggling so much. Sleeping with her once shouldn't have been enough to turn everything upside down.

But it had. And I had no idea what to do about it.

There were too many kids hanging out around the lockers for me to do anything other than hold my hand out for a fist bump when we got to my classroom. She bumped her fist against mine, then stumbled a little as she started down the hall.

"Oops," she said, letting out a nervous laugh. She brushed her hair off her face, shifting her glasses a little, and had to stop to readjust them. Rolling her eyes and shaking her head slightly, she turned and walked away.

My eyes followed her until she disappeared into her classroom, then I reluctantly turned and did the same.

Somehow, I managed to make it through the rest of the day, and by the time I was on the field for practice, I was somewhat composed. Football was a much better distraction than teaching math. The team was looking good, still working hard, and morale was high. Exactly what any coach would want heading into the playoffs.

By the time I left to go home, I was more than half convinced that I actually was fine. Something about barking at teenage football players in the cold air had cleared my head. Sure, I'd slept with Penelope, but it didn't have to be a big deal. We were adults. We'd both wanted it. So why not?

Feeling lighter than I had all day, I pulled into the driveway. The sight of her car made me crack a smile, but I firmly ignored the way the reminder of her presence tugged at my chest.

Inside, I found her curled up in the corner of the couch with a book and one of my mom's throw blankets over her lap. She looked up at me and smiled.

The urge to kiss her—to pull off all her clothes and devour her—hit me like a ton of bricks. I wanted her. I wanted her so bad, I could already taste her.

But she was my best friend. I couldn't do that to her. Not unless I could give her everything.

And that, I couldn't do.

CHAPTER 24

Penelope

As soon as Theo walked in the door, my heart fluttered. I swallowed hard, willing my face to be still—to look normal.

"Hey," he said.

"Hi."

For a second, he hesitated, his eyes on me. It looked like he wanted to say something else. But he didn't. Without another word, he walked away, disappearing down the hall and into his bedroom.

It felt like my heart dropped right through the couch and onto the floor. I set my book down—I'd hardly been aware of what I was reading anyway—and pulled the blanket higher up my lap.

Regrets. Theo had regrets.

I should have said no.

Not that I'd wanted to say no. My desire for him had been overwhelming. But maybe we could have avoided the mess we were in.

Because it felt like everything was unraveling.

I'd tried so hard to be nonchalant in the morning, as if everything was fine. We were still just friends. Roommates getting ready for our workday. Like nothing extraordinary had happened the night before.

But on the inside? I'd been a mess.

Still was.

It wasn't that I regretted sleeping with him. I just hated this feeling of awkward separation. Like we suddenly didn't know how to be around each other.

He was trying as hard as I was to pretend nothing had changed. I could hear it in his voice and see it in the way he looked at me.

I wondered if he'd been half as distracted at school as I had. I'd fumbled and stumbled and forgotten things, losing my train of thought mid-lecture during at least four different classes. I'd almost started my juniors and seniors on a project we'd already finished, and my freshman and sophomores were so confused when I'd asked them to set up their stations for painting, when they were supposed to be doing sketches.

And lunch with him? Agony. He'd been right there next to me, but the entire time I'd felt the gulf between us. So close, yet so far away.

I didn't know what I should do. Go talk to him? Tell him I was sorry, could we please just be friends again?

Everything was too complicated. I had big feelings for Theo Haven, and not because we'd slept together. Not even because it had been the single most incredible night of my life. I very much had more-than-friends feelings, but they were for a man I couldn't have.

Or at least, a man I couldn't keep. Because he was leaving.

Even if our night together had been as good for him as it was for me—which was hard to believe—we couldn't take the next step. Where would that lead? Dating for a while, and then what? A long-distance relationship? For how long?

I couldn't leave Grandma Colleen. She didn't have anyone else.

Besides, I was getting ahead of myself. I had no reason to believe Theo wanted a relationship. In fact, I had every reason to believe he didn't. He'd told me so himself.

There was only one thing to do. Keep my tangled mess of feelings to myself and wait for Theo to realize he didn't need to regret sleeping with me. We could still be friends, and everything would be fine.

He didn't come out right away, so I decided to make dinner. I'd cooked last, and we'd eased into a pattern of taking turns, but I didn't mind. It would give me something to do. Keep my mind off Theo and all my feelings for a while.

There was ground beef defrosted in the fridge, so I decided on spaghetti. It was simple, but one of my favorite comfort foods. I set to work browning the meat and boiling water for pasta.

I found a jar of marinara sauce in the cupboard but didn't see any spaghetti noodles. It seemed like I'd bought some, but after rooting around, I didn't find any.

The lack of spaghetti almost made me burst into tears in the middle of the kitchen.

I took a shaky breath and bit my lower lip to keep the tears from spilling. What was wrong with me? We had other pastas, I could totally make do. I grabbed a box of linguine and set it next to the stove.

The water came to a boil, and I put some pasta in the pot. The steam fogged up my glasses. Stepping back, I took them off to wipe them clean.

The fuzzy outline of Theo appeared in the kitchen doorway, startling me so much I yelped and dropped my glasses.

"Sorry," Theo said, and I could see his form crouch down to pick them up for me. "I didn't mean to scare you."

"I didn't hear you coming."

He straightened and moved in front of me. The first thing that came into focus as he gently slipped on my glasses was his face. That handsome face with deep blue eyes and a chiseled, stubbly jaw.

My traitorous body tingled at his proximity. His hair was damp, and he smelled deliciously clean. Almost of their own accord, my lips parted, and I lifted my chin.

Something like pain, or maybe just concern, crossed his features. Then his eyes flicked to the side to look past me.

"Uh, Pen?"

"Yeah?"

He pointed at the stove behind me. "There's a lot going on over there."

"Oh!" I whipped around and sure enough, the meat sauce was bubbling, splattering red all over the stovetop, and the pasta was on the verge of boiling over.

I fumbled for the dials and only succeeded in turning the other two burners on. Realizing my mistake, I turned them off and reduced the heat on the sauce and pasta. I gave the meat sauce a quick stir—I'd clean up the mess later—and swirled the pasta so it wouldn't stick to the pot.

When I turned around, Theo was watching me with a subtle smile that puckered his dimples.

"We're fine." I adjusted my glasses, not because they were crooked, but because I was so jumpy. "What I mean is, dinner is fine. Nothing burned. There's a bit of a mess, but that's okay. Messes happen."

"Thanks for cooking. I was just coming out to see if you were hungry."

"I don't mind." I glanced over my shoulder at the stove to make sure nothing was going awry again. "Spaghetti is easy, especially when you use jarred sauce. But it's not actually spaghetti, it's linguine, because we don't have spaghetti noodles, even though I could have sworn I bought some."

He opened his mouth but paused, like he wasn't sure what to make of my babbling. "Linguine will be great."

"So great." My voice probably had too much enthusiasm, but I was still trying to keep from crying over the lack of spaghetti. I turned back to the stove and stirred things again. "Can you peek in the fridge and see if there's Parmesan? I forgot to look."

I heard the fridge door open as I stirred the pasta.

"Yep, right here," he said.

"That's good. I guess you can have spaghetti that's not spaghetti but linguine with meat sauce without Parmesan, but really, who wants that?"

I stopped babbling—thankfully—and focused on the food, although there wasn't really anything for me to do. I stirred a few more times and adjusted the heat, as if it were necessary.

"Hey, Pen?"

The softness of his voice felt like a caress. Pressing my lips together so I didn't keep babbling at him—or burst into tears over pasta—I turned.

He opened his mouth to say something, but my phone buzzed on the counter. Craning my neck, I glanced at the screen. It was the assisted living center.

"Sorry, it's Grandma Colleen. I should take that."

"Of course. Go ahead."

I turned off the stove to avoid burning our dinner, then picked up my phone to answer. "Hello?"

"Penelope, this is Janine at Tilikum Assisted Living."

"Hi, Janine. Is everything all right?"

"Yes, but I wanted to let you know your grandma had a minor incident today. She's fine, I'm only calling to keep you updated."

Despite Janine's reassurance, a sick feeling spread through me. "What happened?"

"She felt lightheaded and nauseated. She was able to call for assistance and our medical team responded."

"What was wrong? How is she now?"

"Her doctor believes it was related to some recent medication changes. She's much better now. The symptoms subsided, and we'll be monitoring her closely."

"Can I talk to her?"

"Of course. I'll put you through to her room."

"Thank you."

Theo's brow furrowed with concern. "Is she okay?"

I nodded as the phone rang. "Sounds minor. They were just letting me know. Her phone is ringing."

"Hello?" she answered.

"Hi, Grandma. It's Penelope."

"Goodness, did they call you?"

"Yes, just now. Janine said you had a dizzy spell."

"It was a bunch of nothing. I'm all right. They didn't need to worry you over it."

"Well, I'm glad they called anyway. How are you feeling?"

"Just fine. It didn't last long. I felt a bit sick and clammy, then thought I might tumble out of my chair. Don't worry, I didn't. Felt a bit faint is all. My doctor says I'm fine. Made some medication adjustments and it shouldn't happen again."

"I'm so glad."

"You'll be stuck with me a while longer, I'm afraid."

I laughed a little. "Let's hope so. Can I come over?"

"What, now? That's not necessary."

"I want to anyway. It'll make me feel better."

"All right, if you insist. Have you eaten yet? I ate earlier, but it must be about time for you to have dinner."

"Actually, I was just about to have some spaghetti."

"Eat first, for goodness' sake. No reason to rush."

"Okay, quick dinner and then I'll be over. Can I bring you anything?"

"Not that I can think of. See you later, Penny."

"All right. Love you."

"Love you, too."

With a sigh of relief, I ended the call and set down my phone. "She's okay. She felt faint and sick, so she called for assistance. Her doctor thinks it was due to a medication change. It's nothing serious, but I'm going to check on her after dinner to make sure."

"Really glad she's okay," he said.

"Me too." I glanced at the food on the stove. "Let's eat."

Piling pasta and sauce on two plates, we took our food to the table. While we ate, we chatted about school and the football team. That seemed to melt some of the tension. Then the conversation shifted to Morris and the mysterious notes.

The longer we talked, the easier it felt. The gap between us seemed to be closing. When he made a joke and we both laughed—just like usual—I took it as a good sign.

Maybe our friendship wasn't ruined after all.

After we finished eating, he took our dishes to the kitchen to clean up. I gazed at him for a moment, and the longing I felt so deeply rose to the surface.

I let out a slow breath. I was going to have to learn to live with all those feelings, at least until he was gone.

And one thing was certain. I could not wind up in his bed again.

CHAPTER 25

Theo

I finished loading the dishwasher while Pen wiped down the stove. She'd seemed jumpy when I'd first come home, but I'd brushed it off. Sometimes she was like that.

It was cute.

Truth be told, I'd been jumpy, too. Which was not like me. But walking in and finding her curled up on the couch had felt like being punched in the gut. I couldn't decide if I felt guilty over what had already happened or wanted to drag her to my bed and lose myself in her.

Both. Definitely both. I'd coped by taking a shower.

Fortunately, sharing a meal seemed to have cut the tension for both of us. It felt like things were calming down—returning to normal. Granted, I'd almost lost my mind and kissed her again before the call from the assisted living home. Her grandma's dizzy spell had saved my ass.

She finished cleaning up and went to her room. Probably to grab a sweater or something, since she was leaving to see her grandma. It was odd, but I didn't really want her to go. Not that I didn't want her to visit her grandma. That was great. But with the rest of the evening stretched out before me, it felt a little bleak without her.

I really needed to get my head together.

"Hey, Theo?" she asked as she came out of her room. She'd put her hair up and changed into jeans and a T-shirt with a green cardigan.

"Yeah?"

"I know visiting someone's grandma in assisted living is probably not the most exciting thing in the world. But, do you want to maybe come with me?"

My mouth turned up in a grin. "I'd love to."

Her smile filled my chest with warmth.

We put on shoes and coats, then headed out. I offered to drive, so we climbed into my truck, and she gave me directions.

I was genuinely excited. Pen had told me so many stories about Grandma Colleen, I was looking forward to meeting her.

We arrived and parked out front, and Pen led me through the automatic doors that opened as we approached. While Pen signed us in, I helped myself to a piece of chocolate from a bowl on the counter. The place was decked out for fall, with pumpkins and leafy garlands everywhere.

Just past the entry was a large gathering space with a big two-sided gas fireplace in the middle. On the near side were couches and armchairs. Residents looked up as we walked in, smiles crossing their faces. And they weren't smiling at me. It was all for Penelope.

"Hello, Miss Penelope!"

"Hi, Penelope!"

"Good evening, Penelope!"

She said hi, smiling and waving at each of them in turn. It didn't surprise me that she knew them all by name.

I followed her past the fireplace to an area with small tables. One had a half-finished puzzle laid out on it, and several residents sat at others, some with books or magazines, others with mugs of coffee or tea. A cabinet had a coffee and tea station, and two TVs mounted on the wall played a reality show with the subtitles on.

Penelope approached a table where an elderly woman in a wheelchair sat flipping through a magazine. Her long white hair was pulled back in a low ponytail and she was dressed in a pale blue sweater.

"Grandma Colleen," Pen said. "I thought you'd be up in your apartment getting some rest."

She set her magazine on the table. "Oh, Penny, don't be silly. I'm in a wheelchair. All I do is rest."

"How are you feeling? Any more dizzy spells?"

"Not a one. I'm fit as a fiddle." Colleen's eyes flicked to me and the corners of her mouth turned up in an amused smile. "Did we bring someone?"

"Oh, yes." Penelope glanced at me, nervously biting her lower lip. "Grandma, this is my friend Theo."

"Nice to meet you." I stepped forward and offered my hand. Hers was soft as we shook.

"Very nice to meet you, Theo." Her eyes moved up and down. "Please, sit."

The fact that she was openly staring didn't bother me. I liked that she wasn't trying to hide her curiosity. Made her seem honest.

Penelope and I took seats at her table. Colleen didn't stop staring.

"Um..." Pen looked between me and her grandma, like she wasn't sure what was happening. "Grandma, I should tell you something."

I glanced at Pen with alarm. She wasn't going to tell her that we—

"Theo is a Haven."

That seemed like a weird thing to bring up. Not as weird as the other thing would have been, though.

"Is he, now?" Colleen said. "One of Paul's?"

I nodded. "Yes, ma'am. Do you know my dad?"

"Not well," Colleen said. "I'm afraid I was always on the wrong side of the feud for that."

Her mention of the feud made me crack a smile. "Those were good times. Mostly. I'm glad it's over, though. Having to hate another family for no reason was kind of tiring."

"It does help when there's a reason."

I knew enough about her personal feud with Maury Haven to know what she was talking about. Back in the day, I wouldn't have given prank advice to someone on the Bailey side, but since this was just between the two of them…

"Do you have your own kitchen?" I asked.

"I do, although I don't use it much. Why?"

"Have you put any of his stuff in Jell-O yet?"

Colleen's mouth curled in a devious smile. I decided then and there that I liked her. "I have not."

"It's a good one," I said. "Just make sure you keep it in the fridge long enough. And don't make the mistake of freezing it, thinking it'll set faster. It just freezes and then melts into liquid once it starts to warm up. Makes a mess, and it isn't even funny."

"If only I could get ahold of his teeth," Colleen said.

Pen laughed. "Grandma, please don't put Maury's teeth in Jell-O."

"Why not?"

"Because that's disgusting."

Colleen tapped her chin. "I'll think of something. Although he's been keeping a close eye on me lately. I might have to call in a favor."

"A favor?" Penelope asked. "What kind of favor?"

She patted Pen's hand. "Nothing you need to worry about."

"I want to hear how it goes," I said. "Especially if you manage to get his teeth."

"So, tell me, Theo," she said, and I could hear the subject change coming. "How do you know my granddaughter?"

"We work together."

"Theo's a math teacher and the head football coach," Pen added.

Colleen didn't take her eyes off me. "I see. And you offered Penny a room in your house?"

"Yes, ma'am. She needed a place to stay, and I had an extra room."

"Wasn't that nice of you?" Her eyes narrowed, her voice and expression edging on suspicious.

"It was so nice," Pen said, either dismissing or ignoring the tone in her grandmother's question. "I don't know what I would have done without him. I would have found a place to live eventually, but this worked out great. Theo's moving to South Carolina, but we've already talked about it, and I can rent his house when he's gone. I won't even have to move again."

Keeping her eyes on me, Colleen crossed her arms. I held her gaze, my expression neutral. I didn't want her to get the wrong impression—thinking I was out to take advantage of her granddaughter—but I wasn't going to let her intimidate me, either.

"South Carolina?" she asked. "When?"

"Next summer."

"Have you ever been married?"

"No."

"Are you currently in a relationship?"

"No."

"How well do you know my granddaughter?"

Penelope tried to interrupt her rapid-fire questions. "Grandma, please."

I answered anyway. "We met at the beginning of last school year when she transferred to the high school. We've been friends ever since."

"Just friends?"

Keeping my eyes locked with Colleen's, I leaned forward. "She's one of the best friends I've ever had. So if the interrogation is to figure out whether I'm a danger to her, the answer is no. She's safe with me."

And she was. Sure, we'd given in to temptation and slept together. But that didn't mean I was out to use Penelope. I cared about her. And I took our friendship seriously.

Colleen nodded slowly as she processed my answers. "Good. I'm glad to hear it."

Something, or maybe someone, else seemed to catch Colleen's eye. She sat up straighter in her wheelchair and her lip curled in a sneer.

Maury Haven wheeled himself to a table nearby. He was in his eighties—at least—and was my great-uncle on my dad's side.

He glared back, wrinkling his prominent nose as if he'd smelled something unpleasant.

"Maury," Colleen said, her tone icy.

"Colleen," he snapped back.

Penelope met my eyes and shrugged.

Maury pointed a remote at one of the TVs and changed it to a local news channel. The subtitles popped up, but he cranked up the volume anyway.

"Do you mind?" Colleen asked.

"Sorry," Maury said, pressing the volume again. "Let me turn it up for you."

It looked like Colleen was about to protest, but Penelope stopped her with a hand on her arm and pointed at the screen.

"Look!"

The headline read *Human Remains Found Near Raven Falls.*

Shaking her head, Colleen clicked her tongue. "Terrible."

"Where's Raven Falls?" Penelope asked.

"East of here," I said. "I think about an hour north of Spokane."

A journalist was interviewing a police officer at the scene. Penelope grabbed my arm and pointed at the TV. "Theo."

I didn't know what she was so worked up about. "Yeah, it's awful. I hope the family can get some closure."

"No. Look." She kept pointing.

"What am I looking at?"

"The crime scene," she said. "Look where they are."

I still didn't know what she was talking about. The cop was standing in a field of brown grass with a few small pine trees. There might have been water—a river, probably—behind him in the distance, and beyond that, a rocky hill rose into the cloudy sky. An old barn stood off to one side, not far from where he and the journalist were standing. The paint was faded to a dull gray and the large doors were crooked, hanging like a little kid's loose teeth.

"I think I've been through Raven Falls once," I said. "But I don't know where that is."

"Neither do I, but it looks exactly like an Edwin Morris painting."

She moved her arm to point at the wall above the coffee and tea station. "That painting. I've stared at it hundreds of times. I'd know it anywhere."

I looked between the painting and the TV screen a few times, trying to match the two images, but the interview ended, and it went back to the newsroom.

"What are you talking about, Penny?" Colleen asked.

"I swear that crime scene was the same as the painting over there." She gestured again.

"Well, how could that be?" Colleen asked.

"I don't know, but I'm telling you, it was."

"See if you can find that news story online," I said as I stood.

"Where are you going?" Pen asked.

I pointed to the painting.

Before she could ask what I meant—or tell me not to take it off the wall—I went over to the coffee and tea station. The painting did look strikingly similar—especially the barn with the crooked doors. I wanted to know if this one had a note in the back.

One of the staff watched me with confusion as I lifted it from the hook on the wall. I smiled. "Just need to borrow this for a minute. She's an art teacher."

That wasn't much of an explanation, but she didn't stop me, so I brought the painting to our table.

"See?" Pen held up her phone next to it.

The paused news story on the screen showed the crime scene. I quickly compared the details. She was right. It looked exactly the same.

Without a word, we flipped the painting over and started running our fingers over the back of the frame.

"What on earth are you two doing?" Colleen asked.

Penelope gasped. "Here."

I felt the spot. Something stuck out of the frame, just enough that I could feel it with the pads of my fingers.

Pen knew what she was doing, so I held the painting while she unfastened the back. She loosened it enough that she was able to get a grip on the edge of the paper and draw it out.

I gently set the painting aside while Penelope unfolded the note.

What have I done?

I met Penelope's gaze. We were both wide-eyed, and without needing to say a word, I knew an identical thought had just run through our minds. Had Edwin Morris killed someone and painted the scene of the crime?

Had he been murdered? Or was he a murderer?

"One of you better explain what's happening," Colleen said.

"It's a long story." Penelope folded the note and hastily tucked it in her purse. "I promise I'll fill you in on everything soon."

I glanced around. The other residents seemed uninterested in what we were doing. Probably because the TV volume was so loud. Pen refastened the back of the painting, and I took it to hang it on the wall.

"False alarm," I said to no one in particular once the painting was back in place. "Thought there was an art emergency, but everything is fine."

That got me a few glances, but no one seemed to care. Or they couldn't hear over the weather report blaring from the TV. Either way worked.

I went back to our table where Penelope was standing, saying goodbye to Colleen.

"I'm sorry we can't stay longer," she said.

"I'll be fine." Colleen waved her hand. "I don't know what you're up to, but be careful."

"I will," she said. "Don't worry about me. And call me if you have another dizzy spell or anything like that."

Colleen's eyes flicked to me again. "All right, Penny. See you later."

Penelope hugged her grandma, and I offered a distracted goodbye.

My mind raced as we walked out to my truck. What were the chances Edwin Morris had painted the scene where a body would later be found, and it wasn't a coincidence? Especially with that note.

Suddenly, the whole thing seemed like a much bigger deal—one I wasn't sure I wanted to be a part of. Hunting killers was Garrett's job, not mine. And every time one of my brothers got mixed up in something bigger than him, things went bad. Really bad.

I hadn't resolved to never date again because, in my family, relationships seemed to come with a hefty side of danger. But it was one of many reasons to *maintain* my no-dating rule.

Not that I was dating Penelope.

We got in my truck, and I made a snap decision. That was the difference. I wasn't dating Penelope, and I wasn't going to. So I could help her figure out what happened to Edwin Morris, even if it turned out he was much more than he seemed. It wasn't going to lead us into unexpected danger for which we had no way to be prepared. That particular curse seemed to follow my brothers, but it had always been tied to their love lives.

Pen was just a friend.

I totally had this.

"Are you thinking what I'm thinking?" I asked.

She nodded, her eyes wide. "I think Edwin Morris murdered that woman."

"And painted where he did it. Or at least where he left her body."

"Do you think that's what the other notes mean? He had more victims?"

"I think that's exactly what they mean."

She adjusted her glasses. "I was not expecting this. Edwin Morris a murderer? What do we do?"

I tapped the steering wheel. "I think we try to find the pattern. Find the locations in those other paintings."

"And see if we find a body?"

"Yeah."

She hesitated for a second, then met my eyes. "You're right. The fact that this one painting might match the site of a body isn't enough. But if there are more…"

"The police will take it seriously."

"Now I feel a little bit bad for suspecting his son. And Amanda."

"I don't know. Those two still might have something to do with it. Maybe he was a murderer *and* he was murdered."

"True, that's possible. How are we going to find out if the other paintings are real places?"

"Remember what the lady at the gallery was saying? How most of Morris's paintings are general landscapes. But a few have a defining feature or a landmark, like the barn in that one. And didn't the other one with a note have a cabin?"

"It did. And the one I have at home has that big rock formation by the creek."

"Exactly. I bet we can find out where they are. They could be local."

"The background in the creek painting does look like it's around here."

"Agreed."

"I'm a little creeped out at the idea of hunting for murder victims. But all we need is a little bit of evidence and law enforcement can do the rest, right?"

"Absolutely. No shovels needed."

She snort-laughed. "I'm sorry. Laughing at that is very morbid."

"It's all kinds of absurd, when you think about it." I turned on the truck. "Ready, Detective Fallbrook?"

"Ready, Detective Haven."

"By the way." I put the truck in reverse. "Penny?"

She groaned. "Don't even think about it. Grandma Colleen is the only person who calls me Penny."

Grinning at her, I chuckled. She smiled back.

Just friends, Theo. Just friends.

That was the only way this was going to work—and the only way she wasn't going to get hurt.

CHAPTER 26

Theo

Despite not needing to be anywhere, I woke up early Saturday morning. I sat at the dining table with my laptop and a cup of coffee, scrolling through hiking blogs. The Morris mystery was a good distraction. And I needed it.

My team had won again last night. Decisively. But it wasn't the game that kept creeping into my mind while I searched for locations that matched Morris's paintings. It was the scent of Pen's shampoo wafting from her bathroom. The tea collection on the kitchen counter. Her coat hanging by the door.

Her presence was everywhere. As it should have been. I wanted her to feel comfortable—like she really lived there, not like it was a temporary place to crash.

Before I could think too deeply about the confusing mix of feelings tugging at my chest, her bedroom door opened. She marched to the dining room, and the contrast between her serious expression and straight spine—she seemed very sure of something—and her messy bun made me crack a smile.

"Morning, Pentacular."

"Morning. I've decided something."

I raised my eyebrows.

She put her hands on her hips and her tone was decisive. "I'm getting the rest of my stuff from Sean's house."

My smile grew. "Awesome. How can I help?"

"Well…" She paused and touched her lips with her fingertip. "I'm not sure. I woke up this morning and decided I've procrastinated too long. I called a moving company and they can do it next weekend. So I just need to call Sean and tell him."

"You still have your key, right? You should make sure he won't be there."

"Good idea. I don't need him breathing down my neck while I pack the rest of my things."

"No, definitely not."

She produced her phone from her pocket and wandered into the living room. I waited, my brow furrowing with concern. If he made things hard on her…

"Sean, hi. I just want to—" She paused. "No… That's not… Sean, listen."

Tension rippled down my back and my jaw hitched.

"Can we be grown-ups about this, please?"

She held the phone away from her ear and rolled her eyes.

"Are you done?" she asked.

I flexed my fists, my body coiled like a spring.

"You can't hold my stuff hostage," she said, and for the first time, there was a rare note of anger in her voice.

That was it. I was done. I got up, marched over to her, and held out my hand. Eyeing me with confusion, she gave me her phone.

I put it to my ear. "Fuck you," I said, then ended the call and handed it back to her.

She gaped at me. "I know he was being a jerk, but I don't know if that was very helpful."

"I know it wasn't. But screw that guy."

I ran my hand through my hair. This was kind of my fault. I'd pissed him off when I'd kissed Pen at the Timberbeast. Granted, he was a dick anyway, so he might have caused trouble for her regardless. But I'd probably made it worse.

Which meant it was up to me to take care of it.

"I should have just texted him," she said. "I'll do that. I'll tell him the movers are coming next Saturday."

"No, don't worry about the movers. I'll get your stuff." I'd already pulled out my phone and started group-texting my brothers. "He wants to be difficult? He can deal with me."

"You don't have to do that."

"We both know this is partially my fault." I met her eyes, and with the way her cheeks flushed, I knew she understood what I meant.

"It's not your fault he's a jerk."

"No, but I'm still getting your stuff back." My lips turned up in a grin. "Besides, this is going to be fun."

"Should I be concerned?"

"Not a bit."

"Are you sure about this?"

I paused and looked her in the eyes. I didn't want to steamroll her. "If it's important to you to do this yourself, I won't get in your way. But if the only goal is to get your things out of his house, let me do it for you. I want to."

"I don't have anything to prove. I just want my stuff."

"Consider it done. What's still there that's yours?"

"Let's see. The tall dresser in the bedroom, plus the clothes in it. There are some more clothes and shoes in the closet—those should be obvious. The bed is mine, but I don't want that back. The dining set and the bookshelf, plus all the books. He didn't have anything on the walls when I moved in, so the art is all mine."

"Got it." I typed her list on my phone while she talked. "What else?"

"I think I got most of my art supplies, but I was in a hurry, so if you could check the storage room in the garage, that would be great. And the hall closet has my winter coat and snow boots. Some of the towels and stuff were mine, but I don't care about those. Oh, and kitchen stuff. There are some mugs I'd love to get back, but the rest of it isn't a big deal."

"I should be able to figure it out."

"Thank you. Again. You keep riding in on your white horse and saving the day."

"What are friends for?"

"I just hope I can make it up to you someday."

"No need." Without thinking, I stepped in and wrapped my arms around her.

Oh, shit. Shouldn't have done that.

Too late. I held her tight, breathing in her scent. She hugged me back, and for a second, I closed my eyes, letting the feel of her body next to mine sink in.

She let go first, so I dropped my arms and stepped away. My phone was buzzing with replies from my brothers, so I pushed away the temptation of her warmth and checked my messages.

Luke: What time?

Josiah: Address.

Zachary: I'm in. This is going to be fun.

Garrett: Off duty today. I'll be there.

I got the address from Penelope, sent it to my brothers, and we agreed to meet there in half an hour.

My mouth turned up in a slow grin. I agreed with Z. It was going to be fun.

Sean's house was on the other side of town. Pen had texted him to let him know movers were coming to get her things. The fact that the movers were a bunch of Havens? That was just semantics.

My brothers and I parked in a line along the street. Luke was in his Chevelle, but Josiah, Zachary, and I all had trucks, and Garrett had a big SUV. That would give us plenty of space to haul her stuff.

I got out and did a double take. Josiah wasn't alone. Our dad got out of the passenger seat and tipped his chin to me. With a subtle smile, I nodded back.

Sean had no idea what was coming for him.

Even on the outside of the house, there were signs of Penelope. The porch was decorated with pumpkins and a colorful fall wreath hung on the door.

My dad and brothers fell in behind me, letting me take the lead as we approached. I balled my hand into a fist and knocked several times. Hard.

The door swung open, and Sean's eyes widened. Dude looked rough—probably hungover. He had dark circles under his eyes, and he wore a rumpled T-shirt and a pair of stained sweats.

His gaze moved back and forth across the wall of Havens on his doorstep. "What's going on?"

"We're the movers." I walked in, forcing him to get out of my way.

Sean stepped aside as my dad and brothers came in behind me.

"You guys can't just come in here. I'll call the cops."

"Cops are already here." Garrett was in street clothes, but even without his uniform, his air of authority was unmistakable. Crossing his arms, he stood in front of Sean to keep him in place—and out of our way.

Ignoring the douchebag, I turned to my family. "All right, I've got boxes and tape in my truck. She has clothes in the bedroom and the hall closet, plus the tall dresser, the bookshelf, and all the books. Dining set is hers. Any art on the walls goes, too. I'll handle the kitchen and check for more of her art supplies. And we should do a sweep, looking for anything she might have forgotten to mention. Ready? Break."

Garrett stayed in the entry to keep an eye on Sean the Shit while the rest of us spread out. Dad and Josiah headed for my truck to get the tape and boxes while Zachary and Luke tackled the bedroom.

I headed for the storage room to make sure she hadn't left any art supplies or canvases. The garage was cold, and the small storage room wasn't any warmer. That was where she'd been painting? There was a space heater on the floor, but come on. That was just embarrassing. What sort of man would push his woman's passion to the side like that?

A guy who wasn't a man at all.

I went back into the house to get a few boxes and shot him a glare. Fuck that guy. Back in Pen's little studio, I packed the few supplies she'd left and took them to my truck.

Zachary and Luke had already loaded her dresser into one of the trucks and put the rest of her clothes in Luke's Chevelle. The dining table and chairs were secured, and I directed Dad and Josiah to put the artwork they'd taken from the walls into my truck or Luke's car. Someone had even removed the wreath from the front door.

Josiah helped me tackle the kitchen. We packed a teakettle and a bunch of mugs, plus some glass storage containers, a few pots and pans and other cooking supplies, and a blender.

After loading those into our vehicles, I walked back in to check on the rest of the house. Sean tried to follow me, but without a word, Garrett casually stepped in front of him and shook his head.

"What else?" Luke asked. "We got all the obvious stuff out of the bedroom and bathroom. And there were a few coats and stuff in the hall closet."

"Bookshelf and books are done," Josiah said.

"Couches?" Zachary asked, pointing to the living room.

"No," Sean said. "Those are mine."

That made me want to take them. I gave them a once-over. Didn't really look like something Penelope would have picked out, and she hadn't mentioned them. "Leave 'em."

Zachary seemed to make an executive decision about the TV. It was mounted to the wall, but that didn't stop him. Neither did Sean's protests. He and Luke got it unfastened and took it out to one of the trucks while Garrett kept Sean corralled.

"What about the rest of the bedroom furniture?" Josiah asked.

I scowled. "She definitely doesn't want any of that."

"Does she want to burn it?" Zachary asked, sounding hopeful as he came back inside.

I was about to say no, but that did give me an idea. "Take the bedding."

"Will do," Z said.

"You can't do that," Sean said.

I glared at him. "Watch me."

Josiah and my dad went through the living and dining areas, grabbing random stuff and putting it in boxes while I finished in the kitchen. Zachary took the bedding—including a bunch of pillows—out to one of the vehicles, then came back and stood on a chair to remove the battery from the smoke detector. He dropped it into an open box, all while grinning at Sean.

I walked through the house, giving it a final look while my brothers took the last of the boxes to my truck. From what I could tell, we'd packed everything.

Garrett moved aside as I approached Sean. I had Pen's house key to return to him.

He wanted to hit me. I could see it in his eyes. Garrett shifted behind me. He could see it, too.

I kind of wanted him to hit me. Give me an excuse to smash my fist in his face.

With a hard expression, I held out the key. "Don't bother her again."

Unfortunately—or maybe fortunately, considering Garrett was right there—Sean didn't take a shot at me. Just held out his hand so I could drop the key in his palm.

Sean glowered at us as we started to leave, his face reddening all the way to his scalp. Dad and Josiah ignored him. Luke glared back. Zachary grinned, looking like he was about to say something snarky. I shoved him out the door. Garrett slipped on his aviators and walked out.

I was about to follow when Sean spoke.

"Tell that bitch—"

Before he could finish, I had him by the shirt and shoved him against the wall. My voice was hard as steel. "Do not call her that."

Fear flashed across his face. Good. He should have been afraid of me. I was more than willing to take this guy out on Pen's behalf.

Would Garrett have to arrest me? Maybe.

Worth it.

"Give me a reason," I growled. "Please."

Sean swallowed hard and held his hands out in a gesture of surrender. I let go and took a step back.

Pathetic.

Without another word, I walked out, not bothering to close the door behind me.

CHAPTER 27

Penelope

The chicken-and-rice soup simmering on the stove smelled delicious. I opened the pot and gave it a stir. I figured Theo would be hungry when he got back, and the least I could do was make dinner.

I hoped the move-out was going well. I still felt a little bad about not going myself. But Theo had insisted he'd handle it. And after the way Sean had yelled at me on the phone that morning, I was glad I didn't have to deal with him.

Theo had said help was coming, so I knew at least one of his brothers had gone with him. That was good. I didn't have a lot of big furniture, but at least a few things would require two people to carry them.

Considering everything Theo was doing—and had done—for me, cooking dinner wasn't much. But it was better than nothing. And it did smell good.

For a second, my mind wandered to another way I could thank him. My vision blurred as I lost myself in a momentary fantasy involving me, Theo, the couch, and a total lack of clothing.

Blinking, I stepped back from the stove and fanned myself. That was not happening.

My hormones had other opinions, as did my lady parts, but they weren't calling the shots. I was. And Theo and I were not sleeping together again.

I heard what sounded like someone pulling up outside. Was Theo back already? I thought moving everything out would have taken longer. The engine rumble grew, which seemed odd. Why was it so loud? I went to the front window to look.

It was loud because it wasn't just Theo.

Theo's truck pulled into the driveway while two more trucks, an SUV, and a blue muscle car parked outside the house. They were packed with stuff.

I went outside and watched, open-mouthed. Although I didn't know his family well, I'd seen every one of them. It wasn't just one of his brothers, either. It was all of them. And his dad.

Theo came over with a grin.

"No wonder you finished so fast," I said. "They all came to help?"

"Of course they did." He turned and raised his voice. "Most of her stuff can go in the garage for now. We'll take it from there."

The Haven men started unloading the vehicles. One of them—Josiah maybe?—tipped his chin to me as he carried a box into the garage.

"Thank you," I called and turned back to Theo. "That's so nice of them to help."

"Yeah. They annoy me sometimes, but brothers do that. They're good guys."

My eyebrows drew in as one of his brothers carried a TV into the garage. "I don't think the TV was mine."

Theo shrugged. "It is now."

"Did Sean give you any trouble?"

"He wanted to, but no."

"What did he do?"

One corner of Theo's mouth lifted, revealing his dimple. "Threatened to call the cops. But Garrett was there, so we already had that covered."

"I made soup, but I don't think there's enough for everyone."

Theo leaned toward the opened door and inhaled. "Is that what smells so good? Don't worry about it. I'll buy them a round at the Timberbeast next time we're all there." He jerked his thumb over his shoulder. "I need to finish unloading, but I'll be in soon."

"Okay. Tell them all I said thank you so much in case they didn't hear me."

He smiled. "I will."

Theo went to his truck as Luke brought over one of my paintings.

"Do you want this inside?" he asked.

"Yes, that would be great. Here, I'll take it."

He handed me the canvas. "It's pretty."

"Thank you. And thank you so much for…all this. It's a huge help."

"No problem. There were enough of us, it went pretty fast. Plus, I'm not gonna lie, it was kinda fun. Especially when Theo almost put a fist through your ex's face."

My eyes widened. "Theo did what?"

"Your ex started to mouth off. For a second, I thought Theo was going to lay him out."

Theo getting in a fight with Sean? It was hard to imagine. Theo was so easygoing. Hard to imagine from Sean, too, but mostly because he'd gotten a bit out of shape in the last couple years. Theo would have destroyed him.

"I'm glad no one got hurt," I said.

"Yeah, well, it wouldn't have been Theo getting hurt. Except maybe his knuckles." Luke shrugged. "Anyway, you did the right thing."

I nodded. "Thank you again."

"Mel says hi, by the way. She'll probably call you later." He backed up. "Good luck unpacking and everything."

I took the canvas inside and leaned it against a wall in the living room where it wouldn't be in the way, then went to the kitchen to check the soup. I had it on a low simmer, so it was fine.

In what felt like no time at all, Theo came inside, and I heard the other engines starting up and fading away.

He paused in the kitchen and inhaled again. "Pen, that smells so good."

"Thanks. Good timing. I think it's ready."

We filled two bowls and sat down at the dining table together. Theo's happy moans were music to my ears as he enjoyed his dinner. It felt good to do something nice for him that he genuinely appreciated, even if it was a small thing.

And even if his moans reminded me of my couch fantasy.

My mind continuing to go places I didn't want, I retreated to my studio after dinner. I needed to spend some time painting my feelings. Although it wasn't only my emotions that were getting the best of me. My more primal urges were doing their best to get my attention, too.

After a while, Theo poked his head in. "Hey, Pen? I have something for you."

"As if you haven't done enough already."

"Trust me, this is awesome." He came in with an armful of bedding—sheets and a big comforter.

It wasn't just any bedding. It was my bedding from the other house.

"Oh, gosh. Thank you, but I didn't want that back. I'm not going to use it."

He gave me a mischievous grin. "I know. I thought you might want to burn it."

"Burn it?"

"Yeah. There's a firepit in the backyard. Zachary suggested we burn the whole bed, but I thought that was a little much, especially here in town. I don't want to bring the fire department down on us. But the bedding?" He raised it up a little.

I snort-laughed. "That's ridiculous. And I love it. Let's do it."

"Awesome."

I put my painting supplies down while he took the armful of bedding out to the backyard. He'd already prepped the firepit with wood, so we could enjoy a little fire once the rest of it burned away.

We piled everything onto the wood, and he handed me a small box of matches.

"You do the honors."

I took out a match and struck it. "Here goes nothing." Reaching out, I held the flame to a piece of sheet. It caught, and Theo lit another match to start the fire on the other side.

Soon, the whole pile was in flames. We stood back as the heat beat against us, and I couldn't help but smile.

"This was a great idea," I said. "Who knew it would be so satisfying? It's like my old life is going up in flames."

"It was time."

"It sure was. Is it possible for me to say thank you too much? Because thank you."

He gently nudged me with his elbow. "You're welcome. Like I said, this is what friends are for."

Friends. He was right, it was what friends were for. And that was what we were. And it was great. I was so grateful to have Theo as a friend. He'd come through for me when I desperately needed him. Friendship didn't get much better than that.

I was free.

But there was a little part of me, deep inside, that wished he'd put his arm around me as we stood by the fire. Who longed for the feel of his strong body, his thick arms, his warm embrace.

I had to let that go. Wishing for something I couldn't have was only asking for heartbreak.

CHAPTER 28

Theo

The scent of vanilla and sugar swirled around me as I walked into Angel Cakes Bakery. My sister-in-law Harper ran it, and her treats were off the charts. Just a few days after we'd retrieved Pen's stuff from the jerk's house, she'd mentioned cinnamon rolls sounded good. It had been on my mind to get her some ever since.

Just being a good roommate.

"I'll be right with you," Harper called from the back.

"Take your time. It's just me."

The exposed brick wall was painted white, and a pink scalloped border ran around the perimeter of the room near the ceiling. A shelf next to the door had bread and bagged cookies, and the pastry case was filled with temptation—cookies, cupcakes, brownies, and, luckily for me, cinnamon rolls.

Score one for Theo.

Harper came out from the kitchen dressed in a white Angel Cakes apron. Her blond hair was tied back in a low ponytail, and she wore a pink floral headband.

"Hey, Theo," she said. "Great game last night. Congrats on another win."

"Thanks." I couldn't help but smile. We'd won the night before. "Owen sure played a great game."

A proud grin stole across her face. She was married to Garrett, Owen's dad, and had a close relationship with her stepson. "Football is officially my favorite sport. I love watching him play."

"Yeah, same."

"Anyway, what can I get you?"

"Two cinnamon rolls, please."

"Coming right up."

She put the confections in a pink to-go box and rang up the total. I paid and thanked her, telling her I'd see her soon.

Outside, I squinted at the brightness and slipped my sunglasses on. It was chilly, but the sun was out, and the blue sky stretched over the mountain peaks, already tipped with white.

A squirrel darted up the sidewalk right in front of me, and I almost tripped. I hesitated in case there were more. Sure enough, three others bounded along, their bushy gray tails bouncing. Their cheeks bulged, stuffed with something. Nuts, most likely. I wondered if they'd just raided enemy squirrel territory. Word on the street was a new feud had been brewing in Tilikum—a battle between squirrel factions, each side stealing the other's winter stashes.

"Careful out there," I said to the passing squirrels.

I got in my truck and put the box on the passenger seat. The scent of cinnamon filled the cab and I couldn't wait to get home and dig into one.

And see the smile on Pen's face when I showed her my sugary surprise.

I was walking on thin ice with her. Being roommates was great. I had no regrets about that. But things were different, and I wasn't sure how to handle it.

It wasn't just that she was single now, although the lack of a shitty boyfriend had taken down a very big barrier that had kept her friend-zoned. And while I couldn't get that night out of my head, no matter how hard I tried, it wasn't that we'd given in to temptation and slept together.

It was more than that. Living with her meant she wasn't just my work friend anymore. I saw her every morning, sleepy-eyed and adorable. We hung out during our off-hours. Ate meals together. Ran errands and watched TV. Every night, I watched her go to her room, and a part of me wished she was heading to my bed, not hers.

I was drawn to her like a moth to a flame. And knowing she was sleeping one room away was turning into a special type of torture. Especially because I'd already had a taste.

When I got home, I brought the cinnamon rolls inside and found her at the dining table with her laptop. She swam in my too-big-for-her hoodie and her hair was up in a ponytail. My mouth turned up in a grin. I probably shouldn't have enjoyed seeing her in my hoodie as much as I did. But I kind of loved it.

"Penriffic." I closed the door with my foot and held up the box. "I have a surprise."

She sat up straighter and peeked over the top of her laptop screen. "Are those what I think they are?"

"If you're thinking cinnamon rolls, then yes."

"You're kidding. I've been craving cinnamon rolls."

"I know." I set the box on the table. "You said something at lunch the other day."

Her lips parted and she gazed at me.

"What?" I asked.

"Nothing." She shook her head a little. "This is really nice. Thank you."

"No problem. They sounded good to me, too."

I grabbed a couple plates from the kitchen and poured myself another cup of coffee, then brought everything to the table. Pen clasped her hands beneath her chin and scrunched her shoulders while I lifted each cinnamon roll onto a plate. They were huge—almost as big as her face.

"Oh my gosh, they smell so good," she said.

I sat down next to her, hesitating while she peeled off a chunk and took the first bite.

Her eyes rolled back, fluttering closed, and she moaned. "Oh, yes."

Maybe cinnamon rolls had been a bad idea.

My blood ran hot as I watched her, and I was gripped by the desire to lick the cinnamon-laced frosting off the corner of her mouth.

"Have you tried yours yet?" she asked. "This is the best cinnamon roll I've ever had."

I tore my eyes away and shoved a big bite in my mouth. "Mm-hmm. Really good."

"I'm glad you're home. And not just because of these." She paused and took a deep breath. "I think I found the creek."

"*The* creek? As in the one in the painting?"

She nodded with excitement and shifted her laptop so I could see the screen. "First, I found this. It's from a hiking website. Don't you think that picture looks like the place?"

Tilting my head, I scrutinized the photo. She was right. It did look like the place Morris had painted, from the curve of the creek bed to the big rock formation looming above.

"Here's another one from a different angle." She clicked to another tab. "This one is from a hiking blog."

There was no doubt. It had to be the location in Morris's painting. The rock formation was especially distinctive.

"Where is it?"

"Not far outside town. According to the blog post, it's a pretty flat out-and-back hike."

The corner of my mouth lifted in a grin. "Do you have anything going on today?"

"I do," she said decisively.

"You do?" I twisted toward her. "What?"

She pointed at the screen. "Hiking out there to see if we can find anything."

"Let's do it, Penlicious." Damn it, I'd basically just called her delicious. Thankfully, she didn't seem to notice, her focus remaining on the laptop. "We should get a dog."

That did get her attention. She knitted her eyebrows together. "We should what?"

"For the day," I said. "Not like, get a dog together. I mean borrow one. You know, for the nose."

"Oh. That makes much more sense. But how does one borrow a dog for the day?"

"Easy, when your brother and sister-in-law have two. I'm sure Josiah and Audrey won't mind if we take Max and Maggie for a hike."

"Great idea." She pulled off another piece of cinnamon roll and popped it into her mouth.

I broke off a chunk of cinnamon roll and got up. Although I wanted to stay close to her, I was feeling too many things. I needed to keep my distance. "I'll go call Josiah. Let me know when you're ready. No rush."

"Sure. Let me just finish this. Or maybe half of it. If I eat the whole thing, I'll be in a carb coma in an hour."

"No kidding."

Forcing myself to leave the temptation of Pen as she tantalizingly licked cinnamon off her fingers, I went to my room to call my brother.

The early November air was cold, but at least it was dry. I was wearing one of my THS hoodies and a pair of joggers with my hiking boots. Pen had put on my hoodie again, along with black leggings and hiking boots.

Josiah and Audrey were happy to let us borrow their dogs for a while. Max and Maggie were mixed-breed rescues and both had the excited, happy energy of dogs who get to go on an unexpected adventure.

We parked at the trailhead and got out. The dogs zigzagged around Penelope, getting her legs tangled in their leashes. Once we figured out how to make them sit, we were able to unravel her.

We set out on the trail, letting the dogs sniff as they went. They seemed to understand the concept of hiking and kept their noses to the ground but moved forward at a good clip. We'd come equipped with treats from Audrey and strict instructions not to let them off leash. If Max found something stinky, he'd roll in it.

Our conversation as we hiked centered around the cabin painting, particularly where it might be. There were literally hundreds of lakes in the Cascades. Although we'd narrowed it down somewhat—many were too remote for a cabin—we hadn't run across anything that matched the painting.

But maybe we wouldn't need to. If there was evidence at the creek, it might not matter.

"You know the woman who was found in Raven Falls?" Pen asked. "Did the news ever report how her body was discovered?"

"Good question." I pulled my phone out of my pocket and Pen took Max's leash so I could do a quick search.

We kept walking while I scanned the article I found. "Here it is. It says hikers discovered the remains when they were digging a latrine hole. They notified local law enforcement."

"That makes sense. If someone wanted to hide a body, they'd do it in a spot that's hidden or secluded."

"Which is also where you'd dig a latrine hole." I clicked to go back to my search results. "There's an updated article, too. Looks like the victim was identified—a woman from Spokane who went missing twenty years ago."

"Twenty years? That's a long time."

"Makes you wonder if she was the first."

"That's what I was thinking. If Morris really did it, do you think his wife knows?"

I slipped my phone back in my pocket and took Max's leash while Pen kept Maggie's.

"I don't know. Twenty years is a long time to keep a secret like that. Especially if there was more than one. I guess he could have threatened to kill her if she ever told anyone."

"The whole thing is so strange. I keep trying to imagine Edwin Morris the painter as a murderer. It's hard to fathom. He was so soft-spoken. I know that doesn't necessarily mean anything. Sometimes serial killers seem totally normal to the people around them."

"Did you ever see him and his wife together? Did she seem afraid of him?"

"Not that I can remember. She was at the picnic on the last day of class, and they seemed… I don't know, like a normal couple, I guess. Not very affectionate, but she didn't seem afraid of him or anything."

Max paused to sniff the trunk of a tree. We waited while he peed on it, then started walking again. The trail turned and rose in an incline. Both dogs wanted to race up the hill, but we kept them to a reasonable pace.

"Oh my gosh, I forgot to tell you." She grabbed my arm in her excitement, and I felt a zap of electricity at her touch. "Yesterday after school, I saw Ashley and Jeremy in the parking lot together. I think they might have been about to kiss."

"Are you serious?"

"Well… Okay, I don't know if they were going to kiss or not. Derek was out there, and he yelled something across the parking lot at them. Probably just telling them to have a nice weekend or whatever."

"Freaking Derek."

"I know, right?" She laughed. "I guess two teachers walking to their cars at the same time after work isn't really news. But for a second, I thought I was about to get proof they're together."

"That would have been a breakthrough."

"I just have this feeling about them. I swear they're secretly dating."

I nodded. I thought so, too.

The question of whether Ashley and Jeremy were dating brought another question to my mind. What about Penelope? Was she going to start over? Put herself out there and start dating again?

Why did I hate that idea so much? Just the thought of Penelope dating made me want to punch him in the face. And he wasn't even a real person, just a theoretical date.

Because seriously, fuck that guy.

The trail evened out again and veered right, passing through a thicket of trees. Something caught Max's attention and he stopped to sniff the trunks. Maggie joined him.

I listened, catching the sound of moving water as it carried through the air. "The creek."

Pen gave the leash a gentle tug. "Max, Maggie, let's go!"

The sound of the creek grew as we hurried through the trees. Finally, the trail emerged into a clearing. The creek flowed from higher up the hill, cascading down over smooth rocks, and the gray outcropping loomed just ahead. Deciduous trees blazed with fall color and the red and brown leaves swirled in the trickling water.

Pen got out her phone and brought up a photo of Morris's painting. "What do you think?"

"This has to be the place." I pointed to the rock formation. "Look, that angle right there. It's exactly the same."

"I agree. He definitely painted this spot."

"The question is, what else did he do here?"

Max tugged on the leash, trying to get closer to the water. Penelope moved ahead, taking slow steps while Maggie sniffed the ground.

"If someone were going to dispose of a body, I don't think they'd do it near the water," she said. "Too much chance that erosion would uncover it."

"Yeah, agreed." I followed Pen, nudging Max a little so he'd stay with me. "Probably off the trail, too. Even if he came out here at night, he wouldn't want hikers to find it later."

The dogs kept sniffing as we walked off trail. I scanned the ground, looking for areas where Morris could have dug a hole and covered it up again. There were enough leaves and pine needles that concealing the burial spot wouldn't have been difficult.

Suddenly, Max started digging. Pen and I stopped and looked at each other, wide-eyed.

Was he going to find something?

"Good boy, Max," Penelope said.

Maggie stopped and watched her doggy brother, her head tilted to one side, as if she were curious. Max was a dog on a mission. He dug furiously, tossing dirt behind him until he had a sizable hole in the ground.

"What's in there, Max?" I asked.

He stopped and shoved his nose into the dirt. I had a sudden vision of him emerging with a human tibia in his mouth. I glanced at Pen. By the way her brow furrowed, I was pretty sure she was thinking the same thing.

Max jerked his head out of the dirt with something in his mouth, and his tail wagged fast, like he was quite pleased with himself.

"What did he find?" Pen asked.

It was a little smaller than a football, and so covered in dirt, I couldn't make out any details.

"Max, sit," I said, and he did.

I crouched in front of him and winced. Whatever he had, it was gross. Bits of something dangled off it, looking like rotten flesh hanging from a zombie's body. The scent of decomposition was strong.

I'd channeled my brother Garrett enough to think of bringing gloves. I slipped them on and held out my hands.

"Drop it, Max."

He didn't move.

"Drop it. Be a good boy."

Still nothing.

"Max, drop it," I said.

Finally, he opened his mouth and let the…whatever it was…fall into my open hands.

Penelope clamped her hands over her mouth. Max's tail beat against the ground, rustling through the leaves and pine needles, while Maggie idly sniffed around the spot where he'd dug.

The sickly sweet scent of rotting meat filled my nose. I poked at the thing and brushed some of the dirt off, trying to figure out what it was.

"Oh for fuck's sake," I said, pinching it with two fingers so I could lift it. "It's a rotisserie chicken. Or what's left of one."

Penelope crouched down to look closer. "Oh my gosh, you're right."

"It's just what's left of someone's picnic." I stood and tossed it deeper into the woods so Max wouldn't get it.

"Should we keep looking?" Pen asked as she straightened.

"Yeah. Buried hiker garbage doesn't mean there's not something else out here."

We let the dogs sniff around for a while, but neither of them found anything worth digging up. Max wanted to keep circling back to his hole, but I didn't want to know what other half-rotted food he'd find there, so I guided him away.

After combing the area for a while, we decided to pack it in. We hiked back to my truck and gave the dogs some water and treats. Then we loaded up and took them back to Josiah and Audrey's house.

"That was harder than I thought it would be," Penelope said when we were back in my truck. "I guess I figured we'd be able to tell exactly where to look. Which doesn't make sense, when I think about it. If he really did hide a body, he would have done his best to make sure it wasn't easy to find."

"I thought the dogs would find more than a rotting chicken," I said with a chuckle. "But I guess cute rescues aren't quite the same as trained cadaver dogs."

"Do you think there might be something out there and we just don't know where to look?"

"Maybe. I keep going back and forth on telling Garrett. I might as well, but I doubt he'll be able to do anything. It's a pretty loose theory we have." I backed out of the driveway and started up the street. "I'll tell you one thing, though."

"What?"

"I'm not opposed to going back. And I'm going to keep looking for that cabin."

"You're not giving up?" she asked.

"Nope."

"Good. Me neither."

She shivered, and I glanced at her. "Still cold?"

"I should have worn more layers. It's like my bones are cold."

I turned up the heat and angled the vent to blow the warm air toward her. "Let's get you home."

She smiled and, not for the first time, I had a feeling I was in trouble.

CHAPTER 29

Theo

After dropping off the dogs, Pen and I grabbed takeout from the Copper Kettle Diner. When we got home, she changed into a sweatshirt and a pair of blue lounge pants, and I ditched my joggers for pajamas.

We settled on the couch with our dinner. Pen sat sideways with her back against the armrest and her feet on the center cushion. I took the other corner and crossed an ankle over my knee.

Apparently the hike had made me hungry and I inhaled my food in no time. Since Pen was still eating, I decided to give Garrett a call. We hadn't found anything at the creek, but my gut told me he should know about the woman in Raven Falls and how the location matched one of the Morris paintings with a hidden note.

"What's up, Theo?" he answered.

"Got a minute?"

"Sure."

"You know how I told you about that note my friend Penelope found hidden in a painting?"

"Rings a bell, yeah."

"We found more."

"I probably don't want to know how, do I?"

"Don't worry. I'm pretty sure we didn't do anything illegal." I winked at Pen.

She giggled behind her hand.

Garrett sighed. "Okay, so you found notes hidden in paintings. Where are you going with this?"

"Hear me out. Hikers discovered a body outside a town called Raven Falls. It was a woman who went missing twenty years ago. But here's the thing. That artist—Edwin Morris? He painted the spot where she was found. And there was a note in that painting."

"Huh." He paused. "All right, that's mildly interesting."

"It's not mildly interesting. It's suspicious as hell."

"How do you know he painted that exact location?"

"There's a barn and the details all match. It's definitely the same place. And the note says *What have I done*?"

He grunted. "Okay, that is suspicious."

"Exactly!" I gave Pen a thumbs-up. "We also found the location of another one of his paintings—one that also had a hidden note. We hiked out there today. We didn't find anything, but that doesn't mean there's nothing there."

"Where is it?"

I gave him the location of the trailhead and a rough description of where we'd gone.

"Got it," Garrett said. "That's not far from town."

"We borrowed Max and Maggie, but all they found were the buried remains of someone's lunch."

"Well, if there's anything out there to be found, it might be too old or buried too deep for their noses to pick up on it."

"That's what I was thinking."

"I gotta be honest, you got me. I'm curious. I might head out there tomorrow since the weather is supposed to be dry."

"Awesome, man. Thanks. Let me know if you find anything."

"Will do. Talk to you later."

I ended the call and put my phone on the coffee table. "Garrett's going to take a look."

"Oh good. I'm glad he listened to you." She sat up suddenly, wincing, and put her to-go container on the coffee table. "Ouch."

"You okay?"

She reached down to rub her lower leg. "Yeah, I just got a leg cramp."

"Here, let me."

I scooted to the middle of the couch and put her legs in my lap. She leaned back against the armrest as I bent her leg so I could massage her calf.

Her pants were in the way, so I pushed them up to her knee and dug my thumbs into the muscle. By her sharp intake of breath, I could tell it hurt.

"Too hard?" I asked.

"No, I think that's what it needs."

I kept massaging, working from beneath the tight spot over the knot in her muscle. Pausing a few times, I stretched her leg straight and turned her ankle, then went back to massaging.

Her body relaxed and I could feel the knot ease. But I didn't stop. I massaged her lower leg from ankle to knee, running both hands up her smooth skin.

Touching her was intoxicating. My heart rate picked up and pressure built in my groin as I continued, not ready to let her go. From the corner of my eye, I saw her lick her lips. That tiny flick of her tongue sent a jolt through me.

Leaning her head against the armrest, she let out a long breath with the barest hint of a moan. I stopped, gently pushed her legs off my lap, and stood.

She lifted her head to look at me, her expression surprised.

"Sorry," I said.

"That's okay. It felt really good."

Swallowing hard, I ran my hands through my hair. It wasn't just that massaging her leg was arousing. It was. But I had weeks' worth of pent-up desire begging to be set free.

"Are you all right?" she asked, bending her knees and drawing her legs close to her body.

"Yeah, fine." I walked aimlessly around the living room. "I just need a minute."

"Are you sure?"

"Yeah, I'm good." I ran my hands through my hair again while I paced. Maybe I needed a cold shower. Did that actually work?

She watched me with concern, and I stopped, looking her in the eyes. I opened my mouth to reassure her that everything was fine. That she didn't need to be worried. But that was not what I said.

"I want you, Pen. I want you so fucking bad. I keep trying to tell myself I shouldn't. I can't let it happen again."

"That's what I keep saying to myself, too."

It wasn't helping to hear her admit she'd been thinking about it, too. "Exactly. You're my best friend. And it's great being roommates. So, we can't…"

She shook her head slowly. "No. We can't."

"Because if we did…" I wasn't sure how to finish. Because if we did, what?

"If we did, we'd probably do it again after that."

"Exactly."

"Because it was… Well, I don't know about you, but it was really good for me. I didn't have a chance to tell you that, and it seemed like it would be weird if I did. But it was amazing."

"Right?" I asked, my voice enthusiastic. "It was the best."

"The best? Really?"

"Oh yeah."

She hesitated, her lips moving, but for a second, no sound came out. "So it was good for you, too? Not just average?"

I rubbed my hands up and down my face. "Pen, it was incredible. There's nothing average about you."

She tucked her hair behind her ear. "But of course we can't do it again."

"Right, no. We can't."

"Because…"

She didn't finish, and I was having a very hard time remembering why.

I moved over to the couch and lowered myself down next to her. Her eyes were on mine as I put a hand on her knee.

"This would be a bad idea," I said, my voice low.

"Very bad," she whispered.

"Friends shouldn't do this."

She shook her head slowly, but a flush crept across her cheeks.

"Except…" I tipped one of her legs outward.

Her eyebrows lifted and she licked her lips again. "Except, maybe?"

"If we both want to?"

She nodded.

And the dam broke.

Surging in, I took her lips with mine. Her legs wrapped around my waist, and I could feel her heat through our clothes. Growling into her mouth, I kissed her deeply as I rolled my hips, pressing myself against her.

Her frantic whimpers as I rubbed her center were music to my ears. As much as I wanted to be inside her, dry humping her to climax would be fucking awesome.

With my hand gripping her ass, I found a rhythm she clearly liked and kept at it, utterly relentless. In moments, her lips parted, her breath quickened, and her body shook. She leaned her head back, and I watched her come with gasping moans.

Fuck, yes.

Still breathing hard, she met my eyes. I gently removed her glasses and set them aside, then kissed her again.

"Now I'm going to rip your clothes off," I said low into her ear, "and fuck you until you can't breathe."

She helped me pull off her clothes and I shucked mine, kicking them out of the way. I manhandled her onto her knees with her hands braced on the back of the couch and ran my hands down her waist and over her hips to cup her ass. She looked back over her shoulder.

"Look at you. This is so hot."

Kneeling on the edge of the couch, I groaned as I slid inside her. Holding her hips, I thrust in and out, reveling in the intensity. She held on, arching her back, and moved with me.

Soon, we were lost in a rhythm. My grip on her hips was tight and she pressed herself into me each time I thrust. I groaned at the feel of her—the way she wrapped around me so perfectly. Pressure built and every moan and whimper that came from her lips brought me closer to my breaking point.

I wanted to make sure she came again, but I didn't have to wait. She started to move faster, and I matched her pace. Her breathy string of yeses spurred me on until I was driving into her, buried deep.

The sight of her body, the sound of her moans, and the feel of being inside her were too much. One more hard thrust, and I came unglued.

We came together in an overwhelming burst of heat and pressure. I groaned, moving my hips with the pulses of pleasure as they rippled through my body. I held there, deep inside her, breathing hard as I came down the other side, then finally pulled out.

I stood, and with a little smile, she got up. Standing in front of the couch, I drew her into my arms and held her for a long moment, rubbing slow circles across her bare skin.

She stepped back and gestured toward the bathroom. I watched her go, slow-blinking in my daze.

Our first time had not been a fluke. There was no denying it. We were incredible together.

It was too early to go to bed, and a part of me thought I should just get dressed and go on with our evening. Not as if nothing had happened, but without a lot of post-sex contact. That would be better, right?

Except I hated that idea.

I didn't want to put my clothes on and go back to sitting on the couch with her. I wanted to hold her. Wrap her in my arms and feel her skin against mine.

Maybe that wasn't what friends turned roommates who were now apparently fucking should do. But I didn't give a shit.

Leaving my clothes on the floor, I grabbed her glasses and moved to the hallway to wait, propping my shoulder against the wall a couple of feet from the bathroom door.

She came out and gasped. "That's you, right?"

I grinned and moved closer so I could slide her glasses onto her face. Then I leaned in and kissed her. "It's me."

Without explanation, I took her hand and led her into my bedroom. She didn't protest as I drew her into bed and pulled the covers over us.

She took her glasses off again and set them on the nightstand, then leaned her head on my chest. I put my arm around her and held her close.

With my body sated and her skin against mine, I drifted for a while. I was relaxed, but more than that, I was happy. In a way I hadn't been in a long time.

Or maybe ever.

CHAPTER 30

Penelope

The warmth of Theo's body lulled me into a deep state of relaxation. I didn't know how long we'd been lying in his bed together, but I probably needed to get up. Otherwise, I was going to fall asleep.

I started to move, but he held me tight. His embrace made me smile, and I wondered if he was awake. I lifted my head to find him looking at me with a hint of a grin puckering his dimples.

"Trying to get away?" he asked.

"No. I just thought I should get up before I fall asleep on you."

"But this is so comfortable."

"True." I nestled my head against him and ran my fingers across his dusting of chest hair. "But…"

"Stay with me tonight, Pen."

I squeezed my eyes shut. I wanted to—so badly. But was it a good idea?

"How about this?" He moved, rolling me onto my back, and braced himself over me. His mouth dipped to mine in a slow, wet kiss. "How about I fuck you again? Then we'll see if you want to go anywhere."

I was powerless to resist. Letting my legs fall open, I drew him onto me, my body inexplicably hungry for him.

And he was right. When we finished, he'd taken everything

out of me. I fell asleep in his arms, languid, warm, and utterly satisfied.

I woke slowly and stretched, wondering what time it was. Theo lay on his side, facing me, his breathing slow and even. Moving carefully so I wouldn't disturb him, I rolled over and grabbed my glasses from the nightstand.

With the world in focus, I turned onto my back and looked at the ceiling. I was in Theo's bed, after doing exactly what I'd told myself I was not going to do again—not once, but twice.

But oh my word, it had been amazing. The couch? Unreal. Two orgasms. Two! As if that hadn't been enough, a short time later he'd done it again in his bed.

Three orgasms in one night? That had to have been a dream.

But my body told me it was very real.

I glanced at Theo, still sleeping soundly, and my mouth turned up in a smile. I liked waking up next to Theo Haven. Especially after a night like that.

My heart tried to speak up, fluttering with barely suppressed emotion. I tamped it down. I knew those feelings were there, but for now, the best thing I could do was ignore them. I'd gone into it with my eyes wide open. Theo and I were friends, and we weren't going to be more.

Friends with benefits? That was fine. I'd enjoy what we did have while I could. It would be worth it.

I hoped.

It wasn't long before he stirred. Seeing me, he smiled and drew me against him. Spooning with him in the morning after a night of mind-blowing sex wasn't exactly making it easy to keep my heart out of it. But he felt so good, I couldn't resist.

Eventually, we got up and started our day. There wasn't any tension or awkwardness like the first time we'd slept together. There were smiles, a few touches, and even a kiss in the kitchen.

After we'd showered and dressed, we took a trip to the grocery store. And when we got back, he helped me prep our lunches. We chatted about the upcoming week—what we had going on at school and the game coming up on Friday. Everything between us felt natural. As if we'd passed into a new phase of our friendship and both knew—and understood—that it was temporary.

I invited Theo to visit Grandma with me again, and he accepted. So once the kitchen had been cleaned up, we put on our coats and went to the assisted living center. Like it was all the most normal way to spend a day together.

We didn't see Grandma in the common area downstairs, so went up to check her apartment. She opened the door with a smile and didn't seem at all surprised to see Theo.

"Come in, come in," she said, wheeling herself back into the living area. "If you're hungry for a snack, we can go downstairs, but otherwise, we can have tea. I even have hot water ready."

"Tea is perfect," I said. "Theo, do you want anything?"

"I'm good, thanks."

While I went into her small kitchen to pour some tea, she invited Theo to sit. Her living room had a small couch and an armchair, plenty of room for a small group to gather. An old TV sat on a cabinet against the wall, and there were a few pictures on the walls, mostly of me as a child. A small side table was covered with a stack of books and a few old magazines.

"Is your tea still hot, Grandma?" I asked as I poured hot water over a tea bag in one of her mugs. "Can I get you more?"

"Mine is fine. Thank you, Penny."

I brought my tea into the living room but paused. Her gaze moved between me and Theo, scrutinizing us through narrowed eyes.

"Well," she said, as if she'd come to some conclusion.

I stood there for a second, frozen. She knew.

Theo and I had already slept together once before she'd met him the first time. But after the previous night, things were different between us. And she could tell.

It was hard to keep from glancing at Theo, but I had a feeling I'd turn beet red if I did. With my mug of tea in hand, I went to the couch and sat on the opposite corner from him.

"Are you two going to let me in on what's going on?" she asked.

"Um…" I trailed off with no idea how to answer that question. *Theo and I are sleeping together and it's the best I've ever had but we're still just friends?* No.

"With the painting and that news story that had you two so excited," she added.

"Oh!" I laughed. "Right, the painting. Of course that's what you meant. I knew that."

She raised her eyebrows.

I launched into the story, starting with everything we'd seen and heard at the celebration of life. I told her about finding the note in the painting of the creek, and how a body had been discovered in a location that Morris had painted. Theo chimed in with a few details, especially about Amanda and Michael Morris.

"So, you think this man was murdered?" she asked. "Or was he a murderer?"

"We don't know," I said. "Maybe both. But there's definitely something going on with those notes and the places he painted. We found the location of another one of his paintings and hiked out there yesterday. We didn't find anything, but Theo's brother Garrett is a sheriff's deputy, and he's going out there to investigate."

"This is quite the mystery you've uncovered," she said. "It's even better than that silly crime show Maury always wants to watch downstairs."

"Speaking of Maury," Theo said, "did you ever manage to Jell-O his teeth?"

"Not yet." A mischievous smile crossed her face. "But I did return the favor after that glitter card. I sent him one of my own, except…" Her shoulders shook and she covered her mouth. It took her a second before she could finish what she'd been about to say. "Except the one I sent him was filled with—" She cut herself off with laughter again. "Penis confetti. With glitter."

My mouth dropped open. "Grandma!"

Theo laughed and held out his fist toward her. "Yes. Colleen, you are the woman."

She bumped his fist. "Serves him right. There's still glitter in my chair."

"Penis glitter," Theo said, nodding. "Solid prank."

"I'm glad you approve," she said.

We visited for a while longer, and after we finished our tea, she invited us to go downstairs to the common room for a snack. We found a table and Theo and I helped her work on a puzzle while we ate cinnamon sugar muffins.

I was thinking it was about time to go when Theo got a call. He took his phone out of his pocket and raised his eyebrows at me.

"It's Garrett. I'm going to step outside to take this."

"Lovely to see you again, Theo," Grandma said with a smile. "Take good care of my Penny."

"I will, Colleen. See you soon." He rose from his chair and answered the call on his way out front.

Grandma turned her gaze on me. "That boy is in love with you."

"What?" Nervously, I fiddled with my glasses and tucked my hair behind my ear. "No, he's not. We're just friends."

She shook her head. "Mm-hmm. Either he's head over heels for you, or I'm going batty in my old age. And I assure you, I'm sharp as a tack."

"Of course you are. But Theo isn't in love with me. That's not possible."

"That's a silly thing to say. Why isn't it possible?"

"Because that's not what he wants. He doesn't want a relationship.

He has a plan. He's moving to South Carolina to be a college football coach and he's going to stay single."

A small smile crossed her lips. "Love ruins the best-laid plans."

I glanced away. "That isn't what's going on. And it's fine. I just got out of a relationship anyway."

She batted her hand. "Oh, that was hardly a relationship. Maybe at first, but it hadn't been for a while. Don't let that hold you back."

"Still, I told you Theo doesn't want a relationship. And whatever is going on between us, it's good."

"All I'm saying is, I just spent the last couple of hours watching him watch you. And that's a man with stars in his eyes." She reached over and patted my hand. "Even if he doesn't realize it yet. Sometimes it takes them a while to see what's right in front of them."

I sighed. I appreciated what she was trying to do, but she was wrong. Theo wasn't in love with me. She was seeing something that simply wasn't there.

"I really don't think so, but I'm not going to argue with you," I said.

"You'll see. You both will, eventually. Hopefully before it's too late." She wheeled herself back from the table. "In any case, I'm ready for a rest. I'll see you later."

I stood and leaned down to hug her. "Have a good week. Love you."

"Love you too, Penny."

I watched her wheel toward the elevator, then went in search of Theo. He was on his way back, meeting me just inside the automatic doors. We stepped outside into the cold air to head back to his truck.

"Did Garrett have news?" I asked.

"Are you ready for this?" He paused. "There's a body."

My eyes went wide. "At the creek? How did he find it?"

"I don't know. He didn't give me the details. Just that they uncovered human remains off the trail, not far from the creek."

I put a hand on my chest. "This means we might be right. Morris painted the locations of the bodies."

"Garrett was quick to add that this doesn't mean it was Morris. They need more before they can call him a suspect."

"Like a link between him and the victims."

"Exactly."

I let out a long breath. "Well, at least the authorities are looking into it now. That's good."

His mouth turned up in a grin, his dimples showing up in full force. "That's because of you, Penlock Holmes. Nice work."

I smiled, his praise enveloping me like a warm hug.

We got into his truck, and I settled in to consider everything. Surprise at Garrett's news mingled with curiosity about what Grandma had said. Theo in love with me? No. Like I'd told her, it wasn't possible. She was just seeing the afterglow of the previous night.

But my heart? It wasn't listening to reason and clung to the possibility—however remote—that somehow Grandma was right.

CHAPTER 31

Theo

Prepping for our first playoff game—and school in general—kept me busy all week. And the fact that Pen and I spent more nights together in my bed than in our separate rooms probably should have worried me.

But it was so good, I couldn't bring myself to keep my distance.

Besides, we were on the same page. We'd just added a new dimension to our friendship.

We'd met with Garrett Thursday night to go over what we knew and show him the notes we'd found. The body at the creek had already been identified as a woman in her late twenties who'd disappeared five years earlier from nearby Wenatchee.

Garrett took the possibility that Morris had something to do with both victims seriously, but made it clear that they didn't have enough to consider Morris a suspect. Our theory that he'd intentionally painted the sites where the bodies were found was interesting, but so far, just a theory. And could be a coincidence.

I didn't think so, but the ins and outs of law enforcement investigations were Garrett's area.

Football was mine, and Friday night, my kids killed it. Away games were always tough—harder mentally—but they'd played like they already knew they were going to win. They were just showing the other team.

It had been a great way to end the week, especially since Pen had made the two-and-a-half-hour drive to watch the game. We'd both slept in the next day and spent a leisurely day together—mostly in bed.

I woke up Sunday to a text from my mom asking if I wanted to join them at Christmas Village. It was still November, but Christmas Village had expanded to open in the fall with a pumpkin patch and hayrides. Personally, I was in for the hot cocoa and kettle corn.

Penelope had slept in her own room Saturday night. Probably for the best. I liked it when she stayed in bed with me, but we were walking a thin line.

I got up, and when I came out of my bedroom, Penelope's door was open, but I didn't see her in there. She wasn't in the kitchen or in the living room, either. Had she gone somewhere? A quick check out front confirmed her car was in the driveway. She could have gone for a walk. The sky was clear, but it was pretty cold out, so I doubted that was the case.

I went back down the hallway and approached her art studio. The door was ajar, and I could hear the faint sound of her humming. Quietly, I moved closer, my mouth turning up in the hint of a smile. She was still in her tank top and pajama pants with her hair in a ponytail. Palette in one hand and paintbrush in the other, her back was to me, and I watched as she took a step away from her easel and tilted her head, as if considering.

Still humming softly, she painted a few strokes, pausing to dip her brush into the paint. From what I could see, she was painting a creek. It wasn't the same scene in the Morris piece. This was her own. The creek curved around wet rocks and the sky was a brilliant blue.

It was stunning.

I watched her for a moment, captivated, until my chest started to ache. Pulling myself from the scene I couldn't get enough of, I turned and went to the kitchen to make some coffee. I didn't want to interrupt her.

Halfway through my first cup, she emerged. She had a few flecks of white paint on her cheek and a bit of blue on her nose.

"I didn't hear you get up." She put her palette and brush in the sink and came to the table. "How's your head? I was worried you might be getting a migraine."

"Really?" Instinctively, I stretched my neck. Everything felt fine. "No, I think I'm okay."

"That's good."

"What made you worry I was getting a migraine?"

"Oh, I don't know. Sometimes you make a face like your head hurts and rub the back of your neck. You did it a few times yesterday."

I stared at her for a second, struck by the fact that she'd noticed. I wasn't sure what to do with that, so I tried to brush off the feeling. "I'm good. What are you up to today? You know, since we're no longer hunting for bodies."

She laughed. "My lack of amateur detective work has left my schedule remarkably open."

"My family is going to Christmas Village. Any interest in wandering around with a bunch of Havens? I can't promise my brothers will behave themselves, but there will be hot cocoa and kettle corn."

"Hot cocoa and kettle corn sound fantastic. When do we need to leave?"

I checked the time. "We have a couple of hours, so take your time."

"I'll go shower." She stood. "I probably have paint on me. Do I have paint on my face?"

"A little."

"You should have told me."

I smiled. She was so damn cute. "I would have if we were leaving the house. But you're cute with paint on your nose."

Her cheeks flushed and she stumbled backward. "Yeah, well… I don't want paint on me when we go to the Village. So, I'll just go shower now."

She went down the hallway and I let out a long breath, tempted to follow her into the shower.

The air was crisp as Penelope and I got out of my truck at Christmas Village. Hay bales, cornstalks, and pumpkins stood on either side of the big *Cook Family Farm* sign, and the transition from fall to Christmas decor was already beginning. Twinkle lights were strung along the walkways and six-foot candy canes flanked the entrance.

Penelope was dressed in jeans with boots and my Timberwolves hoodie. She'd basically stolen it at this point, and I had no desire to get it back from her. I liked seeing her wear it too much.

Kind of like she was mine.

Although she wasn't. Not like that.

We walked past the entrance and the scent of sugar filled the air. Congregated in an open space just inside was practically my entire family.

Mom had Garrett and Harper's daughter Isla in her arms, and Dad was carrying Emily, Zachary and Marigold's daughter. Both babies were bundled up against the cold with little knit hats on their heads.

Josiah's daughter, Abby, was strapped to his chest in a baby carrier. She had a similar knit hat, as did my older nieces and nephews—Annika and Levi's kids. Even Owen had one. I had a feeling Mom had made all of them.

I lifted my hand in greeting as we approached. "Hey, everyone. Do you all know my friend, Penelope?"

After a chorus of greetings, Marigold stepped in to give her a hug. So did Melanie. Luke gave me a knowing glance, but I ignored him. Zachary's look was longer, and less subtle, but I ignored him, too.

Owen lifted a hand and gave her a shy smile. "Hi, Ms. Fallbrook."

"Hi, Owen," she said with a smile. "I bet it's weird to see your teacher outside of school."

"Wait, Penelope is Ms. Fallbrook?" Luke asked. "*The* Ms. Fallbrook?"

Owen's eyes widened in alarm, and he shook his head at Luke. "No."

Garrett grinned at his son, and I chuckled. Owen had once admitted to having a crush on Penelope when she'd been his middle school art teacher.

"What do you mean, *the* Ms. Fallbrook?" Penelope asked.

Luke glanced at Owen and seemed to decide to take pity on him. "He just said you were one of his favorite teachers."

"That's sweet," she said. "Thanks, Owen."

Owen let out a relieved breath and Luke winked at him.

I just shook my head. Owen wasn't the only one who got confusing feelings around Penelope.

"It's nice to meet everybody," Penelope said.

"Since we're all here, should we walk around?" Mom asked.

Owen reached for his baby sister and took her from Mom. She giggled and batted at his face.

"Yes, please," Annika said. Her son, Will, was jumping up and down in front of her. "I think someone needs to get his wiggles out."

Our group started down the path, and Penelope settled in beside me with her hands stuffed in the pocket of my hoodie. We wandered past an apple cider donut stand and a booth selling local honey and jars of spices. The big kids ran around the adults, laughing and joking with their aunts and uncles.

When we stopped at a few of the little shops to browse the Christmas decor, I made sure to look carefully at the ornaments Penelope lingered over so I'd remember which ones she liked. Roommates could get each other Christmas gifts, right? That wasn't weird.

Gradually, we separated into smaller groups as people meandered around. Annika's kids wanted to see the reindeer and their guard donkey, Horace. I'd promised Pen hot cocoa and kettle corn, so we moved farther along the path to a booth selling both.

The kettle corn came in big bags, so I bought one for us to share, along with two cups of cocoa. Pen took hers with a smile, and we moved across the path to get out of the way.

She sipped her cocoa, getting whipped cream on her lip. As much as I wanted to kiss it off, I held back.

I glanced away as she licked her lips and had to do a double take. Was that Amanda? A man held her hand and led her to one of the little shops. He looked around, as if he were checking his surroundings, and I caught a glimpse of his face. It was Michael Morris.

"Pen," I whispered, nudging her with my elbow. "Look."

"Look where? What am I looking at?"

Instead of going into the shop, Michael led Amanda around the side of the building.

"I just saw Amanda with Michael Morris."

"Where?"

"They went around the side of that shop over there."

"But why would they be together?" she asked.

I shrugged. Without saying another word, we casually walked past the shop and stopped on the path, pretending to dig into our bag of kettle corn. I angled so I could just see behind the small building and took a handful.

The couple clearly thought they were out of sight. Michael put his arms around her and brought her in for a long kiss.

"He's married," Pen whispered. "And I don't think it's to her."

He broke the kiss, and they started talking. I wondered if we could get close enough to hear. Nodding toward the shop, I took Pen's hand. We hurried around the other side and took careful steps toward the back. We couldn't see them, but their voices carried enough that we could hear their conversation.

"I just don't understand why you have to cancel," Amanda said.

"I told you, it's not a good time," Michael answered. "I have some things I have to handle."

"What things?"

"Things you don't need to worry about."

"You mean her." Her tone had an edge of anger.

"It's not about that."

"Of course it is. Everything is about her."

"Will you stop?" he snapped. "I already told you, I'm going to take care of it. She's at her parents' anyway. I doubt she's coming back this time. I'm not worried about her."

"Then what's going on?"

"I think somebody knows."

"About—"

"Shh. Don't. Not here."

"But, how? It's not possible."

"It shouldn't be possible. But Curt keeps asking questions."

"He gives me the creeps," she said.

"You and me both. Listen, I just need to lie low for a while. If Curt keeps poking his nose where it doesn't belong, eventually he's going to—"

"No," she said, interrupting him. "We made sure."

"I know we did. But if we leave now, it'll look suspicious. I promise, I'll make it up to you once everything dies down."

They went quiet and Penelope raised her eyebrows at me, as if to ask what I thought they were doing. I shifted enough to glance around the corner. He had her pushed up against the building.

I grabbed Penelope's hand, and we quickly moved back to the path. "They were making out back there."

"Ew."

"Yeah, I wish I could unsee that."

"I have so many questions right now," she said as we walked. "They're the ones having an affair?"

"It looks like it."

"I wonder if they were the ones having an affair all along, and Amanda was never with Edwin."

"Or she went for the son after the father died."

Pen winced. "Could be. But what was Michael talking about when he said he thinks someone knows? He couldn't have meant the bodies that were found?"

"I don't see how he'd know about that, unless he's got a friend in the sheriff's office or something. They're not even investigating his father."

"Whatever he was talking about, Amanda was in on it."

Our eyes met and I knew we were thinking the same thing. Did they kill Michael's father? Was the murderer also a victim?

Maybe we'd been right all along, and Morris's death had been foul play.

My vision shimmered around the edges, and I blinked a few times, hoping it would go away. A spasm of pain hit me out of nowhere, shooting up my neck and radiating across the back of my head.

"Shit," I mumbled, grabbing the back of my neck.

"Are you okay?"

I blinked again, but it was coming on fast. "Not really."

"Is it a migraine?"

"Yeah."

She put her hand on my chest. "Let's get you home. I'll drive."

"No, I can…" I trailed off. It felt like someone was jamming an ice pick into the back of my skull.

"I got it." She took the bag of kettle corn and slipped her hand into mine. "Let's go."

With my vision starting to blur and the pain making me nauseated, I went with Pen to my truck, and she drove me home.

CHAPTER 32

Theo

The frustration of missing school—and especially practice—ate at me. I'd been hoping I'd sleep off the worst of the migraine overnight, but when my alarm went off Monday morning, it was clear I wasn't going anywhere for a while.

Pen had checked on me before she left, softly touching my forehead and asking if I needed anything. I was used to handling them on my own, so I assured her I'd be fine in a few hours. Maybe even make it in by lunch.

Unfortunately, I'd taken a turn for the worse around eleven and I'd spent the next several hours in bed.

The good news was, by the afternoon, the worst of it seemed to be over. The throbbing had abated and my vision was normal. I wouldn't make it to practice, but Coach Lewis would have things well in hand. I didn't like it, but I didn't need to worry about the team. Even with another playoff game at the end of the week.

I was hitting the stage where boredom was starting to take over when I heard the front door open. The smile was automatic. Pen was home.

Opening my eyes, I glanced at the time. She must have left the instant the bell rang to get home so fast.

A moment later, my bedroom door quietly opened.

"Theo?" she whispered.

"I'm awake. Come on in."

She came in and sat on the edge of the bed. Her long hair spilled around her shoulders and she tucked a lock behind her ear. "How are you feeling?"

"Better. It's almost over."

"Good." She caressed my forehead and ran her fingers through my hair.

Her touch felt amazing. I closed my eyes and took a deep breath.

"Do you need anything?" she asked, still speaking softly.

Maybe just you, Pen.

"No," I said. "I actually think I'm ready to get up."

"Are you sure?" She stroked my hair again.

I wanted to pull her in bed with me, but I had a feeling my body wasn't ready for that. If she kept touching me, however, all bets were off.

"Yeah, I'm sure." I sat up and stretched my neck a little from side to side. "I'm glad you're home. I was getting bored. How was school?"

"Oh, you know, school. I did find out something, but if you need to keep resting, it can wait."

"Did you finally catch Jeremy and Ashley?"

"No, but this is even better."

"Let me get up and get some water," I said. "Then spill the tea, Pentagon."

We went to the kitchen, and I downed a big glass of water, then poured more and took it to the couch. She sat, and by the way she fidgeted with her glasses, I could tell she was excited.

"So what's up?" I asked.

"Okay." She took a deep breath. "I've been doing some digging online, trying to find a link between the missing women and Morris. Since you weren't at school today, I stayed in my classroom during lunch and spent some time searching. Theo, I found something."

"What?"

"The woman they found at the creek took one of Morris's painting classes less than a month before she went missing."

"No shit?"

She nodded. "I've thought of that before. The Raven Falls woman went missing so long ago, it was hard to find anything about her. But the woman at the creek posted pictures from when she took Edwin's class."

"Good sleuthing, Detective."

"Thanks, but that's not all. Once I found that connection, I did some more searching on the Raven Falls woman, and I found the link."

"Did she take one of his classes, too?"

"She did. I found an old blog she used to keep. I can't believe it still exists, although I guess someone would have had to delete it. Don't they say the internet is forever? Anyway, one of her last entries was about taking Morris's class."

"So there's a link between both women and Morris. That has to be enough for Garrett to treat him as a suspect."

"It should be. And I bet they can get a warrant or whatever so they can search the class records. See if any other former students have been reported missing over the years."

I held out my fist and she bumped it. "You're a freaking genius."

"I don't know about that. I bet the sheriff's office already figured all this stuff out."

"Maybe not, Detective Fallbrook." I grinned at her. "Who knows, we might solve this mystery yet."

"I'm not sure what will happen, considering the suspect is deceased. But at least the families will have answers."

"And we know he can't kill anyone else, so there's that."

"That is good news," she said with a smile, but a second later, her expression changed. "You know what's creepy?"

"What?"

"I took his class. Do you think he ever looked at me and…"

"Thought about killing you?"

"Yeah. Obviously he didn't kill every one of his students. He must have had some criteria. I wonder what it was."

Just the idea of Penelope in danger sent a ripple of tension through my back. I didn't know how I could suddenly want to unalive a dude who was already dead, but if he'd even thought about hurting her—

My phone rang and I grabbed it off the coffee table. It was Kevin Wilkins, the athletic director from Carolina.

For some reason, I didn't want to answer that call in front of Pen. I stared at my phone as it buzzed again.

"Do you need to take that?" she asked.

"Yeah. It's the athletic director from Carolina."

"Oh." She stood, and the drop in her voice was unmistakable. "That's important. Go ahead, I'll give you privacy."

I answered the call as I watched her disappear into her bedroom.

"Hey, Kevin."

"Hi, Theo. Is this a good time? Just wanted to touch base about a few things."

"Yeah, go ahead."

I wandered around the living room aimlessly as he talked. He wanted to know my thoughts on the latest game film he'd sent. I had ideas, but my brain was still fuzzy from the migraine. I did my best to share some feedback, all while trying not to fixate on Penelope's forlorn expression when she'd left the room.

The back of my neck stiffened as the call went on, and a pulse of pain reverberated through the right side of my head. I probably should have stayed in bed longer. The strain of trying to keep up with Kevin's conversation quickly got to me. Fortunately, he seemed satisfied and told me to have a good night.

Another throb of pain hit me as I ended the call. Shit. I needed to deal with it or I was in for a relapse.

I went to the kitchen and took another dose of my medication. While I was at it, I downed another glass of water in case I was dehydrated. Penelope came out, moving so quietly, I almost didn't hear her.

"Is everything okay?" she asked.

Inadvertently, I winced. "Yeah. He just wanted to chat about some stuff."

"Is your migraine coming back?"

"Little bit."

"What do you need?"

"Just to lie down." It was getting hard to think. "And ice, I guess."

"Come on."

She took my hand and led me to my bedroom. I was about to protest that she didn't need to do anything, but my head throbbed again. I lay on the bed, and she disappeared. When she returned, she had an ice pack. I put it on my forehead and closed my eyes.

I could feel her silent presence as she sat on the edge of my bed. After a while—it was hard to tell how long—she scooted closer and put her hand on my chest. I kept hold of the ice pack to keep it in place and laid my other hand over hers.

Her touch was warm and relaxing. The throbbing stopped, although I knew I wasn't out of the woods. Hopefully my meds would kick in, and between that and resting with ice, I'd be okay by morning.

I lost track of time for a while. Maybe I'd fallen asleep. When I came to, Penelope was still there. She'd stretched out and was lying next to me with her hand on my chest. I squeezed her hand, and she shifted a little.

"Do you need anything?" she whispered. "Dinner?"

"No," I said, my voice low. "I just need to stay here."

"Okay."

I felt her settle back on the bed. I wanted to tell her she didn't need to stay. But it felt so good to have her beside me—just knowing she was there—I couldn't seem to say it.

The pain continued to recede, but my brain was still fuzzy. All I could think as I drifted off to sleep was one word.

Stay.

And I wasn't sure if I was thinking about Penelope, or me.

CHAPTER 33

Penelope

I spent the night with Theo so I'd be there if he needed anything. Not that he did. He slept, and my contribution was mostly to move the ice pack off the bed when it slipped off his forehead.

But I also stayed because it felt good to be close to him.

I woke first and got up quietly in case he still needed to sleep. A little while later, I heard him moving around, and he came out dressed and ready for work. The migraine was gone.

He thanked me for staying with him. I wanted to slip into his embrace and feel his arms around me. But I didn't. We needed to get to school, and I needed to stop myself from making things complicated.

I wasn't Theo Haven's girlfriend, so I shouldn't act like I was.

School turned out to be more chaotic than usual. The fire alarm went off halfway through third period and we had to evacuate. We stood out in the cold while the fire department investigated. Rumors flew through the student body that someone had pulled the alarm on purpose, but it turned out to be a malfunction. We were given the all clear and slowly filed back into the building.

The rest of the day was an exercise in futility as my fellow faculty and I did our best to move on with our usual schedule. The students' focus, however, was mostly nonexistent. By the last period of the day,

I was ready to give them all crayons and construction paper, as if they were toddlers.

The final bell rang, and I sank into the chair at my desk while the students scurried out of the art room. I took a moment to do nothing but stare at the wall.

Some days are like that when you're a teacher.

My hesitation meant I wouldn't catch Theo before he went to practice. But that was probably for the best. Sleeping next to him the night before hadn't been a sexual thing, but somehow that gave me even bigger feelings.

Not his girlfriend, I told myself again. *So don't act like you are.*

Fishing my phone out of my purse to check my messages, I smiled when I saw a text from Melanie. She'd reached out the other day to see if I wanted to get together for coffee, and was confirming that we were still on for that afternoon. I replied that I was looking forward to it.

I had a bit of time to kill, so I got caught up on some prep work and grading. Despite the tiring day, I felt a renewed burst of energy as I packed up to leave my classroom. Regardless of what was going on—or not going on—with Theo, I had a new friend.

It's possible I was a little bit too excited about that. Being on the shy side made new friendships challenging for me, but it actually felt like Melanie was someone I could hang out with—even once Theo was gone.

The faint sound of the football team practicing filtered over the parking lot as I walked to my car. My heart decided to treat me to a tug of longing, and I let out a sigh. As often as I kept telling myself I could be intimate with Theo without the rest of it—without my heart getting involved—deep down, I knew I couldn't.

Despite my best efforts, I was falling for him.

But I wasn't going to let that ruin my friend-date with Melanie. So I headed into town and found parking outside the Steaming Mug.

Tilikum's coffee shop had a great vibe, with the scent of coffee in the air and soft music in the background. I didn't see Melanie, so I found an open table and took a seat.

I only had to wait a few minutes before she came in. She greeted me with a warm hug, and we went to the front counter to order. I decided on a matcha latte, and she ordered a decaf mocha. Once our drinks came out, we took them back to the table and sat.

"Sorry if I made you wait," Melanie said. "I lost track of time."

"I was only here for a few minutes."

"Good. How are you? What's new? What's going on in your life?"

I'm sleeping with your soon-to-be brother-in-law and probably can't handle it.

Thankfully, I didn't say that.

"Well, the fire alarm malfunctioned at school, so I had to wrangle a bunch of squirrelly high schoolers who decided one interruption was enough to throw off an entire day."

"Oof. That's not great. I'm telling you, teachers are saints. I don't know how you do it."

"It has its challenges, but I really love it."

"Why? I'm not asking because I don't believe that you love it. I just mean, what it is about teaching that you love?"

I adjusted my glasses. "There are a lot of things. It's so satisfying when I can help bring out their creativity, whether they have innate talent or not. But mostly I love being able to show them that beauty exists in the world, and hopefully impress on them why it's important. There's so much ugliness out there, I feel like beauty—in art or anywhere—gives us hope."

"Well, that's amazing." She smiled. "I love that."

"What about you? What's going on in your life?"

She tapped her chin. "Let's see. I started recording the new season of *Enchanted Hollow*."

"What's that?"

"It's a cartoon. I'm a voice actor and I play the evil queen on the show."

"Do you really? What a cool job."

"I'm not going to lie, it really is. That's keeping me busy. Plus, despite my insistence I'd never get married again, I'm planning a wedding. Leave it to Luke Haven to prove me wrong." She rolled her eyes.

A wedding. I tried not to let the topic weigh on me, but I couldn't help feeling a dip of sadness. I wanted to be married. To have a partner. Someone to share my life with.

To be my best friend and so much more.

"Do you have a date set and everything?" I asked, trying very hard to keep my tangled emotions out of my voice.

"We're working on an exact date, but it'll be next spring. We'll have it at Salishan Cellars, the winery down in Echo Creek."

"That's a beautiful location."

"It really is. Luke's brothers and his sister got married there, so at this point it's basically tradition. And it's where he took me for our second first date, so that makes it even more special."

"That's so sweet."

"Thanks. Amazingly enough, I'm excited. I don't mean to sound cynical, but I made the mistake of marrying an idiot the first time around. I'm still getting used to the idea that I got it right this time."

"No judgment here. I got all too close to marrying an idiot."

"What stopped you?" She tilted her head. "I know that's a personal question, but I'm really nosy. And I think I've told you I have no filter."

I took a sip of my drink. "That's okay, it's a good question. I guess I finally realized how wrong we were for each other. I'd been ignoring the signs for so long, but I couldn't anymore. I still don't know why he thought he wanted to marry me."

"Comfort, maybe? If you were together for a while, he probably figured that's just what you do."

"I think that's exactly what it was. And being comfortable is okay, but when that's all you have, it isn't enough. Especially when one of you is a huge jerk."

"You should want more. Even if you're not a drama queen like me, and I suspect that you aren't, a good relationship should have at least a little heat."

My cheeks warmed and I glanced down at my mug. I knew she didn't mean that type of heat, but memories flashed through my mind—Theo, and me, and the couch…

"Uh-oh," she said. "Pen. Can I call you Pen? Something happened with Theo, didn't it?"

"Is it that obvious?"

She sighed with a slight shake of her head. "What is it about those Haven brothers?"

"I don't know, but I'm worried I made a big mistake. Theo's moving. Not only that, he made it clear he doesn't want a relationship. I shouldn't have…but I did…and it was…but now…"

"But now you caught feelings."

"Big ones."

She reached over and squeezed my hand. "Does he know?"

"That I have feelings?" I sat up straighter in my chair and adjusted my glasses again. "No. Oh my goodness, no. I hope not. I've been trying very hard to make sure he doesn't."

"And you don't think you should tell him?"

"No." I glanced down again. "I knew what I was getting into. We both did. It's not like he ever claimed he could give me something he can't. I know where he stands. We're friends, and we…you know… But it can't ever be more than that."

"This is heartbreaking." She pressed her hand to her chest, then started gesturing as she talked. "You're so sweet, and Theo is such a great guy. Except when he's doing that guy thing he's doing right now, which is being an idiot. How can he not see that everything he needs is right in front of him. Literally. You live in his house. You're *right there*."

I couldn't help but laugh. "Maybe I'm not what he needs. Maybe he needs to move to South Carolina and be a college football coach."

She waved that off. "Not a chance."

I laughed again, but there wasn't much authenticity in it. I wanted what she was saying to be true. But I couldn't afford to get my hopes up.

"Well, right now it is what it is." And I really needed to change the subject. "Tell me more about the cartoon you're in."

I had a feeling Melanie knew what I was doing—redirecting the conversation away from anything me and Theo—but she went along with it. She talked about her role, and her acting career in general, plus what it had been like to move back to Tilikum. I had to laugh as she described her relationship with Luke. They'd gotten off to a rocky start. But they'd been through a lot together, and she was obviously happy.

So happy. I wondered what that would feel like.

It started getting late, and she had to get going, so we hugged and said goodbye. Even with my complicated feelings for Theo lingering on my mind, I left with a little spring in my step. I'd had such a nice time, and it seemed like Melanie and I had started an actual friendship—one that would last.

There was something to make me happy.

I went out to my car and checked my phone. I had a missed call, but didn't recognize the number. They'd left a voicemail, so I tapped to check.

"Hi, Ms. Fallbrook," a man's voice said. "My name is Curt Redfern and I'm a friend of the Morris family. If you could give me a call back when you have a minute, I would appreciate it."

That was odd. I remembered Curt from the celebration of life. He'd been with Gina Morris. I also remembered almost getting caught by him at the gallery when Theo and I had been sleuthing. But why would he call me?

Oh, no. Had he found out we'd been in the gallery and taken one of Edwin's notes? But that was a month ago. How could he know?

Taking a deep breath, I decided not to procrastinate out of worry, brought up the number, and hit Send.

"This is Curt," he answered.

"Hi, this is Penelope Fallbrook. I'm returning your call."

"Of course, Ms. Fallbrook. Thank you. Sorry to call you out of the blue, but I'm helping Mrs. Morris with some of her late husband's affairs. In going through the storage area in the gallery, I discovered one of your paintings from a class you took with Mr. Morris. I'm assuming you'd like to have it. It's quite beautiful."

I let out a relieved breath. He didn't know. "Thank you. I don't even remember what it would have been."

"It looks like a vineyard."

"Oh. I did take the class where we painted at a vineyard. I didn't realize I'd left one of my paintings. Or that he would have kept it."

"There are quite a few paintings from students, actually. He was the type to never throw things away. I'm just going through them and reaching out if I can decipher the name, and if we have contact info."

"I see. Thank you. I appreciate that."

"Are you local? Would it be possible to swing by the gallery?"

"Sure, I can do that. When is the gallery open?"

"It's closed, I'm afraid. Permanently. But I can meet you when it's convenient. I'm there now, or we can arrange another time."

"Now would be fine. I'm out and about anyway."

"Great. I appreciate that. Do you know where it is?"

"Yes, I do. I'm not far from there, so I'll see you shortly."

"Thanks again, Ms. Fallbrook."

I ended the call, disappointed to hear the gallery was closing. But it made sense. Running an art gallery had to be a lot of work. And Gina Morris was probably just trying to put the pieces of her life together after the loss of her husband.

Theo would be at practice a little longer, but since it was unofficially my night to cook, I decided to leave him a message in case he beat me home. I brought up his number and hit Send, not surprised that it went straight to voicemail. He usually kept his phone off during the day, as well as during practice.

"Hey, it's me," I said after his greeting. "I'm stopping by the gallery for a few minutes before I go home. They have one of my paintings and want to return it to me. I was thinking of making soup for dinner if that sounds good to you. I—"

I hesitated. Oh gosh, I'd almost said *I love you.*

"See you later."

I ended the call and let out a breath. Friend disaster averted. I couldn't just blurt out "I love you" to Theo. Where had that even come from?

With a shake of my head, I turned on my car and headed for the gallery.

CHAPTER 34

Theo

It had been a day.

There was always so much to do after missing work. Add to that the shitty feeling of a migraine hangover, the normal craziness of high school kids, and a fire alarm malfunction, and it had been especially chaotic.

I'd hardly seen Penelope. Which sucked. It happened that way sometimes, but I'd been hoping she'd come out of her classroom after the last bell. I'd thanked her that morning for the way she'd taken care of me during my migraine, but I hadn't said enough. We'd been busy getting ready for the day, but I'd wanted to…

Hold her? Kiss her? Something.

Instead, she'd given me the lunch she'd packed for me, and we'd been on our way. And she still hadn't emerged from her classroom by the time I had to get down to the field for practice.

We'd been in the same building all day. How could I miss her?

I didn't have time to contemplate any of it, though. Practice was not going well.

The team's focus was all over the place—certainly not on the field. We had a big game Friday, and my patience was wearing thin. More than once, I had to step back and take a breath to keep from laying into one of the kids. As it was, they'd already spent a good portion of practice running laps.

None of us were in a good mood.

"Hey, Coach," Coach Lewis called.

I whirled around and opened my mouth to snap at him. Not that he'd done anything wrong. My fuse was just short.

"Yeah?" I managed.

"Someone's here asking for you. He's out front."

"Who?"

"Says his name is Sean."

Sean? What the fuck did that guy want?

I nodded in acknowledgment and yelled at the team to get back on the field and run the last play again.

"I'll be right back," I said to Coach Lewis. "Don't let them keep messing around."

"No problem."

I walked around the side of the building and through the opening in the fence. Sure enough, there was Sean, dressed in a dark coat and jeans with a gray hat on his head.

"Sorry to bug you at work," he said as I approached.

I crossed my arms. "What do you want?"

He held his hands up. "I'm not here to cause trouble. There's something I thought Penelope should know, but I figured it would be best if I didn't contact her directly."

"What is it?"

"It's probably nothing, but I noticed a car on the street in front of the house a couple times. Seemed weird. It's not one of the neighbors, you know? So the other day, I went out there and looked. I recognized the lady. It was that painter guy's wife. The one who died."

"Morris?"

"Yeah. His wife. Kinda looks like a skeleton. It's why I remembered who she was."

Gina Morris did have a bit of a skeletal face.

"So, you think you saw Edwin Morris's wife outside your house?"

"A couple times at least. Maybe three."

"Why do you think that has anything to do with Penelope?"

He shrugged. "Maybe it doesn't. But she knew them, at least a little. No idea why that woman would be looking for Penelope, but I couldn't think of any other reason she'd be parked on my street, sitting in her car."

That *was* weird.

"That's all she did? She didn't come up to the house or anything?"

"Not while I was there. She never came to the door. Just sat out there. I thought maybe she was looking for Penelope and didn't know she'd moved. But then why not come to the door and ask for her? The whole thing weirded me out, which is why I figured she should know."

"Thanks." I didn't like Sean any more than I ever had, but I respected him for coming to tell me. It was the right thing to do. I stepped closer and held out my hand. "I appreciate it."

He took my hand and shook it. "No problem."

As Sean turned and left, I checked the time on my watch. I was anxious to get home, but practice wasn't over, so I went back to the field.

The team didn't give me much chance to think about what Sean had said. I had to be on top of them every moment. Finally, in the last twenty minutes or so, they got their collective shit together and started executing. I shouted encouragement instead of correction, and like the flip of a switch, morale turned. They were fired up and ready for their next playoff game.

Time ran out, but we ran a few more plays to solidify the formation. When I released them to the locker room, everyone was in a much better mood—including me.

The aftereffects of the previous day's migraine started to catch up with me on the way home. It was a bit like a hangover. I was fatigued, my head was fuzzy, and my body ached. I knew I'd feel better after a meal—and I probably needed water—as well as a good night's sleep.

Which made me think of Pen, and sleeping next to her the night before.

I'd been too out of it for anything to happen. But it hadn't been about that. It had felt good just having her there—being close to her.

When I got home, it took me a minute before I realized she wasn't there. I'd held it together all day and my brain was freaking tired. I hadn't even noticed her car wasn't outside.

I stood in the kitchen, feeling like a kid who'd just dropped his ice cream cone. In a puddle. While being rained on.

What was wrong with me? Hadn't she said something about meeting Melanie at the Steaming Mug? She was probably still there.

And why was I suddenly jealous of Melanie for getting to spend the afternoon with Pen?

I kicked off my shoes and sat down on the couch, then closed my eyes and ran my fingers through my hair. I was just tired. It had been a long day and I was still recovering. That was all.

Or was it?

Opening my eyes, I looked around. Signs of Penelope were everywhere. Her shoes by the door, her teakettle—not to mention an entire basket of tea—in the kitchen. She'd added little touches all over, stuff I'd hardly noticed until that moment. Fall decorations, throw pillows on the couch, a mirror near the front door.

And her paintings. I knew the ones that were hers without needing to see the signatures. She had a distinct style—somehow both realistic and whimsical. For some reason, it made me wonder how she was doing on her creek painting.

I got up and went to the spare room she'd transformed into a studio. It was there, on the easel, and as far as I could tell, it looked finished. I could practically hear the creek trickling past the smooth rocks. Smell the pine. Sunlight streamed down through the surrounding trees and reflected off the water.

It was captivating.

Just like her.

And standing in the doorway of that room, staring at her painting, it hit me square in the chest.

I was in love with her.

Why then? No idea. I should have realized it a thousand times before. And maybe I had, but I'd been too afraid to admit it.

I couldn't deny it anymore.

Clutching my chest like I was having a heart attack, I staggered back to the living room. What was I going to do? I was leaving, moving across the country.

Or was I?

What if I didn't? What if I turned down the job and stayed?

Was I actually thinking about altering my plans for her? Could I turn down my dream job?

Fuck. I collapsed onto the couch again. I didn't want to go. Didn't want to leave her. Suddenly the thought of moving across the country seemed absurd. There was no job that mattered more than she did.

Except, what if she didn't want me?

Or, more to the point, what if she didn't want me *enough*?

Twice, I'd been there. Twice, a woman had seemed to want me—seemed to want what I did. And I'd been wrong. Neither of them had wanted me enough to stay.

Kind of like my biological father.

I didn't think about that guy very often, but once in a while something would remind me that he existed. That the man who'd fathered me had abandoned his entire family—my mom and my brothers. He'd tried to drop back into my life when I made it to the pros, and dropped right back out again as soon as I'd been injured. Asshole.

If I stayed, would Penelope?

My brow furrowed and I sat up. Where was she? It was all well and good to be alone while I had a mini panic attack over realizing I was in love with my best friend. But why wasn't she home?

I was the worst at checking my phone. It had been off all day and I hadn't thought to turn it on again when I left practice. It wasn't in my pocket. What had I done with it?

After checking around the house, I looked in my truck. It wasn't there, either. Damn it. I'd probably left it at school. I didn't usually do that, but my post-migraine brain fog had been making it hard to think, especially right after practice.

I was starving, so I took a few minutes to grab a snack and drink some water. My head was gradually clearing, and as it did, my realization about Pen didn't go away. It wasn't a post-migraine delusion. I was in love with her.

And I knew before I left to go get my phone that I loved her enough to take the risk.

CHAPTER 35

Penelope

There wasn't any parking outside the gallery, but I found a spot a couple blocks up the street. Dark gray clouds hung low in the sky, almost as if they were pressing on the town, and a bitter wind cut through my jacket. I crossed my arms and walked quickly so I could get out of the cold.

The gallery looked different, even from the outside—empty and devoid of life. It reminded me of the time I saw my pet hamster after it had died. I'd been about nine years old, and the little ball of fluff had been unrecognizable, as if without the spirit of life animating it, it had turned into a different sort of thing. Not a pet at all.

Whatever life had been in the Painter's Loft, it was gone.

With that unsettling thought, I tried the door. Locked. The windows were dark and curtained, making it difficult to tell if anyone was inside. But Curt had said he'd meet me, so I knocked. A gust of wind blew, and I shivered, hunkering down in my coat.

A man I recognized as Curt Redfern opened the door. He was dressed in a long-sleeved shirt and khakis, and he was taller than I remembered.

"Ms. Fallbrook?"

"Yes, that's me. Penelope is fine."

Gesturing for me to come in, he stepped aside. "I'm Curt. Thanks again for stopping by."

"No problem. I appreciate you reaching out."

"You do very nice work," he said. "I'm glad we're able to return your piece."

He shut the door, and the warmth of the gallery was a relief after the cold wind outside. The walls were bare, and the space was cluttered with boxes. Sheets of canvas covered the windows, blocking out the rapidly waning daylight.

"Thank you, Curt," a woman's voice said.

Gina Morris emerged from the shadows at the back of the gallery. Her silver hair was styled in a smooth chin-length bob and her red lipstick stood out against her skin. She was dressed in a formfitting black shirt with long sleeves and black pants, and her matching black heels clicked on the wood floor as she walked toward us.

Curt smiled at her and walked away, disappearing into the back.

"Ms. Fallbrook." Gina held out a long-fingered hand. "So nice to see you."

I took her hand, although she let go almost before we'd actually shaken.

"Hi, Mrs. Morris. Um, thanks for reaching out about my painting."

She waved that off, as if it was of no importance. "Of course. It's been quite the process, getting ready to close."

"I'm sure it's a lot of work."

She glanced around. "Indeed. This place was Edwin's baby, not mine. I thought about keeping it open, but in the end, I realized it's time to move on."

"That's understandable."

"Are you married?"

I blinked in surprise at her question. "No, I'm not."

She nodded slowly and seemed to look past me. "It has its advantages, I suppose."

I tucked my hair behind my ear, not sure what to say.

"I'm so sorry," she said after a brief pause. "I'm being rude. Forgive me, it's difficult not to be preoccupied these days."

"You don't need to apologize. You've been through a lot."

"I'm sure you remember the classroom." She gestured toward the back of the gallery. "We've been using it as a staging area as we sort through everything. Your painting is back here."

She turned and walked away, so I followed. The classroom was much as I remembered it when Theo and I were there last, with stacks of paintings against the walls and others on display easels covered with canvas cloths.

Gina paused and looked around wistfully. "Believe it or not, this was Edwin's favorite place. I think he enjoyed teaching even more than painting."

That made me smile. "I can relate to that. I'm a high school teacher."

"Are you? How nice. What do you teach?"

"Art, actually. And I manage to throw in a bit of art history."

"That's lovely." She hesitated, as if a thought had occurred to her. "I was just about to pour myself some tea. Will you join me? I don't have proper mugs, just paper cups. But I do have lids, so you could take it with you."

"Sure, that would be great. Thank you."

An electric teakettle and a ceramic teapot that had been used for beverages and snacks during Edwin's classes sat on a side table. She poured tea into two cups and handed one to me.

"It's English breakfast," she said. "If you'd like sugar or a lid, everything is on the table there."

"Thank you."

She took a sip of her tea. I tried mine and it had already cooled enough to drink. She'd brewed it stronger than I usually did, but it wasn't bad.

"Do you mind if I ask about the gallery?" I said. "Is someone going to reopen it, or do you know yet?"

"It's possible. I have an interested buyer who'd like to reopen."

I took another sip. "I hope so. We need an art gallery in Tilikum. And this classroom is such a wonderful space."

She gestured to a wooden folding chair that was already open and unfolded another for herself. I lowered myself into the seat.

"His classes were very popular."

"I loved his class. He had such a gift. Not all artists can convey what they do in a way that encourages their students the way he did. I learned so much from him."

She smiled, but there was something odd about it, like her mouth smiled but her eyes didn't. "That's nice to hear."

A hint of discomfort crept through me, and I took another sip of tea, more to give my hands something to do than because I wanted to keep drinking it.

"He was good at teaching technique," I said, feeling the need to keep the conversation going. "But it was more than that. He made his students believe they could be more. That they could be artists."

She nodded along as I spoke but didn't reply.

I couldn't think of anything else to say. Maybe I was upsetting her by talking about her late husband. I adjusted my glasses nervously and it took me a second to realize there was something off about my vision. I moved my glasses again, but it didn't go away.

That was odd.

"I'm sorry, I don't mean to talk about something…something…" I couldn't seem to find the word.

Gina tilted her head, looking at me curiously.

"Sorry. Something painful."

"It's all right. I know Edwin was…special to you. And to many of his students."

I nodded, and a second later, I realized my eyes had closed. When had that happened? And why?

"I think I should go." I tried to stand but my head swam, and the room seemed to tilt sideways. "I don't feel well."

Gina didn't move. Just sat in her chair and watched me try—and fail—to stand.

My legs felt weak and shaky, and the cup slipped from my hand, splashing tea all over the floor. My eyes were so heavy, it was hard to keep them open. And when I tried to speak, my voice sounded far away, as if someone else were speaking.

"What's…? I don't… Can't…"

As fuzziness crowded my consciousness and the edges of my vision went gray, I wondered with a detached sense of horror if I'd been drugged.

Gina rose from her seat. I swayed, almost falling to the floor, but she caught me. Sliding her arms around me, she dragged me off the chair. I tried to move, to at least bend my knees and attempt to stand, but I had no strength. My legs wouldn't respond.

"Why?" I managed to get out, although my voice barely worked.

She didn't answer. Just kept dragging me across the floor. Fear tried to seize me, bubbling up from deep inside, but it wasn't strong enough to cut through the haze. Blackness crept in, and the last thing I remembered was a blast of cold air from outside.

CHAPTER 36

Theo

After wolfing down a quick snack, I left to find my phone. Pen would probably be home before I got back, but I figured it would be better if I had it rather than waiting until the next day. Especially if I'd left it out in the open. I wouldn't put it past one of my students to play a prank on their teacher by hiding it or something.

Plus, I still felt an undercurrent of worry. I knew Pen was with Melanie. But I didn't like what Sean had said about seeing Gina Morris outside his house. I had no idea why she'd be looking for Penelope, especially in a way that had such stalker vibes.

Granted, Sean could have been wrong. It might have been someone else, and he just thought it was Gina Morris.

Because seriously, why? What would someone like Gina Morris want with Pen? It couldn't be about her late husband and his connection to the two victims. No one knew Pen had figured that out. I hadn't even had a chance to tell Garrett yet.

None of it sat well with me. Which was why I turned toward downtown instead of heading straight for school. I'd pop into the Steaming Mug and see that she was fine.

More importantly, I was going to tell her how I felt about her.

Maybe that was the silver lining of her not being home. I'd had a chance to freak out for a minute and now I could give some thought to what I was going to say to her.

Although, as soon as I found a parking spot outside the Steaming Mug, I had a feeling rehearsing what I was going to say would be pointless. The words "Penelope, I'm in love with you" were already on the tip of my tongue. As soon as I saw her, I'd crack wide open. Even if I made a scene.

I hurried through the biting wind and flung the door open. A few people looked up from their drinks as the blast of cold air blew inside. Sucking in a breath, as if I couldn't hold it in another second and was about to announce my love for her from the doorway, I scanned the coffee shop.

But she wasn't there. Neither was Melanie.

Letting out the breath, my shoulders slumped. Well, shit.

I went back to my truck and headed to school, tapping the steering wheel as if I was mimicking a drum solo. There was no music playing, though. I was just edgy.

The parking lot was over half full—there was a volleyball game—which also meant the building was already unlocked. Grateful for small, convenient miracles, I went in and was hit with the scent of popcorn from the concession stand in the commons. I nodded to a few people and headed upstairs to my classroom.

My phone wasn't in my desk drawer, where I often kept it during the school day. I rifled through the clutter on my desk, and there it was.

That was a relief. I'd been afraid it might have fallen out of my pocket on the field during practice.

I powered it on, and it took a second for everything to load. I had a few texts, but none were from Penelope. A voicemail notification popped up, so I swiped to listen.

"Hey, it's me," Penelope said. "I'm stopping by the gallery for a few minutes before I go home. They have one of my paintings and want to return it to me. I was thinking of making soup for dinner if that sounds good to you. I—" There was a slight pause. "See you later."

The gallery?

A knot of dread formed in the pit of my stomach. Something was wrong. Very, very wrong.

I called her number. It rang. No answer. Another ring. Another. Still nothing. It rang again and went to voicemail.

"Hi, this is Penelope. Leave a message. Or just text me."

I didn't bother leaving a message.

But I did not like that she hadn't answered.

Why would they have had one of her paintings? It was too suspicious for comfort. Did Gina Morris know the sheriff's office was about to open an investigation into her late husband? *Could* she know?

My gut was screaming at me, every cell in my body telling me this was not okay. Gina Morris had been trying to stalk her; she was at the gallery and not answering her phone. I couldn't quite connect those dots, but somehow I knew they didn't lead anywhere good.

I ran down the stairs, heedless of the parents and students milling around the commons. The sun set so early that time of year, it was already dark outside, and the floodlights in the parking lot seemed to emphasize the heavy clouds hanging low in the sky.

My phone buzzed with a text as I got in my truck, but it was just Luke. I glanced at it on the off chance it had to do with Penelope—since she'd been with Melanie earlier—but it was something about football.

I pulled out of the parking lot and drove back downtown. There was a popular restaurant next to the gallery, and despite the cold, it was busy and parking was nonexistent. After circling a couple times, I settled on a spot a couple blocks away.

With my heart beating hard, I flew out of my truck and jogged down the sidewalk. The gallery was so dark, it looked abandoned. The windows were covered and not a sliver of light showed from inside. Either they'd put up some seriously effective blackout curtains, or no one was in there—at least not in the main gallery area.

Still, I pounded on the door. Maybe they were up in the loft, and it only looked like the place was one step from being haunted.

No one answered. I knocked again, harder, and waited. Still nothing.

"Fuck."

I pulled out my phone and tried calling her again. No answer.

Hunkering down in my coat against the wind, I went around the building to the alley that led behind the gallery. Pen and I had escaped out the back door the day we'd been sleuthing in disguise. Maybe it would be open. Or if someone was inside, they'd hear me knock and come answer.

The alley was dark. I found the door and tried the knob. Locked. I pounded on it—hard—and waited.

Nothing. No sound except the wind.

Where was she? Panic started to rise, and my heart raced as I jogged back to my truck. I needed to keep my head—not freak out. I'd probably just missed her. And if her phone was on silent, she wouldn't have heard my calls.

Very likely, everything was fine, and she was at home making soup wondering why I was so late. I wasn't going to panic over nothing. I'd go home, find her there, and scoop her into my arms. Then I'd tell her how I felt about her, and hope she wanted me to stay.

CHAPTER 37

Penelope

The sound of arguing drew me toward consciousness.

Confusion muddled my brain. Why were my parents fighting again? I wished they'd stop doing that.

But no, it couldn't be my parents. I wasn't a child anymore. And they hadn't been in the same room in years.

Who was arguing?

"This isn't what we talked about," a man's voice said. It was vaguely familiar, although I couldn't place him. He sounded concerned.

"Stop worrying so much," a woman said. I knew her voice, too. I'd heard it before.

"What did you use on her?"

"Does it matter?"

"Yes, it matters. What if she doesn't wake up?"

A strange thought came into my mind. They were talking about me.

"She'll wake up," the woman said, her tone filled with irritation.

"I still don't see why you had to do that."

"She's not your concern. I'll handle this. You need to go get rid of her car."

"What are you going to do with her?"

"I just told you, she's not your concern."

"But—"

"Excuse me?" she snapped, cutting him off. "When did you develop a conscience?"

"You didn't say anything about—"

"I'll explain this one more time, since it appears I haven't made myself clear."

I forced my eyes open, but I wasn't wearing my glasses. All I could see was the fuzzy outline of two people. It looked like the smaller one—was that Gina Morris?—was sticking her finger in the man's face.

"All you need to worry about right now is getting rid of her car. That's it. That's your job. When I'm finished here, I'll pick you up, and you'll help me with the rest. Or you can keep arguing with me. Don't forget, the feds would love to know about all the things you have hidden away on your computer. But I'm sure you'd have nothing to worry about. Prison is so kind to predators like you." She paused. "The choice is yours."

The man made a gurgling sound in his throat and moved away from her.

"Fine." He sounded defeated.

My stomach roiled with nausea, and I squeezed my eyes shut. I heard his footsteps walking away, and a moment later, a door opened and shut.

Where was I?

My mind struggled to catch up—to make sense of what was happening. I'd been at the gallery, talking to Gina. She must have put something in my tea. Had she moved me? I felt disconnected from my memories, but I had the fuzzy sense that I'd been in a car.

A cold sweat broke out on my forehead. It felt as if I was lying down—on a couch, maybe. Wishing my head would clear, I forced my eyes open. I was so confused.

"There you are," Gina said.

Was it Gina? It seemed like it was.

I moved my mouth, trying to speak, but it was hard to get anything out. "What…?"

She stepped close enough that her features came into focus. It was definitely Gina Morris. She gazed at me with cold, dead eyes.

"What's…what's going on?"

"What's going on, my dear, is you're here to suffer the consequences of your actions."

"Actions?"

She pulled a chair over and sat, leaning forward so her face was close to mine. "You don't need to pretend, Penelope. I know the truth."

"About what?"

"You and my husband."

"What?"

She shook her head slowly. "I knew all along. He always thought he was so clever, as if I wouldn't find out. But I always did. I tracked down each one of them and made sure they got what was coming to them. Now it's your turn."

I didn't understand what she was talking about. The haze in my brain made it hard to think.

"I don't…" I tried to lift my hand to rub my eyes, but my limbs wouldn't cooperate.

Without saying anything else, she pinched my upper arm. I felt a prick and a slight stinging.

"What is that?" I asked. "What are you doing?"

She didn't answer for a moment, then held up a syringe. "It's insulin."

"Did you just inject me?"

"That's right, Penelope. I did. The upside is, it's almost untraceable. If they found you right away, they'd probably detect the GHB I put in your tea. But I didn't give you enough to kill you. Cause of death would remain uncertain. Not that they'll find you." She paused. "The downside is, it takes a bit of time to drop your blood sugar enough to kill you."

"But…why?"

"Don't play stupid with me. They always think the wife doesn't know. What did he tell you? Did he say he'd leave me for you?"

"Edwin?"

"Of course, Edwin. He was lying, you know. He never would have left me for any of them. You were never special."

Wait… My brain struggled with what she had said, trying to make sense of it through the haze. She thought I had an affair with her husband?

"No. I didn't. I never." I took a breath, trying to make the words come. "I didn't have an affair. Amanda did."

"Amanda? My son's mistress? No, she's always had her heart set on breaking up *his* marriage, not mine."

"But I didn't."

"Why does every one of you deny it? These are your last moments on earth, Penelope. There's no point in pretending anymore. I told you, I already know. I always knew."

"No," I insisted.

"Don't lie to me," she said through gritted teeth. "I hate it when people lie to me."

"I'm not."

"You don't know what it's like. To be married to a man people admire. Especially women. They thought being an artist made him so interesting and sensitive. They'd confide in him, tell him all their dirtiest, darkest secrets. It wasn't his fault when they started throwing themselves at him. What man could resist that sort of attention? He was sensitive, and it made him weak."

"But I didn't—"

"My mistake was thinking it would end when we got older. He got gray and fat and they still didn't care. You didn't care. Why would a woman who's young and beautiful let a man like him sweat all over her? What did you think you were going to get from him?"

"Nothing."

"That's right. Nothing. That's all I ever got from him."

I stared at her as realization washed over me—as the fullness of what she was saying sank in.

"It was you," I said. "You killed them."

That seemed to surprise her. She pulled away slightly and her face went fuzzy again. "Did I?"

"The women they found. It was you."

"I don't suppose there's any harm in admitting it to you. You'll be dead soon. But do satisfy my curiosity. How did you know?"

"His paintings. He painted the places where you buried the bodies."

She let out a slight laugh. "Indeed, he did. It seemed to help him cope with his guilt."

"But he didn't kill them. You did?"

"They died by my hand, but make no mistake, it was his fault. He should have resisted temptation. He should have stayed faithful to his wife. It was only fitting he help me get rid of them."

The confusion began to recede, and things became surprisingly clear. She was trying to kill me, but it wasn't because Theo and I had discovered the truth about Edwin's paintings. She wasn't trying to cover his tracks or silence me so the truth wouldn't come out.

She thought I'd had an affair with her husband. She thought he'd had affairs with other students, too. She'd killed them because of it, and now she was going to kill me.

"Gina, I didn't." My chest felt heavy, like I couldn't breathe, as panic rose. "I didn't have an affair with him."

"Here we go again."

"I swear it. I didn't."

"He painted you! Your face. After he promised he'd never do it again. The dirty liar promised me. I couldn't take it anymore. What wife could?"

"Painted me? He painted landscapes."

"No, his favorites were the paintings of his women. His whores."

She practically spat the word. “I never let anyone see them. They were too humiliating. Once I found out who they were, I burned them. Just like I’ll burn yours when you’re gone.”

“Did you kill him, too?”

“Of course I did.” She sighed. “I almost regret that. I loved him. Even after everything he did to me, I loved that man. But I couldn’t go on living like that. You were his last. I made sure of it.”

“I swear,” I said, the words coming out in a sob. “Nothing ever happened. I was just a student.”

“You want me to show you?” She got up and stormed out of my line of sight.

I tried to reach out to feel what was around me, hoping my hands might fumble onto my glasses so I could see more clearly. But my body still wouldn’t cooperate. My limbs were so heavy it was hard to move.

Trying to get up, I turned, but I couldn’t get my legs beneath me. I rolled off the couch and onto the floor with a hard thump.

“Don’t be stupid,” Gina said. “You’re not going anywhere until I get rid of you.”

She crouched in front of me, holding a small canvas. I squinted, trying to bring it into focus, and she moved it closer to my face.

“See?” Her voice was low. “It’s you.”

It was the profile of a woman who did look remarkably like me. Maybe it was me. She had long brown hair and glasses, and her nose and chin were shaped like mine.

“That doesn’t mean I had an affair with him.”

“That’s what these always meant. He painted the students he took to bed.”

“No,” I sobbed. “No. I would never.”

She pushed me over so I was on my back, one shoulder wedged against the front of the couch. My head was starting to swim again and a strange sense of euphoria swept through me. I realized with an odd sense of detachment that I was smiling. I wanted to laugh. Why? What was so funny?

Gina seemed to leave again, her footsteps fading away. I laughed out loud, although the sound of it was feeble. I had no idea why I was laughing. It felt like my grip on reality was unraveling. She'd injected me with insulin, and it was probably dropping my blood sugar dangerously low.

I was going to die. And I couldn't seem to stop giggling.

CHAPTER 38

Theo

After circling downtown to see if I could spot Pen's car—I couldn't—I headed home. Filled with restless energy, I fidgeted and tapped on the steering wheel as I drove.

She's at home. She has to be.

Dread poured through me when I turned onto our street. The driveway was empty. She wasn't there.

Fuck.

I parked and went inside, just in case she'd put her car in the garage. Which she never did, but I was getting desperate.

"Pen?" I called, going from room to room. "Pen, are you here?"

The bedrooms and bathrooms were empty. No sign of her in her studio. No car in the garage. I checked the kitchen, looking for any indication she'd been home. Maybe she'd started dinner and realized she needed something from the store. But the kitchen was clean.

I tried calling again. Still no answer.

Maybe she'd gone to see Colleen. I looked up the number for the assisted living center and called.

She wasn't there, either. I talked to two different people, and both confirmed they hadn't seen Penelope Fallbrook since the previous weekend.

I decided to call Melanie since she'd seen her last.

"Hey, Theo," she answered.

"Is Penelope with you?"

"No. We were at the Steaming Mug earlier, but I'm home now."

"Did she say where she was going?"

Melanie hesitated. "I assumed she was going home, but I guess she didn't say specifically."

"She didn't mention anything about going to the Painter's Loft? The art gallery downtown?"

"No. What's going on? You sound worried."

"I don't know where she is and she's not answering her phone."

"Should we be concerned?"

"Maybe."

Her voice muffled. "Luke, Theo's on the phone. He's worried about Penelope."

A second later, my brother got on. "What's up?"

"Fuck, how do I even explain this?"

"I don't know. Summarize?"

"A local artist died, and Pen and I think he was a serial killer who painted the locations of the bodies. And maybe someone killed him, too. And his wife might have been stalking Pen, but at her old house. Pen left me a message saying she was stopping by the art gallery and now she's not answering her phone, and I don't know where she is."

"So, the serial killer is dead."

"Yeah."

"But the serial killer's wife was stalking Penelope?"

"Possibly."

"And the gallery?"

"Belonged to the artist and his wife."

"The serial killer and the maybe stalker."

"Yes. And Pen doesn't know the wife might have been stalking her."

"Which means she could have walked right into a spider's web and not known it."

"Exactly!"

"You obviously checked the gallery and she's not there."

"Right."

"Have you called Garrett?" he asked.

"Not yet. I called Melanie since she was with her earlier."

"And you're sure she's not at the gallery?"

"I don't think so. It's closed and locked up. Looked totally dark."

He paused. "How locked?"

I knew what he meant. My brothers and I all knew how to pick locks. It had been a basic Tilikum feud skill.

"Go," I said. "See if you can get in. I'll call Garrett."

"Don't tell him what I'm doing."

"I won't."

"I'll get Josiah and Zachary to check around town. Maybe she's just out shopping or something."

"That's what I keep hoping. But my gut tells me something's wrong."

"I get it. Call me if you find her. And don't leave your phone somewhere."

I rolled my eyes. "Yeah, I know. Be careful."

"You too."

He ended the call, and I brought up Garrett's number and hit Send. It rang, but no answer. I didn't leave a message; I'd call him back.

Just in case, I called Pen again. Still nothing.

"Damn it."

As glad as I was to have Luke checking the gallery, at least to rule it out, I knew she wasn't there.

Gina Morris. I didn't know what she'd want with Penelope, but she was the only real lead I had. If they weren't at the gallery, where else would they be? Her house? She probably lived in town, but I didn't know where.

I didn't have time for this. How could I find out where Gina Morris lived—fast?

It hit me like a shock of lightning. Amanda. If she was having an affair with Michael Morris, chances were she'd know where Gina lived. I'd had her number once, from when Aunt Louise had set me up with her. I had to still have it. I never cleaned out my contacts. I probably still had people from high school in there.

Sure enough, there she was. But would she answer? That was a good question. I hit Send.

"Hello?"

"Amanda? It's Theo Haven. I know this is weird. Please don't hang up."

"Oh. Hi." She sounded understandably surprised. "What's up?"

"Do you know where Gina Morris lives?"

"Um, yeah. Why?"

"I'm looking for my girlfriend and I think she might be with Gina." Okay, so she wasn't actually my girlfriend, but that was my dumbass fault, and as soon as I found her, I was going to fix that. "She probably just left her phone on silent, but I'll be honest, I'm a little worried about her. I want to swing by and see if she's there."

"Sure, but…what made you think to call me?"

I winced but decided there was no point in lying to her. "I kind of saw you with Michael Morris at Christmas Village."

"Oh god."

"Look, that's none of my business. I just need to know where Gina lives."

"Sure." She didn't know the address off the top of her head, but she gave me directions and a description.

"Thanks, Amanda."

"No problem. I hope she's okay."

"Yeah, me too."

I rushed to my truck and pulled out of the driveway. According to Amanda, Gina Morris lived in the southeast corner of town. I ran through the directions in my head as I drove so I wouldn't forget, and repeatedly picked up my phone, hoping Pen would call.

She didn't.

The drive felt like an hour, even if the clock on my phone insisted I pulled up out front less than ten minutes later. Amanda had said I couldn't miss it, and she was right. The house had a circular driveway, a wraparound porch, and a dark red door.

The knot of dread in my stomach tightened. I'd been hoping to find Penelope's car, but the driveway was empty, as were the spaces in front of the garage.

I got out and went to the front door. The house reminded me of the gallery—dark and seemingly empty. Glancing in a window, it looked like a move in-progress. There were boxes everywhere—some stacked, others flat or with open tops.

I knocked and waited. Nothing. Not a sound. I knocked again. "Mrs. Morris?"

Still nothing.

"Penelope?"

I beat on the door with the back of my fist. If someone was in the house, they'd have to hear me.

No answer. Not even the faint sound of footsteps.

I checked the knob. Locked. With a frustrated growl, I went looking for another door. There were two—one on the side of the house, and double glass doors in the back. Also locked. I knocked on both, but still no indication anyone was there.

Where the fuck were they?

I jogged over to the garage. Amazingly, the side door was unlocked. I didn't bother worrying about breaking and entering. I'd explain later. I just needed to find Pen.

"Penelope?" I called.

The garage was cold and dark. I flipped on a light, revealing… nothing. Just a typical garage with storage shelves, a cluttered work bench, and a midsize SUV parked on one side. The other space had a car covered by a canvas cloth. I crept in and tried the door leading into the house, but it was locked.

Since there weren't any other places to look, I left and jogged back to the front of the house. Feeling increasingly frantic, I looked in the windows. Something was wrong. I didn't know how I knew, but I was absolutely certain.

Was it possible I was freaking out over nothing? Yeah. Did I care? Nope. I was going to find Penelope by any means necessary.

Even if it meant Garrett wound up arresting me.

I didn't have anything on me to pick a door lock, so I decided to try the windows. Several were within reach, but were solid glass—not the kind that opened. One of the side windows looked like it would open, but it wouldn't budge.

Breaking the glass was not a good option, especially because I didn't know if Pen was actually inside. But I had to get in. She was in trouble.

I went to the front of the house and looked up. The second-story windows were closed, but if I could climb onto the porch roof, I could reach them. Maybe I'd be able to get one open.

Using the railing, I hoisted myself up and grabbed the gutter, hoping I didn't rip it off the edge. It took my weight as I pulled myself up and over, and I scrambled onto the roof.

The pitch was shallow, making it easy to stand. Ignoring the sound of a car driving by—*nothing to see here, just a guy on a roof in the dark*—I checked the front windows. Locked.

Careful not to slip, I made my way around to the side of the house. There was one window, leading into a dark room. I tried to lift it, and it moved. Not much, but if I could get it to slip a little more, I'd be able to get my fingers underneath.

Gritting my teeth, I splayed my hands against the cold glass and pushed upward. It opened a centimeter or two—just enough that I knew I had to keep trying.

"Come on, you bastard."

Finally, I opened it enough to wedge my hands in the gap. It still stuck, but with a stronger grip, I managed to create enough space to get in.

I squeezed through and stood. The dark room looked like it was used for storage. There were easels, canvases, empty picture frames, and plastic totes stacked on shelves. I crept across the room, careful not to trip or knock anything over, and eased open the door. It led into an equally dark hallway.

Fuck, this was crazy. I hoped Gina Morris wasn't big on firearms for home defense.

"Hello?" I called. "Sorry for breaking in. I'm looking for Penelope Fallbrook. Pen, are you here?"

Silence.

With a deep breath, I started down the hallway, checking rooms. A closet. A bedroom that appeared to be partially packed, and another that was empty. A large bathroom. A master bedroom that was obviously lived in, but no sign of Gina. Or Penelope.

I hurried down the stairs, calling for Penelope again. There were boxes and disassembled furniture, even dishes in the sink. But no Gina Morris, and definitely no Penelope.

There was one last door I hadn't tried. Easing it open, I peered into the dark room.

"Pen? Are you in here?"

I flipped on the light. Nothing. Just an empty room.

"Fuck."

My phone rang and I almost fumbled it trying to see who was calling. Garrett.

"I can't find Penelope and I think something's wrong," I said, not bothering with bullshit like hello.

"Okay, slow down," he said, his voice infuriatingly calm. "What's going on?"

"Penelope. She went to the Morrises' gallery for some reason, and no one's seen her since. And I think Gina Morris was trying to stalk her. Something's wrong. She's in trouble."

"Where are you?"

I hesitated, glancing around, and decided fuck it. "Gina Morris's kitchen. I broke in. Penelope isn't here."

"You broke in…" He trailed off. "Fuck, Theo. Okay, we'll deal with that later. Where did you last see her?"

I headed for the front door. She wasn't there, so no reason to stay. "School. She met Melanie at the Steaming Mug after work. I already talked to Mel. She figured Pen was going home after that, but Pen left me a voicemail saying she was stopping by the gallery first."

"And that's the last time you heard from her?"

"Yes." I shut the door behind me and went to my truck. "I checked the gallery, but it's locked. Seemed empty. Checked my place. Don't think she's been there. So I came here."

"She has her car?"

"Yeah." I got in my truck and started the engine.

"What's the make and model?"

"Honda CRV. Silver. I don't know the license plate."

"That's okay. We'll find it. I'm downtown, so meet me outside Harper's bakery. We'll go from there."

"Got it." I drove around the curve in the driveway and turned onto the street.

Garrett ended the call, and I headed back toward town, the knot of dread sitting heavily in the pit of my stomach.

CHAPTER 39

Theo

Garrett's police cruiser was parked in the lot behind Angel Cakes Bakery. He stood next to it, in uniform, talking to someone on his radio.

I got out and my breath misted. It was getting colder by the minute.

"We're working on tracking down her car," Garrett said. "And the neighboring agencies have been alerted. Is there anywhere else she could be?"

"I called the assisted living center where her grandma lives. She hasn't been there. And I had to go back to school to find my phone. I don't think she was there. I circled through town and didn't see her, but I could have missed her car."

"What makes you think Gina Morris was stalking her?"

"Pen's ex told me. He saw Gina parked outside his house. Sounds like more than once."

"He's sure it was her?"

"She's hard to forget. Has a distinctive look. I don't know what Gina would want with Pen, but it's weird."

"Did Penelope know them?"

"Kind of. She took one of his painting classes a few months ago. Which reminds me, Pen found a link between Edwin Morris and both of those women. They each took one of his classes not long before they disappeared."

I froze, my mouth slightly open as I realized what I'd just said. And what it might mean.

"Holy shit, Garrett. Those women took one of his classes and disappeared. Wound up dead. Pen took his class and she's missing. Edwin's dead, but what if he wasn't the killer? What if it was Gina?"

Garrett started to answer, but I kept talking.

"That would mean Penelope might be in the hands of a fucking serial killer."

"Stay calm. It's possible, but we don't know that yet."

"Calm? How the fuck am I supposed to stay calm?"

My phone rang—Luke.

"What'd you find?" I answered.

"Nothing. No one's here."

"Fuck."

"Sorry, man. Did you get ahold of Garrett?"

"Yeah, I'm with him now."

"Good. Josiah just texted. He's looking, but he hasn't seen her. Neither has Z."

A voice came on over Garrett's radio. "Squad seven, this is squad four."

"Go ahead, squad four," Garrett answered.

"I gotta go," I said to Luke. "I'll call you back."

"I've got your silver Honda CRV. Ran the plates. It's registered to Penelope Fallbrook. But unless Penelope is an adult male, she's not driving the vehicle."

"What's your location?" Garrett asked.

I shifted my weight onto the balls of my feet, ready to move, my heart racing.

"Highway two, just north of milepost ninety-nine."

Garrett met my eyes and nodded to his car. I ran around to the passenger side and got in.

"Squad four, I'm on my way to your location," Garrett said as he got into the driver's seat. "Go ahead and make contact with the driver."

"Ten-four, squad seven," the other deputy said. "Dispatch, put me out at a traffic stop, highway two, north of milepost ninety-nine. Possible stolen vehicle belonging to a missing person."

Garrett sped out of the parking lot and headed for the highway. Milepost ninety-nine was just north of town. We weren't far.

But who the fuck was driving Pen's car? And where was she?

The radio chatter continued as the other deputy talked to dispatch. Then a few moments of silence. Garrett kept driving.

"Squad seven, this is squad four."

"Go ahead, squad four," Garrett said.

"Driver claims he's Ms. Fallbrook's friend and borrowed her car with permission."

"Well, that's bullshit," Garrett said. "Who is he?"

"ID says Curt Redfern. Tilikum address."

Garrett glanced at me. "Do you know who that is?"

My voice was strangely calm. "Friend of Gina Morris."

"Fuck," Garrett said under his breath, then keyed his mic again. "Squad four, don't let him leave."

"Copy that, squad seven."

I still didn't know what was going on, but it wasn't good. The thought of something happening to Penelope made my blood run hot with rage. If anyone so much as touched her, I'd kill them.

The lights of the other deputy's car lit up the road as we approached.

Garrett pulled over. "Stay here."

"No—"

"Just wait."

"You know I can't do that."

He stopped arguing.

I got out, but as much as I wanted to rush over to Penelope's car, drag that piece of shit out, and pummel him until he told me where she was, I let Garrett take the lead.

The other deputy joined Garrett, handing him the guy's ID. They approached Penelope's car while I hung back a few feet.

"Mr. Redfern," Garrett said. "Will you step out of the car, please?"

Curt seemed to hesitate, but a second later, the door opened, and he stepped out.

"Hands where I can see them," Garrett said.

"Look, this doesn't have anything to do with me," Curt said, holding his hands shoulder height, his palms facing out.

"What doesn't?" Garrett asked.

Curt just shook his head.

"Why are you driving this car?"

"Penelope. She asked me to."

"You sure about that?"

I gritted my teeth together and clenched my hands into fists. Curt's eyes darted toward me, then back to Garrett.

"Yeah, I'm sure."

"This car is stolen." Garrett's voice was matter-of-fact. "And the owner is missing. What can you tell us about that?"

Curt shook his head but didn't reply.

"Listen." Garrett took a step closer. "We want to find her. And I think you know where she is. Why don't you tell us before this gets worse for you?"

Curt's eyes darted around again. I'd never wanted to hurt someone so badly in my entire life. It took every last shred of self-control not to tackle him to the ground.

"Gina has her," he said finally. "Gina Morris. I don't know what she's going to do. Gina wouldn't say."

"Where?" I snapped.

"My house," Curt said. "This isn't my fault. I swear. Gina didn't tell me what she was doing. I think she drugged her, and she made me help move her. Insisted on taking her to my place, not hers. Then she told me to get rid of the car."

Garrett held up Curt's license. "This your address? This is where she is?"

"Yeah, but it's not my fault." His tone was anxious. "I didn't do anything. Gina made me help her."

I heard Garrett tell the other deputy to take Curt in as I raced to get back in his car. I didn't give a shit what happened to Curt. We had to get to Penelope before it was too late.

Garrett got in and talked to dispatch while he turned the car around and started back toward town. We flew down the highway, lights flashing.

We'll get to her in time. We have to.

I'd never been so scared in my life. Not even when I'd been lying on the field wondering if I'd just been paralyzed.

We arrived at a nondescript house in a residential neighborhood. A small SUV was parked out front. Garrett didn't bother telling me to wait in the car. He got out and I followed him to the front door.

Blinds covered the windows, so I couldn't see inside. Garrett drew his weapon and motioned for me to stand back. He checked the knob. Locked.

He rattled the door again and seemed to check for something. I was about to ask him what the fuck he was doing when he nailed the door with a swift kick. Wood splintered. He kicked it again and it swung inward.

"Tilikum Sheriff's Department," he announced as he rushed inside.

I followed, close on his heels, looking frantically for Penelope. A woman screamed. It was Gina Morris. Garrett raised his weapon, shouting instructions.

"Where is she?" I yelled.

She didn't answer. Just raised her hands and started babbling about it being a mistake.

Ignoring Gina, I barreled deeper into the house.

As soon as I saw Pen, my heart nearly stopped.

She lay on the hardwood floor, one arm stretched out, as if she'd been reaching for something. Her eyes were closed and I couldn't tell if she was breathing.

"Garrett! Ambulance!"

I rushed to her side and knelt. Her forehead was clammy with cold sweat. Pressing my fingers to her neck, I found her pulse, but it was weak and slow.

"Pen," I said, brushing her hair off her face. "Come on, baby, hang in there. Please don't go."

Taking her hand in mine, I looked over my shoulder and shouted at Gina. "What the fuck did you do to her?"

No one answered. I was dimly aware of Garrett talking. Moments later, another deputy came in. I wanted to gather Penelope in my arms, but I was afraid to move her. I didn't know what had happened—if she had injuries I couldn't see.

So I leaned my forehead against hers and whispered to her, my heart ready to crack wide open if she slipped away. "Please stay with me, Pen. Please stay."

I didn't know how long it took for the paramedics to arrive. Probably minutes. But every second felt like an hour—every heartbeat felt like it might be her last.

Finally, a commotion behind me caught my attention. Paramedics rushed in.

I hopped to my feet and got out of their way. Sick with fear, I watched while they took her vitals and prepped a stretcher.

"Insulin!" Garrett shouted. "She gave her insulin! Check her glucose."

One of the paramedics pricked her finger. I held my breath until the meter beeped.

"Forty-nine," he said. "She needs a glucagon injection."

Another paramedic handed him a syringe. He cleaned her upper arm with an alcohol wipe and administered the injection.

"What's going on?" I asked.

"Her blood sugar is dangerously low." The paramedic stood. "Glucagon will help get her glucose back up, but depending on how much insulin she was given, she might need more. We're going to take her in."

The paramedics moved her onto the stretcher. She was still unconscious, and the color had drained from her face.

"Is she going to wake up?"

"It can take ten minutes or so."

I followed them as they took her out to the ambulance, ignoring the chaos of flashing lights and onlooking neighbors outside. Without asking if I could, I climbed in with her. There was no way I was leaving her, even for a moment.

They started an IV as we drove away, but it was several minutes later and she still hadn't responded.

I let the paramedics do their job, hating this helpless feeling.

If only I'd figured it out sooner.

By the time we stopped at the emergency entrance to the hospital, I was ready to tear the ambulance apart. Why wasn't she waking up? What had Gina done to her?

I got out and moved aside so they could bring her out on the stretcher. Right as they raised it to wheel her inside, her eyes fluttered open.

"It's okay." I rushed to her and placed my palm against her cheek. "We've got you. Everything's going to be all right."

She squinted. "Theo?"

"Yeah. It's me."

Closing her eyes with a sigh of relief, she smiled. And it was the most beautiful thing I'd ever seen.

"Theo," she said again.

"Hang in there. We're at the hospital, okay?"

She nodded, and I stayed by her side while the paramedics wheeled her in.

She was met by a flurry of medical personnel. They talked to the paramedics and asked her questions while they worked. Someone checked her glucose again. It was rising.

Still surrounded by doctors and nurses, she turned toward me and squinted. "Theo?"

"Yeah. I'm still here."

"Please don't go."

"I'm not going anywhere. I'll be right here."

She nodded.

And I meant it. I wasn't going anywhere. As long as she wanted me, I'd stay.

CHAPTER 40

Penelope

The chaos of activity surrounding me had died down, but my head was still fuzzy. I knew I was in a hospital, although I didn't remember arriving or how I got there. Nausea came in waves, making me want to keep my eyes closed.

Someone squeezed my hand, and I opened my eyes, wishing I had my glasses.

"Theo?" I asked.

"Hey, Pentastic. I'm here."

My stomach hurt, so I closed my eyes and took a few deep breaths. He softly brushed the hair from my forehead.

"Stay with me, Pen."

"I just feel sick."

"They said that might happen. Shouldn't last long. Do you know where you are?"

"Hospital?"

"Yeah."

"Where is she? Where's Gina?"

"Garrett got her. You're safe."

I opened my eyes again and my stomach didn't protest. But I still couldn't quite make out Theo's face.

"Do you have my glasses?"

"No, I don't know where they are. But Melanie's going to our place to see if she can find an extra pair." He helped me raise the bed so I was sitting up, then leaned closer so his features came into focus. "Can you see me now?"

I nodded. "How did I get here?"

"Ambulance."

"It was her. It was Gina. She killed those women, and her husband. She was trying to kill me."

"I know. She injected you with insulin. Probably how she killed the others, too."

"She thought I had an affair with Edwin."

"What?"

"That's why she did it. She told me he had affairs with the others, so she killed them. And I was the last one. She killed him to make sure of it."

"Why would she think that?"

"I didn't, Theo. I swear—"

He gently placed a finger on my lips. "No. I know you didn't. That's not what I mean. Do you know what made her think you did?"

"He painted my portrait. She said he painted the others, too. But I don't know if he actually had an affair with any of them."

He shook his head and touched my face. "I'm so glad you're all right."

"How did they find me?"

"You're not going to believe this," Theo said, "but it started with Sean."

"Sean? How?"

"He came to practice. God, it was just this afternoon, but it feels like it was a week ago. Anyway, he saw Gina parked outside his house a few times and thought it was weird. Like she might be stalking you or something. He didn't want to bug you, but he thought you should know. So he told me."

"That was good of him."

"It was. He did the right thing, I gotta give him that. So when I got your message that you'd gone to the gallery, I knew something wasn't right. I looked everywhere for you. Luke broke into the gallery, but don't tell Garrett. I even broke into Gina's house."

"Did you really?"

He cracked a smile. "Through a window. But you weren't there. You were at that Curt guy's house. Somehow she roped him into helping her."

"I remember them arguing. It sounded like she had dirt on him. She threatened him if he wouldn't do what she said—something about his computer and going to prison."

"I'm sure Garrett and his crew will figure it out. We found Curt driving your car. He caved pretty quick and admitted where you were. That's how we found you."

Tears stung my eyes. "I thought I was going to die."

"Yeah, I was worried about that, too. I've never been so scared in my entire life."

"You said we. We found you. Were you there?"

He nodded again, pain and worry flashing across his face. "Yeah, I was with Garrett. Once he got Curt to admit where you were, we got there as fast as we could. You were unconscious on the floor."

"Oh, Theo."

"I thought you might be…you know."

A few tears broke free and trailed down my cheeks. "You saved me?"

I didn't know why that surprised me so much. But I'd never had someone in my life who would go to such lengths for me.

Who would even notice if I was gone.

"Of course I did. Pen, I—"

"There you are." Melanie burst in—I recognized her voice—carrying what looked like a pink box. "Sorry I didn't get here sooner. Harper made me pick up cookies to bring over." She set the box on the foot of the bed.

"But I did find a pair of glasses. I hope they're yours. Although I don't think Theo wears glasses, so they must be." It took her a moment of digging through her purse before she produced my glasses with a triumphant, "Ta-da!" and handed them to Theo.

He slipped the glasses on for me and, not for the first time, his dimples were the first thing I saw.

"That's so much better," I said. "Thank you."

"How are you?" Melanie asked. "Luke said you were missing, and then we heard Theo found you, but you were on your way to the hospital."

"Yeah, it's been a weird day. I'm all right now."

"Good." Her eyes moved between Theo and me. "You know what? I'll hear the story later. You've had enough excitement for now. I'll just leave the cookies."

"Thanks for grabbing her glasses, Mel," Theo said.

"Happy to," she said with a smile, looking back and forth between us again. "Call me when you're home. And let me know if you need anything. I mean it."

"I will," I said. "Thank you."

She seemed like she was about to leave when she moved around Theo and gave me a big hug. Gratefully, I hugged her back. After another round of goodbyes and promises to call, she left.

A nurse came in to check on me and said I was doing well. My blood sugar was stable, and the drug Gina had put in my tea was wearing off. They didn't expect me to have any complications, but wanted me to stay a bit longer, just to make sure.

Theo sat down beside me again after she left. He took my hand and held it in both of his, and his forehead creased with concern.

"You aren't getting a migraine, are you?" I asked.

"No." His voice was soft. "Don't worry about me. I'm not the one who almost got killed today."

"Yeah, but stress can trigger them, right?"

He smiled. "I'm fine. Promise."

"If you need to go home and rest, it's okay."

"I'm not going anywhere."

"I know, but—"

"Pen, listen—"

"Hey." Garrett poked his head around the curtain. "Sorry to interrupt."

Dressed in his deputy uniform, Garrett stepped in and gestured to the pink box. "Was my wife here?"

"No, Melanie brought them," Theo said. "What's up?"

"I just wanted to see how things are going." His eyes moved to mine. "How are you doing?"

"Getting better. My head still feels a little fuzzy, but it's wearing off. And the nurse said my blood sugar is stable."

"Good. So glad to hear it."

"Thank you for everything."

He smiled. "Just doing my job."

"Gina Morris is locked up, right?" Theo asked. "Permanently?"

"She's in custody. She's not being particularly cooperative, so I decided to let her hang out in a cell for a while."

"She told me everything," I said. "Or most of it, at least."

"Do you want to give me a statement now?" Garrett asked. "We can wait until you feel up to it."

"No, I can do it now. I don't want to forget anything."

Garrett took notes while I recounted what I remembered—everything from my arrival at the gallery to waking up in the hospital. I told him about the tea Gina gave me, the argument I'd overheard between her and Curt, and everything Gina had said about Edwin and the other murders.

"I don't know how many women she killed, but I got the impression it was several at least," I said. "Edwin probably painted the locations of all of them."

"I bet if you go through his paintings, you'll find them," Theo said. "Or at least more clues as to where they left the bodies."

"That's one of the first things we'll do," Garrett said. "We've already secured the gallery and the Morris residence."

"I also don't know how Gina killed Edwin if she was out of town when he died," I said. "Unless the newspaper was wrong about that."

"She claims she was visiting her sister," Garrett said. "We'll interview the sister and see what she says about it. I'm betting Gina came back early from that visit, and the sister lied to give her an alibi."

"What about Curt what's-his-name?" Theo asked.

"Oh, he's happy to talk," Garrett said, and I didn't miss the undercurrent of disdain in his voice. "He just wants to stay out of prison."

"I don't think he knew Gina was trying to kill me," I said.

"That's what he told us, too," Garrett said. "It'll be up to the prosecuting attorney to sort it all out."

"You know I *had* to break into Gina's house, right?" Theo asked. "I didn't have a choice."

Garrett held up his hands. "I don't know a thing about that."

"Thanks, man."

"Like I said, just doing my job."

"Oh, shit," Theo said. "Do Josiah and Zachary know we found her? I totally forgot they were out looking."

"Yeah, Luke called them. They've been busy keeping their wives from coming down here to make sure Penelope is okay."

Theo grinned. "That tracks."

"I'll let you get some rest," Garrett said. "We might have some follow-up questions, but I'll let you know."

"Thank you," I said. "Really. I feel like I keep saying it, but thank you so much."

With a smile, Garrett nodded, then turned to Theo. "Take care of her."

"Always," Theo said.

Always. That word hung in the air, like the last note of a song.

A sad song.

Because Theo wouldn't always be there. And that reality was breaking my heart in two.

Tears gathered in the corners of my eyes as Garrett left. I didn't want to cry, especially in front of Theo. But the tidal wave of emotion crashed over me, leaving destruction in its wake.

"Hey." He pressed his palm to my cheek. "What's wrong? Are you feeling sick again?"

"No."

The concern in his eyes made everything worse. Why did he have to be so good? So kind and caring and handsome and sweet. Why did the best man I'd ever known have to be someone I couldn't keep?

My resolve to pretend everything was okay crumbled as the cracks in my heart grew. I couldn't do it anymore. Couldn't stop the words from tumbling from my lips.

"I want you to stay," I said, my voice shaky. "I know it's selfish, and I should want what's best for you. And I shouldn't have caught feelings, but I did. I keep trying to pretend I didn't and it's fine, but it's not fine, Theo. Nothing is fine."

And then he did the strangest thing. He smiled.

It wasn't just any smile. It was a wide, dimpled, bright, ecstatic smile.

Then it got worse. He laughed.

"Don't laugh at me," I sobbed. "I've had a horrible day."

"My beautiful Penelope." He cupped my cheeks and leaned in, planting a soft kiss on my lips. "I'm not laughing at you."

"Yes, you are."

"No, I swear I'm not. Pen, before I realized you were missing, I was trying to figure out how to tell you. I'm in love with you."

I blinked a few times. "Am I hallucinating?"

"No, this is real. I'm so in love with you. And if you want me to…" He hesitated and the raw vulnerability in his eyes brought fresh tears to mine. "If you want me, I'll stay."

My lips parted and I stared at him as the tears rolled down my cheeks. Had he just said he'd stay? For me?

"It's all I want. I'd go with you if you asked me to, but—"

"No," he said. "It wouldn't be the right thing. You need to be here. And I need to be with you."

"Can we go back to the part where you said you're in love with me? Because if you really said that, you just turned the worst day of my life into the best."

He smiled and kissed me again. "I love you."

"I love you, too. I love you so much and I want you to stay."

"That's all I wanted to hear. Well, that and *We found her* and *She's fine*."

I laughed softly. "You did find me."

"I wasn't going to stop until I did."

He kissed me again, deep and slow. It sounded like a nurse came in, but he didn't stop, and I didn't care.

Theo had saved me. He'd searched for me, he loved me, and he was going to stay.

CHAPTER 41

Penelope

Although I felt fine, Principal Larson insisted I take the rest of the week off. I was worried I'd be bored with Theo at school and football practice, but it wound up not being as bad as I'd expected. Melanie invited me to lunch twice, I met Marigold for coffee, Audrey and Harper invited me to have tea and cookies—which meant I got to play with their babies—and Marlene and I went Christmas shopping. It actually turned into a pretty amazing week.

Okay, so I'd almost been murdered by a serial killer, but aside from that—amazing.

The awesomeness culminated on Friday night with another Timberwolves postseason win. Luke, Melanie, and I drove the two hours to the game, so we were there, along with most of the Haven clan, to cheer them on. One more win, and they'd be going to state.

I screamed so much, I completely lost my voice. But later that night, Theo said I sounded cute when I was all raspy. And we celebrated together—in bed.

Saturday, we went to the assisted living home to visit Grandma. I'd talked to her on the phone the day after my ordeal, so she knew what had happened. But I hadn't visited with her since, and I knew she was anxious to see me with her own eyes.

It was the weekend before Thanksgiving, and Tilikum Gardens

Village was decked out with paper turkeys, cornucopias, and *Happy Thanksgiving* signs. Apparently, word about what had happened to me had already spread. As soon as Theo and I walked in, we were accosted by residents and staff, all anxious to make sure I was really okay.

After many reassurances that I was fine, Theo and I made our way across the common area to Grandma.

She had her wheelchair pulled up to a table with a puzzle spread out in front of her. I didn't miss the tears that gathered in her eyes as we approached.

She pushed back from the table and held out her arms. "Oh, Penny."

"Hi, Grandma."

I leaned down to hug her, and she held me tight.

"My darling girl. I'm so glad you're all right."

"I'm fine. I promise."

I straightened, and she held out her arms for Theo.

"Come here, young man. I don't know how to thank you."

He hugged her, bringing tears to my eyes. I dabbed beneath my glasses before they could fall.

"My goodness." She waved her hands in front of her face, as if to dry her eyes, then wheeled herself back to the table. "Come on, now, have a seat. I'm done making a scene. What a week it's been."

Theo and I sat, and he gave me a subtle smile that puckered his dimples. Despite everything I'd been through, I couldn't stop smiling.

"So it really was the wife all along." Grandma shook her head. "Terrible business. How did she do it?"

"Theo's brother Garrett said she finally confessed to everything," I said. "She did the same thing to the other victims that she tried to do with me—drugged them and injected them with a high dose of insulin."

"Her husband as well?"

I nodded. "Sadly, yes. He was diabetic, so that's how she got it.

And because he wasn't in the best health anyway, no one thought his death was suspicious."

"And she claimed she was out of town when it happened," Theo added. "But the whole story about her coming home from her sister's and finding him was a lie. Garrett said the sister already confirmed she left early."

"How many other victims were there?" Grandma asked. "Do they know yet?"

"Probably five," I said. "That's how many notes they've uncovered in his paintings. There could be more, but I hope not."

"I suppose we were wrong about it being the son," she said. "Although, I still say that was a good theory."

Theo and I shared a glance. We'd learned a lot about the Morris family drama that week.

"Michael didn't have anything to do with his father's death, but it came out in the investigation that he stole a bunch of money from his mother," I said. "I guess it was money he thought he was getting from his father, but didn't. I don't know the details, but he's facing criminal charges as well."

"Yeah, his life is a dumpster fire," Theo said. "His wife left him. And I don't know what's happening between him and Amanda, but it sounds like she might have bailed on him as soon as law enforcement got involved. She's under investigation as well, although she hasn't been arrested."

"Can't say I feel sorry for him," Grandma said.

"Nope," Theo said. "Not a bit."

"What do you think will happen to the man who was helping her?" Grandma asked. "What was his name?"

"Curt Redfern," I said. "And we don't know yet. He'll probably be brought up on charges. But as far as we know, he wasn't involved with the other murders. He'd been a friend of the family for a long time and stepped in to help Gina after Edwin died."

"It looks like she was blackmailing him," Theo said. "Apparently he has an affinity for… let's just say a certain type of explicit content that is highly illegal. I don't know how Gina found out about it, but she was holding that over him so he'd help do her dirty work."

"Disgusting," Grandma said. "Both of them, disgusting."

"So disgusting," I agreed.

Grandma reached across the table and took my hand in hers. "Thank goodness neither of them will hurt anyone else."

"Exactly," I said. "It's over."

"Colleen!" an elderly male voice called out. "Colleen Wilson!"

A subtle grin crossed Grandma's face as Maury Haven wheeled himself out of the elevator. His face was red, and a vein protruded from his forehead. He had something in his lap and my eyes widened when I realized what it was.

A plate with jiggly red Jell-O in the shape of an egg.

Oh, no.

Maury's lips seemed oddly loose, and his jaw looked as if it didn't fit together quite right.

"You she-devil," he spat, pointing at her.

Yep, no teeth.

Theo put a fist to his mouth, trying to keep from laughing. I gaped at Maury, horrified, as he wheeled his way across the room to our table.

Grandma pressed her fingertips together. "Well, hello Maury. How are you today?"

He picked up the plate, sending ripples through the red gelatin. I could see the outline of his dentures inside.

"How am I? How do you think I am? You did this!"

She batted her eyelashes at him. "Me? How could I have possibly done that?"

Theo coughed to cover his laugh.

"I know it was you," Maury said, his wrinkled face twisting in a scowl. "Admit it."

Grandma took a deep breath. "Fine. It was me. I Jell-O'ed your teeth."

For a long moment, they stared at each other—eyes narrowed and shoulders set. My heart started to race. Had she gone too far? What was he going to do?

Out of nowhere, Maury's face erupted in a wide, toothless grin. He laughed, a loud guffaw that carried through the entire room.

Grandma followed, laughing so hard she was almost wheezing.

Theo laughed along with them, but I couldn't stop staring open-mouthed.

"You are a dickens, Colleen," Maury said, his shoulders still shaking. "But this might be your best yet. How on earth did you do it?"

She dabbed the corners of her eyes. "As if I'd tell you."

Maury shook his head. "Left it right outside my door, too. I don't know how you pulled this off, but it's one for the record books. Well done, Colleen. Well done."

"Thank you, Maury."

"You know I have to get you back, though."

"Oh, of course."

"Good," Maury said with a nod and slid the plate onto the table. "Want to help me get my teeth? I could get some spoons."

Theo laughed again and I tried not to gag.

"No, thank you," I said with a slight shudder.

"You sure?" He scooped some Jell-O off the top and slurped it up. "It's good. Strawberry."

I shook my head. Theo kept laughing.

"No one wants to eat that, Maury," Grandma said. "It has your teeth in it."

"We could just eat around them." He shrugged and put the plate back in his lap. "If this stuff stains, you owe me denture tablets."

"They'll be fine." Grandma waved a hand. "Go get your teeth. You look like a newt."

Maury chuckled as he wheeled himself back to the elevator.

Still open-mouthed, I turned to her. "How did you do that?"

She shrugged. "I had to call in a favor, but it was worth it."

"What kind of favor?"

"Don't you worry about it, Penny." She reached over and patted my hand. "But many thanks to you, Theo. It took me a while to pull it off, but it was an excellent suggestion."

"That was well played, Colleen." He reached his fist across the table.

With a big smile, Grandma bumped his fist with hers.

"So, Theo," she said, her tone indicating a change of subject, "have you figured out that you're in love with my granddaughter yet, or do I need to intervene?"

Theo smiled. "No, ma'am, no intervention necessary. I'm very much in love with your granddaughter." He took my hand. "And I'm staying here in Tilikum."

"I knew you would." She nodded appreciatively. "Didn't take you as long to figure it out as I thought it might. Maybe some of the Havens have good heads on their shoulders."

"A few of us aren't complete idiots."

"That's good to hear," she said. "I'm happy for you both. You make a beautiful couple."

"Thanks, Grandma," I said.

The cafeteria had opened for breakfast, so we joined her for omelets. Theo gave her a few more prank suggestions—none of them involving dentures, thankfully—and we made plans to come over for a Thanksgiving meal on Thursday. Hers would be midday, and the Havens were celebrating later, so we'd have time for both.

It would be a lot of food, but a lot of family, too. I couldn't wait.

After a long visit—we helped finish her puzzle—it was time to say goodbye. I hugged her again and tried not to tear up at her whispered, "I love you, Penny."

I loved her, too. So much.

Theo held my hand on the way out to his truck. Outside, a few flakes of snow drifted from the low-hanging clouds and our breath misted as we walked. We got in and he turned on the engine.

"You know what?" He glanced back at the building. "I forgot something. I'll be right back."

"What did you forget?"

"My phone. I think I set it on the table."

"Do you want me to come?"

"No, I'll just run in and grab it. You stay warm." He leaned across the center console and gave me a quick kiss. "I'll be right back."

He got out of the truck, and it was odd, but I thought I caught the outline of his phone in his back pocket.

But maybe not. The pocket was probably just worn.

Time ticked by and he didn't return. He must not have found his phone. It made me wonder if he'd actually left it at home.

Finally, he came back and got in. With that dimpled smile that made my insides swirl, he leaned over and kissed me. "Sorry. Found it."

We drove away, and I couldn't stop smiling. Whether from the Jell-O prank or seeing Theo fist-bump Grandma Colleen, or just because I was so deliriously happy, I didn't know.

Probably all of the above.

CHAPTER 42

Theo

I didn't know about Pen, but I was already full, and Haven Thanksgiving hadn't even begun.

We'd spent the early afternoon with Grandma at the assisted living center, and the food was fantastic. And when we arrived at my parents' place for holiday meal number two, there was a counter full of appetizers. I felt like I'd been eating all day.

The house smelled amazing, though, so I intentionally moved away from the snacks. Had to leave room for turkey.

Everyone was there, including all the nieces and nephews. The house was filled with commotion, conversation, and laughter as babies were passed around, kids played, and adults chatted about everything from sports to parenting to wedding plans.

Once again, I watched, knowing I had a big announcement to make. They didn't know I was staying, or that Penelope and I were more than friends.

A lot more.

Cracking a smile, I watched as she sat in the living room, huddled with Melanie and Marigold over wedding magazines and a big binder. I knew how much it meant to her to have made new friends. Having a work bestie was one thing, but she needed more. And seeing her bond with the women in my family was like the whipped cream on top of a slice of homemade pumpkin pie—kinda made things perfect.

I'd already contacted Kevin at Carolina to let him know I had to rescind my acceptance of their offer. He was disappointed, but understood and thanked me for letting him know well in advance. They had plenty of time to find another candidate.

After that conversation, I'd been left with a profound sense of peace. I had no doubt I'd done the right thing.

I caught sight of Owen out of the corner of my eye. He held his baby sister, Isla, and laughed as she tried to grab the crackers he was eating. Picking my way across the room, I stepped over my nephew Will and made my way to Owen.

Isla grabbed his nose. With a chuckle, he took her hand and pretended to nibble on her fingers, making her squeal with laughter.

"Hi, Uncle Theo." He gently stopped Isla from batting him in the face.

"Hey, can I talk to you for a minute?"

"Sure. About the game? Don't worry, I'll get a good night's sleep even though we don't have school tomorrow."

"No, I'm not worried about the game." I hesitated, glancing around. I wanted the chance to tell Owen privately first, so I gestured for him to come with me.

He followed me down the hallway. "Is everything okay?"

"Yeah, fine. There's just something I need to tell everyone, and I wanted you to hear it first." I stopped, and Isla leaned toward me, so I scooped her into my arms. "Hi, sweetheart."

She smacked me on the nose and giggled.

"Sorry, I accidentally taught her to do that," Owen said.

"She's fine." I kissed her little fingers. "Anyway, I'm not taking the college job. I decided to stay."

His eyes lit up and he cracked a smile. It made him look so much like his dad. "Really? That's awesome."

"Yeah, so you're stuck with me as your coach for two more years. Hope that isn't bad news."

"It's great news. I was kinda hoping you'd stay. Not just for football. It would be weird without you."

"Yeah, I'm meant to be here." Isla tried to grab my nose, and Owen reached over to take her.

"Thanks, Uncle Theo. Glad you're staying."

"Me too."

We went back to the living room, and Owen handed Isla to their dad. Pen was still engrossed in conversation with Melanie and Marigold, and there seemed to be a lull in the frenzy of cooking. Mom sipped a glass of wine while she chatted with Audrey and Josiah, and Dad had my twin nieces in his lap.

Looked like as good a time as any.

"Hey, everybody," I said, raising my voice above the din of conversation. "Can I say something real quick?"

The noise quieted and all eyes moved to me. Even the babies looked in my direction.

Penelope adjusted her glasses and watched me with a little smile on her face.

"I think everyone knows her already, but I'd like to introduce my *girlfriend*," I said, emphasizing the word, "Penelope."

There was a chorus of *awww*s, a few people gasped, and Melanie wrapped her in a big hug.

Pen's cheeks flushed, and she lifted her hand in a shy wave.

"I also wanted to let you all know that I've come to a big decision. I declined the job at Carolina. I'm staying."

Zachary raised his arms in the air. "Yes! I knew it." He turned to Luke. "Pay up, brother. I was right."

Luke shook his head as he got out his wallet and handed Zachary a twenty. "You called it."

"You guys bet on whether Theo would stay?" Josiah asked.

"Of course we did." Zachary moved over to the couch and held his hand out. "Come on, Dad. You too. Pay up."

Dad scowled and the girls had to scramble off his lap so he could dig a bill out of his pocket.

"Paul," Mom said, her tone gently scolding.

Dad just grunted and handed the twenty to Zachary while Marigold shook her head at her husband.

"What?" Zachary asked. "I was betting on you, Theo. Unlike these sorry excuses for Havens, I believed in you."

"I don't know if that's a compliment or not, but whatever," I said. "Enjoy your winnings."

Grinning, he held up the money. "Oh, I will."

"If there aren't any other big announcements," Mom said, "it's time to start getting dinner on the table."

We all looked around at each other, but no one spoke up, and several people joined Mom in the kitchen.

The truth was, I would have another announcement soon. It wasn't quite time for that yet, but I had a plan.

The scent of food wafted through the house as the last of the dinner preparations were made. I wandered toward the chaos in the kitchen to see if they needed help. Penelope joined me, but it looked like staying out of the way was the better option.

Taking Pen's hand, I showed her the family photos in the hallway. She especially loved the one of the six of us boys with baby Annika in the middle. There were more of us as kids, and Mom had rearranged things so she could add wedding photos and pictures of all her grandchildren.

The front door flew open, and Aunt Louise came in, followed by Uncle George. Her tracksuit was brown and orange and she carried a pie covered with foil. George shut the door behind her and gave me a nod.

"Happy Thanksgiving," Aunt Louise said with a smile. "Theo, I'm so glad you're here. I have the best news. Let me give this to your mom. Don't move."

I glanced at Pen and shrugged. "My aunt. She's a whirlwind."

Aunt Louise and Uncle George went back to the kitchen, and a moment later, Louise returned.

"We're not staying," she said. "We ate already. I brought over a cherry pie, and I was hoping to see you, my handsome nephew."

I opened my mouth to introduce her to Pen, but she didn't give me the chance.

"I was talking to my friend Linda, and would you guess where her daughter lives now?"

I had no idea who she was talking about. "I don't know. Who's Linda's daughter?"

"Willow Johnson," she said, as if I should have known. "You remember."

I didn't, but she didn't give me a chance to say that, either.

"Are you ready for this?" She clasped her hands to her chest. "South Carolina. Isn't that serendipitous? And that's not all. She's in town for the holiday, and I already set up a date for you on Saturday."

I opened my mouth to reply, then glanced at Penelope. The poor thing looked like she wanted to crawl into a hole.

Putting my arm around her, I drew her against me. "Aunt Louise, I haven't had the chance to introduce you to my girlfriend, Penelope Fallbrook."

Louise gasped and she put her fingers over her mouth. "Oh dear. Oh my. This is…?"

With a big grin, I nodded.

"Goodness, Theo, you should have told me. Here I am making a fool of myself in front of your lovely new friend. My dear, I am so sorry. I didn't realize. But you can't blame an aunt for trying. I have their best interests at heart, I assure you. And here I thought for sure I'd found the one."

"It's okay, Aunt Louise," I said. "You didn't know."

She let out a heavy sigh. "I suppose I'll have to tell Linda to cancel. Maybe it's for the best. I'm not actually sure if Willow agreed to the date, but of course I assumed she would."

"I'm sure Willow will be fine," I said.

"She will, although she won't do better than one of my nephews."

Louise gasped again. "I'm fresh out of nephews. Except for…you know. But there isn't much I can do about him."

"I guess you'll have to find a new hobby."

"Nonsense. There are plenty of eligible bachelors in this town. My gift won't go to waste." She smiled at Penelope. "So lovely to meet you, dear."

"Nice to meet you, too."

"George, honey!" she called as she made her way back to the kitchen. "Time to go!"

Leaning down, I placed a soft kiss on Pen's lips. "I am so sorry about that."

"It's all right. I wasn't worried or anything. I just didn't know what to say."

"Most of us don't know what to say when Aunt Louise puts on her matchmaking hat. But that was a new level of awkward, even for her."

Aunt Louise and Uncle George left, and the hustle and bustle in the kitchen continued. I caught part of Dad and Josiah's conversation about the size of our growing family and whether they might be able to extend the dining room. It was a log home, so that wouldn't be an easy feat. Josiah suggested an addition—a big gathering space off the kitchen, extending into the back. Dad seemed excited about the idea, and I had a feeling I knew what I'd be doing next summer.

Mom emerged from the kitchen and seemed as if she was about announce that dinner was served—or at least ask for more help—when her phone rang, the chiming ringtone carrying over the noise of clattering dishes and multiple conversations. She picked up her phone from a side table and a look of alarm crossed her features.

Something about her reaction caught everyone's attention. The room went quiet, and we all stared at her, as if an unspoken signal had clued us all in to who it was.

Reese.

"Hello?" she answered, then paused. "It is you. Happy Thanksgiving."

My brothers and I cast glances at each other. What were we going to do? He'd never called when we were there before.

"Actually, we're all here," Mom said, and looked around at everyone watching her. "Yes, I think they do."

Penelope squeezed my hand. Anger pulsed through me, followed by something else. Sadness, maybe. I was mad at my brother, sure. But I also missed him.

"No, I know you can't," Mom said. "That's okay, I'm just so glad to hear from you. How are you? Is everything all right?"

We waited in silence while she listened.

"Good. I'm happy to hear that." She paused again, listening. "They're all wonderful. Growing up so fast."

Zachary moved like he was going to try to take the phone from Mom, but Luke stopped him. Josiah shook his head.

Dad watched his wife, his expression impossible to read.

"All right, thank you for calling." She briefly closed her eyes. "I love you, too, Reese."

Mom lowered her phone, and the babies started to babble, breaking the tense silence. She took a deep breath as if to steady herself. "Before you ask, I don't know where he is. He never tells me. But he's doing fine."

After another moment, conversations rose again. Dad moved toward Mom and led her down the hallway. That was what she needed—her husband comforting her, not her other kids hounding her with questions she couldn't answer.

"I guess every family has a bit of drama," I said to Pen. "My brother Reese left Tilikum and hasn't been back. None of us really knows why."

"That's so sad."

"It is. I was mad at him for a long time, but at this point, I don't think I'd punch him in the face if I saw him."

She smiled. "That's good at least."

"Zachary would, though." I glanced at Z having an animated discussion with Luke and Josiah—undoubtedly about Reese. "Unless his wife stopped him."

"Marigold seems like she's good at keeping the peace."

"Yeah, she's probably the only woman in the world who can handle him."

As if to prove me right, Marigold deftly stepped in front of Zachary and distracted him with their daughter, Emily. It worked like a charm. Moments later, he was making her laugh.

It didn't take long for Mom and Dad to reappear. Mom didn't try to hide her emotions, but she made it clear she wanted to enjoy a nice holiday dinner.

So that was what we did.

The dining room was packed, and the food was delicious. There was more talk about building an addition to accommodate our numbers. I alternated between holding Pen's hand and resting my hand on her thigh as we ate, enjoying the satisfaction of knowing she was one of the reasons our family was growing—and would hopefully be the reason it grew even more.

And when the conversation turned to the upcoming football game, it was all I could do not to smile like an idiot. Not because I was confident my team was going to win, although I was. But because it wasn't going to be just any football game. And my entire family was going to be there to see it.

Even more importantly, Penelope wasn't going to see it coming.

CHAPTER 43

Penelope

Maybe it was the stadium lights glinting off tiny flakes of snow, but the air seemed to sparkle with excitement as I parked at Tilikum High School. I was dressed in my green and white hat, and I'd put on Theo's hoodie. It was a little big on me, but I loved wearing it, even when it was cold enough that I had to put a coat on over it.

"Are you sure you're going to be warm enough?" I asked.

Grandma sat next to me, bundled in her winter coat, hat, and scarf. "I'll be fine."

Theo had invited her to come to the game, and I'd been surprised at how excited she was. She'd never been a sports fan, and tended to prefer staying home, especially when the weather was cold. But she'd enthusiastically accepted.

I was excited to have her there. It was a part of my life I wanted to share with her.

I'd picked her up and managed to get her wheelchair in the back. She waited while I got it back out and moved it over to the passenger side. She was able to maneuver herself from the car into her seat, and I spread a blanket over her lap to help keep her warm.

We made our way to the stadium behind the school. The game hadn't even begun, and the crowd roared, students and their families chanting along with well-known cheers. It was the first time in recent memory that the Timberwolves had made it to the playoffs, and they were one game away from going to state.

My heart fluttered and my body tingled with nervousness. Theo had been his usual calm, confident self all day, but I knew him too well to miss the hint of anticipation in his eyes. Fortunately, it had looked more like excitement than nerves.

After showing my staff ID, I pushed Grandma up the ramp to the bleachers. I went to the railing and looked down. Theo was on the sideline dressed in a thick black coat, talking to his players.

I remembered the game earlier in the season when I'd come while waiting for a pizza order. That Penelope seemed like a different person.

It was hard to believe how far I'd come, and how much had changed in such a short period of time. I was living a different life—one that was infinitely better.

One I hoped would last forever.

As if he could sense my presence, Theo turned, his dimples appearing with his smile. I was so excited, I bounced up and down, waving like a dork. Then I held out my fist. He did the same, but instead of spreading his fingers wide and making an explosion sound, he lifted his hand to his mouth and blew me a kiss.

Biting my lip, I giggled and waved again.

I loved him so much.

There was a designated wheelchair spot in the front row, so I moved Grandma and took the seat next to her. A moment later, Melanie and Luke arrived. Melanie rushed over and gave me a big hug. I introduced her to Grandma, and they took the seats next to me.

Theo's parents, siblings, nieces and nephews arrived—including the babies, all bundled up against the cold. They packed in behind us, taking up several rows. Melanie's parents came, too, as did the other big Tilikum family, the Baileys.

"I've never been so nervous for a football game," Melanie said. "I miss not caring about sports. This is so stressful."

"They're going to do great," I said.

"Pickle?"

"What?"

She held out a large dill pickle. "Do you want one? I have plenty."

"No, thanks."

With a shrug, she took a bite.

The cheerleaders started another cheer while the players warmed up on the field. I pulled my hands into the sleeves of my coat to keep them warm and watched Theo confer with Coach Lewis on the sidelines. He glanced up, and for a second, our eyes met. His subtle smile sent a shiver down my spine—one that had nothing to do with the cold.

The announcer came on and welcomed everyone to the game. The roar of the crowd was so loud, he had to wait for us to quiet down before he could continue. Timberwolves fans clapped politely as the visiting team was announced and each player took the field.

When it was time for the home team, we all surged to our feet. Each starting player was announced to renewed cheers. Our entire section went wild when Owen's name was called, and again when head coach Theo Haven was introduced. Theo lifted his hand in a wave and our eyes met again.

So many butterflies.

Grandma raised her eyebrows at me as I sat down.

"What?" I asked.

"Nothing."

The announcer's voice boomed over the loudspeaker again. "Before we begin, we'd like to thank the faculty of Tilikum High School. Can any faculty members in attendance come down to the field?"

"That's you." Melanie nudged me. "Get down there."

Suddenly self-conscious, I hesitated, glancing around to see if any of my coworkers were there. Theo was on the field, of course, but would I be the only other one?

Derek got up from his spot and walked down the stairs to the field. So did Jeremy and Sharon. That probably meant I needed to go, too.

"Go on, Penny," Grandma said.

With a deep breath, I got up and adjusted my glasses. Melanie cheered for me, her voice carrying over the din. My coworkers lined up in a row, and Theo made his way to the end so I could stand next to him. I gave him a grateful smile. He winked back.

"Ladies and gentlemen, our Tilikum High School faculty."

The crowd clapped and a few people whistled. Snow fell softly around us, and the lights were bright from where I stood. I lifted my hand in a little wave and was ready to dart back to the bleachers, when Theo slipped his hand in mine.

Our relationship wasn't a secret, exactly, but we'd been keeping it quiet at school, avoiding any physical contact in front of our students, even hand-holding. Either Theo wasn't thinking about the fact that most of the student body was watching, or he'd decided not to care.

He squeezed my hand, and I squeezed back. Our coworkers went back to the bleachers, but Theo didn't let go. I glanced at him, wondering what was going on. The game was about to start. Didn't he need to take his place on the sideline?

He winked again, then lifted his other hand, as if to tell the crowd to give him a minute.

What was he doing?

Turning to face me, he drew something out of his pocket and slowly lowered himself to one knee.

The crowd went wild.

My mouth dropped open and my eyes widened. Theo Haven, my best friend and the most wonderful man I'd ever known, knelt in front of me with a ring.

An engagement ring.

For me.

He tried to say something, but the crowd was too loud. From the corner of my eye, I could see his players jumping up and down, shouting, and putting their hands on their heads, like they couldn't believe what they were seeing.

Neither could I.

Finally, Theo had to raise a hand again to get the crowd to quiet. A hush settled over the stadium and snowflakes fluttered softly around us.

"Penelope," he began, "you're the best friend I've ever had, and so much more. I love you. And maybe this seems crazy, but I've never been more sure of anything. I want you to be my wife. Will you marry me?"

I was so overwhelmed with happiness, I wasn't sure whether I was laughing or crying. Probably a bit of both.

"Yes," I managed, finally. "Yes!"

With a dimpled grin, he took my hand and slid the ring on my finger.

The crowd erupted in cheers as he stood. Wrapping his arms around me, he picked me up off my feet and twirled me around.

Our lips met in a kiss to renewed whistles and applause. Then he set me on my feet, took my left hand in his, and raised it into the air.

I'd always wondered what it would feel like to score a game-winning touchdown, but getting engaged to Theo Haven was better than any big win. It was everything.

Theo leaned down and spoke close to my ear. "I hope you don't mind the crowd. I just thought this would be fun."

"So fun," I said, smiling so big my face was going to hurt later. "It's perfect."

"And I want everyone to know you're mine."

He kissed me again, his tongue doing things that were slightly inappropriate, considering it was a family-friendly event. But I didn't care. It was the best moment of my entire life.

But the game did need to begin. Theo let go and I hurried off the field to another round of cheers and applause from his family. Melanie gave me a tearful hug and Grandma beamed.

"Oh, Penny," she said. "That was worth the wait."

Was it ever. Theo was worth everything.

The outcome of the game wouldn't have diminished my giddiness by an ounce, but the win was even more exciting. The Timberwolves came out on top, securing their spot at the state finals.

A week later, they played in the biggest game in Tilikum High School history, and became the first Timberwolves team to win the state championship.

It was amazing. And still not as incredible as the moment when Theo Haven got down on one knee. For me.

Because that was the thing—he wanted me. Penelope. The weird art teacher who couldn't see without her glasses and constantly got paint on her face. The girl who'd started to wonder if life was going to pass her by and all her dreams would have been just that—dreams, nothing more.

Until a football coach named Theo Haven came along and became my best friend, my roommate, my boyfriend, and finally, the true love of my life.

EPILOGUE

Theo

THE FOLLOWING SUMMER…

The sun glinted off the blue water and a light breeze rustled through the tropical foliage. Waves crashed against the sand, their soothing rhythm lulling me into deep relaxation. A bead of sweat dripped down my back, but I didn't mind the heat. I was stretched out on a lounge chair on a beach in Hawaii, watching the love of my life.

Penelope's easel was wedged into the sand to keep it steady. Dressed in nothing but a pink and orange bikini, with a palette in one hand and a paintbrush in the other, she tilted her head, scrutinizing her work.

She'd captured the beach beautifully, adding her signature touch of magic to the scene. I didn't know how she did it, but her paintings always had a certain glow, as if she could see the beauty of the natural world in a way the rest of us couldn't.

Our wedding had gone off without a hitch. We'd kept with what had become a Haven family tradition and had it at Salishan Cellars. The winery had been the perfect setting, and the weather couldn't have been better.

Watching her walk down the aisle had been an intense experience. It had hit me just how close I'd come to missing out on the best thing that had ever happened to me. A few wrong moves—a few different choices—and I'd have been heading to South Carolina, alone, convinced I was meant to be that way. That I didn't need anyone else. It wasn't worth the risk.

But Pen? She was worth everything.

She'd been stunning on our wedding day. But to be honest, I was enjoying her on the beach in a bikini just as much.

What can I say? My wife is hot.

She glanced at me over her shoulder. "Are you bored?"

I grinned. "Not even a little bit."

"Are you sure? I can finish this later if you want to do something else."

"Baby, I'm good. Take as long as you want."

"What do you think so far?" She gestured to her painting with the brush.

"It's beautiful."

"Thanks. I'm pretty happy with it."

"You should be."

She used her forearm to brush a strand of hair off her face and managed to swipe her cheek with blue paint. She didn't seem to notice. Still grinning, I shook my head. She was so damn cute.

I half dozed in the sun while she worked, cracking my eyes open every now and then to appreciate her painting—and her curves in that bikini.

The beach started to get busier as people found places to sit around us. As much as I would have loved to be on a private island, alone with Pen, we were teachers, not billionaires. And neither of us minded. We'd spent the week snorkeling, sightseeing, lounging on the beach, and eating delicious food.

Slow, lazy mornings, tangled in the sheets together were the best part.

It all had me thinking. We were starting a new season of life together, and that was great. But was I ready for the next big thing?

I was. Gazing at my wife as she painted, I imagined her with our baby in her belly. I thought about what it would be like to bring a new little Haven home with us. I wanted that. I wanted to have a family with her.

But was she ready? I wasn't going to push her into anything. But the more I thought about it, the more I realized I *was* ready. And I hoped she would be, too.

She stepped back from her painting and tilted her head again. "I think it's finished."

"I love it."

"Thank you. I kind of love it, too. Are you ready to go back to the room? It's getting a little windy."

"Yeah, let's go."

I stood to pack up our things, when a couple walking close to the waterline caught my eye. They were hand in hand, and I squinted, wondering if I was seeing things.

"Pen, is that…?"

"Is what?" She looked around and gasped. "Oh my gosh. It is! It's Jeremy and Ashley. Are they—"

As if to answer her question, they stopped to share a long kiss while the water lapped at their feet.

"We knew it!" Pen said, then covered her mouth. But they were too far away to hear her.

"We called it," I said. "I wonder why they were keeping it a secret?"

"Who knows? Maybe they wanted privacy."

"Or maybe they were trying to stay just friends."

"And caught feelings," she said with a shrug. "It happens."

We watched as they walked farther down the beach. Then I held out my fist, and Pen bumped it.

We weren't bad at this detective stuff.

I helped her pack up our things and carried the canvas and easel back to our hotel. Our room had a balcony with a stunning view of the ocean. I propped her still-wet painting against a wall so it could dry and tucked the easel into a corner.

"What should we do next?" she asked. "Do you want to go swimming? Or are you hungry?"

"I could eat." I sat on the edge of the bed and reached for her. "But first, come here."

Drawing her close, I slid my hands around her waist. She draped her arms over my shoulders as I brought her in for a kiss.

"You have a little paint on your cheek."

"Do I?" She tried to pull away, but I held her tight.

"Just a smudge." I kissed her again. "I've been thinking about something."

"Yeah? What?"

I felt a strange ping of nerves, a lot like I used to feel before taking the field. The hit of excitement made me smile. "Now that you're my wife, maybe it's time we work on changing your name."

"To Haven? Oh, I definitely want to. I'll figure out all the paperwork when we get home. I'm sure it will take some time for the students to get used to it, but they will."

"Not to Haven." I cupped her cheek. "I mean to Mommy."

Her lips parted in surprise. "You mean?"

I nodded. "Pen, I want to have a baby with you."

She took a trembling breath, and tears gathered in the corners of her eyes. "Oh, Theo."

"If you're not ready, it's all right. I've just been thinking about it a lot lately. I want a family with you."

Pushing me down onto the bed, she threw herself on top of me. "I would love to have a baby. I want that so much."

I rolled her onto her back and kissed her deeply. "How about now?"

"I don't think I'm fertile right this second, but we can certainly practice."

"Practice makes perfect."

She giggled as I took off her bikini and ditched my shorts. We came together to the sound of ocean waves crashing on the beach outside. Her body melded with mine as we moved in a steady rhythm, her whimpers and sighs music to my ears.

Later, we lay in bed together, our bodies sated. Her head rested against my chest, and I traced slow circles on her skin.

Leaning in, I kissed her head. "I love you, Pen."

She nestled in closer. "I love you, too. So much."

Looking up at the ceiling, I smiled. I remembered another time when I'd been looking up, only then it had been at the sky over a football stadium. I'd been hit with the crushing realization that my career was over, and my life would never be the same.

And thank goodness for that.

I didn't regret the end of my pro-football career or the struggles that followed. I certainly didn't regret becoming a teacher and coach. As much as I'd loved the rush of being on the field, I was where I was meant to be.

Best of all, I had Pen.

My best friend. The love of my life.

My wife.

Seriously, marry your best friend. I highly recommend it.

My smile grew. Penelope, my wife. It didn't get much better than that.

Except it would. Hopefully, we'd add to the Haven family chaos with babies of our own.

Taking a long, slow breath, I kissed her head again. I loved her so much. Our life together was just beginning, and the best was yet to come.

BONUS EPILOGUE

Theo

THE FOLLOWING AUTUMN...

My stomach growled at the scent wafting from my grill. I was starving, and the giant rib eyes I was cooking were going to be the perfect pregame meal.

It was a Friday, and the Timberwolves' first home game. After winning state the previous year, there was a lot of pressure for a repeat. I wasn't worried. My players were already looking strong. It was going to be a great season.

I pulled the steaks off the grill and brought them inside. Pen looked up from what she was doing and smiled. I couldn't help but smile back. After setting the tray on the counter, I leaned in and kissed her soft lips.

My brow furrowed as I realized she was whisking something in a bowl. "I thought you made potatoes."

"I did make potatoes. They're staying warm in the oven."

"Then what's that?"

Her mouth turned up in a mischievous smile. "Jell-O."

I grinned. What was she up to? "Why're you making Jell-O, Pen?"

"Oh, you know." She lifted a bright green whistle on a black cord.

"Is that Derek's?"

She laughed. "Yeah. He left it sitting in the teachers' lounge, so I grabbed it."

"Good one." I held out my fist and she bumped it with hers. Then we spread our fingers and made a little explosion sound. Derek was the PE teacher at Tilikum High and we'd been trying to prank him for weeks.

She shrugged. "He left it out."

"He definitely brought it on himself." I leaned over and glanced into the bowl. Green. "Nice color choice, too. You nailed this one."

"Thank you. I thought it was fitting."

I kissed her again. She finished mixing the Jell-O and put it in the fridge to set. Then we dished up our dinner and took it to the table.

My mind was on the upcoming game while we ate, a familiar sense of anticipation buzzing through me. I loved game days. The excitement of the players, the roar of the crowd, the tension and triumph. There was nothing like it.

I finished eating and meant to say a quick goodbye to Pen. I needed to get back to school. But her lips felt so good, and the brush of her tongue sent a rush of heat through my veins. One minute we were putting our dishes in the kitchen. The next, we were ripping each other's clothes off and stumbling into the bedroom.

Worth it.

Warm and sated, I braced myself over her, reveling in the feel of her body tangled with mine.

"You're going to be late," she said.

"I know, but you feel so good."

"You can have more of me later."

I kissed her. "Deal. I'll see you at the game."

She nodded, and I kissed her again before getting up to get dressed. She watched me from the bed with a contented smile, and her expression reminded me I'd need to put on my game face before I hit the locker room. It was one thing to gaze at my wife like a lovestruck goof in a post-orgasm daze. Quite another to let my players see me like that.

I left and headed for school. The summer weather had shifted, leaving a chill in the air, especially in the evenings. As I parked my truck, I wondered if Pen had her hoodie. She was going to need it.

It wasn't long before players started arriving, and soon the stands were filled with students and families. After a pregame meeting in the locker room, we went out to warm up on the field. Cheers filled the air. I glanced up into the stands, looking for Pen, but didn't see her yet.

With warm-ups finished, it was just about game time. The announcer came on the loudspeaker and the Timberwolves fans clapped politely while he read off the visiting team's starting lineup.

There was a pause, tension filling the air. A moment later, the pep band began and the crowd surged to their feet. Cheers rose as each of our players were announced. At the end, he announced Coach Theo Haven, and I turned to the crowd to wave.

There was Pen. But she wasn't in the stands, like usual. She stood on the sidelines, holding a big poster board. Giving me a big smile, she turned the sign around and held it up.

Good luck, Coach Daddy!

For a second, I didn't get it. My brow furrowed. Coach what?

I'm ashamed to admit, my players figured it out about three seconds faster than I did. Some of them pointed at the sign while others lifted their helmets in the air and shouted. A ripple spread through the crowd and someone yelled, "Turn around!"

Pen did, showing her sign to everyone in the stands. The crowd went wild.

I stared at her, open-mouthed—gaping like an idiot. *Daddy? Me?* But that meant…

Pen was pregnant?

Tossing my clipboard to the ground, I marched over to her. She dropped the sign, and I scooped her into my arms, lifting her off her feet. I twirled her around as the cheering from the crowd grew.

I set her down and cupped her face in my hands. Her eyes shone and her cheeks were flushed. And her smile. God, it lit up the stadium.

Lit up my entire world.

"Baby?" I asked.

She nodded. "Baby."

Heedless of all the eyes on us, I leaned down and kissed her. My beautiful wife, my best friend, was having my baby. I was going to be a daddy.

"I love you," I said in between kisses. "I love you so much."

"I love you, too."

Glancing up into the stands, I saw my brothers—all of them—at the railing, hollering and cheering their asses off. With one arm, I hauled Pen against me and lifted my other fist into the air.

That, right there, was it. One of the best moments of my life. Better than all the game-winning touchdowns I'd ever scored. Better than any win as a coach.

Moving my hand down, I splayed it across her belly. She placed hers over mine. I'd married my best friend, and as if that hadn't already made me the luckiest guy on the planet, we were having a baby.

I couldn't imagine anything better.

Dear Reader,

Penelope's confrontation with Sean—and Theo's intervention—was a scene I had in my head from the beginning. There's just something about a good fake kiss in front of the crappy ex (especially when the crappy ex is telling our lovely heroine that no one else is going to want her) that makes me want to stand up and cheer.

And swoon. Because ooh, what a kiss.

Please enjoy this fun look at Theo and Pen's supposed-to-be-fake kiss with my notes and doodles. Enjoy!

Love,
Claire

CHAPTER 20

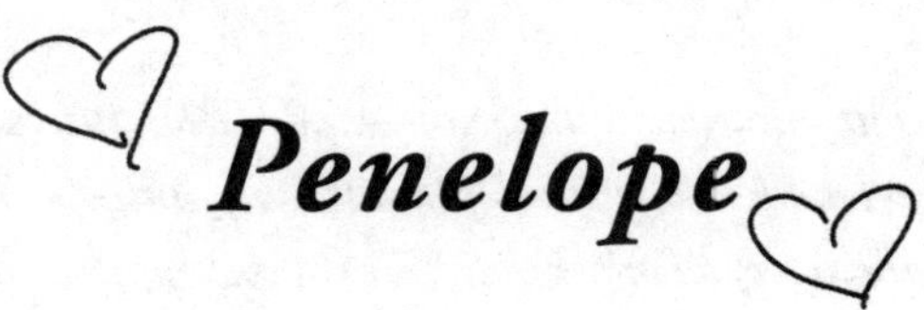

Penelope

I spent Sunday afternoon visiting with Grandma Colleen while Theo went to his parents' house. For once, there weren't any Maury Haven shenanigans. The weather was nice, so we went outside and fed her squirrels for a while, then had dinner in the cafeteria.

It was almost six o'clock by the time I left. My stomach swirled with nervousness as I got in my car and drove to the Timberbeast to meet Sean. It was something I needed to do, but that didn't mean I was looking forward to it.

I parked and got out of my car, glancing down at my black sweater, jeans, and tennis shoes. I wished I would have dressed a little sexier—or at least cuter. It was a perfectly fine visit-your-grandma outfit, but not a great deal-with-your-ex-boyfriend outfit.

Oh, well. I adjusted my glasses, shouldered my purse, and went into the bar. You got this, Pen!

A little smile crossed my lips as soon as I heard the nineties grunge playing in the background. It felt serendipitous. I loved nineties music. Sean hated it. ← He would same

I found him sitting at a table, facing the door. He had a beer, and it looked like he'd ordered a cider for me. I let out a frustrated breath. I wasn't there to have a drink with him. I just wanted to sign the lease paperwork and move on. For real!

He stood with a smile when he saw me.

I walked to his table and stopped.

"Hey, ba—" He closed his mouth before he could finish the word *babe*. "Have a seat."

"What do you need me to sign?"

"It's right here. But have a drink with me. It's the One Tree caramel cinnamon cider that you love."

"Fine." I pulled out the chair and sat. That was one of my favorite ciders, but I wasn't sure if I was going to drink it or not.

"I know you're mad," he said. "And I don't blame you. I've been a real asshole and I'm sorry."

"You left me on the side of the road, at night, thirty minutes from home."

"Yeah, I was pissed off," he said, and his voice was sullen rather than defensive.

"And then you angry texted me half a dozen times."

"I was pretty drunk. I don't remember most of those."

I took a deep breath. "You know what, I have no reason to hold a grudge. Thank you for apologizing. I accept."

He smiled. "Good. I'm glad we got that out of the way."

I was too. I smiled back, feeling like that had been a success. We'd seen each other, cleared the air, and now it was over. I wasn't going to dread running into him in public.

"Is this the paperwork?" I slid it in front of me. It was an agreement stating that I was moving out and, surprisingly, that I didn't owe any additional rent or utilities. I dug a pen out of my purse and signed.

"Now we can both move on." I pushed it back toward Sean.

I noticed someone at the bar and did a double take. Theo sat on one of the stools. He looked over his shoulder and gave me a quick wink. My stomach fluttered and a flush hit my cheeks.

For a hot second, I forgot what I was doing there and started to stand, as if I were being drawn by gravity into Theo's orbit.

"Penelope, wait."

Sean's voice startled me. Blinking in surprise, I looked at him.

"I know I was angry before and I didn't handle it well. You took me by surprise. But I think all this…" He gestured between the two of us. "It's a big mistake."

"What do you mean?"

"I've had time to go over what happened, and I realized I didn't give you a chance to think things through."

"Think what through?"

"Us. Where we're headed."

"We're not headed anywhere. We broke up."

"It was a heated moment. Did you really consider the implications?"

"I don't think I understand what you're getting at."

He rested his forearm on the table and leaned forward. "Are you sure leaving a solid long-term relationship when you're in your midthirties is a good idea?"

My eyes widened and my mouth dropped open. For a second, I was so shocked, I couldn't seem to make any words come out.

"Excuse me?" was all I managed.

"I'm not trying to be a jerk here. It's just reality. I'm a guy who makes good money and who'll eventually take over a business. I'm stable. I'm not going to have any problem finding someone. But you? The cute nerd girl thing you have going on isn't going to last forever."

"What are you saying? I have an expiration date?"

"I don't make the rules. It's not my fault the world works this way." His expression softened. "You made a rash decision, and I want to give you the chance to come back before it's too late."

"Too late for what?"

"Let's just be real about all this, babe. I'm giving you another chance. You should take it. Come home." He gestured to the form I'd signed. "I can rip that up right now."

"Why? Because no one else could possibly want me?"

"I wasn't going to say it, but…" Pressing his lips together, he nodded.

A hand slid across my shoulders, and I looked up to find Theo standing next to my chair.

"Hi, beautiful," he said.

I stared at him in disbelief as he moved his hand to the back of my neck. It was not a friendly touch. It was possessive and intimate—almost dirty. Especially the way he slid his fingers into my hair and leaned down, his grip tightening as if he wasn't going to let me turn away.

With his face mere inches away, he spoke again in a deep voice. "Sorry I'm late."

Before I could respond—or even think—he closed the distance, and his mouth was on mine. The shock of his kiss reverberated through my body, sending sparks that burst between my legs. His lips were firm, but soft, moving over mine like he'd done it a thousand times.

Like he owned me.

And in that moment, he did.

A slight brush of his tongue almost made me moan. But then he pulled away.

My lips parted as we separated, my eyes fluttering open just in time to catch him licking his lips. The corners of his mouth turned up slightly, as if he'd enjoyed that kiss and was savoring the way I'd tasted.

I was dumbstruck, blinking at him like a moron as he straightened.

"Hi," was all I managed to get out.

Theo Haven had just kissed me, and it had short-circuited my brain.

He turned to glance at Sean and his voice was low and even. "You're in my seat."

I was almost afraid to look, but flicked my eyes to the side, risking a peek.

The color drained from Sean's face and his mouth hung open. I couldn't tell if he was mad, or just shocked.

Theo released his grip on my hair but kept a protective hand on the back of my head. His fingers moved, almost as if he wasn't aware of it, sliding through my hair and lightly massaging my scalp. My lips blazed with the heat of his kiss, and his touch was mesmerizing.

Finally, my brain caught up. Theo was pretending to be my new boyfriend—a man who wanted me.

I turned to look Sean directly in the eyes. "What was that you were saying about no one else ever wanting me?"

The grimace of horror that crossed Sean's face almost made me laugh. He'd actually thought he was doing me a favor.

Clearing his throat, he stood and almost crumpled the paper I'd signed in his fist. Without another word, he stormed out.

Theo stopped playing with my hair and the absence of his touch was almost jarring. He walked around the table and took the chair Sean had just vacated.

I opened my mouth, but I didn't know what to say. My mind was a swirl of thoughts and feelings.

That kiss.

But it had been fake.

I resisted the urge to touch my lips. It sure hadn't felt fake.

"Sorry," Theo said, giving me a sheepish grin. "I wasn't going to interfere, but he was seriously pissing me off."

"What are you doing here?"

He hesitated before answering. "I know you don't need me to fight your battles for you, but I wanted to be here, just in case."

I gazed at him for a moment. How did I get so lucky? He was such a great friend.

And an amazing kisser, which—for better or worse—I now knew.

"Thank you."

"You're not mad?" he asked.

"No, I'm not mad. And I sure don't think he's going to bother me again."

"He better not."

My lips still tingled, and I inadvertently rubbed them together. Theo's eyes flicked to my mouth, and I caught a glimpse of his tongue darting across his bottom lip.

I glanced away. The kiss had been fake. He'd only been pretending to be my boyfriend to make a point. The fact that I could still feel his mouth on mine wasn't because it was the best kiss I'd ever had. It was just because he'd surprised me. ~~I hadn't been expecting it.~~

Okay, that was a huge lie. It was the best kiss I'd ever had.

And suddenly, it was killing me to know that I'd never get another one.

Or will she...

I love this moment so much. Theo being protective. A not-so-fake kiss. Sean storming away. Peak swoon!

CHAPTER 21

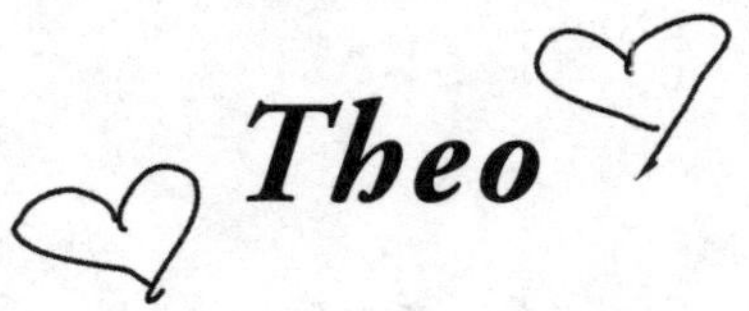

Theo

I shouldn't have done that.

The thought kept running through my mind as I looked at Penelope sitting across from me. I shouldn't have kissed her.

I could have accomplished the same thing without the kiss. All I'd needed to do was touch her shoulder and tell Sean he was in my seat. That would have been enough to get the message across.

But no. I'd leaned down, and a second later, I was kissing her.

I could still feel her lips. Still taste her. And I was hard as steel thinking about what it would be like to taste more of her. To devour that mouth, and the rest of her along with it.

Fuck.

At least she wasn't mad at me for interfering.

She hadn't touched the drink Sean had bought her, which was weirdly gratifying. I wanted to get rid of the last remnants of him, so I grabbed his empty bottle and reached for hers.

"Do you want that, or…?"

"No." She shook her head. "I'm not going to drink it."

"Good." I stood and picked up her cider. Maybe staying for a drink—on me, not the douchebag—would be a good idea. I didn't trust myself to be alone with her yet. "I was thinking about getting a drink. Do you want something?"

"Sure, that sounds nice."

"One of these?" I lifted the cider.

Wrinkling her nose, she adjusted her glasses. "I think he ruined that flavor for me. Maybe just a regular cider."

"On it."

I took the bottles to the bar and waited while Rocco served another customer. Penelope seemed restless. She kept messing with her hair and glasses.

"Be right with you, Theo," Rocco said.

Glancing at him, I tipped my chin, and he disappeared into the back.

When I looked at Penelope again, she was touching her lips with her fingertips. Inadvertently, my tongue darted out and I licked my lips, remembering the way she'd felt. The way her mouth had tasted.

Our eyes met and we both froze. Looking away, she dropped her hand into her lap. I pressed my lips together, as if I could pretend I hadn't been thinking about how it had felt to kiss her.

Damn it. What had I done?

It was fine. I could fix this.

Rocco came out and I ordered a beer and a cider. He handed me the bottles and I paid, then took them to our table.

Just friends, Theo. We're just friends.

I sat and we both took a drink. We needed something to talk about—other than Sean. Or the fact that her mouth felt like—

"How's your grandma?" I asked, cutting off my own thoughts.

"She's fine. She likes to feed the squirrels, so we did that. Then had dinner. Luckily, the food there is good."

"How long has she lived there?"

"About five years. The nice thing is, it was her choice. She can still live independently, but she doesn't have to cook unless she wants to. There's medical help if she needs it. And activities to keep her busy."

"It's nice that you can visit her so often. I'm sure she appreciates that."

"Yeah, we only have each other. It was one of the reasons I wanted to move to Tilikum. I was in Pinecrest before, which isn't far, but it's nice to be able to pop over more easily."

"Sucks that you aren't closer with the rest of your family. Especially your parents. Do you have any contact with them?"

"A little. I usually get a call on my birthday and around the holidays. That's about it."

I shook my head. "Damn. Sorry for bringing up a crappy subject."

"No, it's okay. The good part about all of it was Grandma. My grandpa passed when I was a teenager, so I moved in with her when I was in college. It worked out great for both of us. After that, I got a teaching job in Wenatchee. That wasn't bad. I could still visit. But it made me realize I wanted to settle down here, so I could be as close to her as possible."

I nodded along as she talked. I certainly understood being close to your family. I was still struggling with the reality of leaving mine.

But another thought occurred to me. Penelope probably wouldn't leave Tilikum.

Maybe it would be an option once her grandma had passed on. But then again, maybe not. She'd worked hard and been patient for a long time before finally getting her job at Tilikum High School. This place meant something to her, as did being close to her grandma.

Not that I was thinking about asking her to come to South Carolina with me. That would have been a girlfriend conversation, not a friend conversation. Not even a work-besties-turned-roommates conversation.

But the realization that it wouldn't be an option, no matter what, kind of hurt.

Which was stupid. Just because I'd fake kissed her didn't mean anything had changed. And it definitely didn't mean we were more than friends.

"It's nice that you're so close with your family," she said. "I see them at the games, and it seems like you spend a lot of time with them."

"I think my parents invite me over a lot because they assume I'm lonely."

"Because you're single?"

I nodded. "Probably."

"Can I ask you a weird question?"

I took a drink. "Sure."

"Now I regret saying that. Never mind. I don't need to ask you anything."

"Well, now you have to ask me. What is it?"

"No, I'll just make it awkward."

"You're not going to make it awkward. What do you want to know? I'll tell you anything."

"I was just wondering." She paused, fidgeting with her bottle. "Is there a reason you don't date? I'm not judging you for being single. I'm just curious. You're such a great guy, it's almost impossible to imagine you not getting snatched up by some lucky girl. See? Awkward."

Had she just called me a great guy? A sense of warmth spread through my chest.

"That's not awkward. I get asked that a lot, actually. Mostly by my family. I, um…" I trailed off, trying to decide how much to say. "It's just what's best for me, I guess."

"So it wasn't because something happened? You just like being single?"

"Not exactly." My love life wasn't my favorite topic, but I had a strange desire to tell her. "I was dating a girl in college. We met my senior year and stayed together after I graduated and started playing pro ball. I thought everything was great. She was getting into sports journalism and got a great job working for one of the networks. I was living my dream, playing pro football. It was like we had it all. I actually asked her to marry me."

"Did you? I didn't realize you'd been engaged."

"It didn't last very long. A few weeks after I gave her the ring, I was injured in a game. It was clear pretty quickly that it was a career-ender. Neck and spine injuries are no joke."

"But…" she hesitated. "What did that have to do with your engagement?"

"It was too much for her. The injury, the rehab, the possibility that I'd have ongoing mobility challenges. She called it off."

She huffed. "Are you kidding me? She broke up with you when you were severely injured?"

"Yeah, pretty much."

"That's…" She scrunched her nose. "That's so awful. How could she do that?"

I appreciated that she was angry on my behalf, but I had to fight back a grin. She was cute when she was mad.

"I'm glad it happened. She wasn't the person I thought she was."

"Clearly not." Her voice softened. "So, that was it? You decided to stay single?"

"No. My recovery took a while, and then I went back to school to get my masters. After that, I decided to try dating again. Eventually, I met someone and we hit it off. We dated for a while, and things were getting serious. That was when my migraines got bad."

"Did you get them right after you were injured, or did it take that long for them to start?"

"I had mild ones for a while. I didn't even know they were migraines. But then they started getting really bad. One took me out for about four days, and I had no idea what it was. They were debilitating. Eventually, my doctor and I found ways to get them under control, but for a while, my quality of life was not great."

"So, you were getting serious with someone and the migraines got bad. Are you about to tell me she did what your other ex did? You had medical issues that were too much for her and she bailed?"

"Yeah, that's exactly what happened." I huffed out a resigned laugh and shook my head. "She couldn't imagine herself coping with my migraines for the rest of her life."

Her brow furrowed. "That's not right. If you love someone, you don't leave when things get hard. You stay by their side no matter what."

"I guess she didn't love me." I shrugged. "Anyway, that was it. I decided I was done. I was teaching and coaching, and that was fulfilling enough."

"I can't say I blame you."

Silence settled between us as we finished our drinks. But it wasn't uncomfortable. It felt natural to sit with her, quietly enjoying a beer. Sharing things I didn't usually share with anyone.

After a while, I broke the silence. "You ready to go, or do you want to hang out here?"

"I'm ready to go. The alarm will go off all too early tomorrow."

"Yeah, it will."

We stood, and as she came around the table, she dropped her purse. We both bent to grab it, and I found myself within inches of her face. Again.

Don't kiss her again, Theo. Don't do it.

I picked up her purse and straightened, handing it to her. Her cheeks flushed with a hint of pink as she took it.

Close call.

We went outside and I walked her to her car.

"I'll see you at home," she said.

"Yeah. See you at home."

I backed up a few steps while she got in and watched her pull out of her space and drive away.

See you at home.

That phrase sent a sense of warmth spreading through my chest. There was a very uncomfortable truth brewing inside me—something I kept trying to deny. I liked Penelope. A lot.

And not as a friend.

ACKNOWLEDGMENTS

A big, heartfelt thank-you to everyone who helped make this book happen!

To my early readers for helping me through that messy first draft. This book is SO much better because of your feedback.

To TeamCK for all your behind-the-scenes work. You're the best!

To Lori for another beautiful cover that captures the story.

To everyone at Sourcebooks Casablanca for all your support and for continuing to be an amazing partner in bringing the Haven brothers to bookstores.

And last but certainly not least, to all my readers. I love your beautiful faces!

ABOUT THE AUTHOR

Claire Kingsley is a *USA Today* and #1 Amazon bestselling author of heartwarming, sexy romance, including contemporary romance, romantic comedies, and small-town romantic suspense. She writes fun, quirky heroines, swoony heroes who love big, romantic happily ever afters, and lots of big feels.

She can't imagine life without coffee, great books, and all the crazy characters who inhabit her imagination. She lives in the inland Pacific Northwest with her three kids.

Website: clairekingsleybooks.com
Facebook: clairekingsleybooks
Instagram/TikTok: @clairekingsleybooks

HAVEN BROTHERS

USA Today bestseller Claire Kingsley brings humor and heart to small-town romantic suspense.

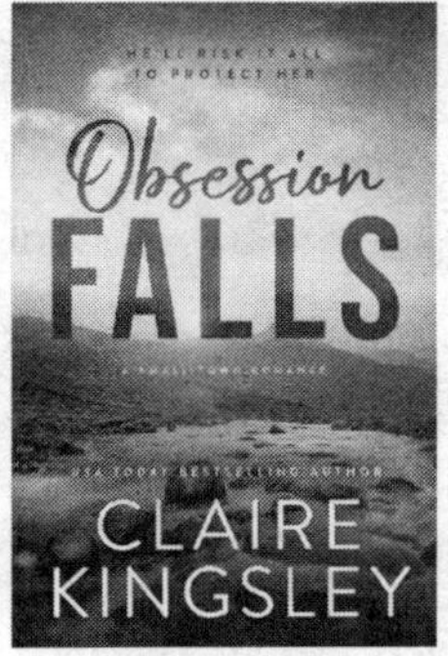

Obsession Falls

Audrey Young could totally handle the mess that is her life. Except someone is stalking her, and she doesn't know who or why. Josiah Haven is the grumpy loner next door. But when Audrey's in danger, Josiah will risk everything—even his heart—to protect her.

Storms and Secrets

Zachary Haven is living a lie, pretending to hate the woman he's always loved. After a brush with death, he's determined to convince Marigold Martin that he's the one. But secrets run deep, and Zachary fears the man who's after Marigold could be more than a romantic rival. He could be the devil himself. And Zachary might be too late to save her.

Temptation Trails

Single dad Garrett Haven risked his heart once and won't do it again. Until he meets Harper Tilburn. The sparks between them are scorching, their attraction undeniable. But when the cold case Garrett is investigating takes a chilling turn, he'll do anything to protect the people he loves and catch a killer before it's too late.

Whispers and Wildfire

Melanie Andolini never thought she'd be starting over in her thirties. Moving back to her hometown is the fresh start she needs—until she runs into her high school ex-boyfriend, Luke Haven, and sparks fly. Their small town might not be big enough for both of them, but he'd do anything to save her from the nightmare in her past.

Captivation Creek

A devastating injury ended Theo Haven's pro-football career, but he's made a good life for himself in his hometown. His work-bestie, Penelope Fallbrook, is one of the best parts of his teaching job. They're just friends—no, *really*. But when Penelope's life comes crashing down, Theo is there to pick up the pieces and offer a place to stay. Together they unravel the mysterious death of a local artist, but doing so just might put a target on their backs.

Peaks and Promises

When Summer Lewis's dangerous ex arrives in town, she turns to Reese Haven, her big, tattooed friend with a security business, to help her disappear. Reese knows exactly where to hide Summer—his hometown, Tilikum—and has the perfect rouse to keep the single mom and her son safe: a fake marriage. As tensions mount and lines blur, their pretend relationship begins to feel anything but.

"Plenty of steam... The danger adds to the satisfying story."

—*Booklist* for *Whispers and Wildfire*